Remember Me Dancing

Ken Parejko

Waubesa Press

The quality fiction imprint of Badger Books Inc.

First Edition
ISBN 1-878569-36-8

Published by Badger Books Inc./Waubesa Press of
Oregon, Wis.
Cover illustration by Terri Shewczyk
Editing/proofreading by J. Allen Kirsch
Printed by BookCrafters of Chelsea, Mich.
Cover color separations by Port to Print of Madison,
Wis.

*Most of the events in this story actually happened at the time
and place affixed within these pages. The author has, however, used
the prerogatives of historical fiction to manipulate time frames and
include incidents which may or may not have occurred.*

To all my family, living and dead, who gathered round to help me write this book. Especially to Grandpa Piotrowski who, though dead 23 years before I was born, stayed patiently at my side till it was finished. And to my mother, and Aunt Catherine, without whom it would not have been possible.

Credits

We gratefully acknowledge use of the following quotations:

Chapter 1: From *The life and Letters of Saint Francis Xavier* by Henry James Coleridge, London, Burns and Oats Publishers, copyright 1972.

Chapters 2, 5, 30: From *Introductory Lectures on Psycho-Analysis* by Sigmund Freud, translated by James Strachey. Reprinted by permission of Liveright Publishing Corp.

Chapters 7, 9, 17, 27: From *Collected Poems by Karol Woytayla,* copyright 1979, 1982 by Libreria Editrice Vaticana, Vatican City. Reprinted by permission of Random House.

Chapters 10, 36: From *Polish Experiences During the Insurrection of 1863-64,* by W.H. Bullock, MacMillan and Co., London, England, copyright 1864.

Chapter 12: From *Pig Earth* by John Berger, Pantheon Books, NY, copyright 1979.

Chapter 13: From *The Nervous Housewife* by Abraham Myerson, Arno Press, copyright 1922.

Chapter 14: From *The Polish Peasant in Europe and America* by William I. Thomas and Forian Znaniecke, Dover Publications, NY, copyright 1958. Used by permission of Dover Publications, Inc., New York, NY.

Chapter 18: From *The Harvest of the Year to the Tiller of the Soil* by Liberty Hyde Bailey, Macmillan Publishing Co., NY, copyright 1927.

Chapter 21: From *Speeches and Writings of M.K. Ghandi,* copyright 1918.

Chapters 26: From *Five Centuries of Polish Poetry 1450-1970* by Jerzy Peterkiewicz and Burns Singer, Oxford Univ. Press, NY, copyright 1970. Used with permission of Oxford University Press.

Chapter 31: From "The Moon Shines on the Moonshine" by Francis DeWitt in *Broadway Brevities of 1920,* Shapiro, Bernstein and Co., NY. Used with permission of Hal Leonard Corporation, Milwaukee, WI.

Chapter 34: From *The Spirit of Man, Art and Literature* by C.G. Jung, Pantheon Books, copyright 1966. Used with permission of Princeton University Press.

Chapter 35: From "The Sheik of Araby," by Harry Smith, Ted Snyder and Francis Wheeler, copyright 1920. Used with permission of EMT Music Publishers, NY, and Ted Snyder Publishing Co., Weehawken, NJ.

Chapter 38: From *Poets of Warsaw Aflame* by Edward Dusza, published by UW-Stevens Point Foundation, Stevens Point, WI, copyright 1977.

1

In all your dealings, conversations, and
friendships with others, so conduct yourself
as if they might one day be your enemies.
— from a letter of St. Francis Xavier

Through high windows thinly etched with frost the morning light fell from a perfect sky into the little church of
St. Francis Xavier. Though it warmed them, warmed their skin,
infant-soft or creased and furrowed with age, and deeper far into
their souls which had somehow survived the long winter, it
seemed too to hold them somehow apart, unmoving, in an almost heartless clarity. Beside the altar Mary, serenely smiling
Queen of Heaven, seemed kept by the light from ever touching
her beloved Joseph.

And in the pews, filled from front to back, they were kept
separate, too, each from the other: husband from wife, mother
from daughter, son from beloved. As though gathered in quiet
congregation they would never be more alone than here, patiently waiting for the priest to scurry out of the sacristy and
begin the Mass.

Then, suddenly, silently as a moth's wing, a hand moved,
fell to test and quiet a rumor from within. Adam Laska, beside

his wife, caught self-consciously Helen's eyes with his. But it was, thank God, only a rumor; with a delicate smile she slipped back to her prayers while Adam folded down Tony's lapel and shushed little Joe and Julia, anxious as he for their mother's sake.

A few rows ahead there rose a subdued cough. Joe Stelmach, the strength of his arms and back breaking through his Sunday best, was enduring the last days of a nasty cold. To cover the sound of his cough he shuffled his boots on the floor and shifted in his seat, feeling meanwhile from behind the silent concern, ardent as his own thoughts.

Beneath the Holy Family, in the front row where the sun spilled in through the south glass, Roman Gruba unbuttoned his overcoat. Bachelor among wives and children, middle-aged, the church's most charitable benefactor, he sat quietly gazing at the altar. The rich fur of his collar hid from behind all but the top of his head; as though he were ashamed to be stuck here between the Brandts and Wolniaks whose pride in their place and the price it had cost them (front pews were ten dollars per annum, twice the normal rate) they made no effort to conceal. Round-faced, moustached Roman Gruba bore that stamp of eccentricity which was his birthright; and he more than anyone other than Father Nowak himself sensed that vast unseen presence which moved among them, sensed too (though here the priest would differ) that they brought it here, not it them.

From the bright, white-plastered walls came faint recollections of incense and beeswax burned: time's flood slowed but never stopped. One by one, here and there, more coats came open, infants unswaddled. Halfway up the north side the Rybarczyks sat silently, Joe and Pauline with the three girls and Peter. Next to Helen, the oldest girl, sat Stanley Topolski, whom everyone called Stash. Beside the thin and frail sixteen-year-old, Stash seemed almost a giant. Yet gentle as he was handsome and though eight years her senior, Stash shared Helen's timidity. Though they sat side by side they did so uncomfortably, for although the congregation had long expected a formal announcement, even this sharing a pew was for them too open a declaration of their intentions. Stash, anyway, was never a man truly at ease in church. He had so few hours to himself, would rather spend them in the woods or down along the river hunting, fishing, or trapping. But that of course was impossible.

Impossible, as we shall see, because of his mother. Piety was a matter of habit with Berenice Topolska. Thirty years and more of prayer had brought her through life's daily battles, both large and small—all the baking, laundering, cleaning, the bearing and burying of her children, the constant tying and untying of the family purse to the point where she even took to bed with her the nagging worry over every last nickel. God-fearing and devout, there was yet something shrewdly vigilant in her eyes, as though she could not give up her incessant calculating and even here continued to figure what there was to gain, what to lose. On her lap Berenice held an open missal. The page was marked with a cross of pink and silver thread she had herself crocheted. She lipped the prayers of Mary: Mother most pure, Mother most chaste, Mother most amiable... Scattered elsewhere in the missal, marking favorite hymns and novenas, were a dozen holy pictures of relatives and friends no longer on this earth, and commemorating the ordination of favorite priests. A single photograph, too, was there, cut lovingly from the *Dziennek Chicagowski*, its newsprint already yellowed, a profile of Archbishop Rhode. The kindly Archbishop was for Berenice the ideal of manhood: spiritual, compassionate, with a saintly passivity. Even Father Nowak, whose whispered instructions to his servers could just now be heard from the sacristy, paled in comparison.

And Frank, her husband, how could he stand up against such gentle and refined a holiness? For Frank was but a farmer. Sitting at the center aisle, he had his huge hands resting on his lap; season after season of wind and weather had furrowed his features, given his face not the polished lustre of saintliness but the strength and character of old weathered oak. With a full black moustache and his dark hair (still rich and supple for a man of fifty-four) parted down the middle, he sat with an unpretentious dignity. One might have been tempted, intoxicated by the bright spring light, to fasten around Frank the epithet of family patriarch. But the word, as he would himself be the first to admit, would just not fit.

Between those two poles of the family, Frank at the one end and Berenice the other, stretched the Topolski children. Alongside her mother, sat twenty-year-old Mary, since the loss of Rose the oldest girl. To Mary her position between her mother and the rest of the family was more than coincidence, more even than symbolic. It was, at that moment, the single most important fact of her life, with which she would not only then but on through the coming days and months struggle in a battle for her very survival. Though she was timid, her heart was strong, and only just opening itself to the world; it would take an unforeseen tragedy of scope far greater than her own to seal it up again. Next to Mary sat Lotti, eighteen, outgoing, vivacious, Mary's principal confidant. Then Bruno, chubby, sixteen, all boy; Angie, Sophie, and Anna, each a year younger. And the baby of the family, Eddie, a baby no more (how the years slip past) but a boy of nine years. There were, all told, nine of them, counting Stash who was sitting by Helen, and Walter, gone to mechanic school in Milwaukee.

It was Ash Wednesday, the first day of March, 1922.

The little white frame church stood patiently beside the river, bravely facing the unbroken woods on the far shore. It had watched, mutely, the wide Wisconsin's flow and freeze and flood for almost fifty years, had seen the Valley change from pinewood to slash to pasture and field. Just across the road, overlain now with three feet of snow, sliced with sleigh and cutter tracks, stood the old Knowlton House, square on the bank of the river, the town's oldest surviving structure. Built in the middle of the last century as an inn for weary travelers who came the thirty miles from Stevens Point to Wausau, it had become in turn a tavern and now, with Prohibition, was being fitted out as a somewhat more respectable tourist house. But the line of its roof, closed at each end with large brick chimneys, already sagged a bit from age and its days, much more than the church's, had slipped irretrievably into the swift current of the past.

Inside the church the north windows rattled lightly from a gust of wind. For March had come in not like a lamb nor a lion, that vain and tropical layabout, but perhaps more suitably like a Siberian tiger, to whose nip and growl the horses, tied to their posts in the churchyard, were only too sensible. Under their shaggy winter coats and thick wool blankets the big Percherons and Belgians, the sleek bay and brown Morgans, faced the cold without complaint. One or two — Laska's poor Kurt, especially — was left to stand unprotected. Reflexively he shivered, his thin flanks proof of the family's economy, and puffed a short breath out into the bright but brittle air.

As though slapped by an unseen hand, they suddenly started, their hooves crunching the crusted snow. From the bell tower above, the church bells loudly cracked the frozen air. Inside, in the light and warmth, Father Nowak had just hurried out of the sacristy.

The congregation stood.

Trailing his long white alb, over which lay the Lenten purple, at the altar the priest genuflected and behind him his servers each followed suit. In their neatly ironed cassocks and lace tunics, their hair meticulously slicked, faces cleaned almost to shining, Henry Ganther and Tony Wolski were hardly recognizable as the pair who'd just the day before pelted Anna and Sophie Topolski, hurrying up the hill from school, with a flurry of icy snowballs.

Father turned and received the silver aspersorium. With it he sprinkled the vessel of ashes, chanting low the Latin only he could understand. A tall, thin man, intensely devout, he faced the congregation and as he approached the Communion rail they flowed toward him, filling the central aisle in a shuffling stream of coats and boots. It was slow, each kneeling to receive the token ashes and with it the priest's muttered prayer, slow almost to the point of tedium.

Mary Topolski shuffled forward with the crowd, pressed in on all sides. The broad back of her father's coat filled her vision to the front. But through a sudden break she caught sight of the priest, bent above the Laska girl; and of Joe Stelmach as he turned piously away to slip back into his pew. Quickly she looked aside, to the grey-tipped hair on her father's neck, then again to the floor where her old and handed-down boots slid inch by inch in what seemed a slow eternity toward the altar.

But at last she too knelt and through half-closed eyes, as she murmured her Hail Mary, saw the priest smear the ashes on her father's forehead, quietly intoning the admonitory prayer: "Remember, man, that you are dust, and unto dust you shall return."

The priest's thumb, cool and faintly greasy, touched her skin, startling her into a tremor of prayer. She lowered her head, thanked God for His mercy, then only half conscious rose to find her seat. Again she knelt, gripping the prayer book, eyes tightly shut, lips running over prayer after prayer. Her head was bowed under a burden of guilt and remorse for sins she, of all people, could never commit. Yet with all that she struggled, too, deep inside, for a life of her own, outside the confines of the family. To come to Mass one day with Joe — or even just to sit quietly and watch him, unashamed — was that too much to ask?

She opened her eyes. The Mass had begun. And now she confessed, with the others, her exceeding sins of thought and word and deed. Three times her hand touched her breast. Through my fault, she muttered, through my fault, through my most grievous fault.

Glory to God on high, Father Nowak sang, his voice carrying them and their thoughts upward. At the pulpit he began the Gospel, first in Polish, then for the few who did not understand, in English.

"Do not lay up for yourselves treasure on earth," he read, his voice clear and absolute as the light which surrounded them, "where rust and moth consume. For where thy treasure is, there also will be thy heart."

To Mary Topolski it was the voice of God Himself she heard; and it was as though the words had rested those thousand years only to be born again especially for her. And her heart, like a fawn bedded in the meadow, lay quivering in fear of the distant sound of the mower.

Father closed the Gospel. Lifting the steel-rimmed glasses from his ears, he wiped the lenses on the end of his sleeve. As he cleared his throat and lay his hands to rest on the pulpit, leaning forward, the congregation relaxed. Prayer books closed; ties and babushkas were discreetly adjusted; children whispered to and turned around.

"Today, my friends," he began, "we were marked with the ashes of the Lord. Today, the first day of Lent, we begin our remembrance of the one singular central act of human history, the suffering and death of our Lord Jesus Christ, upon the Cross, so He might redeem us from our sins."

The priest paused, extracted a handkerchief from the left sleeve of his cassock, wiped his nose. In the congregation, a score of mothers instinctively worried if he was catching a cold. But the white cloth disappeared and he continued, his voice taking on a more familiar tone: the voice of the young priest sitting at the table, declining out of courtesy and not lack of appetite one last *ponchek,* the delicious filled doughnuts Father could not resist.

"Forty days we have to fast," he said, understanding fully what that would mean for the hard-working farmers. "We must discipline ourselves," he asserted. "Just as the Lord disciplined Himself to bear the scourges, the torments, the Cross. Try if you can to be like Him." The priest's eyes fixed on Christ's image beside the altar. "As hard as it may be, always keep His example in your mind." He looked out now over the congregation. "Sacrifice yourselves to Him, as He has sacrificed Himself to you."

And he went on, with a story from his days at the seminary, of how during a lesson on Simon of Cyrene he'd come to realize — suddenly, almost as a revelation — that the real meaning of Lent and of Easter was no more nor less than giving ourselves to God. That the death on the Cross was the death of our own separate wills, to be reborn again within His. To have only one desire left; and that, to have none.

But, as so often happened, he lost them. Though they sat as devoutly still as ever, gazing up at him or blankly staring at the altar, he could see that his words passed over them. He had searched his soul as he always did before a sermon, and could find no more personal nor meaningful way of telling them how utmost Lent must be in each of their lives. While they sat there, he thought, their minds full of potatoes, horses, and heifers due to freshen. "My friends," he said, "as Catholics, Easter must mean everything to you, or it means nothing."

Nothing!

He sighed, ran his hands slowly over the Gospel. "With God's help this will be a specially meaningful Lent for each and every one of us. God be with you all throughout this season and on into the coming year. In the Name of the Father, and of the Son, and of the Holy Spirit."

He began the Mass again, this holy, mysterious ritual, this drama of conflict, betrayal, and suffering. Until at the Consecration, when the bells once more cracked open the suspended silence and He came down among them as they went to meet Him, kneeling at the rail, receiving the bland wafer (Body of Christ), wetting it, swallowing it, taking Him into themselves. And once more, without wanting it, Mary caught sight of Joe as he slipped back to his pew.

As the Mass wound down, the air inside the church grew stale and heavy. So at last as they rose, quickly or stiffly, to stand and wait their turn to join the stream out into the morning, the sky unexpectedly dimmed with thin clouds, the cold air they met came almost as a relief.

Stash Topolski said good-bye to Helen and went to untie the team and hitch them to the sleigh. Lotti and Angie, meanwhile, pulled the canvas off and folded it away under the front seat. As Mary helped to hitch the horses young Eddie petted Prince, the graceful Morgan, and Queen, demanding equal attention, jealously nosed the boy's elbow.

Stash climbed in with the others who'd pulled blankets over their laps. But father and mother were still busy talking with the Tomczaks, so Eddie hopped out of the sleigh and Anna ran after, to the river's edge. There, where the warming sun had struck the river bank, the snow was wet and heavy, tinged faintly blue, a blue as cold and deathlike as the blue veins on Rose's hands. Bending a willow down, Anna broke off four long branches on which little fluffy buds, like the soft pads of a kitten's toes, braved the cold air.

Eddie bent to see where an oak leaf had burned its way deep into the snow. The leaf lay at the bottom of a shaft as deep as his hands, its sides an exact pattern of the leaf's sharp-toothed shape. A caterpillar, all wrapped up in brown and black woolens, moved slowly toward the shaft, and explored the sudden void with its tiny antennae. Eddie lifted the brave little insect. It curled in his hand; he pulled off a glove and dropped it onto his bare skin, where it felt prickly soft. He set it on the snow again. It lay motionless as death.

Packing a big handful of snow, Eddie turned and aimed toward the sleigh—but before he could throw, Mary demanded he drop it. So instead he lifted again the woolly bear, and hiding it in his fists ran to the sleigh to drop it on Angie's lap. But his sister only picked it up and let it fall over the edge of the sleigh where it lay alongside one runner, nestled in one of the girl's deep boot prints.

Holding her little bouquet like a scepter, Anna climbed back among them. They sat and watched the parishioners, broken into little groups, chatting happily away, the children running this way and that, the teenagers standing shyly in separate parties of three and four. The murmur of their voices mixed with the snort of the horses and jangle of the many harnesses.

Father Nowak, now in his heavy fur coat, moved through the crowd. His glasses swept the light from off the snow, flashing it quickly one way, then another. He stopped beside the Tomczaks, took Sophie's hand. Nervously she backed away. But still he held her. Then, smiling, he let her go and put his arm around her husband's shoulder, whispering into Chester's ear. Father stepped back and laughed; suddenly he whirled to catch a running child (was that a Tomczak girl?), picked her up and gave her a hearty hug, then laughingly released her.

Now he turned to the Topolski parents. The children in

the sleigh were too far away to make out what was being said. But their mother nodded her head severely; it must have been important. Father Nowak turned to them, and waved to Henry Ganther, his favorite altar boy, before striding off toward the rectory.

Berenice came to the sleigh, her hands gripping the dashboard. "Father wants to see us," she said. "We won't be long."

She reached over Anna and lifted another blanket off the seat — hers and Frank's — and opened it onto the youngest children's laps. "Eddie," she scolded, "you keep yourself covered!" Anna wanted to show her mother the pussy willows, but she'd already turned her back to hurry off toward the rectory.

By now most of the teams were hitched, and family after family were climbing into their sleighs or cutters and pulling quietly away from the church. A few were already well out onto the river, headed west, in the direction the Topolskis themselves would take toward home. The ice was softening, and after Sunday or perhaps the week after, they would be forced to come the long way to church: up across the bridge which flanked the railroad trestle, just visible on the northwest horizon, then following the road back down south along the river. It would add a half hour to their trip.

As the others left, the churchyard grew quiet, the wind seemed to pick up, and heavier clouds drifted across the sun. Suddenly it felt cold. The younger children huddled under their blankets, their feet bunched together around the jugs of hot water — still warm — lying in the straw. While in the back the older girls sat moving their boots up and down against the floor of the sleigh, holding hands to keep them warm.

Father smiled out from the rectory. "Come in, come in," he said. He already had his fur coat off.

Inside the rectory was warm and almost unnaturally clean. It seemed such a big building for only one man — and Verna, of course, the housekeeper who had her own little room in the back. Frank and Berenice followed the priest down the hallway; he showed them into his office, a neat and sparsely furnished room with white plaster walls and a dark shiny hardwood floor. He stood behind his desk, where above him hung a large, elegantly carved crucifix, in ebony and ivory. This was not the suffering Christ Who hung above Frank and Berenice's bed. Here, instead, was a serene and triumphant Savior, His eyes turned joyfully skyward.

"Please, sit down," Father said.

They sat, uneasily, still wrapped in their heavy coats. Outside under a graying sky they could see the last sleighs pull away, leaving their own to stand alone.

Behind his desk the priest seemed a different person: not the familiar celebrant of the Mass, whose chanting Latin brought them so close to God, nor shepherd out amongst his flock, friendly, cajoling, courteous. Here instead he'd become a figure of authority, interpreter and enforcer of Canon Law. And in his role as an authority he joined the ranks of judges, clerks, and lawyers with whom people like the Topolskis could never be at ease.

It was a role he was self-conscious of and no more at ease with than they were. So he spoke to them instead as the old friend he'd come to be. In whom they'd entrusted the First Communion and Confirmation of their children, the recent burial of their daughter Rose, and some day the marriages which no doubt would come. "Well Frank," he asked, "how are things on the farm?"

Frank Topolski clasped his hands nervously, his eyes resting there, on his thick, work-worn hands. He looked up an instant at the priest, deferentially. *"Dobrze,"* he said. Everything was fine.

"Soon it will be spring, eh? Then you'll have no rest."

The older man smiled, sighed lightly. "We always have enough work, Father."

"Of course," the priest agreed. He winked. "No rest for the wicked, eh?" Frank smiled. "And you, Pani Topolska, have you made any of your famous *czarnina* lately?" There was nothing Father Nowak liked better than a hot bowl of rich blood soup, thick with noodles. And Berenice's was among the best.

"No, Father. Not since Christmas. And now, Lent."

"Of course. But for Easter, perhaps?" he asked slyly.

"For Easter."

The priest shifted in his seat, resting his arms on the desk top. "The children are outside," he said, glancing to the window. "I will be as brief as possible." He looked toward the woman. "I asked you here because something has been bothering me, something I feel obliged to speak with you about." He spoke clearly, as though he had rehearsed the words, yet somewhat distantly. "Ever since last month, when you canceled the banns of Mary's wedding, I have been greatly troubled." He paused, cleared his throat. "Will you announce the banns again after Easter?"

There was no reply. The priest's gaze turned to the man, who was staring blankly at the shiny, neatly arranged desk top, staring as though he wished to lose himself in its wide expanse. The priest spoke again. "What I am asking is, was this only a temporary postponing or is the marriage to be called off completely?"

Berenice spoke, her eyes not afraid to meet his. "We don't know."

"I see." Somehow he didn't believe her. This was the first time he'd personally confronted her with the consequences of her actions — something, he could see, she was not accustomed to. He would rather have let it go. But it needed saying. He picked up the black and silver pen his uncle Tony had given him at Ordination. "I asked you then, Pani Topolska, why you found it necessary to cancel the banns. You had no answer. So I ask you again."

But once more he was not granted the courtesy of a reply.

His eyes turned inward a moment. "I am, of course, your servant in such matters. But still, I feel a duty to speak up for the couple. They seem such a good match." He directed his words to the girl's father. "Don't you think it is safe to say they feel a certain... affection toward one another?" But Frank only looked away, up above the crowded bookcase where hung the painting, in muted greens and blues beneath an ominous charcoal sky, of our Lord at Gethsemane.

"Joe Stelmach is an honest, hard-working lad. I challenge anyone to prove otherwise. He would make a perfect husband for Mary. Why, Joe doesn't even touch the bottle, does he?" His eyes met hers. "Oh, perhaps a beer now and then. We have to forgive them that. I tell you, Pani Topolska, any of the girls in the parish would jump at the chance to be courted by Joe. But he has chosen your Mary. And as for her, you know how much I think of her. There's not a girl in the parish — no, in the diocese for that matter — more obedient and sincerely modest than Mary." The mother's eyes fluttered lightly, in her own small way acknowledging the compliment.

If God would only grant him the guidance to say the right thing. He had in the seminary studied years of rhetoric: invocation, petition, conclusion... invocation, petition, conclusion. He could repeat it in his sleep. But how much out of his depth he

felt, how much he had still to learn about people, the darkness
in their souls and in their hearts. And he felt that the girl's
happiness (how frightened it made him to think of it) and beyond that really her life, were in his hands.

He rose slowly and walked to the window, looking out over
the church and the churchyard which were his home--his pasture, so to speak. Before he had come, just five years before, St.
Francis had been only a mission church. He had been given the
task of raising the funds to build the rectory. He had been the
first priest of the newly organized parish. It was something to
be proud of. Perhaps, he thought, the Bishop had been right in
sending him. Perhaps there really was more to it than just his
being Polish. Yes, he had to admit it. With their age and
experience, superiors can become quite canny about such ap-
pointments.

Yet how he longed, sometimes, to return to Milwaukee, to
the cloistered seminary beside the lake, to those hours and hours
of theology, spent in the august company of Aquinas, Loyola,
Duns Scotus. How they would ignite his spirit! And how long
it had been, God forgive him, since he'd felt that passion of the
mind's discovery of the Lord.

No. There was no philosophy here. Begging, yes, for funds
for this and funds for that. Filling in as lawyer, for those who
could not afford one. Or doctor. Counseling. Selling. Selling
God. It had come to that.

Not that he disliked the people — on the contrary, these
were his kind of people: good, strong, honest folk with a simple
kind of faith he could only admire. That man sitting so nervously behind him, there sat a perfect example. How he looked
up to men like Frank Topolski! Yet he had to ask himself, and
the question seemed to come up more and more often these
days, whether this was what he wanted from life. Had he made
that improbable journey from Posnan to Rome and from Rome
to California and then to Milwaukee, only to end up here in the
backwoods of Wisconsin, unraveling the tangled web they seemed
bound and determined to make of their lives?

In the yard he could see the Topolski sleigh, beyond it the
boarded-up hotel, sagging into the snow. In the sleigh the children were huddled together. Was that Lotti in the front? No
of course not. That was Anna. And what did the Lord have in
mind for them? He shuddered. An early marriage, child upon
child, the working and sweating season after season, right to the

edge of the grave. No wonder life made their women so bitter.
"America," he spoke quietly, breaking away from his
thoughts, "is not the land of our fathers. Yes, I miss the mead-
ows and the woods of Poland too, the smell of her barns and the
taste of her air. But this is my country now. And America's
ways are not the ways of the old country. Perhaps in Poland, I
don't know, but perhaps it is still accepted to choose the man
your daughter will marry. But here, it is different. Even you,
Pani Topolska, even you chose your husband, did you not?" He
turned for a reply. There was none. Again he stared out the
window, his breath fogging the thin glass. "I thought it best to
speak to you today, as Lent is beginning, because now we all
have a good long time to consider these things. I cannot know
your inner hearts," he said, "only God can know that. But if
Mary truly wants to marry Joe..."

"She will do as I tell her," the woman interrupted. There
was impatience in the voice, a rattled warning.

Father Nowak turned, leaned lightly against the edge of
the windowsill. "Of course she will. And my office, as admin-
istrator of the sacraments, requires the same of me. But beyond
the letter of my office there is my own sense of what is right and
what is wrong. Mary, we must all admit, has been greatly upset
by all this."

"Did she tell you that?" the woman asked.

He knew now he had gone at it all wrong. In his heart he
felt a deep sense of failure. He stepped behind his desk, sat
down again.

"No, of course not. But she wears it, like a babushka, this
sorrow of hers, where everyone can see it." He turned to the
man. "What are your feelings about this, Frank?"

The farmer straightened himself in his chair; his hands
lightly gripped his knees. He was like a child in school, being
questioned by the teacher. And he knew none of the answers.
"It's not my business, Father," he said quietly.

Though the priest knew that was not how Frank really felt,
that only time would tell the man's true feelings, his patience
had worn thin. "She is your daughter, isn't she?" he asked.

Frank's eyes turned to the priest. There was sorrow in
them; they cried for understanding.

Father felt ashamed. He retreated to the security of dogma.
"The sacrament of matrimony," he began, "is not to be taken
lightly." His voice droned on, making its pronouncements to

some abstract audience gathered perhaps inside his own mind: certainly not to the man and woman seated so nervously in front of him. "To the Church, whoever is joined here on earth are joined forever also in heaven."

But it was no good. It was like talking to the side of a barn. If only she were a man, he thought. He might know how to deal with her then. But women were as foreign to him as... giraffes. Or airplanes.

"Please," he said, one last time giving voice to his heart. "Think this over. Try to see it from your daughter's perspective. She and Joe, with a real bond of affection, prepared for marriage. Then for what reason only heaven can say, it is all taken away from them..."

He stopped. Enough said. He was only getting in deeper. He breathed out, loudly. "It's cold outside. Your children are waiting." He glanced past Frank to a clock on the wall. "And I must be going. Mrs. Woyta is not at all well. God, I'm afraid, will soon have her with Him. I promised to bring the Sacrament and the ashes right after Mass." He waited for Berenice's natural curiosity to spring at the matter of Mrs. Woyta's illness. But the woman sat proudly silent. And by that he knew just how much he had imposed. He sighed, felt the terrible weight of the struggle which lay ahead.

He pushed back his chair, stood and moved around his desk. The others stood with him. Holding Frank's hand, he said warmly, "Thank you for coming. You know, of course, that it is only out of affection for you and your family that I felt the obligation to bring this up."

He turned to the mother, took her arm at the elbow. "And you too, thank you, Pani. And please, if I may, I would like to stop by and discuss this matter again. When we have more time." But in her eyes he saw no invitation.

"God go with you," he said, leading them to the outer door.

Father Nowak returned to his office to find his bag with the Sacrament. Standing beside his desk, feeling a great weariness flood over him, he turned to glance out the window. There he could see the couple making their way through a shower of dancing snowflakes toward their sleigh. For the man, who stood a head above his wife, so strong in body, clumsy in talk and things of the heart, but behind a team or with a fork or hoe a man of natural, God-given grace, he could feel love, compassion, pity. But beside this man, across the snowy drive, in that short figure wound tight like a spring, he saw walking one of Eve's true daughters.

As he hurried out the back door, into a fine flurry of snow, harassed by anxieties and self-doubt, Father Nowak promised himself to try harder every day, and especially now during Lent, to accept and to love each and all of the sheep in his flock.

2

It really seems as though it is necessary
for us to destroy some other person or thing
in order not to destroy ourselves...
　　　　— Sigmund Freud, *New Introductory*
　　　　Lectures in Psychology

The next morning Lotti and Angie were busy hauling water from the pump, behind the granary, to the big scalding barrel set up nearby. Lent had already begun and the Easter ham was still on the hoof. Though they stepped carefully through the dim dawn, the deep snow still found its way into their boots, and with every step water sloshed out of the buckets at the ends of the yokes. The barrel was large; they had many more trips than they cared to make.

The sun was just coming up between the two tall pines to the east. There was a light south wind; it would be a beautiful day. Stash came out of the barn and lit the pile of pine roots he'd set under the barrel. The roots were full of resin and eager to burn. In a few minutes he had a crackling fire, to which he added oak and hickory brought from the woodshed.

Morning chores were done. Father stopped on his way to breakfast to see how things were coming along. The barrel was now nearly full. The fire, lapping up its sides, had already warmed the water enough to raise a light, thin steam into the cool morning air. Father told Stash to come in and eat while the girls watched the fire.

As usual, the men hurried through breakfast. Frank slipped the big butcher knife out of the cupboard. He stroked it quietly across a whetstone, now and then testing its edge on his thumbnail. It was his best knife and today would have to be sharp enough to shave with.

Stash came down from upstairs with his .22, a single-fire

Winchester he'd bought before going to the service. The gun
was clean and shined darkly. Mary, washing up the breakfast
dishes, winced at the sound of metal on metal as her brother
opened the gun and slid in a shell. The breech clicked shut.
Stash put two more shells in his pocket, just in case.

"You stay in the house, Mary," her father said.

She didn't have to be told. Almost ten years now — ten
years, and how many hundred chickens, ducks and geese, pigs,
cows and calves. Ten years ago it had started. They had brought
the Christmas goose into the basement to butcher it. That was
in Necedah. Her father had dexterously plucked the soft feathers out from behind the big bird's head and held its neck bent
double while with one swift stroke he drew the knife blade
through the artery just behind its skull. Blood spurted out; her
mother caught it in a bowl, with a little vinegar to prevent clot-
ting. Mary watched, from the head of the stairs, a child on her
way to being a woman. Eleven years old. She had seen it often
enough before. But this time — God knows why — she was
fascinated.

The bird made no effort to escape. It seemed itself to be
transfixed by the sight of its blood in a thin stream filling the
bowl. At last — it seemed so long, though it was really only a
matter of minutes — the stream turned to drops, the drops slowed,
stopped. Her father lay the bird on the floor and stood, stretching his cramped leg muscles. There was a moment of calm.
Mary stared down at the bird. Only her mother moved, stirring
the blood and vinegar together. An ocean of pity for the poor
creature poured out of the girl's heart. Seeming to respond, the
bird suddenly flapped its wings and stood. Clumsily it stepped
away, then began dashing about, as though drunk, bumping into
the wall, firewood, the bottom of the stairs. It tried to flap its
wings, as though trying to escape its inevitable fate.

Mary began to cry. Her mother yelled at her to go to her
room. She turned and ran upstairs and fell on the bed, unable
to escape the memory of the gentle bird so timidly facing its
end. She lay there until she heard her parents in the kitchen and
knew the poor bird had died.

Her mother had said Mary felt so sorry for the animals she
would not let them die. That next spring, while they were
butchering chickens, the same thing happened. So Mary was
made to hide upstairs in a closet, where she couldn't hear the
victim's squeals or see their death-throes. Without her watch-

ing, they died as they should. So for ten years now she'd had to hide at butchering time.

Eddie came running down the stairs. In an hour he, Anna and Sophie would have to trudge down the long hill to school. He wanted to stay home today. His mother said no, but he and Sophie could run out and replace the girls by the fire. And they were to begin warming the big rendering kettle which hung nearby from a tripod of green poplar.

Lotti and Angie came in the house, smelling of sharp smoke and damp steam. Bruno followed his father and Stash out of the barn where the three sows were kept with the boar. Stash left the gun outside. The hog pen was in the far corner of the barn, across the aisle from the chickens. Its grey pine rails were smooth and shiny on the inside, rubbed slick by years of soft, pink pigskin. As the men approached, the two breed sows — Katarcyny and Wikta — and the big boar, Janek, came running toward them, hungry for feed. The yearling sow, which had seen her last night turn to day, grunted insistently. Short-Ear, they called her. Because as a tiny piglet, soft and fat with pink rubbery legs which carried her dashing and squealing this way and that, one of her sisters had bit off her left ear. But Short-Ear was a piglet no more. All winter Berenice had sent the girls out with pails of steaming potatoes — the scabby or half-rotted ones — and Short-Ear had turned all that waste into two hundred pounds of pork.

"*Oy, swinia, swinia,*" Frank talked to the animals as he slipped through the gate into the pen. Stash came in after him; Bruno stayed outside, watching. The animals were nervous with hunger. They stood, at a distance, distrust in their eyes, then suddenly bolted around the pen. Hungry sows, the men knew, were dangerous animals. As children they'd been told stories of infants or old men falling into hog pens and being eaten alive.

"*Oy, swinia, swinia,*" Frank chanted, trying to relax the animals. He held a rope, tied into a halter. Short-Ear stood alone now in the far corner; Frank stalked her cautiously. The pig's tiny eyes searched him for some clue to his purpose. Her head was low to the ground, her jowls scraping the hoof-pocked dirt. Man and pig faced one another for a long, still moment, each waiting for the other to make the first move.

Frank lunged. Short-Ear leapt away, squealing noisily. But the halter fell in place. Stash side-stepped Katarcyny and helped his father with the rope. They had Short-Ear now, up against the rail. She squealed pitifully. Frank ran one hand down her long straight spine, calming her with low throaty sounds.

Bruno pulled the gate open. "More!" his father shouted. The boy pulled the gate full open. While Stash held the other pigs cornered in the far end of the pen, Frank pulled Short-Ear out through the gate.

Once in the aisle she followed obediently, past the tails of the cows who had kept her warm all winter and now turned their heads to watch this strange procession, mindlessly chewing their cud. Bruno opened the outside door; only then, tugged out into the sudden white light of the snow, did Short-Ear stop, dig her feet into the snow, and absolutely refuse to go any farther. She turned her head from side to side, trying to understand. And at last within the tiny kernel of her brain she did realize, somehow, that what lay ahead was not exactly in her best interests. Locking her legs firmly, she stood her ground.

Frank pulled at the rope and Bruno and Stash pushed her from behind. She began again to squeal. Even Mary, busy in the kitchen cranking the separator, could hear. She cranked faster, so the noise of the machine might cover the animal's cries. Outside they got Short-Ear moving and half-running, half-skidding, they crossed the snow to the gallus of strong ash beside the steaming barrel.

Short-Ear stood studying the scene. She didn't like what she saw. Nervously she watched as Stash lifted the gun. Her eyes followed Angie and Lotti as they came out of the house and hurried past just as Stash brought the long barrel of the gun within a few inches of her head. She stared at the long stick held motionless between her eyes.

The girls looked away. Eddie and Bruno watched. The loud crack of the gun was followed by the low thud of lead, like an echo, driving itself into the pig's skull. Instantly her legs collapsed and folded onto the ground, almost as though in prayer. From her head flowed a stream of blood. As the girls now turned to see, the sharp warm smell of the animal itself was overlain with the tang of fresh manure.

Working quickly, Frank untied the rope from the animal's head and fastened it and another short rope to its rear feet, just above the hocks. The other ends he threaded over the gallus pulleys. He and the boys hoisted the limp carcass skyward until its nose was just clear of the ground.

Frank pulled the knife from its sheath and stroked it twice

on each side across the stone. The girls looked away again as the knife found the pig's neck, slicing deep into its gullet, from which a sudden gurgle of air, heavy with the smell of its insides, escaped. Cutting into the jugular, the rich red blood streamed down the animal's neck in a thumb-thick rivulet. Stash, kneeling in the snow, caught the blood in a large basin; throwing off his glove, he picked a few long white hairs which floated on the blood's foam. When the flow had slowed significantly, Frank worked the animal's leg, pumping the last of the blood from the heart. Now there was only a single, diminishing trickle, and the animal's muscles shook in a final convulsion. Frank nodded and Stash handed the pan to Bruno, who carefully carried the blood, still warm but grown darker, to the kitchen.

Short-Ear was lowered to the ground, and all hands joined in to push the heavy body up the planks and into the cauldron of hot water. The carcass splashed and sank, not quite covered with water. They left it on that side until their father judged the hairs had softened, then turned and scalded the other side. Then, by pulling with ropes and prying with poles, it was lifted from the water and slid down the planks. Inside the barrel the scalding water was now a thin red color, dirtied with floating hairs and filth; and as the steam rose into the clear morning air, it carried with it a heavy smell of death.

They were just pulling the animal up to hang it again when Berenice called out that the children were to come in and get ready for school. Reluctantly Eddie followed his sisters. Stash and Frank scraped the hair off the pig, until the hide was clean and smooth. Then Frank picked up the sharp knife and sliced down from crotch to head. He pulled back the flesh and reached inside to the steaming innards which gave to the air their own heavy smell. The long windings of intestines fell in a heap on the snow, where they continued their slow peristalsis, apparently unaware of the catastrophe which had taken place around them. The stomach fell alongside. Then the liver came out. Frank held it in his hands, spreading its lobes like the petals of a gigantic scarlet flower. It seemed clean and healthy; he dropped it into a kettle, then threw the animal's heart on top.

The pig's lungs, a soft and spongy pleasant pink, fell onto the ground, where they would be left as a treat for Shep, the family cow dog who sat eagerly watching from a safe distance. Dipping water from a bucket, Frank splashed out the insides of the pig. Satisfied it was clean, he and Stash began the job of cutting the carcass into pieces.

First the head had to come off. Stash tossed it unceremoniously aside. Its rubbery snout stuck up out of the snow, one ear demurely bent over, its eyes shut tight as though in that way it might ignore the carnage surrounding it. From the single ear, the tongue and brains would come a delicious head cheese.

Frank sliced away at the thick layers of fat under the skin, then threw them in chunks into the rendering kettle. The sizzling fat began to melt and fill the air with a greasy smell. The girls kept busy cutting it into smaller pieces and stirring it so it wouldn't burn.

Frank held the remainder of the carcass as Stash sawed a front quarter off, using their fine-toothed meat saw. The quarter was given to Bruno, who manfully threw it over his shoulder and carted it off to the house.

The kitchen, a large room at the back of the house, already crowded with its cream separator, table, cook stove, cupboards, and long bench for washing dishes, was taking on the looks of a butcher shop. Meat was piling higher and higher on the table; scattered on the cupboard were the liver, heart and sweetmeats. Berenice stood at the stove, stirring the blood in a pan to which she'd added slices of meat, sugar, vinegar, barley, and spices. They all loved *keishka*. Especially for breakfast.

Mary was busy with a damp cloth wiping the big slabs of meat clean of hair and dirt. The day's work lay all around them. When Bruno left, they were alone in the kitchen. Berenice peered out the window, then slid the frying pan to a cooler part of the stove. Wiping her hands on her apron, she spoke to Mary. "That can wait. Come with me."

Perplexed, Mary dipped her hands in the warm soapy water, rubbing off blood and fat. As she dried her hands Bruno came in with another quarter, which he plopped on the table, then hurried out again.

Mary stood in the doorway to the dining room. "Sit down," her mother said, pulling a chair away from the table. Mary sat. Her mother went into the guest bedroom, and Mary could just see her as she pulled open the top drawer of the dresser and took out an envelope.

"I want you to write a letter," her mother said, laying the envelope face down on the table. From the living room she brought a sheet of paper and a pencil. Mary stared at her bewildered.

Her mother sat beside her, handed her the pencil, slid the paper to her. "Just write what I say," her mother told her. She sat a moment, closed her eyes.

"Respected Sir," she began. Mary wrote it. Her mother seemed uneasy, her eyes furtive, almost as though she were embarrassed. "Thank you for the letter," she went on. Mary wrote as quickly yet as neatly as she could. "It seems your life is very interesting. You write as an educated man would write. Texas is a long way from the old country. How do you find Army life?"

Her mother paused as the girl caught up. Inside she was a jumble of questions. Who was this "Respected Sir"? Did her mother have a boyfriend? Impossible. And if she did, why wasn't she writing her own letter?

Her mother spoke again. "I will tell you something about myself," she said slowly. "I am twenty years old..." Mary stopped, looked up.

"Write it!" her mother said, pointing to the paper. "Go on!" The girl obeyed. Now she really was confused. "I have four brothers and four sisters. I am the oldest girl since my sister Rose died, last fall, of the flu. My parents come from the old country, the village Tschermesnov, near Gniesno. Do you know it?"

Again the mother waited. Mary's heart was pounding. All morning, because of the butchering, she had been in a nervous state. And now this.

"We have a big farm, mortgage-free. Sixteen cows, eight sheep, pigs, chickens, ducks, and geese. And two cars."

"I help milk, care for the stock, and have learned from my mother to cook, sew, and clean. Perhaps my brother Stash, who has a camera and can make his own pictures, will take a Kodak for you. I would like you to write again, and tell me about your family in the old country."

There was a silence as Mary's hand moved feverishly. "Now," her mother said, her hands closed firmly in her lap, "sign it."

Bruno rushed into the kitchen, dumped a side of ribs on the table. As he was going out, Angie and Lotti came in. They stood in the doorway to the dining room, the cold and smoke coming off their coats. "Father's almost done," Lotti said at last. "He sent us in." She held up the meat saw.

"Did you do the casings?"

Angie shrugged. No one wanted that job.

"Well get out there then and get busy. Take a clean kettle to put them in. And be sure you don't tear them."

Reluctantly the girls turned and in a moment were out the door.

"Sign it," Berenice said again, urgently, under her breath. But Mary stared at her. "Who is he?" she asked. "Who am I writing to?"

"Never mind that. Just sign it. And make the envelope out to this address." She turned the other envelope over, covering all but the return address with her hand. "Go on!"

Reluctantly she put her name at the bottom of the short letter, then wrote on the blank envelope the name and address of this stranger far away in Texas. Then, as her mother told her, their return address: Route 2, Box 1, Dancy, Wisconsin.

Berenice picked the letter up, read it over carefully, folded and inserted it into the envelope.

Mary searched her mind. Had she ever heard of an Anton Walerych? No, never. She stared at the empty tabletop. But when her mother disappeared into the living room to find a stamp, she reached and turned over the other envelope to see the address her mother's hand had so cleverly concealed.

"Marya Popolski, Route 2, Dancy, Wisconsin," it read.

She quickly laid it down again. But this letter, she thought, is for Mary Popolski, who lives six miles down the road. How did her mother come by it? Of course. George Zimmer, the mailman, must have brought it here by mistake. Topolski... Popolski, an easy mistake.

But then her mother had opened it. Knowing it was not for them? She watched her mother lick and set the stamp in place, then pick up and carry the letter which wasn't theirs into the bedroom.

And she will keep it? Mary wondered. Even if it's not ours?

"Back to work," her mother said.

Their eyes met for a long, long moment. Mary felt something strange stir inside her, a mixture of fear and disgust. She was about to speak, to demand that which was rightly hers, but her mother's eyes were too strong, the current between them too one-sided.

Instead she stood, obediently, and pushed the chair into place beneath the table. Her knees were weak, her heart pounding. She found her way into the kitchen. She picked up the damp rag and began again, silently, to wipe the meat clean. As she worked a single tear welled up and fell from the corner of her eye onto the meat. She forced her hand toward it and wiped it off the blood-red, chilling flesh.

3

B utchering took the rest of the day. The chops and loins were fried, then covered with lard in a big barrel in the granary. They would keep that way well into the summer. The hams and bacons lay in the basement, soaking in the curing salts before being smoked. A roast had been put aside for Sunday's dinner. The rest of the meat had been ground up and waited on the back porch to be stuffed into the casings the girls had cleaned.

When the younger children came home from school, they had to help clean up the kitchen. Now all that remained of Short-Ear was a tangle of bones thrown out behind the barn, which Shep would drag home one by one to his place under the porch.

For supper that night they had fresh blood sausage. It was Lent, so they were allowed meat only once a day. It had been a busy day—the girls looked forward to a relaxing evening. But as Mary and Lotti washed the dishes, their mother went up into the attic and brought down a big ticking full of feathers. They knew what that meant.

It was dark outside. Father and Stash were in the barn checking on Brownie, who was due to freshen any day. Bruno and Eddie were in the living room. The girls pulled chairs up around the table. Their mother brought a lamp from the dining room and set it at the center of the table. The cook stove still gave off heat left over from its own hard day's work, and smelled of warm smoldering birch.

Berenice poured a small mound of feathers on the table, and the girls set to work. Their fingers moved regularly, deftly picking a single feather from the pile, pulling the soft part off one side, then the other, and in a smooth and rapid movement reaching out for the next feather. How many thousands and thousands it would take, each meticulously stripped to fill the big feather-filled comforter they called a *pisina*. This, at least, was the last bag of feathers.

Mary wiped her hands and joined her sisters. But her fingers were still damp from the dishwater, and the feathers stuck to her skin. She dried them on her apron, began again. Once she was going she was the fastest of them all.

The girls worked quietly, seriously. They wanted to finish as soon as possible. As the mound of feathers rose, as light as air, they dared not laugh or sneeze.

Angie spoke up, quietly. "Your *pisina* will be done by tomorrow," she said.

Mary blushed. The new feather-tick, which would go into the guest room, would be given to her when she married.

Berenice moved around the table, every movement slow and purposeful so as not to stir the air. Cleaned feathers she lifted by the handful into a ticking. Discarded ribs she put into a bag. When the mound at the center of the table had diminished she poured more out of the big ticking. By now soft down and occasional feathers stuck to the sleeves of her blouse and here and there on her apron-front.

The back door suddenly swung open. Frank stepped in, followed by Stash, and then a cold draft of air which lifted a cloud of feathers and carried them, like gently falling snow, around the room.

"Franchek! Be careful!" Berenice barked, bending to gather up the fallen feathers. Stash gently closed the door. The two men stood on the rug, unsure if they dared even move. Carefully they slipped out of and hung up their coats, then bent to pull off their boots. They moved together to the cook stove to warm their hands and stood, side by side, with their backs to the stove. Stash, in stocking feet, padded in a wide berth around the table and on into the living room. Frank stood motionlessly proud, surveying his busy crew.

"We'll have a new calf by Sunday," he announced. Anna stared at him, smiled. He sighed, padded around the table, to leave the girls to their work. But suddenly he turned and bending, tickled Anna from behind.

"Franchek!" Berenice scolded. But the other girls were giggling now too, and little puffs of down rose and scattered off the table.

Anna wriggled free from her father and bolted away to join

her brothers. Frank stood somewhat embarrassed a moment while the girls straighted up the feathers; then he nonchalantly took Anna's seat, picked up a feather and tugged away at it. The girls smiled to see how clumsy he was. He brought to the table the smell of cold, fresh air. And, as always, of the barn.

From the living room came the sound of Anna and Eddie teasing one another. "Tomorrow," Frank said, "I'm going over to Adam Laska's to see if we can't sign him up. Our first meeting is Saturday."

Berenice was silent. She stood behind Mary, supervising the work. "Now, during Lent?" she remarked at last.

"Even during Lent we have to make a living," Frank replied. He dropped the feather. His hands were too big and clumsy for this kind of work.

Berenice poured the stripped ribs out of Angie's bowl into the bag. A feather which had blown off the table landed on the stove and began to smell. She turned, deftly picked it up and dropped it in with the ribs. "I don't see the sense of it," she confessed.

Frank shrugged.

"You'll only make trouble."

Frank looked up at her. Not often did he assert himself. But this was something he deeply, fundamentally believed in. "So if we have to make trouble, we make trouble." He slid his chair back from the table. "Brother John, he's in the Union, isn't he? And your brother Frank, him too. Every one but us farmers. And nobody works as hard as us." He stopped a moment. "And for what? We have to take what they give us."

"We shouldn't complain," Berenice said. "The farm is paid for"

"Sure it's paid for. But how about Chester, and Adam Laska, and even the Stelmachs?" He glanced at Mary, who was trying to look as though she wasn't listening. "If things keep going the way they are, we'll be the only ones left. The rest'll go bankrupt and move to the city."

He stood up, pushed his chair under the table. The girls were silently rallied behind him. He was a warm man, with a softness and a smile in his eyes, who would tease and — if he had time — play with them. Even when he used the leather thongs of the *pida* on them, they knew they deserved it.

Frank turned to leave. But halfway through the door he stopped. "You remember the story in *Rolnik* about the farmer from Minnesota who shipped his sheep to market and after paying the shipping costs and broker's fees he owed the market five dollars more than he got for the sheep? Well that kind of thing can't go on forever." But it would do no good. Berenice had made up her mind, and when her mind was set, she was hard as bedrock.

Wearily he walked into the living room. Anna was on the floor near the big pot-bellied stove, helping Eddie with his homework. She was a bright child, but for Eddie school was hard. On top of everything else he had to learn English, because Berenice insisted they speak only Polish at home.

"Better finish the feathers," he told Anna. "Then you can come back and help your brother." Anna stood and went into the kitchen. Frank lifted the top of the wood stove and slid a single log down into the crackling fire. He turned the flue open, then collapsed into his favorite chair, beside the stove, and put his stockinged feet up onto the footrest.

Out in the barn or in the field, Frank Topolski worked and looked like a man almost ten years younger than the fifty-four years he had behind him. But here, when he let himself go, it was different.

Stash sat across from him listening to the crystal set he'd built just the week before. With an earphone pressed to his ear, he was meticulously tuning the set. From the radio extended a long wire which, fastened to one leg of the stove, served as a kind of antenna.

Bruno sat in the far corner of the room, beside the lamp, reading the *Dziennek Chicagowski*. He scanned the sports page for mention of Babe Ruth or Christy Mathewson. But though training had started in Florida, there was little said of his favorite sport. Anyway he was having trouble reading Polish. Or English. He lowered the paper long enough to ask his father if he cared to see it. But Frank shook his head and closed his eyes, letting the warmth of the stove soothe his tired muscles.

The clock in the dining room chimed the half hour. Seven thirty. These long winter evenings, spent in the midst of the family, were some of Frank's favorite times. Now, at his age, he needed them to replenish his strength. Because in a month or so, when the fieldwork started before breakfast and wasn't done until dark, there would be no time for relaxing. Fourteen hours a day, nonstop, six days a week.

Yet even while he rested in his chair, his mind kept working. Now was the time to plan out the spring projects. One big job would be clearing the land behind the barn. He and Stash had started on that last year, cutting the trees, blasting stumps, burning roots. But there was still plenty to be done.

And the garage. The family had outgrown the Ford. So in September he'd gone into town and bought the Overland. Both cars —because the roads weren't plowed — now sat up on blocks along the drive. But they needed a garage. Stash, who'd bought the Ford from them with money earned working at the sawmill, had volunteered to do the work. Besides hunting and fishing, carpentry was Stash's passion. No, Frank had to admit, Stash is no farmer. These days he was spending most of his time at Helen's, helping there with the chores. Without pay, of course.

Yes, there would be a wedding this summer. If not Mary's, then Stash's. Either way it meant additional expense. Frank had wanted Stash to take over the farm. But that was out. Then he thought perhaps Walter might. But there would be no talking Walter back home, not after the kind of wages he could make in the city. And Bruno wasn't built for it. Bruno would grow up to be one of those soft, pudgy men who sat behind desks. Eddie? Spoiled. Beyond saving.

Someone, within a few years, would have to help Frank with the chores. Someone to whom he could hand down the farm. For a while he thought for sure it would be Joe Stelmach. And he didn't know anyone he'd rather work with.

Frank opened his eyes and silently watched Stash set the crystal set aside, wrapping the antenna wire around a board. He was a handsome boy, Stash. No, not a boy, a man. Strong and quiet. During the War, Stash had signed up. No big to-do about it. Just went down and signed up. Frank remembered driving Stash to Mauston to catch the troop train. They'd lived at Necedah then. And while Stash was in Texas they'd sold the place and moved here. So when he got out, he came home to a different house. Somehow, ever since, he didn't seem to fit in.

Frank's eyes turned to the table below the big bay window where Stash's picture, in uniform, stood prominently displayed. It made them Americans. It made Frank proud.

It was a dirty war, in the trenches and even here, back home. There were all those ugly scenes between the German-Americans and everyone else. Hell, Frank thought, I'm German. Polish German. It says German on my papers. But it was the ones with names like Schmidt and Mueller, Jaeger, Bock or

Obermann, who had suffered.

In other ways the War had been a blessing. For farmers prices had shot up. And so he'd been able to pay off the Necedah farm, to be rid of that mortgage, which always hung over your neck like a sword about to fall. When he sold that place, he'd had enough to put three thousand down on this one. And just last year they'd paid off the remainder. It was all his now, no one could take it away. He remembered how proudly he'd written to his mother back in the old country. It is ours now, he'd written, a hundred and twenty acres. In Poland it would have been called an estate. Growing up there he'd never dreamed that one day he might own an estate.

There were many things that had happened he'd never dreamed of.

Only now, estate or not, things didn't look so good for farmers. Government loans to help Europe rebuild after the War had been cut off. Immediately dairy exports skidded downward, and prices went down with them. Frank was getting now, for a gallon of cream delivered to the Dancy station, just about half what he'd gotten two years before.

If he were a younger man he might move to the city. But at his age, his future was behind him.

He never thought he'd end up farming. He had a knack with horses, so when they'd come over and he and his brother John ended up in Chicago; he'd gotten a job at a livery stable. Then one Sunday after he and Bernice were married, John came over with a brochure the *Dziennek Chicagowska* had printed about cheap farmland in Wisconsin. John was all excited. They made it sound like the Garden of Eden.

It wasn't. And the funny thing was, John had talked Frank into moving, then stayed behind in the city. Berenice never let him forget that. Because she didn't like the farm life.

He rubbed his hands through his hair. "You going to help with the garage this spring?" he asked Stash. There was a nice stack of lumber in the granary, up in the rafters. It should be plenty dry by now.

Stash nodded.

"For two cars," Frank added. Stash nodded again. "It'll be a busy time for me. You'll have to do most of it yourself." Too bad Walter wasn't home. He could help. "We'll have to buy nails. What else?"

Stash thought a moment. "Hinges for the doors."

Frank interrupted him. "I've got a pair or two in the workshop I brought from Necedah."

"Glass."

"How much do you think the whole thing will cost?"

Stash considered. "Twenty, twenty-five dollars."

"All right. But we want to get it done as soon as the weather breaks. Right after Easter. You'll have to tell Helen's father you're needed here." Though Stash didn't reply, Frank knew he would do as he was told. "Do you want to come with me tomorrow? I'm going over to Laska's to see what Adam thinks about the Union."

Stash answered quietly. "I'll come."

Anna and Sophie suddenly appeared in the middle of the room; they'd come so quietly they startled their father. "All done with the feathers?" he asked.

"All done," Anna answered. She sat again by Eddie, at her father's feet. He bent over to pick a feather from her hair. She looked up at him an instant. He ran his hand over her hair, soft and brown.

Sophie picked the folded newspaper off Bruno's lap. The boy stood and lazily stretched.

"Bruno, you bring in some more wood," his father said. The woodbox by the stove was almost empty. "And ask your mother if she needs any in the kitchen. It should have been done before supper."

But Bruno had done all his barn chores. Hauling in wood was Eddie's job. So he didn't move.

"Get along," his father said. Bruno shrugged and morosely headed for the kitchen.

They heard the back door open and close, then open again as Bruno came in with an armful of firewood. The wood clattered into the box in the kitchen. In a moment he came into the living room with a bigger armful, and walking around Anna, almost tripped on Eddie, who'd resolutely not moved his leg though it was in the way. The logs fell into the box. Eddie grinned at Bruno.

"I'll help," Anna offered.

"Bruno can do it," her father replied.

From the dining room came the quiet chatter of the older girls busy at their needlework. When Bruno had finished filling the woodbox — he worked slowly to emphasize his resistance — the room settled back into its quiet. Frank would like to sit and watch the family for hours and hours. They grew up so fast. Soon, he supposed, he would be a grandfather. That would be something.

Eddie and Anna were finishing up a puzzle the girl had been given for Christmas. Bruno was already upstairs. Stash was quietly leafing through a magazine. It was so warm and quiet by the woodstove.

The next thing Frank knew, Berenice was nudging him awake. "Come on to bed," she was saying. "The children are all asleep."

She carried the lamp with her into the bedroom, leaving him in the dark. He rose, stiffly, ran his fingers through his hair, slipped two big pieces of oak into the stove, turned down the damper, then shuffled after her into the bedroom.

4

The Laska farm — you could hardly call it that, really — was a half hour's cutter ride down on the flats along the Big Eau Pleine. It was a warm, clear morning, with a brisk southwesterly wind, which slowly swung the haymow doors at the Cranshaw place, now abandoned, open and shut, open and shut. And beyond, the Roshak farm, its windows boarded up. Two families gone since last summer. Stash pointed to a spot of red loping across a wide field. A fox. It disappeared into the edge of an alder swamp. Down along this way all the land was wet and full of rocks. Adam's was hardly worth farming — forty acres of marl in one corner that could grow nothing but wet-footed tag alders. Frank knew how hard it must have been for Adam, just to keep his head above water.

They turned into the long drive and now could see the Laska house in a little swale down by the river. It was hardly more than a shack, really, its log walls sided over with tar-paper, its tiny windows and narrow, ill-fitting doors. Behind the house was the barn, itself an old log structure, its roof sagging, a low, long building in which a man of any size at all would have to stoop in order to work. And beside the barn the thatched-roof shed which instantly reminded Frank of the old country.

As they climbed out of the cutter they caught slipping down the wind the acrid smell of smouldering elm. Frank hesitated, for a moment, thought of getting back into the cutter and heading home. Had he become a salesman? Was he really out here pushing these people into something they didn't care about? What good could a Union possibly do for a family like Adam's?

But he walked toward the house. From under the steps Antek growled out at them. Scattered nearby were large tooth-marked bones, cleaned of every last bit of meat or even taste of meat.

Frank stepped up and knocked. After a moment Helen Laska opened the door. A tired-looking woman with a thin face and swollen belly, twenty-five years younger than Frank, she pushed a wayward hair back from her eyes. Dim eyes, she had, from which all desire and enthusiasm had long ago burned out. She smiled when she saw Frank. Behind her, in the clutter of the tiny kitchen, he could see the children, sitting at the table, staring out the door with that sad, frightened look, compounded half of curiosity and half of fear.

"Is Adam home?" Frank asked, standing with one foot up on the steps. Antek chose that moment to begin a loud, pro-longed, senseless barking.

Helen shouted at the dog to shut up. Over the rebellious yelping she told Frank that Adam was in the barn. Frank thanked her and backed off the steps. Antek's head appeared from under the porch, with yellow teeth showing. Helen opened the door wide enough to let a piece of firewood fly and hit the dog's snout. He retreated under the steps with a reproachful whine.

Frank and Stash walked across the yard toward the barn, which squatted like some ancient arthritic animal, exhaling slowly its acrid breath. Frank opened the door and they stepped inside. The tiny windows cut in the long walls did not let in enough light; it took their eyes time to adjust. To their left were stanchioned four cows, little jerseys not carrying much flesh. Eight hundred pounds, Frank guessed, or maybe a little more. Beyond them a narrow pen with two heifers, their rears and sides caked with manure.

Across the aisle in his own stall was Kurt, the big bony workhorse staring out at them from the darkness. Adam was in the stall with the horse, forking manure out into a wheelbarrow. He had his back to the approaching men. The barrow full, Adam set his fork outside the stall and turned around. He was startled to see someone else in the barn.

"Adam," Frank said, offering his hand.

"Frank," Adam replied. "Stash." In his late twenties, Adam

was a thin, wiry man who today sported a two-day stubble of beard. He came out through the gate and carefully latched it, then paused a moment, as though uncertain of himself. "Go on, finish up," Frank said.

Adam lifted the handles and wheeled the barrow down the aisle toward the far end of the barn. With its front he pushed the end door open, and balanced the barrow along a dirt-crusted plank to a big pile ten yards out. There he tipped the barrow, then wheeled it back down the plank inside the barn. He shut the door behind him; again the light dimmed. Turning the wheelbarrow onto its end, he leaned it beside the horse stall.

"How's the family?" he asked Frank.

"Oh they're fine. And yours?"

Adam stood before them, his feet planted heavily on the dirt floor of the barn. Though his clothes were old and dirtied with barn dirt, and his face unshaven and hair unkempt, he carried himself with that pride which comes from hard work, from a spirit not yet broken.

"The family's fine," he said.

"And Kurt?" Frank nodded towards the horse. Hearing his name, the animal moved to them, hoping for a treat. Frank reached out and stroked the long dark muzzle.

He could easily see Kurt hadn't tasted grain for months. Was trying to stay alive on marsh hay. Last summer — no, Frank thought, it was two summers ago already — he'd hurried down to doctor Kurt, who'd broken into Adam's oat-field along the road. Stuffing himself with the sweet, doughy grain, the horse had come down with the founder. Frank really hadn't expected him to survive. But he did. Only his hooves, cracked and laminated, showed the scars of that sudden, indiscreet feast.

"Kurt!" Adam breathed out, shaking his head with the horse and scratching Kurt's ear. "Thanks to you, Frank, he's still alive." Adam turned and grabbed up a handful of coarse hay, pushing it between the rails. The horse's lip curled back and accepted the grass between his teeth. "And thanks to you, too, for Julia and Joe."

"Thank the Lord for them, not me," Frank replied.

Berenice had come as midwife for Adam's youngest two. And Frank, of course, wouldn't let her take any money for that; nor would he accept anything for doctoring the horse. It had been a bone of contention between him and Berenice.

Adam walked to the far end of the barn and returned with

a big armful of straw, which he threw at the horse's feet for bedding. Frank knew this was done for his sake: the manure Adam had hauled out had no straw in it. Kurt lowered his head and picked at the long, dry stalks.

"Let's go in," Adam said. Frank and Stash turned to follow him. Passing the heifers, who stood quietly in deep, hoof-pocked manure, Frank felt a sudden flush of pity for Adam. Even when he'd started, more than twenty years before, Frank had not faced these kinds of odds.

Outside the light glared into their eyes, and the cool fresh air filled their lungs like a drink of cold spring water. Antek crawled out from under the steps and bounded over to meet his master. Adam petted the dog, clicking his tongue and chanting "Antek, hey, Antek." But as they went up the stairs and into the house, Antek growled then tried to rush into the kitchen behind his master. Adam turned and sent a foot in the dog's direction. Antek retreated again under the porch where he took solace in the more courteous, less capricious companionship of a half-chewed cow's knee.

They stepped into the kitchen: small, dark, and hot with the closeness of the cook stove. Julia and Joe, five and three, were sent into the living room to make room for the men. Helen, who'd been kneading bread, wiped her hands and offered them a place to sit. In the small kitchen, the swollen front of her apron only made her more self-conscious.

"Some cocoa or tea?" Adam offered, somewhat nervously taking Frank and Stash's jackets.

"No need," Frank replied.

"Mama, make us some cocoa," the young man said. His wife reached high for the cups in the cupboard and began spooning out the cocoa. Adam took his jacket off and hung it by the door. He suggested that there was more room in the living room.

So they all slipped quietly past Helen. The living room — which was also the parents' bedroom — was cluttered, but clean. From their hiding place on the bed the two children made a dash for the kitchen. Adam caught Joe and gave him a big kiss on the cheek. The boy giggled and squirmed, until his father set him down, when he escaped to the kitchen where he clung to his mother's apron.

Adam gestured his guests onto the simple homecrafted chairs, and sat himself on the edge of the bed, timidly sliding

the thick *pisina* back to make room for himself. Above and
behind him on the pale green wall was a faded oleograph of the
Sacred Heart. *Bose Dom,* it said. God Bless our Home. On
either side, simple crucifixes. And on the wall behind Stash, a
Last Supper.

For a moment they sat in an uncomfortable silence. Frank
knew how embarrassed Adam was of his house. But, by Frank's
reckoning, the value of a house was not to be judged by its size
or the elegance of its furnishings. There was something more to
life than that. He knew of others who, in Adam's situation, had
turned to drink. For them he saw little hope. But Adam would
fight the hard fight clear to the end. It was just that, Frank
realized, which had brought him on this visit: to offer his friend
whatever help he could to win that fight.

Helen came out with the cocoa. Frank and Stash thanked
her, sipping it gratefully. It was thin, made with water, but sweet
and warm.

"I'd offer some *ponchki,*" she said, standing for a moment in
the doorway. "But it's Lent, right?" Frank finished her thought.
Helen smiled, went back to her work in the kitchen.

"Are you shipping cream?" Frank asked his host.

Adam shook his head. "Maybe next month. Duchess is
due around Easter, then Blackfoot. Then maybe I'll start shipping. Now, we use all we get." He shrugged. "Sometimes we
sell a little butter."

Frank had sold butter, for years. But it seemed so long ago
now. The girls used to sit in the kitchen, at the other farm,
with the big jar half full of heavy cream, cradling it in their lap
and sloshing it back and forth. It was slow and tedious; they
had to take turns. Then the butter had to be washed and pressed.
He bought a hand-cranked churn to fit inside the jar. That
made it easier. And finally the tall wooden churn which could
handle three gallons of cream.

But they hadn't sold butter since they moved. Instead he
spun the cream off the milk with the separator, kept it cool
down in the well, then took it down to the cream station every
other day. The girls didn't even make their own butter any more;
Frank bought it at the cream station where it was simply sub-
tracted from their check.

"Price is down, isn't it?" Frank asked. Through the doorway he could see Helen kneading the bread and the two children
sitting at the table, staring back at him. Where were Tony and

the older girls? That's right. They'd be in school.

"You mean the butter price?" Adam asked. "We get twenty-five a pound. Last year, or year before, we were getting forty."

"And your taxes went down by the same amount? And your mortgage payments?"

Adam smiled ironically.

"And the price of oats, or of a shovel or a new plowshare, they all dropped by a third?" Adam held his cup between his hands, was studying Frank. "My taxes have close to doubled in three years," Frank went on. "And everything else along with them. Everything but milk prices. So, I figure we're getting a raw deal." Frank set his cup between his feet. He was no salesman. But he had two essential things going for him. First, he believed in what he was saying. And second, he was a man whose word was implicitly trusted.

"So what can we do about it?" Adam asked.

"Farmers all over the country are organizing."

"Yeah. I heard you were starting a Union," Adam said.

"It's the only chance we've got," Frank replied, leaning forward with his elbows on his knees. Unconsciously, Stash did the same. Frank counted on the fingers of his left hand. "Cranshaws, Roshaks, Detlaffs, I hear Steinbrenners up the road aren't doing too well. How many's that make, right around here, that have had to foreclose?"

Adam sipped his cocoa. "Might be another one pretty soon," he said.

"We're having a meeting." Frank sat up straight. "The first one is just to see if there's enough interest around here to start up a local." He looked Adam in the eye. "Can you come?"

Adam looked away, at the floor, of unfinished fir, grey but spotless. "Well I don't know, Frank," he confessed. "I can see what you're saying and all. But what good's a Union to me?"

He was right. Small subsistence farmers like Adam kept most of their crop right on the farm. Commodity prices hardly affected them at all. But if you were in their position, every penny counted.

"Why are you doing this, Frank?" Adam asked suddenly. "Your place is paid for. You don't have to worry, do you?"

Frank's hand went to his head. "I guess, Adam," he said somewhat self-consciously, "I don't want to be the only farmer left in the town. Think what that would do to the school, the stores, the church."

They looked at one another a moment. "What's the cost?" Adam asked.

"It's two-fifty to join and three dollars for the first year's dues." Adam shook his head slowly from side to side. "I know it sounds like a lot but after the first two-fifty, that's just a quarter a month."

Adam stood up, reached for a small wooden box above the bed. He sat down again, opened the box, moved some coins around, closed it again. He set it carefully on the bed beside him. "Don't have two-fifty, Frank. And sure don't have an extra two bits a month."

"If you can't pay now, we'll carry you till you can. Will you at least come to the meeting? That won't cost a thing. And if you don't like what you hear, well, that's that."

Adam sighed. "When is it?"

"A week from tomorrow. That's the eleventh, at eight o'clock. Down at Roman's place."

Frank stood up. It was time to go. Standing he seemed to take up most of the living room; though he wasn't a big man, now he seemed to dwarf Adam, who was still on the bed. "You came to America to get ahead, right?" he asked.

Adam smiled. "I came to America so the Kaiser wouldn't get me." Frank had already emigrated when, in '93, universal conscription was voted in in the old country. But if he'd still been there, he'd have done just what Adam did. How could you blame him for refusing to serve in the Kaiser's Army when it was the Kaiser's Army that hauled away and executed, without trial, young Polish nationalists? When in the name of the Kaiser the Army swept into farmhouse and shop alike and stole whatever it needed? When the streets were not safe from the men in uniform, and even the Church itself was threatened?"

"I don't blame you," Frank said, "but even so, you want to get ahead, don't you?"

Adam shrugged. "Sure. Everybody wants to get ahead."

"Well we're just trying to help us all get ahead." Now Stash stood up, and Adam with him "If we don't look out for one another," Frank said, "I guess nobody else will." He turned to Stash. "We better go."

In the kitchen, just then, the door banged open and Tony, the oldest boy, ran in. He and the girls were just home from school. Tony rushed on into the living room, but seeing the two strangers, retreated quickly behind his father's leg.

Frank reached out to tug at the boy's ear. "This can't be Tony, can it? What a big boy he is."

"Yeah. He's a big boy all right," Adam said proudly, looking down into his son's upturned face. Only for the word boy, Adam used the dialectal *knop*, instead of the usual *chlopiec*.

Frank put his arm around Adam's shoulder, smiling. "You *kashubas*," he said. "When are you going to learn how to talk?"

Adam reached out and ruffled Frank's hair. "Damned *posnaniak!*" he said, laughing.

Little Tony broke away and Stash chased him into the kitchen, causing in that tiny room a gigantic eruption of giggles and screams from all the children gathered around the table.

5

Thus the ego, driven by the id, confined by the super-ego, repulsed by reality, struggles to master its economic task of bringing about harmony among the forces and influences working upon it; and we can understand how it is that so often we cannot suppress a cry: 'Life is not easy!'
— Sigmund Freud, *New Introductory Lectures on Psychology*

"Can you remember?"

Mary already had her coat on, and stood with her mother at the back door. Eddie, barely awake, slipped into the kitchen to join Anna at breakfast. Fussily he dipped his spoon into the steaming oatmeal. "I'll remember," Mary answered.

But as though she didn't believe her, Berenice took the paper from Mary's hand, found a pencil on the cupboard, and scribbled away impatiently. "Size nine," she said, as she wrote, "but don't pay more than four dollars."

"Black. To match his suit."

"Yes."

Eddie watched with little interest. The girls, on the other hand, would have shown real excitement at the prospect of new shoes for Easter. It seemed all they ever wore were home-mades or hand-me-downs.

"I don't want anything fancy. But not barn shoes either. Understand?"

"Yes." But Mary knew how small the chances were of her bringing a pair home her mother would be satisfied with.

She was handed the list, which one more time she read over carefully. Behind her, in the pale dawn light sifting through the kitchen window, where two African violets were about to burst into bloom, her father could be seen hitching Queen to the cutter.

Her mother fussed at the stove. Mary stood quietly, waiting for permission to leave. But Berenice was thinking out loud. "I've got to start on spring dresses and a shirt for your father," she said, then turned again to Mary. "If you find any nice ginghams, get five or six yards. But no more than twenty cents a yard. And be sure they're colorfast." Berenice poured Eddie a glass of milk, then refilled Anna's. "And two yards of chambray."

Mary took the pencil in hand and added the material to the bottom of the long list. Her mother disappeared into the dining room and came back holding two one-dollar bills.

"Here's some more for the fabric. Now you'd better go. Your father's waiting."

Mary opened her purse and slipped the two dollars alongside the ten her mother had already given her, and folded the list in with the money. As she turned and went out the door, she held the purse tightly to her side.

Even with Queen, who could trot nicely all the way to Point, the trip was still almost two hours. In order to get everything done, they had to start at the first light of the morning. Lotti, Angie, Stash and Bruno were already in the barn doing chores. It was a cold morning, with a brisk westerly breeze. As she walked across the yard, Mary wrapped her scarf more securely around her neck, pulled her babushka forward over her ears.

"All ready?" her father asked her, smiling, as he helped her into the cutter. On cold mornings his limbs, like old oak branches, creaked with stiffness; though he tried to hide it, Mary could see how it hurt him to climb up into the cutter.

A gentle shake of the reins and Queen had them slicing smoothly out the drive, then down the road toward town. Gracefully the horse settled into a gentle trot, seeming to move without any effort at all, as though running were easier for her than just standing still. Only the rhythmic jingle of the harness bells, the thump of her feet on the snow, and the low steady slice of the runners broke the quiet air. As they came down the hill, the cutter began to catch up with Queen; Frank took the reins and clicked his tongue. Across the tracks they turned south. Now the sun, just above the horizon, crept up over the still frozen river, while the wind, coming from the other side, seemed almost to be pushing it back down. On the road there was little traffic. Most of their friends and neighbors could be seen, in the yellow glow of their lanterns, going about their morning chores.

Mary settled in for the long ride. She was glad to be getting away from home — it didn't happen often. And especially she was glad to be in the company of her father, with whom she seldom had a chance to be alone. Wrapped in his big black overcoat, the fur flaps of his hat tied down over his ears, he smiled at her now and then, whistling dance tunes Mary recognized from the records they played on the Victrola. It was almost like a holiday, going into town with her father.

They were far enough from home now that Mary did not know every farm they passed. Her father nudged her arm and pointed. "Look at that place," he said. It was a big, well-kept house, only last summer white-washed. And it was as though the whole place was afire inside, with a bright steady light glowing out of every window. "They must have gas," her father said. "But look at the barn." Far back, on a little rise, stood a sad old barn, whose grey weathered boards sagged as though mortally wounded in the battle against time. "Looks to me like the wife wears the pants at that place," her father said, grinning.

They rode a while. "There," he gestured ahead, "now there's a man's place." A big new barn, with a tall, clean tile silo, stood towering over what was little more than a shack, from which a single dim light hesitantly glowed. "Schmidt brothers," her father added as they swept past. "Bachelors."

The sleigh slid happily along the road, on the right the fields falling back to the woods and on the left the river and river bottoms. "Now over there," her father pointed, "there's a farm where man and wife work together."

A house and barn, standing on a small rise, were surrounded by neat and well-kept outbuildings; the place was a picture of family harmony. Her father was right. He smiled at her, put his arm around her shoulder and gave her a little hug. It was the Stelmach place. As they slipped past, Mary stared at the barn.

Joe would be there now, with his brother George and their father, busy at the morning milking.

The rest of the way they road in silence. Sitting as long as
they had in the cold air, they began to feel chilled. The early
cheerfulness of starting out gave way to a more quiet and thoughtful mood.

Traffic began to pick up — especially after they'd turned
onto County 18, the main east-west artery into the city, which
ran squeezed between the Soo Line tracks on the one side and
the snow-covered expanse of the river on the other. Almost all
the traffic was, like them, headed into town. It seemed that one
of the rules of being a farmer was to stay home during the week
but on Saturday, if there was business to do, you could go into
town.

And so at last they slipped past the huge Box and Lumber
Company which sprawled along the river flats, then crossed the
Clark Street bridge and were suddenly in town. Here they were
only a small drop in a great moving, shifting, noisy stream of
cutters, sleighs and — since the snow in town had been plowed
back — even cars and trucks, the latter of which Queen seemed
not at all to appreciate.

Her father nodded to the big potato warehouse where in
the fall he delivered wagon after wagon of potatoes. "All cleaned
out!" he shouted. From the Sheboygan Creamery came great
puffs of steam which rose into the cold morning air. At a service
station on their right several cars were lined up for their morning meal of gas.

Her father turned Queen left onto Second Street, and in
less than a minute they were in the middle of town. Rynek, they
called it. The public square, alive with activity: people everywhere, walking, in sleighs and cars, yelling to one another or at
their horses, loading and unloading freight, and some just standing and watching the entire spectacle.

"How about some hot cocoa?" her father asked, as he
halted Queen at the hitching rail. "Warm ourselves a little before
we start shopping."

Mary followed her father into the corner restaurant. She
sat at an empty table while her father ordered the drinks. The
restaurant, too, was busy. She didn't know anyone at all.

He brought the two cups of cocoa, and asked if she wanted
a doughnut. But out of habit she couldn't allow herself to spend
the extra pennies. "You sure?" he urged her. "I'm having one."

But she sipped her cocoa and insisted that was enough.

Mary was glad her father was with her. She would have been terrified to come into the restaurant by herself. Yet how exciting it was, watching all these strangers, as they stood to put on their coats, laughing and joking, or sitting and sipping coffee with the morning's first cigarette — how strange and wonderful it was, this bringing her world into contact with theirs. Yet the moment someone else's eyes met hers, she would retreat to her cocoa like a turtle pulling into its shell.

And although her father seemed much more confident than she, inwardly he too was on guard. He knew that some of those innocent-looking strangers regarded him as nothing more than a country rube, ripe for the picking. Well, as he saw it, he wasn't ripe and he sure as hell wasn't about to get picked.

"Do you have lots to do?" he asked Mary. She opened her purse and handed him the list. Berenice's writing, done with a dull pencil on a rough surface, was barely legible. At the bottom was Mary's hand, smooth and patient. "You'll need help at Kleba's," her father remarked. "Why don't we start there then split up?"

Frank and Berenice had begun shopping at John Kleba's the same year they moved to Dancy. John's brother Stanley was the agent who'd sold them the farm. Now John and Frank were good friends. It was good having someone in town you could really trust.

They finished their cocoa; Frank wiped away the sugar left on his moustache. Buttoning up their coats, thoroughly warmed now, they went back outside.

The minute they walked into the store, just two doors down from the restaurant, John Kleba broke away from his work and enthusiastically shook Frank's hand. "Well, Frank, what brings you to town? How are things up your way? A beautiful morning. Beautiful!" He held onto Frank's hand, glanced in Mary's direction. "Let me guess. This one must be..."

"Mary," her father answered. Shyly Mary nodded.

The storekeeper shook his head. "The Good Lord dealt you a handful of queens, Mr. Topolski. And Berenice?"

"She's fine. Stayed home. Sent us down with a list."

Mary handed him the paper.

Mr. Kleba raised his hand high and beckoned to a boy, who had just finished with another customer. "Mark," he said, "see to it Frank gets whatever he needs. You're stopping by for lunch,

Frank?"

Berenice had called Marie the evening before. There was business to be discussed; John's wife had suggested lunch as the perfect time to deal with it. Frank nodded.

"I should be home by twelve-fifteen," John said. "See you then." He put his hand on Frank's arm. It was a busy morning. There were other customers waiting for help.

Mary read the list of groceries to the boy, being careful to find just the right brand and variety of flour, salt, sugar, spices. And a box of sugared fruit for the Easter *babka*.

Frank carried the big sacks of flour out to the cutter. Mary helped with the lighter bags. She handed the boy the ten-dollar bill and carefully counted the change he gave back to her. Then she and her father walked once again back out onto the side-walk. The noise of the people and the stream of horses and cars going this way and that almost made her dizzy. "Why don't we meet here," he emphasized by pointing to the hitching rail, "at, say, eleven-thirty?" He waved across the square to someone he knew. "Is that enough time?"

Mary nodded uncertainly.

Her father squeezed her hand, then stepped up to the rail and untied Queen's reins. In a moment he had pulled easily out into the flow of traffic, swirled around to the other side, and was gone around the bend. Mary, not even certain where she would first go, suddenly felt cold and terribly alone. Frank drove the cutter around the block and parked in front of the big potato warehouse, a large, square, rather mean-looking building. He tied Queen to the scale at which just last fall there had stood the long lines of wagons and trucks with the drivers patiently wait-ing to be scaled and unloaded. Now, except for the traffic in the street, all was quiet.

He pushed the door open into the office. But the grey, dust-coated room was empty. Above Mr. Carley's desk hung the blackboard on which were still written last fall's prices:

Number Ones 85
Number Twos 60

Eighty-five cents a bushel, for the best potatoes in the field. Last year Frank had had one of the worst yields ever. No more than sixty bushels an acre. Prices at least had held up. But his total cash in hand given to him in this very office only a month before Rose died was a hundred and thirty-eight dollars. That was potatoes for you. If prices held and you had a good year, like the last year in Necedah, they could pull you right up out of debt. On the other hand, if prices fell — as they usually did in a good year or if at the wrong time there was too much or too little rain, you could end up with barely enough money to break even. It was one thing you could say for dairying. It wouldn't make you a rich man. Might keep you poor. But if you kept your head and weren't afraid of work, and if on top of that you had a run of good luck, you could at least depend on a regular income. An income which might, as now, decline. But it did so in quite predictable ways. And sometimes, as during the war, it even went up, predictably. Frank wandered into the great empty shell of the warehouse itself, dark, chill, dreary. He wanted to find Mr. Carley, to talk a while about acreages and speculate on prices and get the potato king's opinion on the new Triumph certified seed Frank had been reading about and was planning on trying out. But Mr. Carley was not to be seen.

Frank's footsteps echoed through the gigantic room. Along the sides lay a few odd spuds, not a hundred pounds left of the thousands of tons the building had once held. Now all that was left was that peculiarly earthy, sharp and vaguely repellent smell potatoes brought with them out of the ground.

At the far corner of the building Frank caught sight of a boy who stood pushing a broom, slowly, lazily, raising tiny clouds of fine grey dust. The boy stopped his sweeping to watch Frank approach.

"No," he said insolently, the tip of his cigarette bobbing up and down as he spoke, "Mr. Carley ain't here." And leaning on his broom now. "Nope, don't know when he'll be back."

As Frank turned to leave he knew the boy would stand and watch until he was gone, looking for any excuse not to work.

Frank untied Queen and drove down to the feed store. Inside its tiny office was a tower of Babel; farmers had crowded in from every direction of the compass. There were Norwegians and Germans, Slovenians, Lithuanians and even Russians. Of all, Frank did not recognize a soul.

Beside the stove, his feet propped unceremoniously on an old crate, sat an ancient man with a long white beard. Frank had seen him here before, seemed to recall he was the owner's father. Or father-in-law. It would be quite a long time before the counter cleared away. He wandered in the old man's direction. They exchanged greetings.

"*Gruss Gott,*" Frank said. From out of the man's mouth came a sudden jet of tobacco juice, landing neatly in the nearby spittoon. "*Ach, Mensch!*" the old man said, his voice low and gravelly, his few teeth stained almost black. "Look at them! Can't wait to spend their money. What do you think it grows on trees?" He wiped a tiny dribble of spit from his lower lip. "*Tja,*" he said, "you hear about the old country?" Frank guessed, from the man's accent, that he meant by that Bavaria, or possibly even Austria. "They gonna have their bad times!" It was his favorite topic. He counted on his calloused and gnarled hand. "Inflation," he said, "unemployment, starvation. And inflation."

Frank thought the man was either senile or maybe not quite all there, but had long ago learned that in politics and economics you had to be careful who you called crazy and who you called far-sighted.

At last the counter cleared away. Frank asked if they'd be carrying the new certified potatoes. The clerk had to go to the back office and ask his boss; when he returned he took Frank's name and said they'd be letting him know. He looked in a notebook and said that the certified seed ought to be about twenty cents a bushel more than the Rural Russets or Late Petofskeys. Frank nodded. If what he'd been reading was true, it was worth the difference. He was about to leave when he remembered the soybean seed, and turned back to the counter. He hadn't planted rye for two years now. Rye was a crop of the past, he could see that. Corn. That was where the future lay. And soybeans, too. He asked what varieties they'd have available. It was a matter of finding the right variety for the soil and climate, fertilizing properly, and if the weather held, there you were. He'd even considered in the next year or two giving up on potatoes.

Frank had the clerk put him down for four sacks of seed, which would be arriving early in May. He waved good-bye to the old man at the stove, who'd captured another audience and as far as Frank could tell was repeating the same line to him.

Outside it was quiet and cold. From the west a few clouds covered the sky. He checked his pocket watch. Just after ten. He left Queen tied at the feed store and walked just up the street to the implement dealer. He pushed open the door and stepped inside, where the new line of power equipment was on display. Big McCormick Deerings, 15-30s and, new this year, 10-20s, brought out to compete with the Fordson. Shiny and new, the big steel-wheeled monsters sat next to each other, filled the display-room with the raw power they emanated. Frank stared at the 10-20 just inside the door. It made him feel suddenly weak and very old.

He walked past the tractors and went out back to where the horse-drawn equipment was kept. Here, in the snow, he studied the walking plows. The colter on his was worn thin. The share, too, had seen its better days. But a new plow was twenty-five dollars. Thirty for the sturdier model. He'd have to get by. Maybe by next year, he thought, who knows? I might even have a tractor.

He went back in to look at the 10-20, leaned his arm on the front wheel to study the engine. It looked sturdy enough. But he knew nothing about gas engines. Even with the car, Stash did most of the repairs. He would just be getting himself into a lot of trouble.

A salesman came over to talk. "She'll pull a three-bottom plow for an hour with only two gallons of gas," he pointed out. "Burns kerosene, too. One piece cast frame. Outpull a Fordson any day. And in here," he tapped the side of the massive engine, "ball bearings on the crankshaft. Starting this week, we can offer you this tractor for just seven hundred dollars, and throw in a plow or a disk — whichever you want — at no cost to you."

Frank shook his head, pointed out that seven hundred dollars was about all he could figure on earning in a year.

"Well, one way of changing that," the salesman said, his foot up on the drawbar, "is to put one of these to work for you."

But it didn't figure. To pay for it he'd have to buy more land. And if he had the money to do that, he wouldn't need the tractor. Of course nowadays the way to do it was to go into debt. But that wasn't Frank's way. Once out of debt, he intended to stay that way.

He shrugged, changed the subject. "How's the Equities doing down this way?" There'd been several Farmer's Unions started in the Point area, and Frank was curious to know about them. Superficially at least the salesman seemed sympathetic. After all anything that would help the farmers would help him. Yes, he thought they'd catch hold and in a few years be spread all across the country. Since there weren't any other customers in the store, Frank and the salesman stood beside the tractor for a good half hour and talked weather, farm prices and unions.

✳✳✳

For a long time Mary had been hovering over the bins of shoes; had exasperated the clerks with her indecision; had, in the end, used up every last euphemism she could think of for "nice, but..." At last she settled on two pairs. She vacillated from one to the next, then decided on the lower-priced of the two. Three dollars and fifty cents. But as the clerk wrapped them and the money changed hands, she had second thoughts. She was sure of it. Her mother would prefer the other pair. But it was too late. She was out the door, the parcel of shoes held close, totally convinced she had made the wrong decision.

Then, to the dry goods store. There were hundreds of bolts of material along the wall, from the finest Chinese silk — who could afford that? — to the coarsest muslins fit only for toweling or window curtains. She asked for the chambrays first. That was the easiest. The gingham was another story. She had to find the right color, the right pattern, the right price. She was as careful as if she were out in the fall fields hunting mushrooms. Picking the wrong one could invite disaster. But at last she found a light blue plaid she was sure her mother would like. Then the needles her mother had specified. And a half dozen spools of thread. It used up all but a few cents of the money she'd been given. And most of the morning; it was already eleven o'clock.

She hurried out the store with her new package and was halfway up the street before she came to an abrupt stop. Was she going the wrong way? For one awful moment she stood, the flow of shoppers parting around her, completely lost. And worse: she couldn't remember where she was supposed to meet her father. To those passing she must have been a sorry sight, clutching her purse and packages, staring wildly up and down the street. Then just as suddenly it came back to her. There was Shafton's and behind it the marquee of the Majestic, to which last summer Joe had taken her to the only movie she'd ever seen. So she was on Main. She only had to cross Third and then one more block to the square. Her heart relieved but still heaving, she hesitantly pulled open the door to Steven-Walter's. A gentle bell rang as she closed it. Here all was still and quiet: rows and rows of crucifixes hung on the wall; and across, holy pictures; Bibles, statues and rosaries filled the glass-topped counters. It was a refuge from the outside, a convent in which she could hide herself.

Even the smells reassured her: beeswax of the candles, incense which though unburned filled the air with a sweet spiciness, the wonderful smell of freshly printed books.

She moved along the nearest counter, inhaling the peace, the tranquility, almost as though she was in church. She tried not to draw attention to herself, but an elderly clerk, grey-haired and dignified, came up and asked if she could be of any help.

"I'm looking for a scapular," Mary said, in what was scarcely above a whisper yet seemed in the quiet store to be embarrassingly loud. The lady pulled out a drawer behind her and set it on the counter. Resting on soft blue velvet was a large selection of cloth scapulars. Mary looked through them, one by one. St. Christopher. The Blessed Virgin. That was a nice one. Maybe for Anna, for Confirmation. The Sacred Heart. At last she found what she'd come for: a small rectangle of woven wool, a gentle violet in color, onto which had been appliquéd a smaller square of golden cotton. And on this background a figure of St. Joseph, holding in one arm the baby Jesus and in the other a staff of lilies. Underneath, in tiny letters, *St. Joseph, Patron of the Church, Pray for Us.*

She picked it up. It had hardly any weight. The thick white cord which would hang around the neck was soft and pliable. She turned it over. On the back side the same golden cotton. But here not the image of Joseph, but the papal crown and above it a dove. Beneath, the cross and keys which meant St. Peter and then the words: *Spiritus Domini ductor eius.* She didn't know what that meant. The clerk slipped another drawer onto the counter. "We also have the metal scapulars," she said, holding up a tiny medal, hardly larger than a thumbnail. "They're becoming more and more popular," the clerk added. She handed it to Mary, who held it timidly. The clerk pointed to the tiny image with her long black pen. "The Sacred Heart," she said, then turning it over in Mary's hand, added, "and here, Our Lady."

Mary pretended to be having trouble deciding. But she handed the metal scapular to the lady. "No," she said. "This one." She pointed to the St. Joseph scapular. "How much is it?"

"The cloth scapulars are a dollar and a half. All have been blessed by the Pope." She slid the drawers back into place and wrapped the precious medallion in fine white tissue paper. Mary took the dimes and quarters she'd been saving for six months from a little coin purse and counted them into the clerk's hand. When she snapped the purse shut again it held only a single quarter and two dimes.

With the medallion in her purse she was out the door. And there, across the square, still busy and bustling, she saw her father seated behind Queen.

"Well," he said, helping her into the seat.

"How have you done? Spent all your money I suppose."

Mary nodded. Her parcels she hugged to her lap. But her father picked them up and put them in back with the groceries. The purse, however, she kept with her.

"Let's go for a ride," he said cheerfully. "It's too early for dinner."

So they pulled out into the traffic and turned down Strong, past the big stone courthouse and slowly on down to the depot. A train, just coming in from the south, belched dark smoke and spit sparks out of its stack. A sharp blast from its whistle set Queen on edge. Frank calmed her with cooing noises. They parked by the depot a while, watched the passengers getting off, carrying suitcases, baskets, boxes. There were rich businessmen in fancy furs with tall beaver hats, natty old ladies with elegant purses and shiny leather boots, families with children old and young, and poor old men in rags and women carrying everything from squawking chickens to pots and pans. It was great fun. But when the train tooted again and pulled away, the platform slowly grew deserted. Frank shook the reins and Queen stepped out into the traffic. On Division, where there were many cars and trucks, they had to stay far to the right or their little cutter was in danger of being run over.

They both breathed a sigh of relief when they'd turned onto Normal and skirted under the big elms and maples lining this more pleasant residential section. The street took its name from the normal school, specializing in home economics, agriculture and teacher education, with its Old Main tower rising high above the trees and rooftops, surrounded like a mother hen with a bevy of dormitories and classrooms.

Just past the school was the Klebas' house — in front two white stories with a wide, many-windowed porch. Behind it the single-story kitchen. Like the other houses in the neighborhood, all solid and unpretentious, it had a good-sized yard, ornamented with now leafless lilacs and spireas. In one corner a big red maple. In back, room for a small garden, a clothesline, and the demure little outhouse back by the alley.

Following her father up the steps, Mary speculated to herself on how different life must be here, where, when you look out the window you are looking into your neighbor's. Yet it seemed somehow so peaceful, so pleasant. Unlike the farm, it was all neat and tidy: no mud, no manure, and certainly not all that work, which you could never catch up on even if you worked twenty-four hours a day.

Marie Kleba opened the door. A finely dressed woman of Frank's age, she took his hand and immediately began apologizing that John wasn't home yet, that he always had that last customer to take care of or a shipment of freight come in just at lunch-time but would they please come in anyway. She asked for their coats, which she took and hung neatly in a closet. "Sit down, please," Marie said.

Mary sat beside her on the sofa, its upholstery elegantly brocaded and shining like new. Walnut furniture — little end tables sporting brass electric lamps and knickknacks, the coffee table by the couch, in one corner a piano. Frank sat across from the two women, in a nice Victorian chair he constantly feared — with no reason, really — would collapse under him. On the wallpapered wall behind him was a large gilt-edged mirror which made the room look even larger than it was. And behind the women, next to the big front windows, a nicely framed painting of a pleasant romantic landscape, with sheep and shepherd, sunset and clouds. Though the Klebas were as Catholic as the Topolskis, there were no religious pictures to be seen. Berenice had a word for the house. *"Finya,"* she called it. Elegant, to a fault. Snooty, perhaps.

Yet the Klebas were as friendly and easygoing as anyone. Marie simply liked having nice things around her. And they could afford it. Especially now since the children had grown up, and the store was doing so well. Michael had moved to Portage where he worked for the electric company. Dorothy, though she still lived at home, was in her last year at the normal school. In the fall she would be looking for a teaching position.

Marie sat rather toward the edge of the sofa, her hands clasped together. Without even trying she was graceful and polite. "How was your Christmas, Frank?" she asked. "To think we haven't seen you since..."

"Since Rose's funeral," Frank finished the sentence. Marie glanced down, shook her head slowly. "And now it is almost Easter."

From the kitchen came the deliciously inviting smell of

boiling potatoes and cabbage. Marie straightened an ashtray on the coffee table. "Dorothy and Rose were very close," she said quietly. "I think losing Rose hit her harder than she'd admit. She gave us quite a fright, you know, around Christmas time. Did Berenice mention?" Frank shook his head. "We thought she might be having a breakdown. John thinks it was the pressure of school, but..."

The front door swung open and John Kleba stood suddenly smiling down at them, whisking off his hat and coat. Frank and Marie stood up.

"Oh sit down Frank," he said. "Sorry I'm late." He sniffed the air. "Is lunch ready?"

Marie, already in the dining room, told them all to come and eat. "You're always in such a hurry, John," she shouted.

"They can get along just fine without me," he said, though his guests knew he didn't really mean it. "Come on then," he said, taking the bashful Mary by the arm and leading her into the dining room.

A large dark dining table was set with fine cream china and sterling silverware. Down the middle ran a long linen runner, embroidered at its corners with chirruping birds. At the center, two tall brass candlesticks stood with long tapers like the altar candles in church. By each plate was a cloth napkin, which matched the linen runner.

Mary wished she hadn't come. She just knew every move she would make would be all wrong.

"Sit down, sit down," John said, showing Frank and Mary where to sit. "And Mary, relax, you look like we're going to eat you." He sat down on her right, in the end chair, while Marie came out with bowls of steaming potatoes, cabbage, and boiled ham. Satisfied that everything was ready, she too sat, and they all bowed their heads while John thanked the Lord for the food they had and the company to share it with.

Frank, always a hearty eater, piled his plate high with potatoes and cabbage. Mary, on the other hand, put very little on her plate — and would have put even less had she not been afraid of thereby insulting Marie's cooking.

"It's not homemade ham," John apologized, handing the plate to Frank. "But it's pretty good. We get it down at Trybulas."

Soon they were busy eating and chatting away. John rather monopolized the conversation. Business, he said, was at last picking up after the long recession. But real recovery would have to wait for the fate of the farmers, on whom he and most of the businesses in town depended.

When Marie brought out the coffee — there would be no desserts during Lent — and began carrying dishes back into the kitchen, Mary rose to help. But their hostess insisted she sit and enjoy herself. John lit a cigarette, offered one to Frank, who declined.

"So what's this big business deal you want to talk about, Frank?" John asked, winking at Mary.

Frank turned his spoon over in his hand. "Anna, as you know, wants to be a teacher, like your Dorothy. She will have to come to high school. That is, if she passes her tests."

"Don't you worry about her," Marie said, taking Frank's plate. "She's a smart one."

"Yes," Frank agreed. "And there's nothing she wants more than being a teacher."

"Good for her," Marie said from the kitchen. Her comment, Frank knew, was directed as much to her husband as to Frank. John, it seemed, had a somewhat different opinion than his wife about women working out of the house.

"She could go to Wausau," Frank said, "but Berenice thinks it would be better if she knew someone..."

John put his coffee cup down. "She's welcome here any time," he said.

"We'd rather not put her up with strangers," Frank added.

"Of course not," Marie chimed in, standing behind the chair she'd sat in, holding onto its back. "We'd love to have her."

"We certainly would," John agreed. "Now that takes care of that."

"Not quite," Frank said. "We have to talk about her room and board..."

John interrupted. "Out of the question!" he said, rather loudly. "Michael's room is empty. Dorothy will be gone in the fall. We'll have the whole damned..." he looked at Mary, as though to apologize for the word, "the whole blasted house to ourselves."

"He's right, Frank," Marie said. "Anna can keep us company. Otherwise we'd be alone here, for the first time in..."

"In twenty-six years," John said. He and his wife looked for a moment into each other's eyes.

The last thing Frank wanted was charity. "But there's the matter of board," he said.

"If Anna doesn't peck up any more birdseed than her big sister here," he nodded in Mary's direction, "we wouldn't notice the difference."

"And if Anna could help around the house a little, with some of the light cleaning, cooking, nothing too heavy, mind you, why that would be more than enough," Marie added.

"That's fine," Frank said, "but still I want to pay you something. Whatever you think is fair, for the trouble."

"Anna? Trouble?" Marie put her hand on John's shoulder. "I've got bridge club starting this fall. If she can help out, that's all we want."

But John understood Frank's viewpoint. He slapped the tabletop, rather frightening his wife. "All right, Mr. Topolski," he said in a businesslike voice, "you drive a hard bargain. If you insist on paying us, then pay us you will."

"Now John," Marie interrupted.

"Hush!" he said, squeezing her hand. "Fifty cents a week, room and board." He winked. "Take it or leave it." Frank smiled. "Well?" John stood up, held out his hand. Frank stood, too, and they closed the deal. Already in his mind Frank had visions of hams, eggs, sausages and potatoes he could send down with Anna to square the deal.

"It'll be great just having her here," John said. "Now, I'd better get back to the store before they sell it out from under me."

"That might be a good thing," his wife kidded.

He picked his cup off the table, drained the last of its coffee. Mary stood. "No, no. Don't hurry off on my account."

But Frank edged away from the table. "We've got a little more shopping," he said. "Then the long trip home."

"Of course," John agreed, once again in the living room and putting on his coat. He reached out to hold his friend's hand. "Thanks for stopping in, Frank."

"No. Thanks to you for the meal," Frank protested. "Marie. . ."

"It wasn't anything. Say hello to Berenice for me."

"Can we give you a lift to the store?" Frank asked John, who was on his way out.

"Well, sure, if you've got room," John replied.

Frank patted his stomach. "I think I'm twice as big as when I came, but there oughta be room."

From the cutter, Mary waved to Marie. John patted Queen's

neck as he came around to climb in. "Say, say, Queen," he chanted. "That's a beautiful horse," he said to Frank.

They were squeezed in the cutter, Mary in the middle, as they headed downtown again. John said he usually walked to and from home, it was all the exercise he got anymore.

"Come on out to the farm sometime, I'll put you to work," Frank joked.

The sky had clouded over. The wind, shifted to the south, seemed damp and heavy with snow or sleet. They dropped John off in front of his store, then Frank drove up to Worzalla Brothers to buy a *Lives of the Saints* as an Easter surprise for Berenice. "I forgot to say," he spoke up as they crossed the bridge and headed out of town. "I ran into Alex and Sophie at the hardware store this morning." Mary didn't say a word. "They asked me to stop in on the way home. I said I didn't know if we'd have time. But I think we should stop or their feelings will be hurt."

His eyes met Mary's. She shrugged, her hands nervously clasped around her purse, inside of which was that precious scapular. "Just for a few minutes," he said.

✳✳✳

Alex Stelmach came out of the house and hurried out to meet them. Short and getting chubby, Alex pumped his arms and puffed in and out as he came. Though just two years older than Frank, his hair was already white and thin. But like Frank he was still strong and healthy. The farm showed it.

"Come in, come in," he offered, enthusiastically taking Mary by the arm and helping her down from the cutter. He led her straight toward the house. Frank came up from behind. It was the first chance Mary had had to see Joe's father since the banns had been cancelled. He certainly didn't seem to be holding any grudges.

Sophie, a quiet pleasant woman who radiated the kind of warmth that made you jealous of whoever had her for a mother, stood by the sink in her apron peeling potatoes. She set the knife down and wiped her hands. "Take your coats off. Sit down," she insisted.

"We can't stay long," Frank said, sitting at the kitchen table. "Berenice will wonder where we've been."

"You're big enough to take care of yourselves," Sophie said. She turned to Mary, who sat at the table with her hands in her lap. "Too bad Joe's not here. He's gone down the road to help with a lambing."

"Already?" Frank asked.

Sophie brought them all a cup of tea. "It does seem early, doesn't it?" she wondered aloud. Frank felt right at home here; you could tell by the sparkle in his eyes and the way he sat in his chair, legs spread apart. He thanked Sophie, sipped the tea. Mary, too, had to admit to herself how much more comfortable she was here than at the Kleba's. Her father was just then telling about the arrangements they'd made for Anna. He spoke of it with a certain pride, this crossing of the class lines. It fit in exactly with his plans for Anna.

"She'll be a good teacher," Sophie said. "She loves school, doesn't she?"

Mary spoke up. "She used to sneak off with us, back in Necedah, when she was a year too young. She'd hide under my desk until the teacher found her. He'd pretend to be mad. But he had an extra desk in the corner and he always let her sit in it, as though it was her own."

"She's been helping Mrs. Schrum teach the younger children already," Frank said proudly. "And the other children... well, not you, Mary, but the others, I couldn't make them go to school."

"The day'll come," Alex said, "when everyone'll need a high school education, just to find work."

There ensued a moment's pause, which frightened Mary, afraid as she was that into the vacuum of the conversation might slip the subject of her and Joe.

Frank had had a few words with Alex one afternoon at the store. They all knew Berenice. What had happened was certainly a serious enough offense to hold it against the Topolski family. But instead Sophie and Alex had put their faith in God and expected that, in the end, everything would turn out all right.

Frank set his teacup down. "We'd better be going," he said. For courtesy's sake, it was best to announce your departure several times before actually taking it.

"Nonsense!" Sophie blurted out. "You just got here. And take off your coats or you'll catch cold when you go back outside. It's still winter, you know."

Frank stood and slipped out of his coat, hanging it over the back of his chair. Mary took hers off, too, handing it to Sophie. She followed Joe's mother into the kitchen, talked her out of a knife and stood beside her peeling potatoes. The water, boiling away on the stove, made a cheerful, welcoming sound.

Alex and Frank were talking cows and co-ops. "Joe told me," Alex said, "that as long as he's going over to Wolniaks, he might as well talk them into coming to the meeting."

The potatoes were cut up and dropped into the water to cook. Now Mary began to worry that Joe might come home and find her there. And as much as she wanted to see him, she just wasn't sure how she could handle it. As Berenice had secretly hoped, Mary had taken upon herself the guilt of the wedding cancellation.

At last her father stood up, stretching his legs, and said it really was time to get home before the boys started chores on their own. "Let them," Alex said, waving his hand.

But Frank had his coat on, and stood by the door while Mary got into hers. Frank thanked them for the tea.

"We're glad you stopped," Sophie said, taking Mary's hand in hers. In the grey-haired woman's eyes, Mary could tell she was still considered their future daughter-in-law.

"See you at church," Frank said as they went out the door.

"Tomorrow's Sunday!" Alex exclaimed. "The days sure go by."

As Frank and Mary pulled out of the driveway and turned north to finish their trip home, Mary saw, far to the south, another cutter come up over the hill. It was Joe.

6

M ary was right, about the shoes. Her mother really didn't like them. The heels were too high, she said. Are you sure they aren't girls' shoes?

But it was the style. The other pair wouldn't have been any better.

The next day, Sunday, was not a fast day. So after church they had a big chicken dinner; and the rest of the day was a day off. Stash went for the afternoon to Helen's. Angie ran across the road and came back with the Tomczak children. They all got together — Mary, too — with sleds and toboggans for a sledding party on the long hill which led to town. The sun was bright, the air warm, the snow wet and slippery. It was great fun. There weren't many such days left.

Berenice napped on the bed while Frank dozed off in his chair. In the middle of the afternoon he woke out of sleep and only half awake could hear the distant laughter of the children as they played. For an instant his mind, like a mouse tunneling through dizzying drifts of snow, surfaced onto his childhood, when he too had gone sledding down the snowy hills of Wielkopolska. But it was only for an instant, when he drifted back to a sleep which lasted until suppertime.

During the night the wind shifted and blew a slow, slathering drizzle in from the south. Going out to the barn in the morning, Frank's boots crackled through layers of ice, treacherously slippery. By mid-morning the trees, the house and barn, gates, fences, and even the cars were all wrapped in a glassy skin of ice. Instead of spending the day burning brush on the new clearing, Frank had to work inside. He fussed, at the kitchen table, over harnesses that would need repairing before fieldwork began. But when Mary and Lotti dragged out the clothes washer and filled it with hot water, the close, warm smells of soiled clothing spreading through the room drove him and his harness out to the barn.

The following morning dawned cold and clear; walking to the barn in the faint light of dawn, the sun just clearing the fields to the east, sparkling off the treetops which seemed made of crystal, Frank Topolski moved as though through a fairy-tale world, a world made of dreams come to life. He was near the barn when, coming from the *dompki*, the little woods to the west, he heard a faint, tinkling warble, as though the ice itself was singing. He stopped, startled, and turned to find its source. Listening closely, he made out a lilting melody, sweet and clear, as though one of God's own angels had been sent down to remind man of the glories of His creation. Frank caught sight of a bright red bird, high on an elm branch. As the bird sang, its wings fluttered at its sides. Frank stood in the yellow, glistening dawn, unable to move, as though captured inside a sparkling diamond. After more than fifty springs, the thought of winter's end still stirred his heart.

❊❊❊❊

Mr. Dietzmann was due that morning. He was a Farmer's Union membership representative whom Ben Lang, the county chairman, was sending down. Frank had contacted Ben through an ad in *Rolnik*, the Polish farmers' weekly paper, published in Stevens Point.

So the brush-pile would have to wait a little longer. Finished with morning chores, Frank hauled another harness into the house and sat at the kitchen table. Pushing the sharp-pointed awl through the cowhide, he grew minute by minute more nervous and more certain he didn't want anything to do with all this organizing he'd gotten himself into.

There was a knock at the door. He set the harness aside and, passing the cupboard, stopped to glance in the mirror and slick his hair down. He opened the door.

A neatly dressed young man stood with his hat in hand. "Bill Dietzmann," the man said, offering a handshake.

"Come in," Frank offered, uncomfortable with his English. He took the stranger's coat, fur-lined and heavy, and offered a chair.

Mr. Dietzmann laid a briefcase on the table, quickly glancing around. "Nice place you've got here," he said. "Looks like a new silo out there." He sat down and opened his briefcase.

"Coffee?" Frank asked.

"Please."

Berenice, with one ear cocked in their direction, was busy in the dining room folding linen. She'd been against the Union from the start. Even when Frank read one of his mother's letters to her, telling about the Farmer's Associations which were being started up back in Poland, even then she held out. They had come up by themselves, the hard way; that was between God and them, was nobody else's business.

Frank poured two cups of coffee.

"Thanks," the other man said. He sipped from the cup, breathing out a cozy sigh. It was a cold morning; the coffee warmed him down into his limbs.

Frank sat down across the table from Mr. Dietzmann, picked up the leather he'd been working on. Now and then he glanced up at the young man. There was a self-assurance in him which disquieted Frank. He didn't trust a man who so easily made himself at home in a stranger's house.

"It's good coffee," Mr. Dietzmann said.

"Thank you."

"Getting ready for spring?" He gestured to the leather.

Frank nodded. He slipped the bit through a ring and was sewing an end of leather to hold it in place.

"So, Mr. Topolski, Ben told me you're starting a local down here. How's it coming?"

Frank took his time in answering. He was having to think in Polish, then answer in English. "It's going pretty good," he said.

Mr. Dietzmann pulled a stack of papers from his briefcase. "We're in a membership drive right now," he said, "and every county has a quota to fill. I'm working district four, which includes Marathon County. Ben... Oh, have you met Ben, Mr. Topolski?"

"He called." Frank set the harness aside and held his coffee with both hands.

"I see. Ben's done a marvellous job up here. There are..." He looked through some of his papers. "Yes. There are more than twelve hundred paid-up members in your county. That's tremendous. Really tremendous. In a couple weeks, Ben's having a statewide meeting in Marshfield. The goal is to formulate an organization of buying co-ops to be sure of closer cooperation between the various locals. It's all Ben's doing." He sipped his coffee. "We'd like you to attend, Mr. Topolski."

Frank shrugged.

The man set his papers down. "First I better tell you a little about myself," he said. "I grew up on a farm near Rothschild. So you see, I'm a local boy."

But to Frank there was nothing local about forty miles away.

"I know what it's like, working on a farm. Throwing hay in the hot sun, hauling out manure at forty below. When my older brother took over the farm, I went to Wausau to look for work. Then six years ago I moved down to Milwaukee. Lots of you Polish down there. Well, I sold insurance for a bit, did pretty well, too. But one summer, three years ago, I was home talking to Fred — he's my brother — and he was getting pretty worked up about joining the Union. He talked me into trying out for a job with them. So, here I am. Well, I mean, I started at the bottom, as an Equity Insurance agent. You're aware, aren't you, that as an Equity member, you're eligible for some very good insurance plans?"

No, Frank wasn't aware. But he didn't believe in it anyway. He believed in taking care of himself, not gambling.

Dietzmann plopped a pile of insurance pamphlets in front of Frank. "It's a good way to get your friends to join," he said. "Anyway, the last year and a half I've been covering the district, helping fellows like yourself get started. Mind you, I'm not getting rich. I could be doing a lot better for myself in Milwaukee. But," and he lowered his voice and spoke very seriously, "this is something I believe in." He paused a moment. "How many you think you can sign up?"

Frank thought a bit. "Seven," he said, "maybe eight or nine."

Dietzmann leaned back in his chair. "Good. That's fine. We only need five to start a local." The legs of his chair thumped on the floor. "You'll find that once you're started, you'll pick up members. It's getting through the first few months that's the hardest. Now, I've got some things for you here," he said. He handed Frank a very official-looking document. *American Society of Equity*. Mr. Dietzmann read the bold, large letters across the top. He was fully aware that many of these immigrants couldn't read English. "This is your roster sheet. You're Local No. 183, as you see. Every member has to sign the roster. Then you collect the initiation fee and the first year's dues."

"I see," Frank said.

"The initiation fee all gets sent to Ben. Of the dues you keep twenty-five cents of each three dollars. The rest goes to Ben, and he splits it up between himself, the state and the national organizations." He handed Frank a booklet. "This is the official local handbook. It tells you all you need to know about how the organization runs — what officers to elect, procedures for meetings, so on. By the way, as you see here, every member of your family, between the ages of sixteen and twenty-one, automatically becomes a member with you. How many children do you have?

"Nine," Frank said. "We lost one last fall."

"Oh, I'm sorry to hear that." He stopped a moment. "Do you have any questions?"

Frank couldn't think of any. He felt hot and sweaty and wished he could get out of the house.

"This month," Mr. Dietzmann went on, "we're offering all new members a copy of Dr. Hartwig's *Rural Veterinary Secrets*." He pulled a big black book from out of his briefcase and let it fall open. "It's all in here. Everything you need to know. Ever have a cow rupture her womb, Mr. Topolski?"

Frank nodded.

"Here it is. Cause, symptoms, treatment. Sprained tendons, sweet clover disease. Here, have a look."

Frank took the book, leafed indifferently through it. "I do

my own doctoring," he said.

"Perfect. Then you need something like this. As I was saying, for new members it's only three dollars. By the way you can keep that copy and we'll just bill you when you send in your dues."

"No..."

"That's all right, Mr. Topolski. No trouble at all." He plopped another pile of literature in front of Frank. "Here's more stuff, on the Capper-Volstead Act, the Voight Bill, things like that. We encourage our locals to pass resolutions on controversial issues. You know, it's the locals who hold the reins of this Union. Everybody from Charlie Barrett — you've heard of Mr. Barrett I'm sure, he's the national president — down to Ben Lang, they're all ready to listen to you fellows at the locals. Another thing, we're the only organization that restricts its membership to farmers."

Frank stared out the window. Quietly he asked, "You farm?"

"Well, not exactly," Dietzmann explained. "I grew up on a farm and when I'm home I help Fred out. But you see, I'm on the road most of the time." He handed Frank a business card. "If you have any questions or need help of any kind — we'd be glad to send a speaker down to your meetings — just give me or Ben a call." He straightened the papers out, slipped some of them back into his briefcase. "Well, Mr. Topolski, I know you've got work to do and I've still got one more stop to make before lunch." He stood and slipped into his coat, brushed off one shoulder. "You're right on the county line?"

Frank nodded southward. "Just half a mile."

"Right. That's Jim Weaver's territory down there. Now we've got a spring convention coming up on April 12 over in Edgar. There's some talk of co-op oil stations. Be nice to see you there."

"Yes. Maybe."

"And every June there's a big meeting with a picnic, entertainment for the ladies and all. That's always a good one."

"June. It's a busy time."

"Yes, I'm sure it is."

"I'm not much for meetings," Frank confessed.

"That's what they all say, Mr. Topolski. But once you're there, you'd have a great time."

Berenice suddenly appeared in the doorway.

"Ah," Mr. Dietzmann said, "you must be..."

"Mrs. Topolska," Frank answered, standing up.

"Very nice to meet you."

Dietzmann held out his hand a moment. Berenice did not move.

"Well I've got to be going." He turned to Frank. "Hope to see you at the county meeting. Well, good-bye, then." Frank held the door open for Mr. Dietzmann, then closed it behind him. They could hear his boots crunching through the snow as he walked out to his sleigh; then the sleigh moved, turned around, and was out the drive.

Berenice stood in the doorway to the dining room. In her hand she held her needlework: around the edge of a linen scarf she was making a row of tiny, delicate red roses. Through one, unfinished, she had stuck the needle.

Frank picked up the coffee cups, set them on the cupboard. Suddenly he felt very tired. He lifted the stack of papers and the veterinary manual and walked past Berenice.

"*Tjah,*" she said as he passed. "Lots of books. Are you practicing to learn English?"

Frank stopped in his tracks. He turned to face his wife. "Yes," he said. "I'm practicing to learn English." He set the papers on top of the china cupboard, then stalked outside to work off his frustrations.

7

Even the abyss surrounding the earth now is no
*   burden*
While man is born an infant suckled at his
*   mother's breast.*
— from *The Wall,* by Karol Wojtyla (John Paul II)

There was a ringing in the dark. Long... long... Yes. The telephone. Frank fought to wake his senses, waiting for the next ring. Long... long... short... long. It was theirs. As he swung his legs over the edge of the bed, Berenice turned onto her back.

"The telephone," she said, her voice slurred with sleep.

"I know." He hurried into the living room, stubbed his toe on the stove. The pain cracked him awake. He rounded the doorway, and lifted the receiver just as it was completing another ring. In the darkness he could just make out the hands of the clock. Two-fifteen.

"Yah," he said, clearing his throat. "Yah... Yah... Okay... Yah."

He hung up, padded in his stockinged feet back toward the bedroom. On the night stand he found a match, and lit a lamp.

"Who was it?" Berenice asked.

"Adam. He said Helen wants you to come, right away." Frank sat on the edge of the bed, pulled his nightshirt off and slipped into his pants.

"What did he say?" Berenice leaned on one elbow.

"Her water broke at midnight, and now her pains come every ten minutes."

"You should have let me talk to him," Berenice complained. There was no indication she was going to get up.

"He was sure."

"They always are," Berenice remarked. At last she threw back the covers and sat on the edge of the bed. Frank was already dressed, headed into the living room. "Where'd he call from?"

He stopped. "Huh?"

"Where did Adam call from?"

He stood for a moment, looking at her as she slid her nightgown off. "I don't know. I didn't ask." She had been a handsome woman. The first time he saw her like that. Twenty-eight years ago this summer. It was a long time. "I suppose from Detlaff's," he guessed. "It's the closest phone."

She was slipping into her dress. "If I knew," she said, "I'd call back and talk to him."

He wouldn't be standing around the phone waiting for you to call, Frank thought. He'd have gone back to be with Helen.

Frank lit another lamp and carried it upstairs to the boys' room. Quietly waking Stash, he told him if they weren't back by chore time to go ahead and start without them.

"Yah," Stash's voice was throaty and only half awake.

"Do you need the clock?" his father asked, in a whisper.

"What?"

"Do you need the clock, to wake up?"

"No."

Frank turned to leave. On the other bed, shared by Eddie and Bruno, Eddie lay without covers, his legs curled up to his body for warmth. Frank set the lamp on the dresser and carefully covered him.

Back in the living room, Frank dropped two big sticks of oak into the stove. Berenice had her midwife bag open on the bed and was looking through it. In the kitchen Frank put on his coat and boots, then reached high to the top of the cupboard and slipped a bottle into his pocket.

***

It was a cold night, thinly clouded, with a half-moon lighting the snow which seemed to faintly glow of itself. Queen was asleep. He woke her, gently brought her out into the night. He walked her around to the cutter and soon had her hitched and pulled up to the house. Berenice blew out the lamps and came outside with her bag.

Their eyes adjusted to the darkness. The Tomczak place was deep in sleep. Only Casey woke and barked at them as they passed. Probably woke Chester, Frank thought, and he's wondering what all the fuss is. Berenice will have to call, when we get back.

The landscape seemed dead, as though they were moving through the mind of a great sleeping giant, cold and motionless. Then, far ahead, Frank saw a fleeting shadow shoot across the road. A coyote, he thought. Or maybe a wolf. Who was it said they saw one last month? Berenice's eyes were shut. She hadn't seen it.

***

The Laska place was all lit up. Adam came to the door to meet them. First he thanked them for coming. "Please," he said to Berenice, "hurry."

Frank took his wife's coat; she scurried into the living room, where Helen Laska lay on the bed, breathing quickly, between contractions. Berenice lifted the lamp and set it down toward her feet.

"How are you doing, Helen?" she asked, while moving back the sheets and covers.

"Something isn't right," Helen said.

With one hand Berenice could feel the top of the child's head. It had already dropped down and begun its long journey toward the light. "What do you mean?" she asked. "What doesn't feel right?"

But just then a contraction started. Helen's eyes closed and her face set as she pushed with every ounce of her strength.

This was her fifth child, yet it seemed as hard as the first. Julia, on the other hand, had come so suddenly she almost fell out on the floor. This time she was really frightened.

"That's good," Berenice encouraged her, trying to feel if the child's head was properly placed. It had moved only a little, if at all, during that last contraction.

"How long has it been like this?" she asked.

Helen's eyes stared up at the ceiling. "While Adam was gone."

Berenice looked around for a clock. It was almost three-thirty. "An hour? More?"

Helen nodded.

Berenice blotted up the beads of sweat on the woman's forehead. She'd handled nearly thirty births already. Only three had gone bad. Two were stillbirths and the other died during labor, the cord wrapped around its neck. That was terrible. And it was what worried her now.

She'd never lost a mother. It wasn't her fault about Martha Kubera. At every birth since she always thought of Martha, so young — just seventeen — facing that first birth so bravely. What a long, hard labor it had been.

She placed another pillow under Helen's back, slid her up so she was sitting more than lying. That was important, to let the baby out. Helen was having a bad time of it. Not even thirty, she was half worn out from work and care and was already too old for this. But you took what the Lord gave you and you didn't complain. Berenice dabbed more sweat, reassuring Helen that all would be fine. "Rest," she said, "save your strength."

A little boy, Joseph, had been born to Martha Kubera. That was three years ago already. When she left them that afternoon they were both fine. But two days later Caspar, her husband, showed up at the farm, weeping like a lunatic.

My wife, he said, my wife has died.

Helen's *Hail Mary* was interrupted by another contraction. Berenice held the woman's ankles, giving her something to push against. Low moans came out of the mother's throat. She was ready, the child was ready. Only God wasn't ready. The contraction seemed to wear itself out, like a great wave crashing against a cliff. Finished, Helen sank into a deep fatigue. Berenice picked up the rosary.

"Died?" She'd asked Caspar. "But how? When I left her she was fine."

"She bled to death," he said. "Oh, the blood. During the night. Oh, the blood, the blood!"

"What happened? Did she fall?"

Caspar sat at the kitchen table with his head in his hands. "No, no. Not fall. She must have tore herself, digging potatoes."

"What?" Berenice shouted. "Digging potatoes? Two days from childbirth?"

He spoke quietly. "I needed the help," he said. "I needed the help."

Come to us, Blessed Mary, she prayed, *in this our hour of need...*

"Get out!" she had shouted and the stunned Caspar fled out the door.

He didn't even come to the funeral. Her parents took the baby. Berenice had seen Joseph, just last week in church. A fine, strapping young boy. Caspar, they say, had gone West somewhere and took to drinking. They'd never seen him again.

✳✳✳

Frank pulled the bottle from his coat pocket and offered it to Adam. It was Lent, but he figured that under the circumstances the Lord would forgive them. Adam took two tin cups down from the counter and half filled them with the amber liquid. It was the last bottle remaining of the previous summer's stillings. They sipped together, winced from the liquor's bite.

It was hot in the kitchen. Adam had fired up the cook stove, on which big pots were coming to boil. The lamp on the table flickered, its wick in need of trimming.

After a few moments the warmth of the whiskey calmed the men. They sat opposite one another, in an awkward silence. Suddenly little Tony appeared from the children's tiny bedroom and ran to his father's side. Adam put his arm around the boy's shoulder and told him to go on to bed.

"Is Mommy all right?" the boy asked, staring at Frank as though he wasn't sure if this was a dream or not.

"Pani Topolska's with her. She'll be fine. Now you get back to bed. School in the morning."

Frank poured more whiskey into the cups. Quietly Adam thanked him.

"You know Eddie Barrens?" he asked. But Adam shook his head. "Lives up along the river a couple miles. Last spring, about Easter, he called and asked me to bring Berenice. His

wife was ready, he said. I was in the middle of morning chores.
Eddie sounded like it was a rush, so I let the boys finish. I
decided it would be quicker with the car. Had the Ford then."

Adam was staring at him, out of courtesy trying to follow
the story.

"Everything went fine until just west of Hladceks, I ran
into a sinkhole a good quarter mile long, a low spot where the
frost was just coming up. I got the Ford fifteen, twenty rods out
into it and down we went, up to our axles in mud." Frank took
a sip of whiskey. "Berenice was getting all worked up. But what
could I do? Not a damned thing."

"Well, Hladceks must have seen us, because in a little bit
they came out with a team. Couldn't get us out. They sent their
boy back to the phone, and in half an hour we had three teams,
all hitched onto the front of the Ford, churning away through
that sinkhole. We were almost out of it when the car just shook
itself and came to a halt. The horses couldn't budge it. They'd
pull and pull and the old Ford would crack and creak like they
were going to pull it apart. But it wouldn't move."

"So what'd you do?" Adam's eyes were softening from the
liquor.

"I got down under the car and found the front axle jammed
up against a fence post buried down there in the mud. There
was no way we could pull that car out of there. So we all got
busy and dug the fence post out."

At just that moment a loud high-pitched cry came from
the living room. Adam whirled around. There was a moment's
pause, then again the crying, only this time it didn't stop.

"Congratulations," Frank said, reaching his hand across the
table. "What did you want, a boy or a girl?"

"It don't matter," Adam answered, on his face the look of
a rabbit who'd just escaped from a fox.

A moment later Berenice parted the curtains and came
into the kitchen, wiping her hands on a large piece of boiled
sheeting. "We need some water," she said. Adam stood to help
her. "It's a boy. Everything's fine." She carried a basin of hot
water into the other room. Adam was going to follow her, but
she kept him back. "We're not done yet," she said.

"So," Frank resumed, gesturing Adam to sit again. "Another *knop*, huh?" Adam smiled. Frank raised his cup; they
clinked together. "What's his name?"

Adam tipped the last of the drink down his throat, shut his

eyes. "I don't know."

"Well," said Frank, stretching and at last allowing himself to feel tired, "to finish the story, we finally got the Ford out of the mud and up to Eddie's place, about three hours late."

"Was it born already?"

Frank grinned, pulled the curtain back to peer out into the yard. "That's the good part. It was a false alarm. We went back home — the long way, mind you — and she had the kid the next night, all by herself."

Berenice brought the baby into the kitchen, wrapped in a soft cotton swathing. It seemed so tiny, no bigger than a cat or a squirrel. Wrinkled, red, it squirmed and complained, but appeared perfectly healthy. Frank confessed to seeing a close resemblance to Adam. But the father protested, beaming happily as he poked its nose.

"No," he said, "he's got his mother's big mouth."

"Franchek," Berenice said.

Adam looked at her. "What?"

"She said she wants to call him Franchek. We looked it up. March ninth, today, St. Francis of Rome."

Frank clicked his tongue. "Well, little Franchek," he said, running his finger along the child's soft cheek.

Adam looked at his friend. "Good. I like that. Franchek!"

"You can go in now," Berenice said, lifting the baby out of Adam's hands and following him into the other room.

Frank sat down, suddenly overtaken with drowsiness. He lay his head in his arms, heard but did not see as Adam tiptoed into the children's room, anxious to tell someone. But the children were all asleep. So he sat down beside Frank, too tired to do anything but too happy to sleep.

A faint light was already coming in through the east window when Berenice came out at last and said that everything was taken care of and they could go home.

Frank woke slowly, slipped into his coat. Adam pressed something into his hand. Frank looked. Two dollars. He tried to give it back, but Adam would have none of it. It was a matter of pride. So Frank handed the money to Berenice.

Adam stood beside the stove. He seemed so small and vulnerable, out here all alone, and now with a new baby in the house. *"Djienkuje,* both of you," he said warmly.

Berenice got into her coat, picked up her bag, and they went out the door. Queen was anxious to get home. Once out

the drive they turned into the gradually growing light to the
east. Berenice closed her eyes and slept, and Frank himself was
only half awake. Queen could find her own way home.

8

T he gentle jersey Brownie chose just that morning to go
into labor. She gave Frank no time for a nap; when they
got back from Adam's and he went into the barn to see how
chores were coming along, he could see she was ready. He laid
down a good thick bedding of fresh straw under her and stayed
keeping a close watch while everyone else went in for breakfast.

An hour later there was still no sign of the calf. Brownie
only stared at the wall ahead of her, lowing gently now and then
as though to ask of Frank the reason for her trouble. He began
to worry. It began to look like a breech birth, the calf trying to
come out all turned around. At best that would be difficult; at
worst, he could lose both the calf and his best milker.

He reached inside and found instead something far worse
than a breech birth. Brownie's womb had somehow wound itself
three-fourths of a turn shut. His hand could not go in; the calf
could not come out. He wiped his arm clean on handfuls of the
fresh straw, stood in the aisle trying to think. It was a problem
he'd never encountered before. He wasn't sure what to do. He
seemed to remember, a few years before, Alex Stelmach running
up against a twisted womb. Either way, Frank was going to need
help.

He went into the house. Lotti had brought in the mail.
On the kitchen table was a letter from Poland. Immediately he
recognized his mother's handwriting. Anxiously he washed his
hands. Had something happened back home?

But first he had to make that call. He took the letter with
him into the dining room, cranked the phone and asked for
Stelmach's number. The connection wasn't good.

"Alex?" he shouted. "Frank. Look, I've got a cow with a
twisted womb. Yeah. She's ready to calve but it's turned shut.
No... I thought you did. So what did you do?... Lost the cow
you say?"

"It's my best milker. Did Joe help you out? He did?
Look, could you send him over? I'm going to need some help.

Yeah. Soon as he can. Thanks. I hope so too."

In trying to get the calf out Alex had torn the womb and lost the cow. That was all Frank needed. He sighed, sat down. Joe was leaving right away. It would take a bit until he got here. Frank tore the letter open. He wasn't expecting a letter yet. They'd written at Christmas. Something must have happened. It was reassuring, though, just to see his mother's writing. He read slowly.

Dear Frank, she wrote, *Praise be to Jesus Christ and the holiest Virgin Mary, his mother.*

He whispered to himself, "In centuries of centuries. Amen."

We are in good health and hope this letter finds you and your family the same. We thank you for your letter of Christmastime and the money. I, your mother, bought new shoes for Christmas Mass, from the shoemaker Orlecki, of very nice black leather. Antek bought a wool coat. And from Kostusia Stoyka, who lives beside the church, Marya bought a very nice rosary. And what money was left we put away in case some day we should need it.

"And now we thank you too for the photograph of your family. Such very fine children you have. Your father, God rest his soul, would be very proud. We miss him very much. Especially at Christmastime, I wept for loneliness. He wanted very much to see you again before he went. But we are not always given that which we ask. Now I pray for death to take me to him.

"Now we must tell you that your godfather, Jan Kurchinski, was taken from us the Monday after Candlemas. It got him while he was walking to his daughter's house in the village. Father Stychinski was called and gave him the last rites. So at least he died a holy death. He had eighty-two years on this earth. He was the last one from Tschermesnov who fought in the rebellion of sixty years ago. Now there will be no one to remind us.

Frank crossed himself, turned to the second page.

We also inform you that Antek's wife Julia has given him another son, christened Janek. So once again you are an uncle. We thank the Lord he is a healthy boy. Now he sleeps in his cradle as happy, as they say, as a cat behind the stove in God's house.

It has been a big winter. There is still much snow and the

*wind blows cold. We think of you and Antek remembers to us how
you were wont to jump out of the haycocks and tumble over the
ground, making us all laugh so hard. How long ago that was.*

*It is not the same here as it was. Meat in the village, for those
who have money to buy it, is three times the price of a year ago. The
same for everything else. We fear it will only get worse. In Warsaw
there is much trouble. They say there are many strikes and violence
against the big bosses.*

Mary came down the stairs. Frank glanced up at her and
smiled. There was one last page.

*And now we tell you when we saw your boys in the photo-
graph we thought, they are big enough now to take care of the farm.
Perhaps Franchek can come home to see us one more time before we
die.*

*Do not be angry, son, for our saying this, for it is only because
we want so much to see you again. And we are too old and too poor
to come to you.*

*Katarzyny Pawelka's son Victor, who lives in the state of In-
diana, writes to her saying there are many in America who never set
their feet in a church. We are happy at least you have not forgotten
that you are a Pole, and a Catholic. Without God, who are we?*

*And so we kiss you with our whole heart and wish you every
good, whatever you want from God, and success in your every intention. May you and your family be blessed with a happy and holy
Easter.*

*Your mother, Josephine, and Antek
and Marya.*

Frank set the letter down. So, he thought, he would not
see his godfather again. He hardly remembered Pan Kurchinski
— could recall only vague images of a tall and strong, moustached man who told, over a glass or two of vodka, hair-raising
stories of terrible battles during the Insurrection. Frank and his
friends, as young lads, used to scoff at him and call the stories
lies. But when he grew up, and came across to America, he
realized they were all true. How cruel we are in our youth, he
thought. Age teaches us to be kind.

He slipped the letter inside the envelope and left it on the
table for Berenice to read. "Mary!" he called out. The girl came
out of the kitchen. "Come on," he said, his arm around her

shoulder. "I've got work for you. You have to read to me."

Frank lifted down from the shelf the big volume called *Rural Veterinary Secrets* which Mr. Dietzmann had left a few days before. He handed it to Mary. "Find where it tells about calving problems," he said. They both sat down at the table.

Mary opened the book to the index, found pages dealing with everted womb, breech birth, twin calves. Frank found it hard to listen. His thoughts kept returning to his mother. It would be thirty-three years this summer when he'd last seen her. He and his brother were setting off that sunny morning to hike into Gniesno and there catch the train which would take them to Hamburg and the ship already waiting to bring them over the great ocean. She stood, beside their father, in the doorway of their house. She was crying. He kissed her, then John kissed her. They walked away. He kept turning around to see her. She waved with her handkerchief.

And now his father was dead and buried, and his godfather.

And would he even recognize her? If she stood in a crowd of people at the railroad station could he even pick her out? Yes, of course he could. Or no, perhaps...

Now Mary came to the part about twisted wombs. It was a big job, a risky job. If he lost Brownie, he could never replace her. And then how much harder it would be to pay for a wedding. Did Mary know that? How interconnected it all was. It took a strong man to hold it all together. If it gave way at one spot, the whole thing could come tumbling down.

"Thank you," he said, his hand on Mary's shoulder. She could see the anxiety in his eyes, and would have offered to help, only she knew there was nothing she could do. "You go help your mother now," he said. "And when Joe comes, tell him I'm in the barn."

But as soon as her father was out of the house, Berenice sent Mary upstairs to help her sisters with the *pisina*. She was taking no chances.

It was cool in the spare room upstairs; cool and sweet with the smell of apples. Through the south window a bright warm sunlight shone in, bringing the room to life. The *pisina* ticking was spread on the floor while Angie and Lotti, on opposite sides, were sewing the top to the bottom. One side they would leave open to push in the bags of feathers now lined up against the south wall. Mary stood a moment watching them, then found a needle, threaded it, and kneeled next to Angie.

They sewed quietly a while, making careful stitches which were strong and even. Lotti, near the window, saw a movement on the drive. She leaned over to see. A sleigh had pulled in and was headed toward the barn.

"It's Joe!" she said.

Mary answered quietly, her needle working with a steady rhythm. "Pa needs help with Brownie," she said.

Angie leaned back onto her heels to tie a knot at the end of her thread. Running the thread through her lips, she stopped a moment, staring at Lotti. "I know, Mary. We'll take the window off and you can climb down on the back porch and you and Joe can run off together!"

Mary looked up from her work.

"Don't tease her," Lotti said.

"I'm not teasing. I mean it."

But Mary went on with her stitching. Kneeling there in the bright sun it looked almost as though she was praying. Only to Lotti, the way she bit her lip and refused to talk, she was either awfully mad or at any minute was going to break down and cry.

***

Frank and Bruno brought a heavy plank from the granary to the barn. On the layer of straw beneath Brownie they spread a heavy canvas. The cows on either side of her had been taken out of their stanchions and stood at the far end of the barn munching hay.

Frank was lost in thought when Joe came in the barn. He stood behind Brownie. "She's twisted this way," he demonstrated with his fist. "We'll have to turn her over and try to keep the calf from going with her." He thought a moment, looked up. "Isn't that what you and your pa did?"

Joe nodded. "It's what we tried."

Brownie was lying down. They lifted her legs and turned her onto the tarp. The three of them pulling on the canvas slid her away from the nearest stanchion. Though she was in pain, she made no sound; only now and then she exhaled heavily through her immense nostrils. Frank laid the plank up against her stomach, where the calf could be seen pressing up against the skin. Her udder was fat, engorged with milk. They would have to use extreme care not to damage it.

Frank sent Bruno to stand on the end of the plank resting

on the ground. His weight, and the weight of the plank, were meant to keep the calf from turning. Frank took hold of Brownie's front legs, murmuring to her in low, reassuring tones. Joe held her by the back legs. They put all their strength into a single lift and rolled her away from the plank.

But the end of the plank slipped off, just missing her udder.

They had to turn her back over and reset the plank. Frank had Bruno move up the plank a few steps. There was no alternative but to try again.

This time the plank held and they got Brownie turned onto her back and partway over the other side. But that was not enough. It had to be done several times in order to unwind the womb. So they rolled her back, reset the plank, ran through the whole procedure one more time.

Joe was right. It was hard work. Frank stood up, straightening his aching back. Already he was sweating.

He cleaned his hands, rolled back a sleeve and reached inside her; his arm went in farther than it had before. "It's coming," he said, wiping his arm clean with straw.

They rolled the poor cow over and began again. Bruno stood balanced on the end of the plank. It seemed very strange to him, this rolling a cow over and over. He almost wanted to laugh. But his father was taking it very seriously.

Frank and Joe were about worn out. They couldn't keep it up much longer. "One more time," Frank said.

They pulled her over, set the plank, and heaved again. Frank came around behind her. "I'll check her," he said.

His hand slipped inside. Joe watched his friend's face. Frank was concentrating, his eyes were closed. Then suddenly they opened and he broke into a big smile. "We've got it!" he said excitedly. "I can feel the calf's feet... and her nose. She's coming!"

Joe stood aside as Frank cleaned up. They were both exhausted. "Bruno, bring a bucket of water," Frank said. The cow sucked it up noisily. Her contractions had once again begun. In a few minutes the calf's feet and then its nose were poking out. Frank helped by gently pulling on the feet.

Its head and front legs free, the rest of the calf slipped clear. It was a big heifer calf. Frank found a piece of straw and tickled its nostrils; the calf sneezed its nose clear of the thick mucus, which lay shiny and wet over its entire body. Then, using straw, he wiped the worst of the blood and mucus, lifted it gently, and carried it around to Brownie's head. Immediately she began licking the calf. It lifted its head from the ground, its neck swinging spastically from one side to the other. In a few minutes it struggled to stand, but it had tried too soon. It fell in a tumble at its mother's nose. That, it decided, was where it belonged.

Frank told Bruno to give the cow an extra helping of grain and to stay and keep an eye on her and the calf. If the afterbirth didn't come out, he was to let his father know. Frank scratched between Brownie's horns. She seemed happy now, as though all the trouble and the embarrassment of being rolled back and forth had been worth it. The calf looked fine. By evening, Frank guessed, it would be standing under Brownie, sucking big stomachs full of thick rich colostrum from the bloated udder.

Frank, who'd been up most of the night, was tired but elated. The worry over Brownie slipped away from him. It was because Joe had come, he thought. They worked well together — Joe had been apprenticing to Frank for over a year now, with animal doctoring. They could depend on each other.

"Any more due to freshen?" Joe asked as they walked toward the house, their sleeves rolled up, wiping their hands on mitts full of straw, then stooping to slather them with snow. It was a warm day. Icicles dripped from the house.

"Three this month, two next month."

Joe stopped to pack a handful of snow. "A nice calf." He threw the snowball, just missing the silo. "It's a nice herd you've got, Frank. Put them out on fresh pasture and they'll make you a rich man." They walked onto the back porch, stomped the snow from their feet. Frank picked up the broom and swept the tops of his boots clean of chaff and mud. "Rich enough maybe to afford a wedding?" Joe said slyly.

Frank, about to hand the broom to Joe, broke into a grin, then swung the flat of the broom sharp against Joe's backside. He turned and went into the kitchen.

Berenice was frying potatoes for lunch. The heavy smell of warm lard rose into the air. Joe followed after Frank; but Berenice seemed too busy to return the young man's greeting.

"Thank God," Frank said, slipping out of his boots. "Somehow we managed it. A big healthy heifer." Brownie had given something over six thousand pounds of milk in her last lactation. Daughters like the one born today were to be the backbone of a whole new herd for Frank. "Give us some warm water to clean up, Mother."

Standing at the bench like father and son, Frank and Joe washed their hands, then dried them on towels.

"Thanks, Frank," Joe said, reaching for his coat. "I'd best be going."

"Nonsense. You're staying for lunch. And don't thank me. I'm the one to thank you." Frank pulled a chair away from the table. "Sit down, Joe. How about some coffee?"

Joe really didn't like being in the same room with Mary's mother, not since what had happened with the wedding banns. But Frank insisted. So, reluctantly, he sat at the table. Frank poured two cups of coffee, slid one over to him. Joe was just putting the cup to his lips when Mary appeared suddenly in the dining room. Without looking their way, she turned and hurried into the living room for some thread. Joe set his cup down, braced himself. When Mary reappeared, to go back upstairs, she caught sight of him at the table, stopped abruptly, and stepped back one small step.

Berenice turned around. Wiping her hands on her apron, she stepped toward Mary.

"All done?" she asked.

"I..." But Mary, staring at Joe, had lost her words.

"Well then get up there and finish," her mother said. But Mary didn't move. "Go on!" Berenice urged her.

"Oh let her sit down for a minute," her father protested. He pushed a chair out from the table. "For goodness' sake, it's not like Joe's a stranger. Come on, girl, sit down."

But Mary only stood, like a statue.

And Joe, too, did not move. The last thing he wanted was to cause family trouble. Now he wished he'd gone straight home from the barn.

"Sit down, Mary," Frank insisted. Hesitantly she moved past her mother and sat, but there was a tautness to her; she moved like an animal exploring a trap. She was on the edge of her chair, with both hands gripping the spool of thread.

"Some coffee, Mary?" her father asked. She shook her head. Berenice turned back to the potatoes, to stir them from burning. "Brownie gave us a nice heifer," Frank said proudly.

Joe slid his chair back. "I think maybe I should be going," he said.

In the dining room, the phone rang. Their nerves were on

edge; it startled them. It was their ring. No one moved to get it, until Mary stood and hurried out of the kitchen.

She stood in the doorway. "It's for you," she said to her father, then turned and ran upstairs.

Frank went into the dining room and picked up the phone. Joe sat quietly at the table. Between him and Berenice not a word was exchanged, but in the confines of the kitchen a powerful voltage was building, ready to spark free at any time. He sipped his coffee, growing more nervous by the moment. At last he decided to slip out while Frank was on the phone. He stood and reached for his coat. His hand was on the doorknob when Mary reappeared again; instead of the thread, she held in her hand a small piece of white tissue paper, folded neatly and tied with a bright blue ribbon. Joe recognized the ribbon. He had used it to wrap Mary's Christmas present.

Berenice turned. Her eyes fixed on the paper Mary held in her hand. "Get on upstairs," she demanded. "There's work to do." But the girl didn't move. Berenice stepped toward her. "What's that? Come on, give it here!"

Mary stared right past her, to Joe. Berenice moved closer. Her hand reached out toward Mary's. The girl's eyes turned to her; burned into her like coals through snow. Mary's hand clutched the little gift to her breast. "No!" she said, the force of breath escaping from her almost unconsciously.

Astonished, her mother stopped.

Mary used that instant to rush past her mother and hand the gift to Joe.

"For you," she said, looking up into his eyes.

He smiled, held it in his hands. He leaned toward her, on her forehead left a sudden kiss.

Berenice whirled around. "Joe! Give it here!" she demanded.

But he slipped the little package into his pocket, smiled again at Mary, and was out the door.

He already had the cutter turned around when Frank came running out the back door. "Joe!" Frank shouted Joe pulled the horse to. Frank stood by the cutter, his hands on its side. "Come back in and have some lunch."

"No. I better not."

Frank offered the young man his hand. "Look, Joe..."

"Forget it, Frank," Joe said, holding onto his friend's hand. "Don't worry about it." Their eyes met for a long moment. "Just take care of Mary for me."

"I will."

Joe whistled his horse to start. Frank stepped back a short step. As Joe turned out of the drive, he looked back and saw Frank still standing there, looking tired and almost homeless. He lifted his hand and waved; Joe waved back.

Out on the road, away from the sight of the farm, Joe reached into his pocket and took out the tissue paper. With the reins on his knees, he carefully untied the ribbon and folded back the paper — those hands of his strong enough to turn a cow now meticulously opening the delicate present.

He held it in his palm like he would hold a newborn chick.

"St. Joseph!" he said, the words a simple reflex of the feelings within. He kissed the scapular, unbuttoned his coat and slipped it over his head. He tucked it inside his shirt, where he could feel the holy image close to his heart; and swore to himself to keep it there, day and night, until the day Mary herself took its place.

9

Now observe the abyss that glitters in the eye's reflection. We all bear it in us — when men are gathered together they shift it like a boat on their shoulders.

— from *Abyss* by Karol Wojtyla

A little east and a half mile south of the Topolski place, the Gruba forty, destined never to grow beyond forty acres, lay at the exact southeastern corner of the township, at the end of one of those narrow go-nowhere roads which, like the life history of someone you've just met, can take you into territories you never expected to travel. Access in good weather, on its ungraded dirt, was less than easy; in bad, next to impossible. There were other ways in which the homestead lay on the frontiers of the community. Feliks Gruba had, after all, been one of the county's earliest settlers; and like his son Roman he carried with him a mostly undeserved reputation of eccentricity.

Roman was an only child. That alone set him off from the

crowd. His mother was just nineteen when he was born. In bearing him she contracted and nearly died of puerperal fever, a peril then lurking in every childbirth, more real in fact than the *boginki* which some said lie waiting in lakes and streams, ready to pull unwary young women to their deaths.

But Basia would not go under. After a long and delicate convalescence she recovered, having lost neither more nor less than God's greatest gift to womankind: the ability to bear children. Her grief grew with her health. She turned, for comfort, to her infant son, this bright and laughing miniature of the man she'd loved and married. She doted over the boy, sheltered him with her hovering maternal wings. For the father, holding the child and looking into the depths of his eyes was like holding and looking into a mirror which threw back his own reflection, stripped of the intervening decades. There was a mystery there, even a miracle, noticed though not comprehended.

Roman Gruba's childhood was happy; too happy, perhaps. A childhood rich with the smells of fresh-baked cakes and cookies, of sausages and Easter *babkas,* blueberry pies and custard creams. Of toddling, then running, then stepping defiantly out of the big, sturdy house with its walnut dadoes and quarter-sawn red oak niches, into sun or snow or swimming in the river which marked one edge of the forty. And always his mother was there, to give him what he wanted, or to offer even that which he had not yet desired. They were not a wealthy family, nor were they as poor as most. But Feliks was a carpenter, who built their house meticulously, and with a certain elegance above their station in life.

Twenty years passed, as twenty years could pass. The century was three months old when Basia Gruba, sleighing home from church with her husband and grown-up son, caught a cold. The cold in turn became pneumonia, and within a week, suddenly, astonishingly, she was gone. Like two hemlocks tipped in a great storm, their roots exposed to the bite of the elements, Feliks and the boy lay at the very brink of ruin. The husband fashioned for her a coffin, of walnut and cherry, and in that same sleigh she had come home in, smiling and pointing out the first blush of red high in the maple's branches, he carried her to church. And from the church then to the cemetery beside the river, where in a bitter wind they stood and watched her lowered into the hillside, beneath the towering, shivering pines.

Feliks Gruba stayed on the farm, continued to take what

carpentry he could find. But never again, they said, did his work show the same old meticulousness. Instead of clearing more acres and expanding north as he'd talked about doing, he sold all but two cows and a few pigs. The barn seemed almost overnight to sag; and even the house of which he and his wife had been so proud shed its whitewash and here and there lost a board or two. To the people of the parish Feliks became a charity case: white-bearded, suddenly old, harmlessly eccentric.

His son left home the day after the funeral. He stayed with an uncle in Chicago — his mother's older brother — until, after a month or two, he found work. His first job, with the Pullman Car Company, would be his only; though in it he would grow slowly and steadily upward, from general office boy to machinist to floor foreman.

Neat, punctual, almost scandalously uninterested in the gentle sex, Roman moved into an old farmhouse on the west shores of Lake Calumet, renting there a room from a widowed farm wife, a kindly Mrs. Larson who only wanted company on the long winter nights, wanted only the sound of someone else in the house. Living there on the lake shore was like living a thousand miles from the ash-grey, crowded city. Ducks and geese, and sometimes even the big white graceful swans, would come every spring to pepper its rippled surface on their way to nesting sites far to the north. Roman liked to think that at least a pair or two of the thousands would stop on the shores of the old homestead to settle and raise their family.

Every morning the trolley took him to work; every evening it brought him home again. He was the ideal citizen — sinless, selfless, efficient. A man — and how few there were! — who need not shrink from the burning gaze and stern speech of even a William Jennings Bryan.

Yet someone so careful in his dress, so meticulous in his work, so obviously wanting in the common vices, was inevitably to become the butt of jokes of those mostly poor and uneducated factory hands who worked with him. "Gruba," they would chuckle behind his back, "Gruba wipes himself before he uses the toilet."

He was neither unaware of nor troubled by such remarks. Day by day he built his independence. The lion's share of his paycheck went into savings, which in turn were invested in the municipal bonds which the rapidly growing city so often offered for sale. And, to assuage the adventurer in him, he sent a small part wandering in the jungles of Wall Street. During the War his mother's brother died and left him a small inheritance. With this, and his position at Pullman advanced, he entered the middle class.

One day, about eight months after the Armistice, Roman Gruba returned from work to find a telegraph on his door. "Father very ill," was all it said. "Come immediately. Signed, Father Nowak."

He was given two weeks' leave from work. He hadn't been home for nearly twenty years. Albert Janz, the depot agent, took him from the train to his house. Roman was shocked — nauseated, almost — by what he saw. The house, the barn, the surrounding fields which had grown such tall corn, all had fallen into disrepair and disuse. And inside, on a filthy bed surrounded with ten years' trash and litter, his father lay in an advanced arthritis with complications of pneumonia. Rolling up his sleeves — he actually did that, after the first shock was over, rolled back the fine linen shirt so as not to soil the cuffs — he set about the dual task of nursing his father back to health and transforming the farmhouse to a semblance of decency.

He never did return to Chicago. He sent a telegram to the company, a carefully composed and apologetic letter to Mrs. Larson, had his few personal belongings shipped home, and his savings and bonds, as they came due, transferred to the bank in Wausau.

His father, too far gone really to argue, accepted the son's help. They lived together a further two years, in a kind of quiet unspoken fondness of each other, until one afternoon Roman came in from the barn to find his father dead in his chair by the window. The profusion of flowers lavished on the funeral, the elegant walnut coffin with its heavy silver handles, the luxurious black horse-drawn hearse hired in Stevens Point, all added up to a benchmark funeral, to which for years to come many another was compared. And when he stood in the summer shade watching the coffin disappear into the earth, the bluebirds and a solitary thrush cheering the hour and the day, it was to Roman Gruba as though he were planting the seed of a new life.

What that life would be he did not yet know. The homestead was his now, his alone: his the inheritance and his the responsibility. Those next few days he spent hours at the kitchen window, staring out across the yard, searching for an answer. He thought of selling the place and moving west or south, or even out east. He could. He could start all over, anywhere he wanted. But as he stayed, unsure of his next move, day by day his love for the quiet and seclusion which the farm provided sent roots down which began, without his noticing, to take hold. He was still there when autumn brought its frost to paint the woods. His team became a common sight on the road, loaded high with bricks and lumber, nails, concrete, and hardware. Slowly he began repairing the damages done to the house and barn by his father's neglect. And as he uncovered the plaster and found the meticulous joints his father had laid into place, he would pause and come almost to crying, as he realized the weight of events that had fallen on his father's shoulders.

Roman, having more money than he needed for his simple tastes, did not farm nor look for work. And so he became the township's one and only resident gentleman. Many who were now living in the parish had not known him as a child; he moved among them as a stranger. His neighbors, all of them farmers, had come to distrust first impressions: they'd seen too many clear-blue mornings rain on fresh-cut hay. And so they kept their distance, reserved judgement of him for a later date.

Being neither farmer, nor husband, nor as others who might meet those two criteria, a good-for-nothing drunk, he became instead a local curiosity. With a garden he loved to putter in, he grew some of the nicest tomatoes anyone had ever seen. He kept a few head of stock, which consisted of a single old brown Swiss he christened Mrs. Larson and a head or two of first one and then another of various experimental beef breeds. He had a quartet of beehives, and started an orchard, trying out all types of exotic fruits such as sweet cherries, pears and peaches, most of which he lost to the long, bitter winters. And his Morgans, a beautiful team of light and graceful horses, deep red and as elegant as the swans which graced the April skies, became, though somewhat begrudgingly, the pride of the community.

After his first few years of seclusion Roman began to take an honest, active interest in local affairs. He served several years as town clerk. Always he voted, no matter how minor the election nor odious the candidates. If help was needed — and it often was, with threshing, barn-raising, road repair — he would be there, unasked, unpaid. The spring of '21, when Frank Topolski was out behind the barn burning the marsh and the fire got away from him, Roman Gruba was one of the first to show up and last to leave.

In the old country it was the priest's custom to announce each family's donation during Mass. A custom happily, you might say, left behind. Instead, at St. Francis, Father Nowak posted in the vestibule of the church at about Epiphany time the previous year's totals. The list always attracted its share of attention. And since 1919, the year Roman returned home, the Gruba name had stood at the head of that list. While this could easily have been the perfect cause for envy, Roman was so sincerely devout and obviously selfless that his contributions became instead a cause for community pride.

In the old days in Poland every village claimed for itself a kind of wise-man or wise-woman; someone who took the time to study nature's ways, who preserved the traditions of days long gone. This village *wioz* — or *madra*, if a woman — was consulted about planting or harvesting dates, about what herbs would cure diarrhea in a horse (blueberry leaves, dried), when the storks were due to return to the rooftops (traditionally St. Joseph's Day, March 17), or how to save a dwindling beehive (place a consecrated Host among the bees.) No journey or important project was undertaken without consulting the *wioz*. His advice was as crucial to the village as the priest's blessing. The priest, of course, preached day after day, year after year, against the pagan deviltry which the *wioz* represented. But in the peasant's mind pre-Christian and Christian superstitions were not incompatible. There was, after all, no sense in taking chances.

In a small way, Roman Gruba became for his neighbors something of a village *wioz*. He loved the out-of-doors and so came to know the ways of the animals, their comings and goings, and where the wild ginseng and orchids grew. Always at his lips was some proverb or prediction of the weather. Had they kept a tally of his forecasts he would likely have been found about as accurate as Poor Richard himself; but in simply having the nerve to attempt it, he gained credibility in his advice.

Stanley Topolski — Stash — became something of a disciple to Roman Gruba. Stash admired his neighbor's ways, the dexterity with which he moved through the forest, straight, silent, quick as an Indian. Even as a child, but especially as he grew into adolescence, Stash would steal off and visit his friend, to fish or hunt or go looking for hickory nuts, asking how this and why that, or by just being with him, learning from him the ways of the woods. And, many years later, in his own old age, to those who knew him, Stash himself took on something of the

aspect of the *wioz*: a fisherman of legendary luck, a keen ob-
server of the outdoors, collector of roots and branches, birds'
nests and bones which like sachems contained for him some
mysterious power and made the walls of his house a dust-covered but wonder-filled nature museum.

But about Roman Gruba Berenice Topolski felt quite dif-
ferently. Fundamentally and irreversibly she distrusted him,
possibly because he was a bachelor. Sophie Tomczak came on a
visit, a few days after Roman had moved back in with his father,
to fill Berenice in on the history of that family. When Berenice
heard the phrase "old bachelor" attached to the name Roman
Gruba, she needed to know nothing more about him. He was
filed away into that already-crowded mental compartment bearing the label "dangerous." She had, after all, six daughters to
look after. And the very next day she let it be known to those
six daughters that Mr. Gruba and his house were, in the strongest of terms, *"streng verboten!"*

At that time she hadn't met Mr. Gruba. Indeed she wasn't
the slightest bit interested in doing so. Like the wolves rumored
to prowl the big woods to the north and west he was, though
never confronted, always to be wary of.

The girls obeyed. At church, when Roman happened to
look their way or politely nod, they ignored him. If they chanced
upon him in town they moved to the other side of the street or
walked right past him as though he were invisible. He took
such behavior in stride, and had no expectations it would change.
But there was that grace in youth which, though it obeyed the
unkind order, suspected in time its motivation.

Every summer the female component of the Topolski family climbed into the wagon, piled high with buckets and wash-
tubs, and pulled by the gentle Queen, would pass right by the
Gruba place on their way to the biggest blueberry marsh in
twenty miles, just a quarter mile beyond. And again, after a full
day's picking, baked in the sun, nagged by deerflies, they would
return, exhausted but with hours of work still ahead of them,
their buckets and tubs filled with many gallons of berries: each
a tiny waxed globe, blue or jet-black, hazed like grapes, unfor-
gettably sweet and spicy. Sold by the bucket or quart to neighbors and strangers alike, in good years the income derived from
the blueberries, added to that from the strawberry patch, would
rival the income Frank earned at farming. And the girls' reward
for their work, bent over the blueberries, their fingers moving

through the bushes like a plague of locusts through the fields of Egypt, was this: at the very end of the season, for each her own big, fresh, steaming-hot blueberry pie which, devoured in a day or two, left little appetite for more of the same.

As they passed the Gruba place those early August mornings, the dew still heavy on the weeds, the dust from their wheels coating the goldenrod just coming into bloom, sometimes they would catch sight of Roman out in his garden, leaning on a hoe; or hanging his laundry on the line from tree to house; or swinging a scythe in easy, steady arcs through the weeds in his yard, each rhythmical cut making a quiet whisper in the grass. As he saw them pass, he would smile and wave. If their mother sat, as she most often did, sternly in the front seat, they would not return his greetings. But sometimes she would send the girls down to pick without her. Then Rose, being the oldest, or Lotti, being the most outgoing, might smile back to the "old bachelor" — or even wave a quick, guilty little wave.

About a month after Roman's father died the girls came past on the first outing of that year's season. After four long weeks alone in the farmhouse, he needed someone to talk to. He watched for several days as the wagon full of girls passed, until one morning they went by, their buckets and tubs jangling on the rough road, without their mother. When the wagon had disappeared down towards the marsh, he hurried out to the ice-house, where under great piles of sawdust a few blocks of ice still remained, and pulled up a big bucket of heavy cream he'd been saving in the well. As he worked he smiled, even found himself whistling.

And when the girls came up from the marsh that afternoon, tired, thirsty, stinging with fly bites, he hurried out to the end of his drive and shouted for them to stop and have some ice cream.

With their eyes they consulted each other, and Rose nearly brought Queen to a stop. But habit and caution won out. Anna and Sophie, on the back of the wagon, their legs dangling almost to the ground, stared at him until they went over a little knoll and he was out of sight.

The next day, when they were returning home once again late in the afternoon, Roman met them with a tall stack of bowls and spoons and the big wooden bucket full of cold and delicious ice cream. As they came past, he spooned great dollops of it into a bowl and held it towards them. This was too much. Rose pulled Queen to. Lotti accepted the first bowl, hesitantly, and tasted it. Roman meanwhile scooped bowl after bowl full and exuberantly handed them around to the other girls. Without moving off the wagon or saying a single word, they sat in the afternoon heat, their big wide-brimmed hats shading their faces, eagerly devouring the delicious treat. When they were done, Roman collected the empty dishes, then passed around a cup full of cold well water. He felt like a father on Christmas morning who'd just watched as his children tore open their presents. Now the girls smiled — though still they would not go so far as to talk to him.

There came an awkward moment. Rose shook the reins. The wagon jerked ahead. Roman watched them disappear, wiping the last traces of the sweet cream from their lips, the two in back still staring at him, the almost-empty bucket hanging from his hand. Only when they were gone did he sit down, in the shade, and enjoy — truly enjoy — a bowlful for himself.

Within a few days it had come to this: the girls would meet the quiet bachelor at the end of his drive, park the wagon, and shyly walk, huddled together like little chicks, to the shade of the big oak beside his house where they would sit and gulp big spoonfuls of the ice cream, into which they dropped fistfuls of blueberries. And the summer of '21, the last year they had Rose with them, they would pick as fast as they could, hurrying through the day to fill the buckets and tubs, so they could leave a half hour early and stop for the treat they had now come to expect. By then the real reward of blueberry picking was not the pie their mother baked them at the end of the season, but the secret, clandestine, sinfully delicious ice cream stolen, as it were, right from under her eyes.

And as much as they enjoyed their treat, that much more did Roman himself relish their company — the laughter in their eyes, the embarrassed giggles and blushes as he came round with seconds. It was a high point of his year. But he was not ignorant of the culpability of his actions. To squelch any rumors which might get started, the previous September when he met Frank on the road headed to Point with a big load of potatoes, he stopped his neighbor to talk. Roman brought the subject around to the berries by asking how well they'd done that summer.

"Good," Frank said. "It was a good year."

"I thought so," Roman answered. "You know, you're lucky

to have such hard-working girls." Frank nodded. Roman hesitated. "Did they tell you," he went on, "they sometimes stop for
a drink of water?" Frank showed no reaction. "And sometimes,"
Roman confessed, "I give them ice cream." Frank stared at
Roman. "Do you mind?"

Now Frank broke into a smile. "Mind? No, of course not.
It's nice of you." It was the beginning of their friendship.

A few days later, when Frank was alone in the living room
with Rose, he asked her, suddenly, if they ever stopped at the
Gruba place when they were out berry-picking. The girl looked
him in the eye, could see that he knew. But before she could
answer, he confessed that he'd had a talk with Roman and told
her it was perfectly all right, and that there was no need to tell
their mother.

At Rose's funeral, a big bouquet of two dozen scarlet roses,
in November an exorbitant expense, sat anonymously donated at
the foot of her coffin.

And a month later, Roman phoned Frank and asked a favor: Could he come down to look at one of his horses? Roman
thought it was strangles. It was. Frank saved the animal. Stopping by a few days later to check on the horse, Frank accepted
the invitation to a bottle of homemade beer and mentioned,
casually, his interest in the Farmer's Union. Suddenly Roman
became animated. Unionism was one of his secret passions. He
had organized down at the shop; for a while was even shop
steward. And though he had investments of his own on Wall
Street, and was therefore a small-time capitalist, at the same
time he'd even flirted with the Wobblies.

But at heart he was neither capitalist nor radical — just a
diehard, farm-born Progressive. In the '20 campaign he'd worked
actively, taking the train down to Point each morning, coming
home late in the evening after a long day spent canvassing. That
fall he had the opportunity to meet and talk with the great Bob
LaFollette, Senator and possible candidate for the presidency.
Roman would never forget shaking the acerbic little Senator's
hand and the few words they exchanged.

So Frank had stumbled across an unexpected ally, without
whose help he might not have gone on with organizing the local.
And when it came time for their first meeting, Roman volunteered his own house. Its living room, he argued, was plenty
large for however many showed up, and there they wouldn't be
interrupted by either women or children. Frank, who'd all along

been somewhat anxious about holding the meetings at his own house, quickly accepted.

***

Saturday night Bruno was drafted into helping the girls finish the chores while Stash and his father cleaned up and changed clothes. They arrived at Roman's a full half hour before the meeting was due to start. Stash went into the living room where, in helping Roman renovate the house, he had learned so much of his carpentry. While Roman put water on the stove for coffee, Frank carried a lamp down into the basement and came back up with a case of beer.

"Who would have guessed," he said, setting the rattling bottles onto the floor, "that here in America, the land of the free, you'd be a criminal just for having a beer?"

"Damned near enough to make a man into a Socialist," Roman snorted. Now from the stove came the delicious smell of coffee brewing.

"Or a Democrat?" Frank asked, with a wink.

Roman turned. "Now, just a minute..."

In the south window of the kitchen, just above the sink Roman had installed with its hand pump, were three tins full of tomato plants. From each plant two tiny leaves were bent to-ward the window. Frank gently lifted one of the cans, studied the plants, then ran his hand lightly over them and smelled his fingertips. The deep, spicy smell which along with new-cut hay and corn growing in the hot sun was to him one of the hundred smells of the color green, took him ahead half a year to the rich foliage and juicy red fruits of the garden.

"Berenice's aren't up yet," he observed, setting the plants back onto the windowsill.

"Put 'em in on Washington's Birthday," Roman replied, tak-ing cups down from the cupboard. "A family tradition."

There was a knock at the door. Roman went to open it. "Come on in," he said. It was Alex and Joe Stelmach. Now with them the kitchen seemed smaller. Alex and Joe took off their coats, threw them on the table. Seeing the case of beer, Joe smiled.

"What you got here, a speakeasy?"

Roman handed him a bottle-opener. "Help yourself."

"Frank?" Joe held out an opened bottle.

"Sure."

The four of them stood for a moment in silence, running

the cold beer down their throats. "And Stash?" Joe asked.

"He's in the other room." Joe took him a beer.

Within a few minutes of each other, Chester Tomczak arrived and then Ed Wolniak. Already, Frank thought, that's seven. And it wasn't quite eight o'clock yet.

They went into the living room. Stash and Roman were looking at an article in *Wallace's Farmer*. Someone knocked on the back door. Frank went to see who it was.

"Henryk!" he said, surprised. Henry and Gertrude Bollom, good friends of the Topolskis', lived an hour's ride to the west, far enough that Frank hadn't expected Henry to come.

"*Guten abend,*" Henry said. "It's all right I come, no?"

"Of course it's all right. Come on in. Care for a beer?"

Henry and Frank came into the living room, where Stash was reading from the magazine. Henry pointed a work-worn finger at an ad for a tractor. "That's what you need, Frank," he said.

"That's right, Frank," Alex said, "weren't you down in Point last week shopping for a tractor?"

Frank shook his head. Everyone had seated themselves. "Can't even go pee without everyone knowing about it. No, not shopping. Just looking."

Chester Tomczak took the bottle from his lips, belched quietly. "Last summer," he said, "we was down by my brother's and there was this poor guy trying to get a big McCormick-Deering alongside his manure pile so he could load the spreader. We pulled over to watch." The others sat around paying close attention, while trying to look uninterested. "That tractor was like a great big hog slipping around there in the mud, squealing and grunting and getting itself in deeper and deeper. By the time we left, he was up to his axles. Nope," he asserted. "You wouldn't catch me on one. Why, any half-baked team would have had that spreader loaded, out in the field, and unloaded before he even got himself unstuck."

Nobody wanted to disagree. Only Alex looked like he might have something to add. But he didn't say it.

There was a quiet knock at the door. Roman went into the kitchen and returned in a minute followed by young Adam Laska. Frank smiled and reached out to shake his hand.

Joe Stelmach stood, shook Adam's hand. "Say, I hear you're a pa again," he said. "Don't you ever get any sleep?"

"Well, not since the baby arrived," Adam said, blushing.

"Just you wait till you're married, Joe," Chester retorted. "You'll have more pups running around the yard than my Casey has fleas."

Everybody laughed. Adam sat down next to Stash, turned down a beer which Roman offered him.

Alex's bottle thunked onto the floor. "I've been thinking," he said.

"Watch out!" Joe kidded.

"About them tractors. You know all of us used to say trucks would never catch on. But you go to the city and there's more trucks than wagons."

Chester sat back with his hands clasped across his belly. "That may be true, Alex," he said, "but if I was to go out and buy a tractor it'd take two men to do the job of one. Somebody driving the tractor and somebody else on the machinery."

"Not if you had power machinery," Frank argued.

"So what you're saying, Frank, is I've got to not only buy the tractor but a brand new cultivator, a plow, a spreader," he enumerated on his right hand. "A harrow, rake, mower, reaper. The whole kit and caboodle. No thanks," he said. "Not me. Maybe out west where the farms are big enough."

Joe came round to Frank's defense. "They say one man can plow ten acres a day with a 10-20."

"Not in my clay!" Ed Wolniak chirped.

"Worse thing," Joe's father added, "is like they say, there ain't no way to get them tractors to breed."

That got a laugh.

When the phone rang, Roman went to answer. He called out for Frank to come. While Frank was in the other room the men sat around in silence. Stash and Roman lit cigarettes. Alex pulled out a cigar and chewed on it.

"That was Joe Rybarczyk," Frank said as he came back in the room. "Got a cow down so he can't make it." He checked the clock on the mantle. Quarter after eight. Counting Stash, there were nine of them. He couldn't think of anyone else that might be coming. Again they sat in silence, waiting for Frank to start the meeting. But he didn't really know how.

Behind him hung a big oval portrait of Roman's mother, Basia, an elegant woman in a fine chiffon blouse. The picture reminded Chester of Roman's parents. Basia had been a fine dancer; deep in her eyes he had often caught a glimpse of something wild trying to get out.

"Hey, Roman," he asked across the quiet room, "how come you never got married?" Chester never was afraid to say exactly what he was thinking.

Roman stared at him a moment. Nervously the others waited. At last he smiled. "Hey, Chester," he said, his eyes lit up, "how come you all wanted to meet at my place tonight?"

There was a short release of laughter and the room was quiet again. Roman brought the coffee and cups out from the kitchen. Only Adam, who didn't have a beer, took a cup.

"So what do you think of Harding?" Chester said to Roman. It seemed like he was always trying to back the bachelor into a corner. Maybe it was jealousy because Roman didn't have to work. But Roman just sat down with a derisive snort. "I thought you were a Republican," Chester said.

"A LaFollette Republican," Roman clarified.

"Back to normalcy," Alex added. "That's Harding's way. More like back to bankruptcy."

"Well I'm one man didn't vote for him," Ed Wolniak announced.

The Democrats had courted the ethnic vote, and certainly most of the Polish immigrants voted Democratic. But even the ethnic vote could not hold back the Republican tide of '20. The defection of the German Americans played its part. They were Democratic until 1916, when Wilson slipped from his stand of neutrality on the War, and in '20 they flocked to the Socialists. Wherever there was a majority of ethnic Germans — which meant a good part of Wisconsin — there were Socialist mayors, aldermen, and representatives. By then Wilson, and the Democrats, had lost most other ethnic groups, too.

Only the Poles remained steadfastly Democratic. They credited Wilson — quite properly — with insisting that after the War there be an independent Poland, something the world had not seen for many years. But now, after the defeat of 1920, which he saw as an abrogation of his policies, Wilson was already a broken man, sliding quickly toward his end.

"Mark my words," Roman said, "the man to watch is Cox's running mate." They listened carefully; they all knew how well Roman kept up on his politics. "Franklin Roosevelt," he said. "That man is going places."

Roman had liked Wilson, had liked his style, which was however too sophisticated for the times. He considered Wilson's fate one of the real tragedies of American politics. "When the

War ended," he said, "and Wilson was up there with Lincoln and Washington as a great President, we all cheered him and what he stood for. And just two years later everybody was climbing on top of themselves for a chance to spit on him. Take the League, for example, the first honest attempt at a way to world peace. And Harding treats it like a bum leg he'd rather have cut off."

"That's all true," Alex Stelmach admitted. "But as long as we're stringing up the Republicans, we might as well use the strongest rope we've got."

"You mean farm prices?" Frank asked.

"I do not. I mean Prohibition."

"I'll drink to that," Joe added. They all raised their bottles.

"It's got so government's got nothing better to do than send revenue agents out sniffing up and down the countryside," Chester complained.

"They been out your way?" Roman asked.

"No. And they damned well better not either."

There was a silence then, to affirm Chester's defiance. Frank glanced up at the clock. Close to eight-thirty. The room was quiet. Someone would have to get them turned in the right direction. Roman took on the job himself.

"Well Frank," he said, setting his beer bottle aside, "what do you think?"

Frank, suddenly the center of attention, was unnerved, standing in front of them all. But he had called the meeting. So it was up to him.

"I suppose," he sighed. He turned and picked up a pile of handbooks, and passed them around. "I guess what we want here," he said, nervously holding one of the handbooks, "is to organize ourselves to beat the prices we've been getting. Maybe we can talk about co-op marketing."

Roman helped his friend along. "They say over in North Dakota the co-ops are going real good. Paying three or four cents more on a pound of butter."

"Makes sense," Joe added. "Cuts out the middleman."

"You talking about starting up a creamery?" Chester asked.

Frank glanced at Adam, who'd been quiet all this while. Adam's uncle owned the cream station in town. "No," Frank said. "It'd take more than a half dozen of us to do that."

"There's a co-op general store down in Junction," Joe observed.

"Yeah, but that's not Equity," Ed ventured.

"No. It's A.C.A." Roman had stopped there several times. Frank spoke up. "Besides there's already two stores in Dancy. They wouldn't be too happy if we started another. However, you know we all go down to Point to buy our supplies and our equipment. If we could establish a farm outlet close by..."

"You're talking big money there," Chester observed.

"Now I'll probably regret saying this," Roman piped up, "but if you guys get this thing organized, I might just underwrite you a certain amount..."

Eyebrows went up around the room.

"Thanks," Frank said. "But that's a long way off. Meanwhile there are other things we can do. With spring coming we'll be shopping around for fertilizers." He turned to the stack of papers on the table, found what he was looking for. "We can buy it from the Union." He handed the sheet to Roman.

"Potato grower," Roman said, his finger moving across the page, "is forty dollars and seventy-five cents a ton."

Alex was thinking aloud. "Forty dollars a ton, that's pretty good."

Roman continued. "That's freight on board in Milwaukee. The catch is, you've got to buy it in one-car lots, bagged in hundred twenty-five pound sacks."

"We couldn't use a whole carload between us," Chester said. Most of them didn't use commercial fertilizer. It was something Frank had started, a few years back, and the Stelmachs and a few others had followed suit. But thirty tons would last them most of their lives.

Roman handed the paper back to Frank. Maybe, Frank felt for a moment, maybe I was all wrong even to try. He held the paper in his hand, unable to think of anything further to say.

"As I understand it," Roman came to the rescue, "as an officially organized local, you fellows can pass resolutions and send them on to the state."

"You mean the capital?" Alex asked.

"No. The state union convention "

"So what good's a resolution?" Chester asked.

"I don't know," Frank replied. "But we've got to let somebody out there know how we feel. Like about the way we're importing more butter than we're exporting." Frank had read about it in *Rolnik*. "That's bound to hurt us right where it hurts the most."

But moving these men seemed harder than moving a big pine stump.

"Well, how about potatoes?" Joe asked. "Couldn't we pool our crops and market them together? I mean, straight to the city, rent a boxcar or something."

"Sounds like a good idea," Ed Wolniak said.

"Stash has been picking up farm reports out of Stevens Point on his crystal set," Frank added. "If we can keep on top of prices, we could hold them until they went up."

But they all knew that wasn't practical. Where could they hold that many potatoes? It was a good idea all right, but...

Chester was sitting back with a look of skepticism written all over his face. Ed, Joe and Roman were staring at the floor, their elbows on their knees. Alex, who'd finally lit his cigar, was drawing on it thoughtfully. And Adam seemed miles away, tucked into his corner.

"There's a meeting a week from Wednesday," Frank said, "in Marshfield, about a wool pool and co-op oil stations. Anybody interested?" Nobody moved. "I don't blame you," Frank admitted. "I'm not much for meetings, either."

Frank didn't want to drag the thing out any more than he needed to. "I don't know what you fellows are thinking," he said. "Maybe we oughta just forget the whole thing."

"Not yet," Alex said. "Not yet, Frank. I think we oughta have another meeting, see who else we can get. Maybe if everybody comes back with one good idea for a resolution..."

"Sounds good to me," Ed Wolniak agreed.

"Well that's all I've got to say," Frank admitted. But Roman was forming a word silently with his lips. Frank tried to make out what it was.

"Dues!" Roman said, clearing his throat.

"Oh, yeah. It's two-fifty to join and three dollars for the first year. That's five-fifty. And if you're interested," he added, "once you join you can get this book for three dollars." He held his copy of the veterinary manual up. "Far as I can tell, it's pretty good. It and Joe here helped me out of a mess a few days back."

Nobody moved. Frank was afraid the whole thing had fallen flat. But then Alex stood up and reached for his wallet.

"Who do we pay?" he asked.

Frank shrugged.

Roman reminded Frank that they had to elect officers. Alex

sat down again. Ed Wolniak nominated Frank for president. The vote was unanimous.

"You need a vice president," Roman suggested. The men looked from one to another. Alex suggested Ed.

"Hell, I can't even read," Ed objected.

Roman turned to Joe. "Joe?"

Joe stared at the floor, shrugged noncommittally.

"It's Joe then," Roman said. Again it was unanimous.

"And for treasurer and secretary I nominate Roman," Alex said. The last vote of the evening was another uncontested vote.

"That's it then," Frank said. "Try to bring somebody along to the next meeting. That way we can double our membership."

"When's the next meeting?" Ed asked.

Frank shrugged.

"We better wait till after Easter," Alex said. "The women-folk don't cater to us going out during Lent."

"How about the Saturday after Easter?" There were no objections.

One by one they stood up, poured coffee, milled around. A short line had formed by Roman, who was putting their money into a cigar box and scribbling their names on the roster. Alex and Ed had already paid. Frank was surprised to see Chester in line.

They had the five they needed to start. Frank smiled to himself. Outside of killing themselves out in the fields there had to be something they could do to get ahead. And the idea that as individuals they could make a difference, it was what America was all about.

Frank couldn't find Adam. He went into the kitchen and there the young man was already in his coat. "Thanks for coming," Frank said, holding out his hand. "If it's the money..."

"No," Adam replied. "All that talk about fertilizer and tractors and pooling potatoes. Hell, I don't sell two hundred dollars worth a year all put together. I'm out of my class here."

"I understand," Frank assured him. "Maybe some other time."

"Yeah,"

"How's the boy?"

"Fine. Keeps us up all night."

"You planning a christening?"

"Got to talk to Father first."

"Right."

"Well..."

"Good night, Adam."

Frank knew that Adam had come without any plans of joining. He'd come only out of respect for the man who'd doctored his stock and who'd helped his children into the world. But that he had come at all only made Frank like the man that much more.

And the others, too — even Chester, who had put his money down. And now Frank felt the full burden of what he'd taken on, of following through, of making the Union work.

The others were leaving, one by one. Henry Bollom, who hadn't seen Frank for several weeks, stayed the longest to chat. They talked a little about the cancelled wedding. Mary was Henry's favorite of the Topolski girls. He shook his head from side to side, clicked his tongue.

When he left it was already nine-thirty. Frank yawned. He and Stash were alone in the kitchen. Roman came to join them, plopped the roster on the table. It looked like a legal contract.

"Frank Topolski!" Roman said. "President of Local 183 of the Farmer's Cooperative and Educational Union!" He put his hand on his friend's shoulder. "Make you feel any taller?"

Frank shook his head. "Shorter."

They spent some time cleaning up the empty beer bottles and coffee cups. "What you need, Mr. Treasurer, is a woman," Frank kidded.

Roman shook his head. He picked up the cigar box. "Almost forty dollars," he said. "What do we do with it?"

"We keep twenty-five cents of each annual dues. The rest goes to the county."

Roman stood holding the box open, piling the bills into a neat pile. "Seems a shame, keeping two dollars and sending all the rest."

Frank shrugged. That was the way it was.

They put their coats on. Roman handed Stash the leftover literature. Frank now looked really tired.

Roman held the door open and they walked out into the night, where to Frank the unbroken darkness falling away on every side seemed more desolate than ever, and the press of the night's and the morrow's duties more burdensome perhaps than he could bear. Stash would help, yes, as now the boy took the reins and pulled away from the warmth and light of the big farmhouse out onto the narrow, sleigh-rutted road.

And Joe. You could depend on Joe. And Roman. He smiled to himself, basked for an instant in the warmth of a friendship which seemed only to have just begun. But he was leaving his friends behind. It was the road ahead that he feared. And for that they weren't enough. They just weren't enough. The sky, he thought, only half awake as Stash guided the cutter through the countryside, dull white below and above a deep unending black, peopled with its timid, hesitant stars, the sky is too deep, too great a burden for any man to bear.

10

It is this constant habit of looking forward,
which distinguishes Polish women from those
of every other nation. You can see that they
believe they have a mission to fulfill, and make
it the business of their lives to fulfill it.
       — from *Polish Experiences During the*
            Insurrection of 1863-4, by W.H. Bullock

Monday, wash day, was an overcast, grey day on which the thermometer refused to rise above freezing. All morning the girls took their turn at cranking the machine; by lunchtime only Frank's barn clothes remained to be done. When he and Bruno were finished eating and hurried off on errands into town, Berenice slipped away into her room for a nap. The girls cleaned off the table and did the dishes.

Three big kettles of water were heating on the stove. The fire, which during lunch had been left to subside, was coaxed back to life; at the bottom of the kettles little bubbles began to form, only to rise and be replaced by more until at last the water steamed and spoke to Mary, standing above it, in little bubbling noises.

Done with the dishes, Angie and Lotti had lamps to clean, trim, and refill. It seemed a perpetual job. As Father Nowak might put it, man's natural state was darkness and only through God's grace and hard work could he dwell in the light. They all looked ahead to summer, when the days would be long and the lamps hardly used. Angie, pouring kerosene, overfilled one of the lamps and though she hurried to wipe it up, the sweet smell of the oil floated through the house, intermingled itself with the pungent birch smoke and the bright, clean smell of laundry soap.

Standing at the stove, Mary saw a movement outside. She pulled the curtain back. Yes. It was a sleigh. Someone was coming to visit. Now Shep was barking and had run off the porch.

She carried the heavy kettle to the machine and carefully poured the water into the washer. Clouds of warm, sharp steam rose into the air. She set the empty kettle on the floor. There was a knock at the door.

Wiping her hands, she pulled the door open. It was Gertrude and Henry Bollom. "Come in," Mary said, stepping back. Mrs. Bollom stepped inside: a short, stocky woman with a round face, blonde hair and bright blue eyes, wrapped in a heavy overcoat and her head covered with a scarf. Gertrude smiled warmly, untying her scarf. Her husband followed, a tall thin man with a square, jutting jaw and one arm held stiffly across his chest.

"Maria," Gertrude said. "Is your mother *nach Heim?*"

Mary nodded. "Taking a nap."

Mrs. Bollom looked puzzled a moment. "Ah! Sleeping? Of course. I forget."

Lotti and Angie appeared in the doorway. They greeted their guests, who stood rather timidly just inside the door. Mary turned to lift a bucket of water and pour it into the empty kettle.

"*Vielleicht* I come back some other time?" Mrs. Bollom asked. She and Henry spoke no Polish, only German and the little English they had to use with the Topolski children.

"No, no. Stay," Lotti insisted. "She'll be up in a bit."

"Is okay?"

"Yes," Lotti assured her.

Gertrude turned and said something to Mary in rapid-fire German. Of the girls, only Mary could understand any of it. Henry nodded to the girls and backed out of the door. As she was taking off her coat, Gertrude explained that Henry had some business in Mosinee, and she thought it would be nice to spend the afternoon visiting Berenice.

Angie took the woman's coat into the dining room. Lotti asked if they should wake their mother.

"No, no," Gertrude objected. "Let her sleep. She deserves it, no? And you, Maria? You are making the wash?" Mrs. Bollom peered into the washing machine, from which rose a steamy, soapy smell heavy with the odor of the barn. "For Frank!" she said, looking up and pinching her nose. Mary smiled.

Gertrude followed the other girls into the dining room. "Cleaning lamps!" she chirped, clapping her hands together. Her light, soprano voice and fine little gestures made her seem so quaint to the girls. "You know, the brother of my Henry, he lives in Minnesota, he put on what they call..." She searched for the word. *"Karbid, auf Deutsch."*

Lotti nodded. "Carbide, yes."

Gertrude's hands rose, fluttering like butterflies. "Makes gas," she said, "Very nice!"

Above the sound of the gears turning and the sloshing agitator Mary could hear the three of them in the dining room. She stopped a moment, saw that Gertrude had picked up a rag and joined the girls in cleaning the lamp chimneys.

"Frank is in the barn?" Mrs. Bollom asked.

"No," Angie answered. "Gone to town with Bruno."

"To Knowlton?"

"No. Mosinee."

"Yes? Maybe Henry see him there." She wiped a chimney, held it against the light streaming in from the window to see that it was absolutely clean. "And Stash, he is at Rybarczyks?" Lotti nodded. Gertrude winked. "You will have a wedding soon, no?"

Mary cranked the agitator again, drowning out the chatter in the other room. The clothes clopped back and forth beneath the thick layer of suds. It was hard work. Now and then she would stop to catch her breath, and while resting check the fire in the cook stove.

Lotti and Angie came into the kitchen.

"Mother's awake," Lotti said. "She told us to come help you."

"I need more water for the rinse," Mary said. It was just the job her sisters didn't want, trudging through the wet, slippery snow with the heavy yoke over their shoulders. And if they spilled even a few drops from the bucket, their mother would get mad. She was superstitious about that.

But they had to do it, there was no use in complaining. They slipped into their coats and picked up the empty buckets.

"We'll stop and see if the ewe has lambed," Lotti said as they went out the door. There was an early lambing due any day. It was a sure sign of spring.

As she returned to the machine, Mary noticed that her mother and Gertrude were no longer in the dining room. She could barely hear them, chatting rapidly away. They must have gone into the living room, she thought. Her mother, who'd learned German in school, when the Posnan region was part of Prussia, always seemed so glad for the chance to speak that language which her father refused to speak. Compared to Polish, he would say, it is an ugly language. Unknown to her mother, Mary had over the years picked up enough of it to make fair sense of whatever she might overhear.

Cranking the agitator again, Mary daydreamed about the Bolloms. They were such jolly people, she thought. Especially Gertrude. How different she was from their mother. Of course, Gertrude had only the two boys, grown up now and gone away. But Mary speculated that even with a big family, Mrs. Bollom would be happy-go-lucky. It was just the way she was. When she came in the house, it was like a breath of fresh air.

And she was a grandmother already, with a lap big enough for two grandchildren. She baked such delicious cookies. *Springerlie,* she called them. And she gave the cookies away as though there were no end to them. They called her Oma, sometimes, meaning grandmother.

And Opa Henry, he was different. Always he loved to drink beer and eat those spicy, smoked sausages. He must have known a hundred different kinds of sausages. His left arm he'd hurt years ago on the farm; he carried it bent over in front of him. When he wanted to move it, he had to use his right. And when he danced with Oma, he only put the one arm around her. It looked so clumsy. Yet how they could dance. He was a quiet man, really. Always, it seemed, on the brink of getting mad or breaking into laughter. But never doing either.

She paused to wipe the sweat from her forehead. The two women, in the living room, were talking about Easter, and all the good food it would bring. *Osterkuchen,* Gertrude said. Was it the same as the *babka* they would be having? Then, Gertrude said, when Lent is over, we can dance again.

Gertrude and Henry came by often on Saturday nights to dance. They would drop a record on the Victrola, a Landler or an Oberek, a waltz or a polka, and the two couples would dance in whirling circles around the living room. Upstairs the children would gather at the register and peer down at them. It looked such fun.

Cranking the machine again, Mary remembered back two summers before, when on a Sunday afternoon they'd piled into the Ford and driven to the Bolloms' for a picnic. It was something they did so seldom, it was like a holiday. The youngest Bollom, Otto, was still at home then. Mary remembered how he'd smiled at her and how they'd sat on the blanket in the grass talking and laughing. When she came home that night she couldn't forget him. And then she met Joe.

Of the Bolloms' house she remembered most the big beautiful living room with the lovely wooden clock on the wall that had the little boy and girl who would dance out of their cottage every hour on the hour. They were painted so real. They seemed so happy, swirling around while the bell chimed. It was like a fairy tale. And then they were gone.

It smelled different, too, the Bollom house. Somehow it seemed nicer than their own. As much as she was a homebody and didn't like going into strangers' houses, she would very much have enjoyed going back to the Bolloms'. But since that one time, her parents always went by themselves, to spend the evening dancing.

So the girls did not see Henry and Getrude often. Not even on Sundays, when Oma and Opa went to church in Rozelleville. Mary knew that most Germans were Lutherans — the Bergs, Altenburgers, Plattmans — they all went to the Lutheran church just north of town, whose bells they could hear ringing if they were a little late leaving for Mass. But the Bolloms were German Catholics. Henry had told them about the terrible wars in Germany between the religions. It sounded so different. In Poland everyone was Catholic.

Where Henry and Gertrude came from, it was marshy land, low pine marshes. Like the Necedah swamp, her father had said. And Henry had told them that the river which flowed through his town, where his father and his father's father had been shoemakers, flowed into the Danube. Then he would hum a waltz and whirl around, sometimes with his good arm grabbing one of the girls and twirling her with him. The Blue Danube, he called it. The blue, blue Danube. Such a funny man. Mary tried to imagine a blue river. The Wisconsin was brown, almost as brown sometimes as the water in the washing machine. And sometimes, too, it had suds in it, like the wash-water, from the factories up in Wausau.

She tried to remember the name of the village the Bolloms came from. That was another way they were different. They were already married when they came over. Mary stopped cranking, let the clothes settle to a stillness. Leaning on the washer to catch her breath, she smiled as she thought of how much Oma and Opa must love each other. Her father and mother, and most of the older people she knew, they just lived together, and had families. But Oma and Opa, sometimes they would kiss one another, on the forehead or on the cheek. And Opa loved to tickle his wife or pinch her and make her scream just like they were young kids.

Dachau. Yes. That's it. Because one of their records they danced to was played by a band from there, and Henry was so proud of that.

Mary moved a kettle to the side of the stove to let the water cool down from a rolling boil. Now she could hear fragments of the conversation coming from the living room. Gertrude was talking about a *Kuh* that was *krank,* a cow that was sick. And Berenice mentioned *ein schones Sauglein.* That would be the Laska baby. Only her mother's next sentence, the meaning of which Mary could only guess, sounded bitter and scornful.

She drained the washer into buckets, wishing her sisters were back to help carry them out. But they were probably fooling around in the barn. So she lifted the heavy pails herself and carried them out the back door, into the cool, grey afternoon, and sloshed the water off the porch, where it steamed and turned the snow a frothy, dirty brown. Then she filled the washer with clean, hot rinse water. It was the last of the water, until the girls brought more.

The hot rinse water only added more steam to the already clammy air. Mary was sweating already. Suddenly, from the other room, she heard her own name. "Maria," as Gertrude said it. She turned toward the doorway, so she could hear better, wiping her wet red hands on a towel. "Josef," Gertrude said.

They were talking about her and Joe!

Mary stood motionless, still as a statue, afraid to move a single muscle lest she miss some essential word. And yet, even in standing still, hardly breathing, focusing all her senses into her ears, even then she could catch only some of the words.

"Zu heiraten," Mrs. Bollom said. And *Hochzeit.* That was

German for wedding. Maybe now they were talking about Stash, Mary thought. About Stash and Helen's wedding.

But the voices grew louder, almost as though they were arguing.

"*Wieso?*" her mother asked. "*Wieso? Ich tu...meiner Tochter...mochte.*"

Meine Tochter, she'd said. No, Mary realized, they were talking about her.

And Gertrude now, more calmly, as though trying to soothe an angry child. How reassuring her voice sounded. "*Aber liebe Berenice, sie ist keine Kind.*" She is not a child, Gertrude was saying.

No. She was not a child. No.

"*So lange...in meine Haus lebt, sie ist meine Kind.*"

The clock in the dining room chimed the half hour, but Mary scarcely heard it. It sunk into her mind, what her mother had said, like a stick driven into the pit of her stomach. As long as she lived in this house, she was her child. And her mother would not let her leave until she married.

And since she was, to her, only a child, her mother would choose the man she was to marry.

It was a trap from which there was no way out.

But now suddenly Mary realized that Gertrude was taking her side. That kindly old lady with the squeaky voice and button nose was actually standing up against Berenice. Mary thanked God, and asked the Virgin's help.

How helpless she felt, standing breathlessly, only just able to make out what they were saying, as they argued her fate, her own happiness and future. It took all her will not to break down into tears.

Her mother was speaking again, more quietly, but with that determination which was her trademark — that iron stubbornness which said the world would end before she changed her mind.

"*Nimmer!*" she said. "*Nimmer Josef!*"

Never! Never Joe!

And Gertrude, frustrated, her voice cracking, "*Aber warum, liebe Berenice, warum?*"

There was no answer.

And it echoed in her mind, that one terrible word. Why? Why?

But now she heard her sister Rose's name spoken. It was

her mother talking. "She had a lover, too. Did you know that? Stanley Derkowski. So I told her, no. It's shameless. Let this be a warning to you. You would be better off dead."

There was a moment's pause. It was beyond belief. Had her mother really said that to Rose, that she'd be better off dead, than to marry Stanley?

Then her mother's again voice, dripping with condemnation. "But she was crazy, like a goat, crazy. Do you understand? A goat, in heat."

Gertrude caught her breath. "Berenice!" she said. "To speak so, of the dead .... And your own daughter!"

Mary's legs nearly buckled under her. She leaned on the washer, stood with one hand holding it for support, the other gripped tightly on the towel, hanging helplessly at her side.

And how he'd cried, poor Stanley Derkowski, at the funeral. She'd never seen a grown man cry, like that.

They'd all cried, in their turn. But it was something she could never wash away, that somehow she'd caused her sister's death.

How? Who could tell? God works, as they say, in mysterious ways. By being happy with Joe. Who could tell?

No, Rose, I did not want you to die. No.

And mother did not know what she was saying. How could she know?

But Mary remembered an argument between her mother and Rose; it was why Rose went to the city. And two months later, she was dead.

No. Her mother couldn't have known.

Why?

Why was her mother so set against Joe?

Stash had picked Helen. Not a word about that. And Walter, who could tell who his girlfriends were? It was only the girls she hovered over, like a broody hen. First it was Rose.

And Rose is dead.

So now it is my turn. It's not fair.

It's just not fair.

Mary wiped her forehead again with the towel, and caught among the sweat a small tear, of anger and frustration. Her hand dropped again, the towel dangling to the floor. She stared, unthinking, into the corner, at the cream separator, bright red and shiny clean, to which she came each morning so obediently, as a prisoner to his shackles.

Suddenly the door burst open. Lotti and Angie rushed in. "Twins! She's had twins!" they shouted, setting the buckets on the floor. "Two little lambs!"

But Mary, leaning on the washer, hardly heard what they said. Only she turned to them, uncomprehending, as though she were peering out at them from some other, distant world. And the girls, only a moment before so buoyant, so happy about the lambs, stopped suddenly still, as though confronting death itself. And so she looked, their oldest sister Mary, as though that fragile thread holding body and soul together had, just that instant, burned through.

11

The world will remember and revere Mahatma Gandhi not only for his love for others, but also because of his wisdom. He knows from experience that the inhabitants of India, although there are three hundred million of them, could not win a real war... Obviously, if one is strong and stubborn, the best way to go about getting what one wants is by using force. But if one is a quiet, meek creature, let him lay down and say: 'I came this far, but shall go no further.'
from *Rolnik*, March 17, 1922

I n work and sleep and work again the week passed by. The sky turned blue, the weather cold. By week's end the clouds were back, warming the air just to thawing. The air was heavy with moisture as the wet snow thawed and rose skyward.

By Saturday morning winter was back. Over everything the snow lay thick. So came the spring every year, these timid thawings in which the heart, cold-contracted so many months, loosened just a little, stretched in the warming sun, showed itself timidly like the first chattering chipmunk. Then, suddenly, overnight, a north wind would bring the cold or drifting snow, to hold the heart prisoner until, in time, came the next thaw, each loosening a little longer, a little more confident, each subsequent cold spell a tiny bit less tyrannical.

Halfway over the river a dozen crows cawed as they broke

from one another, the flocking instinct which had held them together all winter now overridden by the urgency to couple and mate. Perhaps in one or two of the tall pines silhouetted against the sky on the opposite shore some had already begun the rough architecture of their homes. Closer by, in the thicket of sumac and lilac beside the Knowlton House, a small flock of robins chirped noisily, as though complaining over whose fault it was for starting north too soon.

The people did not complain. The church was warm. At home there was, thank God, sufficient food and firewood. And if the spring was delayed, so it was. What good was there in complaining?

Father Nowak's sermon, too, had comforted them. He'd spoken of that simple, quiet, prudent man granted the gift of marrying God's mother. The gift of nurturing and teaching and protecting the baby Jesus. Of doing God's work here on earth.

A man, Father said, like them: who did his duty quietly, humbly, and like them, faded into faint and shadowy rumors of what he'd been. A man so close to anonymous we knew little more than his name.

It was the feast day of St. Joseph — the day in Poland the storks were due to return — and though winter had here leapt once more among them, it was the knowledge that he was there, that he was them and they were him, which more than their coats or blankets or the heat rising in waves from the registers took the bite out of the growing cold.

***

As always they lingered after Mass. The Topolski family scattered: Eddie to the other boys and girls who ran around the rectory and played hide-and-seek among the sleighs and cutters, the younger girls to stand timidly at the bottom of the steps trying to ignore and be ignored by a group of neighbor lads joined by Bruno. Stash stood silent sentry beside his Helen, so small, so young, a fragile fawn. And the way he stood so patiently beside her, it seemed as though he were a certain part of his father — the passive, unresisting part — broke free and turned into a world not made for him.

Berenice and Frank chatted with the Tomczaks. And not far off stood Mary, talking with the oldest Tomczak girl, Andrea.

Within the close boundaries of that parish there were few secrets. Mary had approached the door of happiness and, just as she was about to enter, been turned away. In the eyes of those around her she could not help but read an unspoken pity, a common perplexity. She, who wanted so badly to remain anonymous, was singled out, and she knew it. She carried this recognition as a stigma which only pushed her further inside herself. So that as Andrea talked, of Easter hats and dresses, of going off during the summer to visit her uncle, Mary heard hardly a word.

And when she saw Joe standing there beside his father, tall and strong, his brown overcoat open to the wind, it was his presence which consumed her, nearly took her senses away. Their eyes met; she looked away.

Suddenly he was beside her.

"Hello Andrea," he said, tipping his hat. Mary's heart pounded, she caught her breath. How gently he smiled. Yet she could hardly bear to look at him. And though she prayed so often to be beside him, now she would have given anything to be instead within the sheltered circle of her sisters.

"Hello Joe," Andrea answered. Joe smiled. He had his hands in his coat pockets. Realizing he wanted to be alone with Mary, Andrea looked across the churchyard. "Oh, there's Stacy," she said. "I need to see her. Bye!"

Joe watched her go. He reached out, touched Mary's arm. She glanced at him, smiled timidly. He slipped his hand inside his coat. For a moment he searched along his chest, then brought the scapular out for her to see.

"Thank you, Mary," he said. "I wanted to thank you. I wear it day and night, and it reminds me of you."

She looked down. He seemed so close, nearly overwhelmed her with his presence. And yet she wasn't afraid. There was nothing to be afraid of. Since they'd first met she knew she could trust him. He was strong — so strong that without touching her she felt he could crush her — but he was gentle. And not once had he disappointed her, in his strength or in his tenderness.

"I wanted to come to see you," he said almost in a whisper. She glanced at him quickly, to let him know he was right in not coming. "How have you been?" he asked.

How had she been? Did he really want to know? That she'd written to some strange man in Texas? That she'd lain awake night after night praying for Joe and for herself? That her days had gone past in a tired, aching haze? That she had come, almost, to hate her mother — had wished at times she could hate her mother? And in the end, that she had come to hate herself?

He looked in her eyes, saw how weary she was. "I missed you," he said quietly. "Did you miss me?"

She glanced toward her mother, whose back was still to them, knowing that the moment her mother saw them together, she would intervene. And so there was that urgency of the impossible, like a child again and again trying to force a square peg into a round hole, of fitting a whole lifetime into a few moments.

"Yes," she said, not looking at him. "Yes. I missed you." And there was so much to miss: his strength, his gentleness, the way he made the world seem brand new, made so much seem possible, made every moment, every laugh, every gesture seem important, almost holy.

"I have something to tell you," he said, his voice now cautious, as he chose every word. "I heard they're hiring up at the mill in Wausau," he whispered, as though it hurt him to say it. "I'm going up there next week, to see if I can get on."

She stared at him, bewildered. He might as well have slapped her face.

He reached out, touched her hand. "I'm sorry, Mary. I have to get away. It's too much for me, here. You'll have to decide, one day. It's either me, or..."

As though conjured by the mere thought of her name, Berenice was suddenly beside them.

"Come on, Mary," she said, pulling her daughter's arm. "Come on, we're going home."

Joe let go of Mary's hand, but did not back up an inch. He turned. The rest of the girl's family was still scattered around the courtyard. The team had not even been hitched yet. He turned back.

"Good morning, Pani Topolska," he said, politely tipping his hat.

Berenice nodded coldly to him. She tugged at Mary's arm, to lead her away. Mary could feel the eyes of the congregation turning to her.

"I was just telling Mary," Joe said, stepping forward, "that I'll be going to work in Wausau next week." Berenice froze. "Wasn't I, Mary?" But Mary had retreated deep inside herself. "I thought you'd like to know, too," Joe said. And then as though her mother weren't even there, or in spite of the fact that she was there, or perhaps even because she was there, he took hold again of Mary's hand. Clearly, confidently, somewhat loudly, he asked, "Will you write to me?"

Mary, certain that everyone else had heard, felt as though she were being torn apart. She closed her eyes and when she opened them again, one word escaped her lips.

"Yes."

Joe squeezed her hand, held it a moment, then let it fall.

"Good day, Pani Topolska," he said with an ironic politeness. He stood a moment, as though there were something else he wanted to say, as though inside himself he was fighting his own battle. Then, seeming to have won that battle, he smiled at Mary, winked mischievously, turned, and walked away.

✳✳✳

The sleigh cut lightly through the wet snow, which the horses' hoofs threw up in neat little clods. Already they were halfway home. No one, since climbing in, had spoken a word.

Frank, Berenice, and Eddie sat in front; Mary, behind them, with Lotti, facing backwards to Bruno and the other sisters. A few snowflakes floated down, lit on their faces like cold sparks. Now and then another sleigh would go past, headed north. Their father would raise the short whip he seldom had to use, and wave.

At last, just for something to say, Frank spoke to Berenice. "You were talking with Joe?"

"*Tak,*" she answered, pausing a moment. Eddie pointed to a cardinal flashing through the brush. "He said he's going to work in Wausau."

Frank's face turned to hers. "He is?" He stared ahead once more. "I don't understand. He didn't say a word to me." The horses trotted onward. "But Alex will need him, when the field work starts."

"I guess he didn't think of that," Berenice said, somewhat smugly.

The way her mother said it, blaming Joe for leaving, cut through Mary like a blast of cold air.

And since he'd turned and walked away all she could wonder was whether or not she'd ever see him again.

She broke into a shiver she could not control. Sophie stared at her. Lotti held her hand. And as they went along the road toward home, the steady slog of hoofs on snow, the light-hearted jingle of the traces and harness bells, the grey enduring trees on either side, their branches heavily overlain with the winter's snow, it seemed to Mary as though this were a foreign land they travelled through, a land she'd never seen before. And she found it hard to care if she ever saw home again.

12

A culture of survival envisages the future as a sequence of repeated acts for survival. Each act pushes a thread through the eye of a needle and the thread is tradition.

— from *Pig Earth*, by John Berger

Dawn brought bitter cold to the first morning of spring. In lowlands along the river the temperature fell below zero. Once again where the ground was bare it became hard as concrete. From the north came a razor-sharp wind. Lotti leaned over the hole in the smokehouse floor, glad for what little heat the coals provided. Above and around her the hams, bacon and sausages which three weeks before had been Short-Ear hung like great meaty fruits of some fantastic tree of flesh. The split slivers of hickory caught fire; she lay on larger sticks, then over it all a thick carpet of sawdust, to give a smolder that would last. But as the air inside the little building filled with smoke, she stepped outside to catch her breath. Now she welcomed the cold wind. Yet even outside she could smell the smoke in her hair, and how it permeated her coat.

She saw a horse's head clear the hill toward town, then the sleigh and all the rest. It was George Zimmer, the bachelor mailman. Lotti hurried into the smokehouse to check the fire one more time then walked out the drive to meet him. She stepped around the little gobs of manure which had fallen from the dung-cart and frozen solid, each crosshatched with a frosting of thin crystals.

"Morning, Lotti," George said, pulling up. "Cold this morning." Though the Topolski farm was the first stop of his route, already his curly black beard and moustache were coated with ice from his breath. He handed the girl their weekly copy of *Rolnik*, and with a sparkle in his eye handed a letter to her. But when she tried to take it, he pulled the letter away, hiding it behind his back. "From your boyfriend," he said, winking.

Lotti held out her hand. "Please," she said.

The letter was not even for her. It was for Mary. From some man in Waco, Texas. George sat smiling out of his heavy furs, as though waiting for an explanation. But Lotti had none to give. She put the letter into her coat and turned toward the house. She could hear Leo, George's horse, begin his slow and steady plod on up the road, with many miles to go before resting again in the stable.

Even with her coat off the smell of smoke followed Lotti into the dining room. She handed the newspaper, then the letter, to her mother, and like George stood waiting for some solution to this new-found riddle. But the letter was quickly and without a word slipped into her mother's apron.

"Take your father some coffee," her mother said.

Lotti poured the steaming coffee into a tin, wrapped thick with cloths. She slipped into her coat and walked past the smokehouse, from which came a thin drift of smoke. Her father and Stash were behind the barn loading manure. She could hear the thud of the heavy bar against the frozen pile.

Molly, tied to the cart, turned to watch her come. Her father, his breath puffing into the cold air, hefted with a fork a heavy, solid chunk. It fell with a thud, shaking the cart. Stash lifted the bar and plummeted it into the pile, prying back and forth to loosen the frozen manure.

"Ah, Lotti!" her father said, setting his fork against the cart. He looked so old this morning, as she poured the cup full. He held the steaming cup in both hands, warming his fingers which protruded from the ragged gloves, sipping the coffee as it steamed up into his cold and reddened face. His tongue touched the edges of his moustache. He smiled at Lotti. *"Dzienkuje,"* he said.

Lotti poured a cup for Stash. The two men sat on the edge of the cart. They had chipped away, in these two mornings, only a tiny fraction of the winter's pile of manure. Most of the work still lay ahead of them. By noon, they hoped, the warming sun might begin to thaw the pile. Then they could skim a layer off without having to chip away every piece they moved.

***

Berenice opened the envelope. So, she thought, he'd lost no time in his reply. Inside she found two pages of a neat and steady hand. She stood by the window. He seemed a very polite sort of man; his first words were to thank Mary for her letter and compliment her on her penmanship. He added that their farm must indeed be very prosperous to afford them two cars. He had heard of Wisconsin from one of the men in his company, a Lithuanian from Milwaukee. It sounded like a beautiful state.

"I dream, sometime," he wrote, "of visiting Wisconsin."

Berenice smiled to herself.

Walerych told how difficult it was in the Army with a high school education when his superiors hadn't finished grade school. But, he said, he would be getting out in May, and that would all be in the past. He didn't know what he would do when he got out. His brother in Cleveland wanted him to come to work at the foundry.

"But when I am free," he wrote, "I am free, and I will decide what I do."

Already it was hot in Texas. Berenice remembered when Stash came back — he'd been stationed in Texas, too — and told of how they'd stood at inspection in thick woolen pants with the temperature near a hundred. How the sweat poured out of their bodies and the men standing in line dropped one after the other, keeling over into the burning sand. For Stash it meant that making hay would never seem quite as hot again.

The food, Walerych wrote, was mostly bread, meat not fit, as he put it, for a dog, and beans. Mostly beans. He would give anything, he said, for a big plate of mushrooms fried in cream. But even the restaurants in Texas had never heard of mushrooms.

His company had rated very well in an important inspection, for which he seemed to take a good deal of credit. "Another Easter," he wrote, "I will spend alone." And this, his last paragraph:

"Perhaps some day we can meet and I can see this farm of yours and meet your mother and father and all your brothers and sisters."

Berenice slipped the letter back into its envelope. If he wants an invitation, she thought, then I guess that's what he'll get.

***

She arranged after lunch for all the girls but Mary to be out of the house. Again the girl was made to take up the pencil and again, setting it to paper, she battled the urge to refuse. But to disobey would have been a sin — a sin against the Commandments, against her mother, against the family. To sin against her own heart was her only choice.

An unspoken understanding had passed from Berenice to all the girls: whatever sin had caused Rose's death, they were all to blame, and so they all had to do their part in atoning for it. It was Christ's way, the way of suffering, the only way they knew.

Like a machine she copied her mother's dictation. It seemed impossible, that she would write this way to a stranger, would open herself to him this way. But it was her mother's doing, not hers.

Finished, Berenice read the letter over, had Mary address the envelope, inserted the letter, sealed it, and placed it in her pocket. She would deliver it to George herself, in the morning. Once out of their hands, it would be irretrievable, and what had seemed a mere turning of the sod would in the coming days reveal a deep and empty pit toward which she led her frightened but obedient daughter.

✳✳✳

For three days Frank and Stash hauled the manure. Now the most of it was out in the fields, in rows and rows of piles, like so many beads on a rosary which in the coming weeks Frank would have to pause and pray at, one by one, in order to save himself.

It was warmer now, and the manure thawed. But still it was hard work. This was the first spring Frank could not keep up with Stash. When Bruno came out behind the barn to do his share, it was Frank who would rest, leaning against the cart or standing to run his hand along the ridge of Molly's long and sloping nose.

Out in the field just east of the house which he'd seeded last year into alfalfa, Frank talked in low reassuring tones to Molly. The horse seemed to sense her master's weariness, and readily obeyed his commands to stop, back up, or turn. There had always been that kind of understanding between Frank and his animals, which he treated as equals. Heading out in the morning to work, they would share his eagerness. And in the evening, plodding back, it was his tired bones and aching muscles which they felt as much as their own. Through this daily intimacy, they came to adjust themselves to his mood.

The piles stretched now to the far end of the field. Walking beside the cart, the sky broken with big white clouds which the sun dodged now and again to warm the earth and bring it to life again, a cool easterly breeze in his face, tired and aching as he was, Frank was at home. The breeze picked up that heavy but reassuring smell of freshly spread manure and carried it back to the yard and, when a door was open, straight into the house. And somehow — in a way no more mysterious than the turning of manure into corn or oats or bright yellow marigolds — that very odor enriched the air and as he went about his work, fed the fires which kept Frank alive.

13

Of all the living creatures in the world the female of the human species has been the most downtrodden, for to every wretched class of man there was a still more inferior, more abject group, their wives. She was a slave to the slaves, a dependent of the abjectly poor.
— from *The Nervous Housewife*,
by Abraham Myerson (1922)

Despite the hour's work Berenice had put into it, the pile of clothes which needed mending seemed to have grown no smaller. Her needle worked deftly through the shoulder of a shirt Frank had torn throwing silage. Behind the stove rose a dozen loaves of bread, almost ready for the oven, which she was coaxing up to temperature. Soup for dinner was warming on the stove. When the mending was done, there was supper to start with.

The telephone rang. She waited out one complete ring to be sure it was theirs. Impatiently she slipped the needle into the shirt's sleeve and rose to get it.

"*Tjah,*" she said. Above the phone hung a holy picture. She moved a finger across its frame, picking up a light layer of dust.

"Mrs. Topolski? This is Albert at the depot. We got a telegram for you."

Berenice breathed in sharply, staring at the image of Christ, his breast opened so all could see his suffering heart. And she thought: Walter? Has something happened to Walter? Or Father?

"You want me to read it to you?" Though only a mile away, Albert's voice was barely understandable above the crackle of static which clotted the line.

"*Ja, ja,*" Berenice said anxiously.

"Berenice Topolska, RFD2, Dancy, Wisconsin." Albert cleared his throat. He'd made too many of these calls. Especially during the War. It was hardest when it was friends. But it was his job. "Peter Smolinksi killed in car accident Sunday PM stop. Funeral Thursday stop. Will you tell sister Anna stop. Signed, Father."

There was a moment's pause. Berenice breathed a sigh of relief. Then, as though from a thousand miles away, Albert's voice cleared the line. "I'm sorry," he said. "A close relation?"

He was just being nosey. "No," she said, coldly. "My sister's husband."

"Oh?" He sounded confused. "Well. You want a reply?"

"Not now."

She stood in the doorway to the kitchen, crossed herself. "May the souls of the faithful departed through the mercy of God rest in peace, Amen," she muttered.

She sat once again and picked up her work. So, Peter is dead, she thought. And she would have to tell Anna. She was the closest. Always, she'd been the closest. Though Anna was two years younger than her, Berenice had depended on her sister. She was the only one to talk to, about growing up, about marriage, about children. Especially after their mother died. Anna knew things about Berenice no one else knew. And she, about Anna.

And, Berenice thought, she might not even recognize me. Five years had slipped past since they'd seen each other. Locked away in the asylum, her condition, as their father wrote, had only worsened.

She would have to bring it up with Frank. I could go already tomorrow, she thought. But not alone. A hundred miles on the train, it would take all day and most of the night to make the round trip. Little Anna can go with. Sister Anna is her godmother, and her namesake. And besides, her fare would only be half. The work planned for tomorrow, it will have to wait. Always it is best, each day to get what work done you can. Because you never know. Never.

She remembered the first time she'd met Peter. Her sister had come home with him, in Chicago. And she knew from that moment that Anna was making a mistake. His eyes were weak, he would never be a good worker. But no matter how hard she tried she could not convince her sister. Anna was blinded by her love.

But Berenice had been right. Not long after the marriage Peter took to liquor, moving from job to job. Then they followed Frank and her out to the farm in Necedah, put money down on a house not a mile away. Peter spent most of his time and money in the tavern. He gambled. In spite of that, Berenice remembered those times with a certain fondness. At least she and Anna were close together, could visit, could share their hopes and sorrows.

Four years went past and though Berenice's family seemed it would never stop growing, Anna and Peter had no children. Peter blamed Anna, made remarks in front of others. But Anna confessed to her sister one afternoon, her husband no longer came to her bed.

And sometimes he would hit her, in his drunkenness. She started slipping then. Berenice remembered how easily she would go into a bout of tears. How she loved children, sister Anna. Always she brought presents for her nieces and nephews, handing them over with that look in her eye: Why, Lord? Why me?

And how quickly she had fallen.

Berenice slid the loaves of bread into the oven, stood for a moment staring out the window. Frank was in the barn. The girls were upstairs. Soon it would be lunchtime. Then she would tell Frank.

Five years now since I've seen her, she thought. When we moved, we left some stock at the old place and Mary and Lotti stayed behind to care for them. It was late in the fall, Stash had already gone to the service. We shipped the stock up by train and Frank drove down to get the girls and the last of the things. We locked the house up — it seemed so empty — and drove over to Anna's to say good-bye.

The girls stayed in the car. Anna was sitting in her rocking chair, her hands folded limply in her lap. Her dress was filthy, her hair uncombed, her face smudged and smeared. She was staring out into the bleak November afternoon. The room was cold. Frank busied himself relighting the fire. Anna hardly noticed they were there. How thin she'd become, how grey and unhealthy her skin. Berenice already knew how little she was eating, how little she slept.

She stood beside her sister, afraid to look at her — or was it shame, not fear? The words came easy, promises to come to visit or send money so Anna could come to them. But they both knew, without saying it, that that would never be. And Berenice could only think that Anna was blaming her, for moving away and leaving her alone. With Peter.

She bent and kissed the cool grey skin of Anna's forehead. For an instant their eyes met: Berenice hugged her sister. When they turned to leave her there, beside the window of the cold and dismal house, it seemed the light itself was like an ice bath which drew from Anna's spirit the last bit of warmth.

Berenice would never forget that image of her sister, framed against the cold light, a shadow of what she had once been. Almost like looking at a corpse.

The car shuddered and edged away from the house. Halfway out the long drive Berenice glanced back. Through the window, silver with the dim sun's reflection, her sister's face could still be seen, staring out at them — but not at them, beyond them, into an emptiness Berenice herself had now and then to skirt around.

As they neared the end of the drive, the scrub pine on either side patiently, quietly awaiting the onset of the winter, Peter's old Ford turned in and came toward them. Frank slowed, to exchange farewells. But the other car sped past; at the wheel Peter sat grimly staring, as though they weren't even there.

So, Berenice thought, sitting down again to her work, so now he is dead. And that would be the last she would see of him — that thin, grey, unshaven face, the clouded eyes, unseeing, as though intent on escaping the nightmare to which he was so relentlessly being drawn. And into which he'd drawn poor Anna.

Would God forgive him? It was not right. For what he'd done to her, now he is deep in hell. That, then, was that the nightmare he'd driven so blindly toward?

***

Sophie and Eddie and all the other children were in school. Anna wouldn't trade places with them for anything. Already they could hear the train, its running gear rumbling over the bridge two miles to the north. Albert came out and joined them on the platform. The man and woman who had been sitting beside the depot picked up their suitcases and stood at the edge of the platform. Anna didn't know them. He looked like a minister of some kind. He smiled at her.

The locomotive came into view around the bend, big white clouds of steam and smoke puffing from its stack. The train's whistle blew two short blasts. As it came up to the station, the roar of the wheels on the steel tracks was almost loud enough to hurt your ears. And when he threw the engine in reverse, the wheels squealed, the engine puffed noisily, and the whole train creaked to a stop.

Albert helped them onto the car, waved to Anna as she stepped inside. The car was warm; only half its seats were filled. Just as they found a place to sit, the train jerked forward and began accelerating away from the depot. The train-car filled with the smell of coal smoke.

Anna slid in next to the window. Her mother put the big basket in which they had their meals under the seat and sat down next to her. The seat across from them was empty. Anna watched the man and woman who'd gotten on with them find a place far to the front of the car.

Anna could tell, by the way her mother sat so stiffly wrapped in her heavy black coat, her hands on her lap, that she was supposed to be afraid. But she wasn't. She was all eyes and ears, glancing bashfully at the others in the car, then staring out the window. They rattled over the Little Eau Pleine; because the tracks had now separated from the highway, they were passing through a countryside she had never seen. It was fascinating to her, all these strange houses and barns, the marshes and woods that though only five miles from home, might just as well have been a hundred.

The train-car bounced and rattled, its wheels making a steady click-click-click on the track. The other passengers seemed hardly even to notice they were on a train. They sat chatting or knitting — Anna even saw an old man dozing peacefully away. And she wondered, to herself, what if he was supposed to get off back at Dancy, but had slept right through it?

The door at the front of the car pushed open. A cold blast of air blew in and brought with it the noise of the wheels and the rattling couplings. In his uniform and jaunty hat, the conductor came down the aisle. "Junction City," he said, his voice a low monotone. "Junction City. Change here for Millidore, Sherry, Auburndale, Marshfield and all points west. Change here for Stevens Point and all points east."

He sounded to Anna almost like Father Nowak when he was chanting the Latin prayers. He stopped beside the girl and her mother and as he looked over the rest of the car held out his hand. Anna's mother handed him their tickets. The train began to slow down and the conductor steadied himself with one hand while he punched little holes in their tickets. He thanked her mother, smiled at Anna, then slipped his ticket puncher into a leather holster and headed off toward the front of the car.

They stopped at Junction for a few moments. Three people got off, but five came on. A man and a woman sat down across the aisle from them. Anna's mother nodded lightly in their direction.

The train started up again. They sped past farms and villages, over bridges and crossings. It was like a foreign country to Anna. Soon they pulled into Grand Rapids, Wisconsin, where big paper mills and factories filled the air with rolling clouds of dark smoke. Cars and trucks were everywhere. There seemed to be so much going on, and it all seemed to be happening so fast.

Her mother's eyes closed for a few minutes. Anna knew she was worried about the house, about how the girls would manage without her. How many dishes they might break, whether Frank's lunch would get fixed on time. But Anna knew, too, that all that worrying was needless. Her mother always imagined the worst. But the fact was that when she was gone they were all so frightened of her they did everything especially carefully. She'd told them, time and again, that God was watching. Anna never doubted it. And she was convinced, too, that He told her mother exactly how they'd been while she was gone.

The woman across the aisle smiled at Anna every time she glanced shyly in her direction. Seeing her mother's eyes closed, Anna smiled back, but only for an instant, then stared again out the window. They were moving along a highway now on which cars and trucks sped past. When one came toward them, from up ahead, it went by so fast it made it seem they were moving at an impossible speed. At a road crossing the driver of a truck, waiting for the train to go by, waved at them. In a seat ahead of her Anna saw a little boy wave back.

Now it was lunchtime. Other passengers pulled sandwiches, chicken legs, pieces of bread and cake from bags and boxes. Anna was hungry. At last her mother opened her eyes and slid the basket out from under the seat. She spread a dish towel over her knees and gave another to Anna. Then she poured milk from a quart jar into two cups. Anna sipped hers. It tasted good. But it was hard not to spill it, the way the train bounced along.

To Anna's disappointment she was having the same lunch as if she'd gone to school: two thick slices of bread spread with a heavy layer of salted lard. But she was hungry, so it didn't matter. It felt odd eating with all those strangers on the car. When they were finished, her mother folded away the dish towels and set them beside the sandwiches which were left for supper.

They were into the flat pine country already, with little villages like Sprague and Finley no more than a depot and a house or two scattered among the woods. Anna watched out the window closely. Soon they would be coming past their old farm, just north of Necedah. Even her mother watched now: they would be able to see the house from the tracks. Anna wondered what it was like now, after strangers had lived in it five years. She'd never met the new owners. Only they sent their payments every month, sometimes with a nice note about the place. Last year at Christmas the man had written and said that one evening around Thanksgiving he'd looked out the kitchen window and saw Rose standing there looking in at them. But when he went to the door no one was there, not even any tracks in the snow.

That was when she died, in Chicago. Her mother said it was Rose's spirit coming back for one last look at the house in which she'd been born.

There it was. But it looked so old now, the grey siding broken here and there, the windows needing painting. From the chimney, smoke rose into the air. And the old barn looked ready to fall in. Anna wasn't even sure it was the right place. But her mother nodded her head. Yes, that was it. And now she recognized the right of way here, along the tracks she and her sisters used to walk to school.

Then it was gone, around the bend, and already they were slowing for Necedah. That was scary, about Rose. And the night she died, Stash had a dream. He was out in the river in the old boat Uncle Frank had made. Rose and Mary were with him. None of the girls knew how to swim, only the boys. In his dream, Rose fell out of the boat. Stash tried desperately to pull her up. Just as she slipped out of his hands and back under the water, he woke, frightened. He looked at the clock. It was twelve-thirty. And the next morning their mother telegraphed back to them from Chicago. Rose had died during the night, she said. At twelve-thirty.

Anna did not understand things like that. Only it scared her some. But it didn't scare her mother. Ghosts and witches and devils and angels, there were plenty of them in Poland, she said. But Anna wished they would stay there.

For a while they traveled along a stretch of tracks with another train alongside theirs. First the caboose and then one car after another slowly blacked out Anna's sight. They seemed so close, swaying and rattling this way and that. And it was hard to tell if the other train was slowly backing up or if they were passing it. Only now the noise of the wheels was that much louder. And when they were past it, the engine of the other train slowly fading to the rear, Anna breathed a sigh of relief.

In New Lisbon they had to get off their train and wait a half hour for the mainline Train No. 30. It was warm and quiet in the depot, and it felt good to be sitting still for a while. Anna watched the other people, tried to imagine where they lived, where they were going, what their lives were like.

But their train pulled into the station, and they hurried aboard. Now the seats were almost filled, and they had no choice but to sit across from a young couple. Shyly, Anna smiled at them.

"Where are you going?" the man asked her mother. She said they were visiting a sister in Madison.

"Ah." He held one end of his long moustache between his fingers, smoothing it out. "Do you live here?" he gestured to the little town from which the train had just begin to move.

"No," her mother answered. "On a farm, near Dancy." The man shook his head. "North of Stevens Point," her mother said.

"Ah. They grow potatoes up that way, don't they?" The woman next to him reached into her purse and offered Anna a hard candy, wrapped in a shiny gold wrapper. Anna looked at her mother.

"No, please..." her mother began to say.

"Oh, take it," the woman insisted, and set it on Anna's lap. The man smiled at her. Anna didn't know what to do. She had given up candy for Lent; but she couldn't just leave it on her lap.

"I'll save it for later," she said quietly, slipping it into her pocket.

The woman offered a candy to her mother; refused, she opened it herself and popped it into her mouth. It was red. In a few moments the woman's breath smelled like cinnamon. Anna wanted, very badly, to taste her own.

"We're on our honeymoon," the man said suddenly. He picked up his wife's hand and kissed it, looking at her affectionately. Anna looked out the window. "We were in LaCrosse last week. Have you ever been there?"

Anna's mother shook her head.

"It's nice. Now we're going back to Milwaukee." The man seemed so happy he just had to talk to someone. "I'm in trade school there. I'm learning all about electricity." Anna thought her mother would tell him about Walter, that Walter was in trade school in Milwaukee too. Maybe he even knew Walter. But her mother didn't say anything.

The man and woman were sitting in the middle of their seat, right up next to one another. They were holding hands. Only the woman seemed a little embarrassed when the man leaned over and kissed her cheek. It made Anna feel good, to see someone so happy. But it embarrassed her, too.

"Oh look!" the man said, pointing to the window. "Ducks!"

Out on the wide Wisconsin a dozen or more black and white ducks were floating along, diving and playing. Here the river was twice as wide as it was back home. Anna marveled that one river could travel so far. Of course in school Miss Schrum had told them all about the Nile, and the Mississippi, even bigger than the Wisconsin. She tried to guess how long it took water to get from their home to here. She even tried to calculate it, but didn't know how fast the river moved. She was going to ask the man — he looked like he would know — but decided she'd better not.

In Portage once again they had to change trains. The nice woman pressed another candy into Anna's hand as they stood up to get out, and put her finger to her lips so that her mother wouldn't know. When Anna and her mother were out on the platform the woman knocked on her window and waved down at them. And the man appeared, too, as the train pulled away, smiling and waving.

When they got on the next train, the only seat they could find was opposite an old man who sat, hat on his knee, big flowing white whiskers falling across his thin chest. He hardly looked up at them when they sat down. They seemed to embarrass him. Every time his eyes fell on Anna he would blink, his body give a little jerk, and his eyes jump away to stare at the floor at his feet.

Now they were in rich, rolling farm country. There was no snow on the ground at all. Only wide rolling fields of brown, some plowed, some not. And sometimes out in the field they would see a team and a spreader. They even saw some tractors spewing black exhaust into the air as they pulled the manure out onto the field. Anna remembered that her father, at home, was probably busily spreading with his fork the piles he had dumped a few days before. Now, so far from home, she began to grow a little tired. And she missed her father.

Alongside the track stood a little group of children, on their way home from school. They cringed from the noise of the speeding train, but managed to wave, staring up at the cars as they roared past. Anna's hand came up to the window and gently she returned their gesture. Now she wished she was with Sophie and Eddie, walking up the hill on their way home from school. But instead, as the sun slipped toward a tired horizon, like an orange sigh dropping from the clouds and exhaling its melancholy rays, here she was a hundred miles from home, tired and hungry; and it would be dawn tomorrow before she was home again.

They were coming into the outskirts of a city. And she thought, Madison at last. Here there were no farms, only industries and scattered houses. They came past the big rendering plant with the words "Oscar Meyer" written on it. Anna had never seen such a big building. It seemed as big as their whole farm.

Now the train was moving more slowly, weaving from one track to another, skirting past warehouses and freight cars parked on short sidings. The city seemed, from this approach, dirty and dreary. Anna could not imagine herself ever living in such a place.

They moved along a very big lake, its shore crowded with houses, some large and fancy, others nearby hardly more than shacks. And then suddenly they were at the depot, and the train was stopped. Everyone stood up. The conductor moved through the car, "All off for Madison," he was saying.

The air outside was cool. Workmen with black clothes and smudgy faces hurried to clean and oil the engine. Anna had to step aside to not get run over. All around them was a busy, noisy babble of people, cars, trucks, horns blaring, and the engine hissing its steam. Anna took her mother's hand. They walked along the long covered walkway with its smooth red bricks neatly placed in a herringbone pattern. The depot was a long building of tan brick, with many sets of large grey double doors, in and out of which streamed passengers, railroad agents, baggage handlers, newspaper boys and shoeshine boys. Another train, headed north, pulled away from the station, picking up speed, puffing and panting like Shep after he'd chased the cows. Across the tracks Anna saw the big roundhouse with a single locomotive slowly chugging its way onto one of the many tracks which splayed out like spokes of a bicycle wheel.

Anna was glad her mother knew what to do. They would have to take a Northwestern to Mendota. She knew that much. But that meant finding the Northwestern depot.

Her mother asked a man behind the counter where she could get the trolley that went to the Northwestern depot. They went out the back of the station, where rough-looking men tossed baggage onto carts and trucks or into the trunks of big shiny taxis. Across the alley was the Hotel Washington where inside the lobby Anna could see well-dressed businessmen lounging with the day's paper, watching out the window now and then at the activity brought in by the train which had just arrived.

Anna was frightened of the trolley ride. There were strangers pressing in on her from all sides. She held tight to her mother's hand. Some of them must have been from the university. The men were dressed in long fur coats, talked loudly and were full of jokes; the girls had bobbed hair and some even smoked cigarettes. Their silk stockings showed under their elegant coats. Anna was equally repulsed, fascinated, and frightened by them.

The Northwestern depot was even bigger than the one they'd come from. It was made of granite, like a monument or cathedral of some kind. It made Anna feel out of place. Its lobby was shiny marble on the walls and had fancy furniture with big plants in porcelain pots.

Anna was hungry. She wanted to eat supper at the depot. But their train was already at the platform, so they waited until they'd boarded. Soon they were moving north again, at first along the same tracks they'd come in on, then angling off along the other lake. They just had time to finish their sandwiches when they pulled into the Mendota station. The ticket agent told her mother it was just a short walk up that way to the hospital.

Hurrying along beside her mother, the sun low on the horizon, Anna felt exhausted. She had seen so many new and different things, all she could think of was she didn't want to see any more. But, she knew, the hardest was yet to come.

✳✳✳

Ahead lay the hospital compound. Behind the broad expanse of lawn with walks flanked by tall elms brooded a half dozen large brick buildings, heavy, severe. As they made their way onto the grounds, Anna could sense in her mother's step and in her grip the same anxiety she herself was feeling. But still her mother moved on, a mission to fulfill. Without her Anna would have turned and ran away from this place at which white-gowned patients were being herded out of one building and into another.

As they passed the great building into which the patients had disappeared, the door came open and a well-dressed, rather official-looking man stared out at Anna and her mother. Behind him Anna could see a huge, high-ceilinged room in which rows and rows of white-clothed tables were filled with patients eating their suppers. Strange sounds came through the door. Anna looked away, squeezed her mother's hand.

She clung more closely than ever now to her mother's side. They climbed the steps and pulled wide the great doors which led into the main building of the compound. The doors clicked shut behind them.

Inside it was warm and quiet. Directly ahead, behind a large desk sat a woman. Timidly they approached her.

The woman smiled courteously, watched them coming. She was well-dressed and took good care of her looks. "May I help you?" she asked. Her voice was calm and quiet.

Anna held her mother's hand. Her mother cleared her throat — would have to speak English. "I would like to see my sister," she said.

The woman looked very concerned. "I'm sorry, but visiting hours are in the morning only. Our patients are having dinner at this time."

"My sister's husband, he was killed in an accident. We have come all day on the train to tell her."

"Oh. I'm sorry," the receptionist said. And she said it so sincerely, Anna believed her. "Please, take a seat."

Against the far wall was a line of leather-upholstered arm chairs, dark red with elegant carvings on their arms. Anna sat back into one next to her mother, who was on the very edge of her seat. It seemed rather pleasant here. On a big round table beside them was a deeply green fern, healthy and carefully tended. On the walls behind them and across the wide aisle hung paintings of flowers and beautiful landscapes. The floor, of grey and black tile, was covered here and there with pretty rugs. It seemed such a nice place, after all, that Anna began to wonder why they should be ashamed that Aunt Anna lived here.

Now the lady was coming down the hall with a short young man. The man looked even more official than she did. He was dressed in a dark suit and tie, had a little black beard, and walked with soft, easy steps. He stopped in front of Anna's mother, bent slightly forward, and breathing through his nose, held out his hand.

"How do you do! I am Doctor Schilling." Anna's mother held his hand. "Would you come with me, please?"

Anna walked beside her mother down the long carpeted hallway from which on both sides offices opened. At last the doctor showed them into a door which had his name on it.

"Please, sit down." He remained standing behind his large oak desk, until they sat down, when he sat too. "Now, how can I help you?" he asked politely, lighting a cigarette.

Anna's mother spoke. Her voice was nervous. The man listened closely in order to understand. "My sister's husband was killed on Sunday in a car accident. We've come to see her and tell her. Her name is Anna Smolinska."

The man frowned a moment, then his face lit up. "Ah yes!" he said. "Anna." He puffed on his cigarette, regarded them as though from a distance. "May I ask, Mrs..."

"Topolska. Berenice Topolska."

"May I ask, Mrs. Topolska, how long it's been since you've seen you're sister?"

"We are farmers," Berenice said. "It is hard to get away."

"I understand." He smiled. "But how long has it been?" He leaned toward them to tap the ash off his cigarette into a heavy glass ashtray.

"Not since she was here," Berenice said.

"Ah. I don't recall when she was admitted..."

"Five years," Berenice tentatively suggested.

"Ah." He picked up his telephone and spoke into it. "Bring me Anna Smolinska's file, please."

Her mother interrupted. "You might have it Smolinksi,"

she said.

"Thank you." He spelled the name to the other person. When he'd hung up, he leaned back in his chair and stroked his beard. Anna looked around the room. She'd never seen so many books in one place. Tall, glass-fronted cases held them all along the walls and even extra chairs were piled with big heavy volumes. She tried to read the titles, but there were words she'd never seen before.

On the wall behind the doctor was a framed certificate from Harvard College. To Anna he was a funny kind of doctor. His office did not have the usual scale, strange-looking equipment, and bottles full of medicine. It didn't even smell like a doctor's office. On his desk she saw a photograph of a girl about her own age and suddenly realized that this rather strange and solemn man was also a father.

He was looking at Anna. Behind his cigarette smoke he smiled, then stood and excused himself. He went to the door and looked out into the hall. He stood there for a moment. Anna glanced at her mother, who sat staring stiffly out the window toward the setting sun.

The doctor spoke a few words with someone, then came back to them carrying a big folder full of papers. He set it down on his desk, sat again in his chair. Opening the folder wide, he turned from page to page, puffing now and then on his cigarette, which at last he snuffed out in his ashtray. The smoke hung heavy in the still air. Anna's mother leaned toward her and unbuttoned her coat, then opened her own.

The man cleared his throat, slid the papers to one side. "Yes," he said. He spoke slowly, choosing every word with care. "Your sister was admitted in early 1918, diagnosed with acute dementia praecox." He paused to see if that meant anything to them. "I'm afraid," he went on, "there's little we could do for her."

He stood up, ran his hand along some books in the bookcase, but couldn't find what he was looking for. "It's a progressive disease. Recent evidence indicates certain pathologies of the frontal cortex." He placed his hand on the front of his head. "Here."

Anna could not understand what he was talking about. Neither, she knew, could her mother. But her mother had no use for doctors of any kind. Sickness, to her, was a punishment for sin, best cured by priests and prayer, not doctors and medicine.

Anna knew that talking to this young man was merely a formality they had to go through in order to see Aunt Anna.

But she began to wonder if, after all, the doctor would even let them see Aunt Anna.

"There are of course individual etiologies," he was saying. But it was as though he was talking to himself. He walked slowly back and forth behind his desk. He stopped suddenly, turned to them. "Something, with your sister, to do with barrenness, wasn't it?" Berenice nodded. "Ah yes, how interesting." He sat again. "Is there a history of hysteria in your family, Mrs..."

"Topolska."

"Yes. I'm sorry."

Anna's mother sat rigidly holding the big basket in her lap. How out of place she looked. She wanted to answer but was not at all sure of the question.

"Has anyone else," the doctor asked, "your parents, brothers, sisters, grandparents, experienced the same symptoms as your sister Anna?"

"No."

"I see." The doctor sighed. "We've established a department of Occupational Therapy here... You know, making things like towels and birdhouses... It shows quite a lot of promise. Unfortunately, in your sister's case the disease was already quite..." He chose his words carefully, "Quite advanced." He flipped the folder open again, casually skimming the pages. "Incontinent..." He looked up to see if Berenice knew what that meant. He wasn't sure. "Occasional hallucinations, often catatonic and insensate..." He lit another cigarette. "You see, Mrs. Topolska, she may not even recognize you."

Anna's mother stared at him. "We've come very far, all day on the train."

"I see." He thought a moment. "Did she love her husband?" Anna's mother continued to stare at him. It seemed to make him uncomfortable. "I only ask because one has to take into account the effect such news as you bring might have on her."

"Her husband drank," Anna's mother explained. "He was not good to her."

One of the man's eyebrows lifted. "So perhaps the barrenness...?" But he was asking the question of himself. "But did she love him?"

Anna's mother shrugged. "Yes."

Her mother was clearly becoming impatient. How could one talk with a man who asked such questions? Even the priest did not ask such questions. It was God's business, not his.

"I see," he said. At last he let out a great, long sigh. "There is some chance, in informing your sister, of generating unwanted reactions." He thought a moment. "But I honestly doubt she'll even know what you're talking about. And, since you've come this far, I suppose you really ought to see her. But please, do not expect too much..."

He reached for the phone. "Yes. Anna Smolinski. She may be in the refractory. Yes. Right away." As he snuffed out his second cigarette, Anna noticed how womanly his hands were. She had never seen a man before with such immaculate, and delicate, hands. Perhaps, she thought, Father Nowak's. And the office, the books, the rather serious air, it all connected him with the priest rather than with other doctors she'd seen. But she could not imagine this man at the altar, placing the Host between their lips. In comparison Father Nowak came out far ahead.

While they waited, the doctor rapped his fingers on the tabletop. Clearly he was as uncomfortable with them as they were with him. Berenice set the basket on the floor beside her chair. Now that she knew she would at least see her sister, she relaxed a little. And Anna could tell, by her mother's lips, that she was praying. So Anna closed her eyes and said, to herself, an Our Father, hoping the doctor wouldn't notice.

What would Aunt Anna look like? All she could remember was a thin, pale woman who gave them presents but hardly ever smiled. And now the doctor said she was very sick. Did he mean that she coughed a lot or couldn't walk by herself or had some strange kind of lump on her head? Anna wished she was at home.

Outside the door they heard footsteps. The doctor hurriedly stood and went to open the door. Her mother rose, and Anna followed suit. They turned. A man came in, an orderly, rather busy and anxious-looking. And then Aunt Anna. Anna recognized her at once, though she looked much older than she remembered, and walked with a peculiar kind of stiffness. Another orderly came in, an older woman with a gentle face. The doctor took Aunt Anna by the arm and speaking quietly to her, sat her in a chair.

"Your sister's come to see you," he said, leaning close over her, looking into her eyes. She looked up at him, smiling, but didn't even look at Berenice. The doctor put his hand lightly on hers. Now he seemed very kind and considerate. "Would you like to talk to her?" he asked. But Aunt Anna did not respond.

Berenice sat down, leaned toward her sister. "Anna," she said, quietly. *"Jak sie mas,* Anna?"

Anna's eyes flew to her sister's, stopped a moment, then back to the doctor. He looked at Berenice, as though to tell her to go on.

"Anna, it's me, Berenice," she spoke, in a slow and careful Polish, as though she were talking to a child or an old man on his deathbed. The doctor was watching Aunt Anna intensely. "Anna, there's been an accident," Berenice said. "Your husband Peter's been killed in Chicago." But the patient stared forward, as though not even hearing. Or not wanting to hear. "He was killed on Sunday. Do you understand? In a car accident. Father sent a telegram, so I came to tell you. Do you understand?"

They had come so far across the ocean, the two sisters, so long ago. And only now to have this even greater ocean rise up to separate them.

Little Anna could not look away from her aunt's face. There was something wrong with Aunt Anna's eyes. They looked glazed over, as though they were all surface, and nothing they saw sank in. Anna felt sorry for her; she did not look sick, except for her eyes. But to not even recognize your own sister, it meant she really was sick.

Berenice dropped a rosary into her daughter's hands, motioned her to give it to her aunt. Anna stood and placed it into Aunt Anna's cool and motionless palm.

"It's the rosary mother gave me," Berenice said. "Do you remember? It was mother's rosary." But the palm did not seem to notice what it held. Berenice reached over and wound one end around Aunt Anna's fingers, patted lightly her sister's hand. "For you. To pray with."

For a moment little Anna thought her mother would actually cry. But instead she sighed and placed her hand on top of her sister's grey and brittle hair. "Anna, Anna," she crooned. "Can't you hear me, Anna?"

But from the other came no sign at all.

Berenice bent and kissed her sister's forehead, turned wearily away and sat once more. The doctor nodded to the orderlies, who one on either side helped their patient to stand. The rosary hung in a long loop down from Anna's hand, threatening to fall on the floor. The older woman unwound it and carried it devoutly in her own hand. "I'll put it in her room," she whispered to Berenice.

Then they were gone, completely gone, and the door closed behind them. And Anna knew she would never see her aunt again.

The doctor waited a moment. Standing behind his desk he cleared his throat. "I thought for a moment," he said, "she might have recognized you. But I don't think so." He looked down at the floor. He spoke with a subdued voice, as though in church or at a funeral. "It's interesting, though," he said, one hand resting on the desk, the other running over his beard. "With patients such as her, you never know. Really," he said, and then as though making a confession. "You never know."

✳✳✳

It was after ten o'clock when they boarded the train for home. Anna was exhausted. She watched the big blank-eyed warehouses, deserted now, and the ragged shops and slums slip past. Somehow in her mind she blamed these cold and heartless buildings. As though if they could only bring Aunt Anna home, to the farm, she would get better. As though it was the city which made her that way.

As she fell asleep she was thinking of the smell of the barn, of the warm milk right from the cow, of their kitchen and its warmth and delicious smells. She wanted to be in bed with her sisters, snug under the *pisina*. And she wondered if she would ever get home.

Her mother had to wake her, in the middle of the night, to change trains in Portage, and again in New Lisbon. Anna was barely awake, rubbed her eyes, followed her mother out into the cold, fell asleep in each depot, followed her mother again onto the new train. There were strangers all around, sprawled in their seats, their heads resting on pillows or only bunched-up coats. A few sat, puffy-eyed, staring out into the darkness. It was cold on the train, Anna pulled her coat around her, lay her head on her mother's lap.

At one stop she woke and saw a man making his way up the aisle. He was coughing a loud and terrible cough. He looked like he was drunk. But Anna couldn't tell. It might have been the jerking of the car that made him walk that way. She drifted back to sleep.

Her mother did not sleep all night. As the train made its way northward, from tiny village to village, pausing a little longer at the larger towns, she sat patiently embroidering a doily. Her needle pierced the fine linen regularly, mercilessly. And all the while she was blaming herself for her sister's troubles. If they'd stayed behind in Necedah, she might have been able to save Anna. She wanted to stay. But when Frank went and signed the papers on the new place, she had to go.

Or they could have taken Anna with them.

If God had only given Anna one of our children, she thought. Lord knows, she thought, I've had more than my share. He could have given Anna one, even one would have been enough.

How she'd needed Anna when Rose died. How alone she was then, with no one to turn to. Frank, he tried to help, but he was a man. She needed, then, another woman. And there was none.

How close, Berenice remembered, looking out the window where only darkness could be seen, how close I'd come to breaking. We're not even allowed, as men are, to turn to drink. How I envied Frank for his whiskey. But we are not allowed. We have to carry our own burdens and we have to carry the rest of the family too.

And thinking of it that way, in this chattering, bouncing car full of strangers making its way through the cold and utter darkness, she could not help but for an instant envy her sister, whose spirit was already in the arms of God.

But she would not be granted that, until the final moment. She would have to face the long uphill climb. She would have to see the meals cooked, the house cleaned, the clothing made and washed and ironed, the groceries bought, the canning done, the berries planted, hoed, picked and sold, the girls kept washed and chaste, the boys sent off to school or jobs and families of their own, the whole family kept in a thousand and one simple and not-so-simple ways, together.

And on top of all that, there was Mary.

Oh Mary, she thought, Mary. You do not know what I go through for your sake.

***

Little Anna felt clumsy as she stepped off the train. Her legs had fallen asleep, were stiff and stubbornly refused to listen.

She almost tripped; her mother caught her, by the hand, and helped her down.

The sun was already high above the river-bottom elms. There on the platform her father stood, beaming, the arms of his heavy fur coat thrown wide. Behind him, Queen and the cutter. How happy she was to be home! She ran as fast as she could to her father, who squatted down to catch her and give her a great big furry hug.

"Anna!" he said. "We missed you."

He picked her up, whirled her around. She was home, and she never wanted to leave again.

And when he sat her down and turned to look for her mother, they saw she was already in the sleigh, sitting with the big basket on her lap, staring impatiently forward.

"Come on," her father said, taking her hand. "Your mother's waiting."

14

"The solidarity of nature, in the peasant's life, is neither a matter of theoretical curiosity nor an object of purely aesthetic or mystical feelings aroused on special occasions. It has a fundamental practical importance for his everyday life; it is a vital condition of his existence. If he has food and clothing and shelter, if he can defend himself against evil and organize his social life successfully, it is because he is a member of the larger, natural community, which cares for him, as for every other member, and makes for him some voluntary sacrifices... Even the simplest act of using nature's gifts assumes, therefore, a religious character."
— from *The Polish Peasant in Europe and America*, by Thomas and Znaniecki

What little snow remained at April's arrival was quickly rinsed away by a light but drenching rain. The girls were busy washing floors, ceilings, walls, chairs, and anything else which warm water and soap could clean. For next Sunday was Palm Sunday — how quickly it had come — and for Easter morning the house must be as gloriously immaculate as Christ's own soul. And, they hoped, their own.

Berenice sent Angie out for the mail. There was a letter from Walter. Anxiously she sat at the kitchen table and sliced the envelope open. Walter had not been writing as frequently as he'd promised — this was only his second letter since Christmas. Berenice fretted over him constantly. Always he was in her prayers. But she was proud, too, because he'd struck out on his own.

"Our boy Walter," she would say, "who's in Milwaukee." No matter that her friends already knew where he was and why: she was proud to say it. As though getting off the farm automatically meant success. Her words, meanwhile, offered no comfort to Stash. And Frank, if he was handy when she spoke that way, was always just ready to say something about how much he could use Walter's help at home. But he never did.

"Should we take the curtains down from the living room?" Lotti appeared in the doorway to ask her mother.

"Yes, yes." Berenice sent her away impatiently.

She unfolded the letter. Walter greeted her warmly and asked how they were. Already in Milwaukee flowers were springing up. The Archbishop was celebrating a pontifical Mass in the Cathedral on Easter morning. He would go, and think of them; and hoped that Easter morning they would think of him.

There were only three month's school left. Perhaps he would go to Chicago to look for work. Factory mechanics, he'd heard, were earning six dollars a day. But before he went, he would come home for a visit.

He mentioned a girl named Stasia with a hint that he might be bringing her home with him. "You would like her, mother," he wrote. "She is very nice."

He said there was not much else that was new and that he promised to write more often. Saying hello to the rest of the family, he closed.

Berenice dropped the single sheet of paper onto the table.

Tja, she thought to herself, already a girl. Well, she sighed, he's grown-up now, and out on his own.

She set the letter aside; Frank could read it at lunch. Angie threw open the door and set a full bucket of water on the floor, then another. It was drizzling out; her coat was wet. And her boots were thick with mud, where she'd made her way along the path, balancing the buckets on the yoke. Now, as the mud came, hauling in water was almost worse than in the cold of winter. If any was spilled — even the smallest drop — or if they wasted fire or let it go out, all their stock, their mother warned, would get sick.

Angie slipped out of her boots and hung up her coat. She lifted, under close scrutiny, one of the buckets and carefully poured the water into the big kettle on the stove. It was astonishing how much water could be used up in housecleaning.

Angie, of all the sisters most in temperament like her mother — and, most liked by her mother — complained that a hand pump in the kitchen would be nice. They had, after all, had one at the house in Necedah.

"*Tja,*" Berenice said, watching her daughter fill the kettle. "It would be nice."

But it was like asking for the moon. The summer after they'd moved in, urged by Berenice, Frank had tried digging a well just outside the kitchen. Fifteen feet he'd gone down, breaking the hardpan with a bar, scooping it into buckets which Stash and Walter took turns hauling up. And all the while, wondering if the walls of the well might not cave in on him. Or, as he'd read in *Rolnik*, one of the buckets slipping out of the boys' hands and falling onto his head.

Fifteen feet down Frank struck bedrock. There was only one chance: wedging into a crevice half a stick of powder left over from blasting stumps, he covered his well with heavy oak planks and set the powder off.

Berenice, watching from the barn, had been terrified that he would blow half the house away. He didn't. But neither did he budge the bedrock.

So all the dirt they'd hauled, bucket by bucket out of the hole, had to be dumped back in. And the pump out past the granary would have to do.

After lunch Frank and Bruno escaped to the barn. The house was topsy-turvy; they wanted nothing to do with it. In the dining room the table was moved aside so the linoleum could be washed. Shelves were dusted, furniture polished. The kitchen chairs were scrubbed clean of the caked manure left by the men's dirty boots. It was a big job; before they were done, they would have used up most of the week.

On Wednesday Lotti met George at the mailbox. His buggy creaked to a stop; Leo begged Lotti for a treat. But this morning she had none. It was a sure sign of spring, George using his buggy instead of the cutter.

"River's out," he said, handing her the mail. "Goin' out, I

mean."

Lotti met her father as he hurried between the barn and the work shed. She could tell he was upset about something. Often he was in that mood — something had gone wrong, a cow was sick or some tool needed fixing. She stopped, anyway, to tell him what George had said about the river going out. He stared at her, trying to fit that information into the scheme of things which at that moment was propelling him toward the workshop. Lotti was sorry she'd bothered him.

To everyone's surprise, right after lunch he said they were all to get into the wagon and go down to see the river. Berenice demurred; there was too much work to do, she said. But Frank insisted. The river only goes out once a year. There'll be plenty of time, he said, when we get back.

They could hear it even before they could see it. The churning ice-cakes ground against each other with a low growling sound, so deep and powerful it sounded like the earth itself was in some desperate agony. As they approached they could see the surface of the water, from bank to bank white with moving ice.

Frank pulled the wagon on the side of the road and they stood along the bank, already lined with friends and neighbors staring excitedly, to watch in awe. Now and then a big cake of ice, perhaps two feet thick and twenty across, would be pushed up onto its end, and so ride the current until it broke loose and suddenly fell back in with a tremendous splash.

Some of the cakes, the ice a deep turquoise, filled with thin cracks and scattered bubbles, had been pushed up onto the shore where they lay like huge pieces of some impossible puzzle. A gang of adventurous boys were climbing over them, jumping up and down and trying to crack them. Two of the lads stepped out onto a floating cake and rode it downstream a ways. They were showing off. Bruno wanted to join them, but his father told him not to. And just then, as the cake the boys were on began edging out into the dangerous current, the two lads had to jump for their lives. One ended up in the icy water up to his knees.

After they'd taken the rest of the family back home, Frank dragged out his big ice-saw and he and Bruno returned to the river's edge. They cut off big pieces of the ice-cakes and hefted them onto the wagon, to be laid up in the icehouse under a blanket of sawdust. This was old ice, to be sure, which would not last as long as the big blocks Frank had cut from a nearby lake in February, but it was too easy to pass up.

They were to spend the next day hauling ice. But in the morning it rained, so Bruno got a break. Until at noon the sun came out and he and his father hitched the team and started once again down toward the river. The air, the land, the trees — all were so clean and warm and clear it seemed the very first day of Creation. After a morning spent in the house, the girls took a few minutes after lunch to sit on the back steps and drink in the wonderful sun. The air was fresh and so absolutely still they could hear the buzz of the year's first flies as, halfway across the yard, they argued over the last remnants of the spring butchering.

The chickens and ducks were out and seemed as exuberant about the weather as the girls themselves. One of the big white drakes, his face blackened from straining through his bill each of the yard's dozens of puddles, craned his neck toward the sky, stood on tiptoe, fanned his wings, then settled back to fluff and preen himself. Just watching him stretch and enjoy his freedom after the long winter's confinement made the girls feel better.

All across the yard and under the trees of the orchard half a hundred hens, watched over by five insufferable roosters, scratched at the grass, turning over last fall's leaves, tirelessly and with all the solemnity of so many bankers counting their precious dollars, searched for bug, seed, or gravel, to store away in their crops. The grass itself showed signs of greening, and many of the hens pecked at it, stowing away for their own use blade after precious blade. Under the granary, where the dirt was still dry, a clutch of hens had clustered together and were clucking happily away, kicking up fine little showers of earth as they shared a communal dirt bath.

Going back inside to work that afternoon was like walking back into prison. And the next day, too, when in the morning the blackbirds, phoebes, and robins sang from the tops of trees, fences, roofs, anywhere in the world they could find to get closer to God so He might better hear their song of praise.

But even work could not dampen their excitement, their sense of joy at the morning's glory. Life, once again, had triumphed over death. It was the Easter theme, played out by nature herself.

Coming in from the outhouse that next afternoon, Bruno found a wood tick on his arm; and naturally, had to pass from one sister to the next, showing it off, before he yanked off its head and popped it in the stove. Yes, life had indeed triumphed!

One day later a southwest wind brought the temperature, for the first time in six months, up into the sixties. House doors were propped open; roosters crowed more brashly than ever; even the horses were restless, whinnying and begging to be let out of the barn. Most of the cleaning done, the girls were let outside to help their mother put in the early garden. While they scratched away at the still-damp soil, Berenice disappeared into the attic and returned with the old sugar tin in which she'd saved the seeds from last year: lettuce, spinach, radishes, they could all go in. She had Lotti moving the tomato, cabbage, and pepper plants off the windowsills and out into the cold frame, their tiny leaves seeming almost to shiver with the joy of the sun.

As the girls made shallow rows in the cool soil, a bumble-bee buzzed noisily around them, still heavy with the winter's sleep, thick-headed, slow, but inquisitive about these newly-sprouted flowers which alternately bent to the dark earth or turned their beaming faces to the warm and yellow sun. The air was fresh and smelled of the earth, the sun embraced them in its warm arms. When they were done the girls stood together in a little bunch and quietly admired the tiny garden in which they'd set the seeds of a new year's growth.

It was not a good time to be a teacher. Poor Miss Schrum, down at the school, was having quite a time with her students, who just couldn't seem to keep their minds on their studies. What, after all, was the geography of Africa compared with the sweetness of spring?

At lunch she'd let them all outside. Sitting along the south wall of the big block building, like so many turtles on a log, they took with their sandwiches and boiled potatoes as much sun as their bodies could absorb. And when they stood to play, they all rose to find their pants and dresses watermarked with the cool dampness of the earth.

Playing tag, Eddie and Anna stopped long enough to wave to their father and Bruno who were going up the hill with the last load of ice. Bruno looked out at them with unmistakable envy. Tag, blind man's bluff, and I spy seemed much more rea-sonable pastimes than that into which he had been drafted.

Even Miss Schrum was loathe to go inside, it was so pleas-ant in the warming sun. But it was her job, was what she drew her sixty dollars a month for doing. Reluctantly she rang the bell which hung atop its tower, and the children came streaming in, flushed with the excitement of recess, their hair a mess, their shoes and clothes splattered with mud. It seemed to take forever for them to settle down again. As a compromise Miss Schrum agreed to push open the big wide windows which faced the south to at least let in some of the fresh air. It was a mistake. The rest of the afternoon they spent staring longingly out into the free air which seemed only to taunt and laugh at them, as though they were pilloried in stocks for some unstated crime.

Their only crime, Miss Schrum knew, was in being young; so she let them out for an extra recess, and their loud and happy voices filled the school yard once again, overflowed out into the fields and down the roads, so that simultaneously Albert, wheeling a freight cart onto the platform at the depot, and Frank and Bruno Topolski, down at the sawmill filling the wagon with sawdust, and Louis Dupre, down at the Post Office sweeping dried mud off the steps, all stopped a moment to marvel at that sound which suddenly they realized had not been heard for so many months — a sound to them more cheering, more expressive of the signature of life and of God Himself than even the year's first bluebird or the buzz of the courageous and foolhardy flies and bumblebees.

It was a scene repeated all across the country that particular afternoon in April of 1922; yet how terrible it was to think of how many went their ways dead to the sound of either children's laughter or the bluebird's song. So many, in truth, in city, suburb and countryside, that the thought would be unbearable were we not so sure that there was One Who never closed His ears to the joy of children's laughter; and Whose appreciative smile, as He pauses at His work, can be readily felt in the warmth of the newborn sun.

15

Six months' winter is too much!
— from the Dancy News of the
Mosinee Times, April, 1922

It was a procession, bearing their palm branches out into the morning drizzle and in a long, shuffling, singing line around the little white church, a reenactment of the entrance, twenty centuries before, of a poor rag-wrapped preacher, astride a gentle donkey, into the walls of the City of David:

Hail our King
son of David
Redeemer of the World!

It has become almost a cliché, the incongruity of that hour, the myopic crowds unable to see that here was no revolutionary promising to lead them out of the bondage of Caesar's might but a simple man — son not of David but of Joseph — whose only promise was another bondage:

Father, he would pray, *let this cup pass away from me; yet not as I will, but as thou willest.*

It was not what they'd come to hear, that milling throng whose dust already for a thousand years has mingled with the earth of Judea. Turning their backs, they denied Him; and He, in full knowledge of the depths to which His steps would lead Him, began that historic journey from the palm branches to the bitter garden, and afterward the arrest, trial, and suffering upon the Cross, scribbled sarcastically with: *Jesus, King of the Jews.*

On Second Passion Sunday — called by most Palm Sunday — they gathered all across the world in little congregations such as this beside the river or in thronging masses such as saw His Holiness Leo XI at St. Peters, to hear the history of that man, the familiar yet touching story which in the Gospel ends with this poignancy: *Then they rolled a large stone to the entrance of the tomb, and departed.*

All week he would lie in that darkness — and they would lie with him, their hearts encased in stone, until came that Queen of Days when the sheer power of His light would roll back that stone to explode in glories unimagined.

✳✳✳

The Mass was done. They carried their palms with them, down the steps. There was an anxiety in the air: they approached the climax of the liturgical year, on which everything else depended. The week, they knew, would seem a month, and Easter, so close, was yet so far.

"Can we have a talk," Alex suggested to Frank at the bottom of the steps. "About Joe, I mean?"

Joe was not with them. He had done as he had threatened to do, gone to find work in the city. Obviously Sophie and Alex were upset.

"Well, I..." Frank glanced toward Berenice.

"We thought if we all got together, the four of us I mean, maybe we can come to an understanding."

Berenice, naturally, was less than enthusiastic about the idea. What could Alex mean by an "understanding"? It was none of their business, really. Mary was her daughter, not theirs.

But Frank was eager to have the air cleared. All along it had bothered him, not knowing what Alex thought of the situation. "This afternoon?" he offered.

"We've got company," Alex answered. "Tomorrow?"

It was agreed. Berenice turned surly, taciturn. She had, as she saw it, a strategy to contrive, and little time to do it in. But, unknown to her, fate was about to weave another, more formidable pattern, over the coming days.

A pattern of drizzle, which turned by afternoon into a driving sleet, pushed them all inside, the wind slathering the sleet like a cold tongue against the ice-coated windows. It was blowing up a storm. Their father said that Molly had predicted just that, in her anxious whinnying the night before. It blew and rolled outside, like a huge stone up and down their drive, making the pleasure of their own company that much more meaningful. The girls gathered with their needlework at the dining room table — they'd had to light, against the glowering clouds, the kerosene lamp — and chatted in high spirits about the day's events.

Lotti was telling them how during the procession she saw

little Franchek Laska crying miserably until his mother put the palm leaf in his tiny hand, when suddenly he quieted and began waving it about, making gurgling noises deep in his throat.

"Perhaps it means he'll be a priest," her mother suggested.

It was still raining, hard, when Lotti met George Zimmer at the mailbox the next morning. The river was rising at Wausau, he said, was already near to flood stage from all the snow melted to the north. Roads were being washed out. He was excited, and he was worried.

And Mary worried about Joe, wondered where he was and if he was safe.

At noon Sophie Stelmach called. The weather was too bad for them to visit that afternoon. Perhaps the next day, she said.

So it was that Berenice's strategies, of justifying and explaining, became suddenly superfluous.

The mailman had brought a letter. Berenice sat after lunch by the big bay window and opened it. Outside the rain was turning to snow, big wet flakes driven by a strong north wind. Over the house hung a spirit of darkness. What had promised to be a heavy spring rain was turning instead into a bitter reminder of the months gone by.

The letter, from Mr. Walerych, was small talk, mostly. But with two important exceptions: the first being a subtly vague reference to the desire, once free of the Army, to find a spouse and be married. "It's what everyone seems to be doing," he wrote. "And I'm not opposed to the idea." And the second, in his closing paragraph, admitting that he would very much like to come to Wisconsin after mustering out, to visit my "faraway friend," as he put it, "who already seems so much more than a friend."

Berenice held the letter in her lap, the snowflakes flying past just outside the window, so that it seemed to her almost as though the house were scudding across the landscape at a tremendous speed. It made her dizzy. She closed her eyes; the house slowed to a stop. Only one more letter, she thought, and they will coast right downhill into the church. Only more more: in it she must invite him here. That's all that's needed anymore and this Anton Walerych, whoever he is, will be woven into the fabric of the family as easily as a needle is pushed through cloth.

And the other girls, the younger ones, they will learn from it.

She slipped the letter into her apron when she heard Frank

come in the back door, stomping the snow off his boots and coughing. As she stood, outside the window she was astonished to see raging a full-fledged blizzard.

***

All night it snowed and half the next day. School of course was canceled. The Stelmachs could not come over. Even the mail did not come through. According to reports on Stash's crystal set, half the state was snowed under. A number of rivers had reached flood stage and were still rising. Frank, worried about the church, tried to get through to Father Nowak. But the lines must have been down. They could get through only as far as the Tomczaks.

Once again the ground was blanketed deep in snow. The newly planted garden was buried. For the second day the family stayed inside. Now they were tense, moved cautiously past each other, as though afraid the little charges each held inside might accidentally detonate. Even Frank ventured out into the blizzard only for chores and to let the cows out for water. Their hearts and souls had expanded in the warmth of the past days, and now pushed back inside again, it was as though there just wasn't room.

***

By Wednesday morning the snow had finally stopped. Holy Wednesday, it was — Shrove Wednesday, the day for Easter confession. Once again bundled into the sleigh — which they'd hoped, mistakenly, to have seen the last of — they set out against a northeast wind. Under a crystal blue sky, the whiteness of the snow dazzled their eyes. They sat in a kind of shock, as though the spring were an infant son who one day healthy had overnight been taken ill and died.

As they slid down the hill they met George, once again in his cutter, Leo plodding up through the deep snow. Wrapped in his coat, he stopped for a few minutes' talk. It had been terrible, he said, the reports coming in on the telegraph. Highway 18 was closed just outside Stevens Point. Train tracks east of Mosinee were under four feet of water and most trains had been canceled. There was a report that far to the north a father and his young son, trying to ford a flooded road with their team and buggy, had been swept away, their bodies not yet found. No, there was no report of damage in Knowlton; they would have heard if the church were in danger. As far as he knew, the road was passable. The river had already crested and was on its way down. But all this snow, his hand swept across the landscape, if it melts too fast, it will bring trouble again.

Once at the river's edge they could see for themselves just how high the water had been. Trees along the bank were wet two feet above its present level. Some had fought the current but lost; they lay now in the water, weaving back and forth, their roots slowly working loose, soon to be torn away and taken downstream. It was like the story in the Bible, when Noah and his family came down from their ark.

The road was washed away in places, along the sides, but still passable. And the church, it turned out, had been safe. Parked in front, a few sleighs and cutters — a buggy, even, its tires deep in the snow — showed that others had come out for confession.

Inside the church was warm and quiet. Here and there parishioners knelt to examine their conscience or mutter penance. A short line led to the single confessional. The Topolskis knelt, and one by one rose to stand in line. Only for the parents was confession ever easy. Frank had, as usual, been too busy to sin. He did mention the whiskey at Laska's, and the beer at Roman's. And almost came to ask Father about his role in Mary's troubles — for he knew that there were such things as sins of omission. But he kept quiet. It was not mortal. It would wait.

And Berenice — Berenice was untroubled at confession time because she had decided long before that there were certain things, certain womanly or family things, that the Lord need not be troubled with.

Mary stood behind Bruno, her hands folded piously before her. She was the last of the family to go in. She had decided that her urge to disobey her mother, with regard to Walerych, was not a sin. After all, she had obeyed. But it had meant a deep and protracted examination of conscience.

Now she was at the head of the line, waiting only for Bruno to come out. This was the hardest time. It was so hard to know what might and what might not send you to the eternal fires of Hell.

Bruno hurried out of the confessional. It was her turn. She pushed the curtain aside, slipped in. At the sound of the kneeler against the floor, Father cleared his throat and from behind the milky window began his prayers. Mary answered, quietly, crossed herself. Confession was a strange rite — but her first, the hardest, had taken place ten years before and by now, once inside the booth, though her mouth was dry and her heart fluttering, she knew she could rely on the formula.

The last time she had confessed was at Christmas time. She paused, mentioned anger toward her mother — it wasn't really anger, but she could think of no better word to describe it. And having forgotten her prayers two nights — when she'd been thinking of Joe, instead. And being discouraged, sometimes, almost to the point of failing in her faith.

"Is this often?" Father asked.

"Just... sometimes."

She was told to say her prayers every day and to remember God's great sacrifice of His only begotten Son and that way she wouldn't be discouraged because God was always with her, thinking of her and loving her. He asked if there was more. There was not. For penance he assigned five Our Fathers and five Hail Marys. As he muttered the absolution, Mary repeated an act of contrition. To really be rid of her sins, she knew, required perfect contrition: sorrow based not on the fear of Hell, but of the pain it had caused the Lord. It bothered her, sometimes, wondering if her contrition were ever really perfect. She did not want to hurt the Lord. She did not want Christ — any more than she wanted a duck or a pig — to suffer and die. But it was hard, sometimes, seeing the connection between being angry at her mother and Christ's terrible agonies.

Father had her go in peace. She thanked him.

But as she lifted herself from the kneeler, in a lower, more familiar voice, Father whispered to her:

"Mary!"

She stopped, one knee on the kneeler, the other half off. Her breath caught in her throat. How did he know?

Her heart pounded as she bent closer. What could he want? He must know that if she stayed too long, they would all think she had many sins to confess.

Father cleared his throat. "Verna is going away after Easter, for a week. I'll need someone to fill in for her. Could you come, Mary?"

What could she say? It wasn't right to say no to a priest. Yet her mother... Her mouth was dry; she stammered, "I have to ask mother."

His voice carried its disappointment. "Yes, of course." He had hoped she would commit herself. But now, all was lost.

And it was so timely, his housekeeper wanting a week off, a chance to learn the girl's true feelings. There seemed to be something he wanted to tell Mary as a friend — and, if necessary, influence her to stand up for herself. "Yes, of course," he repeated. There was another silence. Mary thought perhaps that would be all, was ready to push herself back up again. But then his voice again, quietly. "How are you, Mary?"

Hesitantly she answered, her voice almost a question. "Fine."

"Tell me," he went on, taking what he saw might be his last chance, "do you still want to marry Joseph?"

There was a moment's pause. "Mother..."

Father interrupted her. "Forget your mother, Mary, just for now." He repeated the question. "Do you still want to marry Joseph?"

Another pause. At last, tentatively, "Yes."

Father moved on his chair behind the screen; she could hear his shoes slide on the floor, the rustle of his cassock. "And if your mother should propose someone else?" It was always possible. He leaned toward her, wishing to God he didn't have to put her through this. But he must know. "Well?" he urged her on.

Her reply caught him off guard. "She has," the girl said, her lips almost touching the window.

He breathed quickly inward, waiting for her to go on. But she would say no more. "Yes?" he asked. "She has?"

And now Mary wondered if it was a mistake to even mention it. If her mother found out... But it was her mother who'd taught them it was a sin to keep anything from a priest. And if he knew, there was always the chance that he would help her.

"We write," she said, "to a man in Texas."

"Texas? Do you know him?"

"Only through our letters."

"I see. And you write with... with marriage in mind?"

"I write what she tells me."

Another indrawn breath. "Thank you, Mary."

"Father..."

"Don't worry, my child. I won't say a word." Again he moved in his seat, as though he had more to say. But after a pause, he blessed her. "God go with you, my child."

"Thank you, Father."

She left the confessional hardly able to walk. She slipped

into her pew, feeling the eyes of all the others on her. Burying her head in her hands she prayed the penance, and prayed on and on until her father signaled it was time to go.

***

On the way home she decided to make no mention of Father's proposal. After all, what good would it do? Her mother would never let her out of the house for a week, especially now. But she had promised the priest that she would ask. She waited until they were home and in the kitchen peeling potatoes for lunch.

Berenice's first reaction was mixed. To have a daughter who was a priest's housekeeper was an honor. Yes, Verna was getting old already. Perhaps if Mary spent that week with Father, when the time came he'd ask her to serve as his new housekeeper. Then there would be no question of her being married.

But she would have to send one of the other girls with. It wouldn't be right, Mary alone with the priest. So she didn't respond to Mary's request. She kept the thought in her head through lunch, turning it over and over to see all sides. And as she lay down for her afternoon nap, Berenice saw the prospect in yet another light. Was Father Nowak trying to turn the girl against her? She and the priest had gotten along well, until this thing with Mary. It was a family matter — why did he have to stick his nose in it? But clearly, she now saw, he meant to.

One week together with him and who could say how Mary's head might be turned. No. It was too big a chance. Fieldwork would be starting soon. Mary was needed at home. Perhaps some other time, she could say. He would just have to find someone else.

***

Between confession and Communion — which in this case would not be until Easter morning — to sin would mean to have to confess again. So the following days allowed for no family discord. They moved more easily now, lubricated as it were by their state of grace. It was understood there would be no arguments — all were on their best behavior. Even Bruno put off hiding his sisters' combs and tying their socks in knots until some future, less sanctified, time.

Only Mary was still troubled. Joe had promised to write, but she'd seen no letters. And how she would have liked to go to the rectory. It would be like a vacation, getting away from her mother. She was twenty-one years old and had never spent a night away from home.

Each day now was one step closer to Christ's resurrection. On the first Holy Thursday, He had gathered His apostles around Him and admonished them to remember Him with bread and wine. It was, though they did not know it, their last supper with Him.

On the farm there was still work to do. The family was scattered into their chores. Mary once again found herself alone in the house with her mother.

"Come, sit down," her mother said.

Mary knew what that meant. Obediently — for to disobey would be a sin — she sat, and lifted the pencil. Her heart was torn, but word for word she copied her mother's dictation. She balked only when it came to inviting this stranger who, though she'd never met him she already hated, to come and visit. It was almost too much. She shivered as she wrote. Never again, having put those words to paper, could she feel worthy of Joe.

She was addressing the envelope when her father came from the barn into the kitchen. Berenice snatched the letter and its envelope away from her and slipped them into her apron.

"Go upstairs," she told Mary abruptly.

The girl disappeared up the stairway just as her father came into the dining room, sensing that something was wrong. Berenice hurried past him toward the kitchen. Then, remembering Walerych's most recent letter, on the table, she turned. But it was too late. Frank had already seen it.

He picked the envelope up. It was addressed to Mary. The return address, written in a man's hand, was Camp MacArthur, Texas. He held the envelope, turning it over as though it were an arrowhead or silver dollar he'd just plowed up in the field. He turned to his wife.

"What's this?" he asked. She reached for the letter, but he held it tightly. "What is it?" he repeated.

"A letter," she said.

"I can see that myself. Who's it from?"

She shrugged. "A friend."

"A friend? What friend?"

With one hand she leaned on the table; with the other, nervously fingered the holy medal around her neck.

"It's a man's writing," he said. "Who is this man?" But she would not answer.

Frank sat down and opened the envelope, pulled the letter

from it. Berenice simply stood watching. His lips moved slowly over the words on the page, as though it was hard for him to comprehend. Marriage? To come to visit in May?

It was beyond his grasp. He looked up at his wife. She looked ready to take on the Devil himself. "What in God's name is this?" he asked. She only shrugged. He set the letter on the table. They both stared at it. "Do you know this man, this... Anton... Walerych?"

"No."

"Does Mary know him?"

"She writes to him."

His eyes widened. "She writes to him? How long has she been writing to him?"

Again Berenice shrugged. "A month. Two."

Frank stared at her as though she were a stranger. He had felt this way toward her only once before, when she'd adamantly refused to sign the mortgage on this farm. She didn't want to leave her sister. Or maybe she wanted to move back to the city — he wasn't sure. But in the end he'd taken the mortgage out himself, and that was that. And now, again, they faced each other across a chasm even thirty years of marriage could not bridge.

He remembered glancing into the dining room when he'd first come in from the barn, the way Berenice was hovering over the girl. "Are you telling her what to write?" he asked. She wouldn't answer. He stood up, gently pushed her aside. "Mary!" he shouted up the stairs.

"No!" Berenice said.

"Mary!" he shouted again.

He picked up the letter and turned with it just as the girl came timidly down the stairs. "Come here," he said softly. "Do you know this man?" he asked, his finger pointing to Walerych's name.

Mary glanced first at her mother, then her father, but would not answer.

"Do you write to him?"

She was like a captured animal, her eyes searching some way out. She nodded, quickly. Yes.

"Where did you get his address?" she glanced again at her mother. "I see," her father said. "And what about Joe?"

Now she stared at him with eyes full of fear, begging him to let up. You are blaming me? she was asking. How can you blame me?

Then, the tears welling up, she could only stare at the table.

Her father put his arm around her shoulder. "Go upstairs," he said, gently, his voice full of weariness.

The girl gone, Berenice adopted a strategy of compromise. "Don't forget, Frank," she said quietly, "it's Holy Week."

But he only turned to her as though she'd slapped his face. Holy Week! Of course it's Holy Week! The perfect chance to take advantage of the girl! But he kept his thoughts to himself.

His hands dropped wearily to his side. She picked up the letter, put it in the envelope and slipped it inside her apron, next to Mary's letter already there. He walked past her to the back door. Bending to slip his boots on, he leaned against the wall as though he were suddenly twenty years older, that much closer to the only peace he felt he could ever find.

He opened the door. Outside a slushy snow was filling the yard. He closed the door and turned as though he had more yet to say. His hand came up, and grasped futilely at the empty air. His fingers squeezed, of their own, until the knuckles showed white. He stared at it, this enormous white fist, as though he'd never seen it before. And the moment he recognized it for what it was, it fell to his side, heavy, useless, clumsy.

He opened the door and walked out into the snow.

✳✳✳

That night was the darkest Mary had ever known. At the supper table they could all feel the tension between their parents, and knew that it was only Holy Week which kept it from erupting. Only Mary knew the source of it. And she could tell, by her father's furtiveness and the calm quietude of her mother, that her father had lost.

Always she had thought: when he finds out, he'll put an end to it. But her last hope was now gone. Like all her dreams, that too was only her heart dancing on the billowing mists of illusion. A wind had come, had blown the mists away, and her heart had fallen, hopeless, exhausted, helpless.

All night long she lay in her bed, next to Lotti, fighting back the flood of tears, staring out into the darkness, into the emptiness of the night and the days and years ahead. Downstairs, as though mocking her, the clock ticked on, measuring her life second by terrible second.

Her lips moved over his name, took the rhythm of the

clock, as she whispered again and again, crying out to him: *Joe.
Joe. Joe. Joe....*

✳✳✳

Father, who prostrated himself at the foot of the bare altar,
wore black. Even the crucifix was gone. All was silent. The
world was without hope. Christ had been taken away.

Slowly rising, the priest paused to genuflect then turned to
the lectern. He read the Passion with a clear and sorrowful
voice, genuflecting and holding the silence at the words: *"And
He gave up His Spirit."*

The Cross, wrapped in a deep and sorrowful purple like a
corpse for burial, was brought from the sanctuary. Slowly Father
unveiled it, one arm and then the other, the feet and then the
head. Taking off his own shoes, he genuflected three times then
knelt to kiss the suffering Christ's feet. And they all came
forward then to kneel and one by one to kiss His feet. And as
they shuffled forward the choir sang, in a low and sorrowful key:

> *Sweet the nails and sweet the wood,*
> *Laden with so sweet a load...*

Holy Saturday dawned cool and cloudy, yet leaning more
toward spring than winter. With only one day left until Easter,
there was so much to do. The girls were busy dyeing eggs:
boiling a dozen in onion skins, to give them a gentle tan, and
another twelve in beet juice mixed with vinegar, leaving a dark
blood red. And there was baking to be done. Now, for the first
time since Lent had begun, the kitchen was once again filled
with the sweet smell of freshly baked cookies and cake. A special Easter *babka* was made, rich with butter and candied fruit,
almonds and raisins. Just the smell of it was too much to bear.
But there would be no tasting it. Today was still a fast day.

Berenice formed little round cheeses rolled in caraway seeds,
which she called *katchki,* or baby ducks. These she set one by
one into the big basket as though they were going back into
their nest. Around them the eggs were set and slices of the
babka. Fresh-baked bread both white and rye, *kieshka* and kielbasa
from the smokehouse, ham, a tiny dish of horseradish, salt, pepper, butter molded into the shape of a little lamb. It all went
into the basket and looked as delicious as it would, in the morning, taste.

Berenice, Mary and Lotti rode in the buggy that afternoon to the church. The snow was mostly melted away and here and there in the ditches the grass showed green. Though the church-yard was filled, all the statues, candles, and crucifixes had been removed from inside the church, which now seemed almost empty.

Father was exuberant. He stood at the altar, sprinkling away at the dozens of baskets with holy water as though he were the rain god watering their fields. Even he was glad that Lent at last had drawn to a close.

How unbearably hungry all that food made him! And now he was receiving invitation after invitation to Easter dinner — more than he could possibly keep. But to not drop by, that would be an insult. And he knew from previous years which was the richest, sweetly chewiest *babka;* whose ham had just the right balance of cure and tenderness; whose vodka — though he would allow himself only one shot all day — was flavored with just the right touch of honey and spices, exactly as he remem-bered it back in Posnan. And for czarnina, of course, he would stop at the Topolskis, whose basket now he blessed and thought of that rich, sweet, warm soup, thick with homemade noodles.

He set the aspersorsium on the Communion rail. "God has granted me two great boons in my life," he said, loudly, to the gathered women as he slipped the long silk stole from around his shoulders. "The first, to study in Rome, and be blessed by His Holiness himself. And the second," he smiled mischie-vously, "to be sent here to St. Francis where within the bounds of a single parish reside all the world's greatest cooks."

They beamed back at him, loved every word of it. He raised his hand. "No. I'm sorry. Not all. Every one, but one." He paused. "My mother. Go now, in peace," he said, blessing them, "and I will see you early enough in the morning."

The church cleared. As Father was removing his vestments in the sacristy, he thought he heard someone still in the front pew. He glanced out into the church. Berenice Topolska stood beside the Communion rail. He set the last vestment carefully into its drawer and went out to her.

"Yes," he said quietly, "Pani Topolska. Come, let us go outside." He held her arm and walked her toward the vestibule. "The long winter, floods, another blizzard, we've survived them all, haven't we? God be thanked!"

They stopped and looked out the opened doors. The pa-rishioners were climbing into their wagons and cheerfully setting off. There was not a man among them. Father was in his glory. The light was soft; in the air, a sense of relief, of having escaped one of the big deaths.

"If the weather holds," Berenice said, "we'll start our field-work next week."

Father stared out into the churchyard. "Yes. And you will be needing Mary at home."

"For planting the potatoes and cleaning the seeds," Berenice sighed. "There is so much to do."

"Of course," Father said, dropping her arm. He stepped down onto the stairway. Berenice followed. He turned to her, seemed distant now, his voice cool and businesslike.

"I'll have to get someone else then, won't I?" Again he looked out over his fold, and beyond them where the river still sped swiftly and treacherously. They stood for a long awkward moment like that, posed on the steps of the church almost as though for a photograph: objects as distant from each other as two statues on a shelf or two images on a picture, though only inches apart never able to touch. And, like statues or images, unable even to move.

Berenice at last broke the spell. "I'll go then," she said, stepping down one step.

Father seemed startled, as though he'd drifted into another world. He turned to her and stared as though he'd forgotten she was there. "What?" he stammered. "Oh. Yes, of course. Of course."

Berenice moved down the steps to the buggy in which Mary and Lotti sat waiting. Prince stamped the ground anxiously. The short, taut figure was almost to the buggy when Father called out to her.

"Pani Topolska!" he shouted, "And Mary and Lotti! God go with you!" His hand came up in an unconscious gesture of blessing.

16

L ike a cat stirring up a mouse's nest, three a.m. stole into the house on padded feet and shook them all awake. Their father moved from room to room and woke them, where they fumbled to light a lamp, and by its yellow glow slid only half awake out of their beds and into their better-than-Sunday best. Hair was combed, in some big yellow or red ribbons tied. In a few moments the house clattered with the sound of footsteps down the stairs. Mass would start at five. It was time to go. Breakfast, already spread out on the kitchen table, would have to wait for their return.

The night still lay heavy over the farmyard. Not a star could be seen in the sky. A westerly breeze blew through their spring coats; they buttoned every button and pulled their collars up. While the girls were getting their baths the night before and the boys their haircuts, Frank and Stash had gone out to the barn where they braided Queen and Prince's tails into long, elegant braids, and tied ribbons in each. And along their manes, too, they tied colorful ribbons, then brushed their coats to a special sheen. Now, let out to be harnessed, the horses seemed proud of how elegant they looked. They pranced and whinnied, demanding the attention of the family climbing into the wagon.

On the way out the drive, the harness-bells singing and the traces jangling, Eddie lay his head on his mother's lap and was soon asleep. The girls, too, were tired enough to sleep; but excitement kept them awake. The ride, through the dark, seemed to be taking forever. By the time they'd crossed the bridge and turned east toward town, a faint glow was beginning to show above the trees. Here the road was full of buggies and wagons all making their way to the church, with their bells and ribbons and the families all dressed in their finest, making a sleepy but cheerful parade.

The doors to the church were open. From inside came the light of what seemed a thousand candles, as though here at last they'd found the chamber in which the sun itself was born. On the altar, spread with beautiful white linen, were glorious bouquets of lilies, whose odors could be smelled even out in the yard. All the holy statues had been returned to their places —

of Joseph, Mary, and St. Francis — and at their feet spread careful little arrangements of flowers. From the sacristy came faint wisps of incense, so that walking into the church was like walking into a gigantic, glowing, sweetly aromatic flower blossom.

The pews were rapidly filling. The Topolskis slipped into their own. Around them were all their friends and neighbors. Roman Gruba, walking past to his place in the front, touched Frank on the shoulder. Across the aisle were the Tomczaks and behind them Adam Laska and his family, little Franchek sleeping happily in his mother's arms. And there in front were the Stelmachs — and like a ghost returned from another world, next to Alex sat his oldest son, Joe.

The big bronze bell in the wooden tower began to sing loudly the miracle of resurrection. They all stood and Father appeared from the sacristy, his white vestments dazzling to see, while the choir sang out:

Alleluia, alleluia, I arose and am still with you!

As the Mass began, while they sang the Sanctus, the congregation had in a very real sense taken their place in heaven; had, through the mystery of faith transcended the earth and water of which they were made, and joining the ranks of the angels sang God's glory with all the rest of the celestial court. Their belief in Christ and His resurrection united these farmers and their wives, mothers and daughters, each with their own particular pains and sorrows, with the timeless chorus which sang at the first dawn of the first day, are singing now, this very moment — can you hear them? — and will sing until... until the last line of the last act of human and divine destiny has played itself out and, satisfied with the performance, the curtain is at last lowered.

Mass was over too soon: they could have stayed through two or three such masses. But a part of them was still slave of the hour. As they filed out into the new dawn, the clouded sky now broken into patches of blue and white, they took their Christ with them; He would be at their sides, in their homes, fields and businesses.

But first they had to show off their new hats and coats, and the men, tolerably uncomfortable in their suits and ties, had to talk excitedly of the fieldwork which lay ahead. From one to the other they went. *"Christus surrexit!"* they said, shaking hands. "Christ is risen!"

Frank Topolski stood, his hands in his coat pockets, talking horses with Alex and Roman. Stash was nearby, with Helen. Berenice chatted with Sophie Tomczak and tried, all the while, to keep an eye on the girls.

The girls had scattered to admire and be admired. Lotti and Angie, arm in arm, headed across to the Tomczak girls, leaving Sophie with Anna, who was so proud of the red ribbon in her hair, though her hand-me-down shoes, scuffed and worn no matter how hard she polished them, kept her feet firmly on the ground. Beside Anna stood Mary, even her spirits lifted up by the exuberance of the day.

Suddenly an arm slipped under hers. Startled, she turned. Handsome in his dark blue suit, a fancy straw hat cocked on his head, Joe stood beside her with a new self-assurance which came from a man who'd gone out into the world. Gently he pulled her aside. "Mary, Mary," he said, taking off his hat to her, "you look wonderful."

She blushed. He seemed like almost another person now: unbearably handsome, six inches taller and a hundred times stronger than before. More than ever she was afraid of him.

"I missed you, Mary," he said, standing close, his hat in his hand. "Why didn't you write?"

She looked into his eyes. "Where would I write to? I didn't know your address."

His forehead wrinkled. "But I sent it to you..."

"I didn't get any letters."

"Twice, I wrote," he said, his eyes darkening. "On my honor. Don't you believe me?"

"Yes," she said, looking down.

"You don't think..."

Her hand came up, touched his arm. "Joe," she whispered, "don't start anything."

Like a phantom materialized out of nothing, Bruno was suddenly beside them. "Time to go!" he crowed to his sister.

"What a swell we've got here!" Joe said, tousling the boy's carefully combed hair and tickling him under the arm. "Run off and find someone else to bother."

Bruno took a playful swat at Joe, then disappeared into the crowd.

"I really need to go," Mary said.

"Not yet." Joe reached into his pocket and with a pencil and a scrap of paper wrote his address. He handed it to her. "Here," he said. "Now if you don't write to me I really will get mad." She held the paper in her hand as though it were a precious currency.

For her, confronting Joe now was almost unbearable. The urge to collapse into his arms and beg his forgiveness and tell how miserable she'd been was so strong she could hardly overcome it. As though in her dreams and thoughts she could actually be closer to him than now, in his presence. Was it her own love for him which frightened her? Was she afraid she could not, in the end, control herself? All she knew for certain was that right now she wished she was with Angie and Lotti and Joe could be somewhere else — but knew, too, that then she would be only that much more miserable.

Suddenly Bruno reappeared. "We have to go," he said. "Mother will be mad."

Like an imp he stared up at them, his outlandish ears standing out from his head, made only the more obvious by his recent haircut. He smiled wickedly — that was his style, pretending to possess some secret about the world with which he could control everyone else. Whereas, in reality, he knew so little of the world that he wasn't even aware how unwelcome he was at the moment. But, welcome or not, his sister took his hand.

Joe reached out and touched her arm. "Write to me?"

And she was thinking: why does he care? By now he could have forgotten me. Perhaps it would be better if he did.

But she nodded, unable to speak, the link between her mind and vocal chords severed by the commotion of her heart. Then quickly she turned away and, still holding Bruno's hand, walked into the crowd. Bruno tried to pull his hand free — did not like being treated as a little boy — though it was really she who needed a hand to cling to.

Joe watched them as they headed toward their wagon. She seemed to him a thing of precious crystal, so fragile, so delicate, vibrating from an inner resonance which might at any moment shatter into a thousand pieces. And, he thought, it was up to him to keep that from happening.

He watched their wagon pull away, hoping Mary would turn and wave or at least look his way. But she disappeared behind the trees, a prisoner surrounded by her retinue of guards.

He sighed, set his hat on his head, ran the toe of his shoe

through the wet gravel, leaving little furrows as though a tiny plow had turned the soil. Then, mechanically, almost against his will, his foot crushed the little furrows into a confused pile. He put his hands into his pockets and shuffled to join his friends who, now that Lent was over, were laughing and planning excursions to dances in town, ice-cream socials, and weddings.

***

From its place of honor at the center of the table, the ham, with its perfect honey glaze, steamed incredible odors all through the room. Around it lay, as though resting in pasture, a little flock of butter lambs, each sporting a bright red pennant. And all around were chicken, kielbasa, *kieshka*, potatoes, peas, a big steaming bowl of hot blood soup, and so many other delectables there was hardly room at the table for plates or people.

Frank said grace. They all sat down to face the duty of the moment, which was to move as much as they could of that great feast from the tabletop into their bellies. Mary, Lotti, and Angie were busy serving the others — ferrying back and forth with pitchers of milk, dishes stacked high with sliced bread, cups of coffee, fetching salt, pepper, sugar and honey. Though too busy to pause, with the delicious smells and sounds of all the others eating, they grew hungrier and hungrier.

Eddie ate too fast — that was predictable. Bruno — though he wasn't alone in this, ate too much — also predictable. One further, confident prognostication about Bruno would be that by the age of twenty he would begin to fill out rather like a cow heavy with calf. But that was a concern not at all of the moment. The girls continued their work of trucking great heaps of mashed potatoes, more peas from the stove, warming the chicken, slicing the ham, until at last Eddie, Bruno and Anna were finished and could replace them in their jobs.

When they were all finished their mother brought in the big babka and more coffee; on the table remained enough for an equal feast the next day. Dirty dishes were hauled into the kitchen where the younger girls now had the job of washing and drying. The rest of the family sat again at the table and picked at their babka, too full and too tired to move.

There was a knock at the door. Anna, in the kitchen, opened it, then smiled broadly.

"Anna!" Father Nowak said, putting his hand on her head. "May I come in?"

From the living room their mother asked who it was.

Father himself stepped into the dining room. "Nobody important," he said. "Just me. Oh, don't stand up, Frank. I see you've left a few bones for the poor."

Frank gestured the priest to sit. "Go get Father a plate," he said to Angie.

"No!" The priest raised both his palms, then lay them on his stomach. "I've just come from the Tomczaks, and I'm stuffed like a goose for the slaughter."

"You mean to tell me," Frank smiled, "you haven't even room for one bowl of *czarnina?*"

"Well..."

Angie went for a bowl. Father Nowak winked at Mary. "It's a good thing for all of us that Easter comes only once a year, isn't it?" Eddie stared at him, wondering what he meant. Father slid the ham toward Bruno. "Here, young man, you'd better have some. You look underfed. Christmas, Easter, and a big wedding," he glanced to Mary, "how could we live without them?"

Angie brought in the bowl of *czarnina.* Berenice sat quietly watching. Father sniffed the steam rising from it, smiled. Picking up a spoonful, he cooled it by blowing, then slipped the soup into his mouth. He chewed lightly, closed his eyes, swallowed. Smacking his lips, he looked at Berenice. "You must have got the recipe from my mother," he said. "Or God Himself."

There came another knocking at the door. Holidays were for visiting. Who could tell who might stop by? Frank stood up, stretched, and went to the door himself.

"Roman! Come in!" Roman Gruba brought a bottle of vodka with him, which he set on the kitchen cupboard. "For you, Frank," he said, taking off his coat.

"Well, *djienkuje bardzo,*" Frank said, lifting the bottle, then putting his hand out. "Happy Easter!"

"Happy Easter!" The two men embraced for a moment.

"Come in, come in," the host said, ushering Roman into the living room. "Sit down and join us."

Roman stood a moment in the doorway. "Father," he said, nodding to the priest. "Pani Topolska. No thanks, Frank. I've already eaten."

"Then eat some more," Frank demanded, offering a chair.

"Maybe just one slice of your ham." Frank slid the ham down to his friend and handed him a carving knife. Father, just finishing his soup, accepted a thin slice into his empty bowl.

Roman chewed the ham satisfyingly. He was about to compliment Frank on it when Frank raised his hand and spoke up. "I know. Don't say anything. It's too dratted salty."

"No. Absolutely not!" Roman protested. "It's perfect. Father?"

The priest swallowed. "Yes. Perfect."

"So, Lent's over and now we can lie, huh?" Frank said. They all smiled. "Come on, then. Let's get into the other room so the girls can clean up."

"Wouldn't you like some *babka?*" Berenice interjected.

"Oh, let them bring it along," Frank said. That, of course, was against house rules. But it was Easter.

Frank led them into the other room. There Mary brought all of them a plate of cake and cup of coffee, Frank accepting these seconds with a groan.

"You'll manage," Father kidded him. "Where's Stash? Ah, don't tell me. I can guess."

Anna and Eddie had gone outside to play with the Tomczak children — their shouts of "Annie, Annie, Over!" could be heard from alongside the granary. The men in the living room, sipping their coffee and chewing the delicious cake, talked quietly away. Only Berenice was left out; she sat in the dining room, needlework again in her hands.

"I understand the Knowlton House will be ready to open soon," Father Nowak observed.

"A speakeasy, eh?" Roman quipped.

"No, not quite." Father chewed the babka, swallowed. "By summer we'll have tourists at Mass."

Roman shook his head. "And we'll have to move to Alaska. We're in just the position the Indians were in fifty years ago. Yes, I'm afraid we're in for an invasion, gentlemen."

Frank, who was half asleep in his favorite chair, offered his opinion. "They've got to go somewhere," he said quietly.

"Long as they're here," Father suggested, "maybe you could hire them to help on the farm."

"Huh! Not likely!"

"I understand you're planting certified seed potatoes this year, Frank," the priest observed.

Frank's eyes opened, his eyebrows rose. "And did you hear the last time I went to the outhouse?" he asked mischievously. "Maybe," he admitted. "A couple acres, anyway."

"And how's the Union going?"

Frank turned to Roman, shrugged. "Oh, kinda slow, I guess."

Again there was a knock at the door. Frank paused to hear who it was. After a moment he could hear a discussion by the back door. He pushed himself up from the chair. "Excuse me. I'd better go see who it is."

Berenice was standing by the door, holding it open but unwilling to step aside and let their guest in.

"Who is it?" Frank asked, yawning. Then, through the open door he saw. "Joe!"

"Hello, Frank." Joe Stelmach was grinning sheepishly, like a child rescued from a snarling dog.

"Oh let him in, Mother," Frank said. "Can't you see he wants in? Come on in," Frank asserted. He held out his hand, and Joe slipped in. As he passed Berenice, it was like steel on flint.

Mary was coming out of the living room with the coffeepot when she met Joe and her father in the dining room. For a moment she stopped dead still; the coffeepot nearly slipped from her hand. Then, smiling at Joe, who'd taken his hat off to her, she slipped past them and into the kitchen. Berenice was watching them like a hawk.

In the living room, Roman stood up. "Well Joe Stelmach! Good to see you!"

And Father Nowak stood, to take Joe's hand. "Joe. Last Sunday when I looked down at your father's pew and you weren't there, it was like I'd lost an old friend."

"Not so old," Roman joked.

"Sit down, Joe," Frank said. "Mary!" he called. The girl appeared in the doorway, timidly. "Bring us another cup of coffee and some babka for Joe." They all sat down. "How's city life treating you, Joe?" Frank asked.

Joe shrugged. "Oh, I don't know."

"I'll bet you miss home-cooking."

Joe smiled, nodded.

"But you're putting away money head over heels, right?" Roman teased.

"I wish!"

Mary appeared with the coffee and cake. "Well, are you going to stand there all day? Don't be afraid, girl. He's not a stranger."

Timidly she handed Joe the cup and plate, then quickly turned and stole out of the room. Joe set his coffee down, bit into the cake. He chewed it a bit, washed it down, then went on. "Forty cents an hour may sound like a lot of money but by the time you take out your room and board and getting to and from work, there ain't much left."

"You working at International Paper?" Roman asked. Joe nodded. The year before there'd been a prolonged and somewhat heated strike at that plant, which had attracted national attention in the papers. It seemed that the companies were using it as a test case. If they could hold the strikers there, they could hold them as far east as New York and even up into Canada. On the other hand, caving in in Wisconsin meant caving in all across the nation. For a while there just about every paper mill president and vice-president from Montreal to Minneapolis was camping out in Wausau, lending their support to the local company. The result?

"Before the strike," Roman remembered, "your job paid, what, probably fifty cents and hour?"

"Fifty-five," Joe corrected him.

"Down to forty. All across the country workers have had to accept that kind of pay cut. That's entrepreneurial capitalism for you!" Roman's voice was bitter.

"It's the dictatorship of Mammon," Father interjected.

"You sticking it out?" Frank asked the boy. "You know, your father could sure use your help once fieldwork starts."

Joe looked at the floor. He was sensitive to that point. No doubt he and Alex had already had their disagreements. "I don't know," he shrugged.

"When you going back?" Roman asked, to get the lad's mind off the subject.

"Tonight. Gotta work tomorrow."

"On Easter Monday?" The priest seemed offended.

"We put half a day in yesterday."

Father shook his head, clicking his tongue.

Outside they could hear the shouts of the children, who'd just been joined by the older girls. The clock in the dining room chimed. Three-thirty. Yes, Frank thought, it was a shame. If we don't take time out to remember the Lord, then why should He remember us?

Father Nowak stood. "I'd best be going," he said. "More stops to make yet. I honestly don't know if I'll last through the day." He patted his stomach. The other three men stood. "Thanks for the coffee and *babka*. I'll compliment Berenice on her *czarnina*. Easter wouldn't be Easter without it. God bless you all," he said, shaking hands around.

Roman quietly suggested he'd best be going too. While Frank saw the two of them out, Joe stood in the living room with his hands behind his back looking out at the children who were running through the yard. And he realized, then, as he'd not realized before, that he was caught between two worlds — too old to join in such games and not yet a man with his own family. He felt as though he had no place in the world. He regretted, then, taking the job in the city; the long hours and nights of loneliness he felt there pressed down on him. How much easier it would be on the farm, with his father and his brother, and friends like Frank. But then every day would be a reminder of the world he'd lost when Mary was taken from him.

It was Easter. He was supposed to be happy. But now it seemed that any chance of his ever being happy had been taken away from him. He wanted to whirl around and confront Berenice with that. But it wouldn't be right. She was Mary's mother, and deserved respect. An argument would only strengthen her resolve. If he was to stand a chance, he would have to be patient.

Frank returned, to stand beside him for a moment, watching the children playing tag. Even Mary ran with them, her bare feet quick on the cool grass. But her father seemed tired. Joe could sense he wanted to take a nap. So when Frank turned to sit and asked Joe to do the same, he thanked them for the coffee and cake and suggested he'd better get home to spend some time with his own folks. "The train leaves at eight," he said, sighing, as though now even the thought of it made him sad.

Anna, Eddie, Bruno and behind them Julia Tomczak dashed in through the front door, half out of breath. Anna slowed, seeing Joe, then walked cautiously up to her father. "Can we play the Victrola?" she asked. It was one of the things they'd given up for Lent.

"We've got company," Frank said, his hand on her head. Her hair, which at Mass had been so perfectly combed, was now a tangle. She glanced at Joe.

"Really, I have to go," Joe said. Under other circumstances he and Frank might have had a good talk; but not today. "Go ahead," he urged little Anna.

Frank stood up, nodded to the girl. She opened the cabinet and slowly searched through the records. The others stood around in a circle. She cranked the machine and dropped the record into place. Joe smiled down at her as she looked up, waiting, the rhythmic scratch of the needle promising the song to come. Suddenly the capricious orchestra and xylophone began the droll comedy of *"Dawniej a Dzisiej,"* which Joe immediately recognized as one of Ulatowski's songs he'd given the family for Christmas last year. He reached out and tousled Anna's hair. The children all sat down, their faces staring up at the machine; one or two moved a finger up and down to the rhythm of the song.

Frank walked his friend to the kitchen. "We miss you up here, you know," he said. "I don't know what I'll do if I need help with a calf."

"Oh, you'll get along," Joe said modestly.

"Maybe. And how about you?"

Joe shrugged. He took Frank's hand.

"There's another Union meeting coming up on Saturday," Frank remembered.

"I'll have to work," Joe said. "Sorry."

They both felt the past slipping away from them, faster than they wanted or could ever change.

"Take care of yourself, Frank."

"You too."

As Joe walked out the door and climbed into his buggy, Frank stood watching. Turning to the end of the drive, Joe took off his hat and waved with it to Mary, who stood beside an apple tree. She looked so much alone, hugging the tree's trunk, staring at Joe as she waved back, as though he really was a stranger she was trying so hard to recognize. And when he'd disappeared below the hill, she still stood there, her hand frozen in its wave, unmoving as a statue. Her father watched her, for a long moment, and it seemed she meant to stand like that for the rest of her life, in that gesture, confused and poignant, composed equally of greeting and farewell.

17

*With work then it begins, the growing
in the heart and in the mind...*
— from *Inspiration*, by Karol Wojtyla

Abruptly the morning quiet was shattered by the sharp rhythmic ring of hammer on steel. The sound rose, with a heavy black smoke, from the workshop. Frank, bent above his anvil, was working a plowshare to a meticulous edge. Wrapped in his big leather apron, spotted with burn-holes and charred here and there like the soul of an unrepentant sinner, he set the share once again in the fire, pumped the bellows to turn the smoke to a bright orange mass whose heat drew drops of sweat from his arms and forehead.

The share, heated to a dull cherry red, he lay with tongs on the anvil and again the ball-peen worked the steel. It was slow work, tedious work. But he loved it, the smell of burning coke and the sharp tang of heated iron, the rhythmic ring and the rebound of the hammer off the metal. It was a skill he'd been drawn to even in the old country, watching the smiths work the shoes and steel. There was a mystery to it, working the cold hard steel into a pliable servant of his own will.

The edge of the share was even: he set it on the dirt floor and let it cool, then drew it out with a file. Again he heated the point, and bent it just right to give the plow its suction. At last satisfied, he heated it one final time, all along the edge, and plunged it into water, where it hissed and gave off great clouds of steam.

The plowshare finished, he worked on a disc blade, making as much use of the heated coke as he could. And from bar steel he cut and pounded out several teeth for his harrow. Side by side he lay them on the floor, wiped his face and hands and untied the big, heavy apron which from the heat of his body and of the fire gave off a faintly sweet and leathery smell. He hung the apron on its nail. Bending, he touched the plowshare. It was warm, but not too hot; he hefted it and carried it out to the plow beside the granary. He slipped the share into its place, with three bolts fastened it onto the standard. Now, carefully, he knelt on the wet ground and bent over the plow as a wrestler might grasp his opponent, adjusting the share and the angle of the land-side. Using the back of his wrench, he scoured the jointer, then turned the beam wheel and squirted heavy oil on its bearing surface until it turned quietly and smoothly.

He stood. The plow was ready. This would be its last season. By next year he would have a sulky plow or, perhaps, a two-bottom tractor plow. He picked up his tools and took them into the workshop. The prelude had finished. Tomorrow, if the weather held, would be the first act of the long drama of opening the soil to seed.

✳✳✳

Mary threw oats to the chickens and let the ducks out of the barn so they could roam the yard. Natural-born comedians, in three pairs they paraded across the drive, dressed in neat white smocks which they meant with all seriousness to wash in the nearest puddle. Quacking low and wiggling their tails, they moved with comical duck steps. Suddenly the leader, the biggest drake, then all the others, stopped dead still to cock their heads and peer at the sky, mistaking a subtle fluff of cloud for some marauding predator. On the move again, they sifted through the luscious mud. One of the drakes mounted his hen, his bill clipping her neck while on her back his feet noiselessly padded. For a moment, as he held her head under water, it looked like he might drown her. But it was over as quickly as it had begun. Unceremoniously flapping their wings, they each went their separate ways.

In the woods beside the drive — the *dompki* — the bloodroot and spring beauties had joined the mayflowers in blossom. Mary was sent by her mother to gather a little bouquet for the dinner table, when they would sit and feast again on the previous day's leftovers. Along the drive she found a cheerful little circle of bloodroot and bent to pull the flowers from the still-folded leaves. How white they were in the broken sun, against the dead brown earth, how brashly they exposed their soft yellow organs. One by one she broke them off and lay them in her hand, each torn stem bleeding on her opened palm.

Carefully stepping over little puddles, she walked deeper into the woods. Here the earth was still covered with a thick blanket of last year's leaves. And here grew the spring beauties, more solitary than the bloodroot, as if too shy to show themselves among company. Their tiny blossoms, a rich creamy white, veined with dainty pink, seemed the most delicate things in all

the world: like the soft, idle hands of a beautiful fairy-tale
princess.   As she broke their fine, long stems, Mary was startled
by a memory — a vague and subtle thing, like the change of
light when a thin cloud subdues the sun — of how as an infant
she would lie in her tiny bed and study her own hands, uncertain
whose they were. How soft they were then, pale and unsullied.

She rose and turned toward the house, the memory gone,
the chaste white blossoms gently clasped in her hands, veined
now with blue and grown darker with the blemishes and wrinkles
of work.

✻✻✻

After dinner — they stuffed themselves almost as badly as
the day before — father and mother used the holiday for a long
afternoon nap.   It was the last rest before the rush of spring
fieldwork overtook them.   Frank dozed in his chair, Berenice on
the bed, while the girls cleaned up the dishes.

The children saw no wisdom in wasting a holiday with
sleep.   It was, after all, Easter Monday — Dingus, they called it.
Threshing Day.   The day the boys came round with long willow
switches to thresh the girls.   The Topolski girls convened and
decided that in numbers there was security; they stayed together
all afternoon, circling in the backyard and quietly throwing a
ball back and forth.   All the while they kept a sharp lookout for
the marauding boys.   But, growing tired of playing catch, they
wandered out into the *dompki* to pick flowers which they would
weave into bracelets and garlands for their hair.   They sat, then,
on the back steps, each wondering to herself if it was possible
that they'd been forgotten.   What would Dingus be without a
threshing?   Even the pretty little floral bracelets on their wrists
could not cheer them from such a dreary prospect.

The afternoon seemed to be running through them like
water through a sieve.   Sophie suggested, sullenly, that they walk
over to Tomczaks to see if Julia had been visited.   But Angie
noted that the boys might come after them while they were
gone.   So instead they moped around the back yard, and it seemed
that nothing, not even the liquid song of the bluebird warbling
away from the orchard, could cheer them up.

And then, like a sudden flash of the sun out of a cloud-
clotted sky, from behind the barn there came a terrible war whoop
and the Tomczak boys and little Henry Ganther charged out at
the girls like savage Indians on the warpath, swinging their willow
sticks this way and that.   The girls screamed all at once, then

scattered in every direction: Sophie and Angie dashing around in front of the house, Mary and Lotti skirting past the boys toward the haymow, while Anna clambered breathlessly up into the granary. But Anna was the first to feel the twigs against her legs; then Lotti and Mary, too, before they could get the big door to the mow pulled open. The boys turned then and went after the other two, and by the sound of it, it was no time before they too had gotten their share.

Bruno and Eddie, who'd mysteriously disappeared earlier in the afternoon, and stolen across the road to crouch beside the Tomczak silo, on the signal of their sisters' screams swooped down on poor little Julia, who though half frightened out of her wits, would have been simply crushed had she been left out.

***

Gathered around the Victrola, the kerosene lamps glowing against the darkness, the children wished that Easter could last all week. Or a month. How quickly it had come and gone, not to return for an entire year. Tomorrow for the young ones school would begin again and, for the others, the long uphill climb of work to the full days of summer. They had eaten their fill for two days and rested and played. These last hours of the holiday they were spending together, their mother working on some needlework, their father in his chair. Even Stash was with them, relaxing with a newspaper.

The arm of the Victrola swept toward the record's end, then began its rhythmic clicking. Lotti rose and lifted the arm, placed another record on the turntable, cranked it up and set the needle down again. It was an old folk song from Poland, which their father had bought for Christmas several years back. *Ojciec i syn*, it was called. *"Father and Son."* The man's baritone carried the simple, catchy tune, alternating with the lilting concertina. It was hard to sit still, the music was so infectious. Suddenly they realized, to their astonishment, that singing along with the scratchy record was the wavering, off-key, rough but cheerful voice of their father.

***

Sixteen hands tall, their shoulders as high as Frank's, with enough weight to crush a man's body against the wall of the barn, they stood outside in the dark, bringing with them the warmth and clean, familiar smell of the stall. Their warm breaths puffed into the chill air. They seemed anxious to start, as though remembering the work from years past, as though they knew in their bones that with the thawing of the earth would come these long days of work, which to them were so much better than being locked long months inside the stall.

Molly's coat shivered as Frank placed on her the collar, adjusting the harness so as not to cut into her throat. He slipped the bit into her mouth and ran his hand down her long, white nose. She lifted her head in acknowledgment.

Dewey lifted a back leg nervously, again and again, sidling over in that direction. But when Frank brought the harness, Dewey stood obediently still, then backed without a single false step between the traces. Frank attached the chains to the rings, and they were ready to go.

"Wait," he told them. "Wait!" They turned their heads, and nodded, their eyes warm and familiar.

He went into the kitchen. The house was still quiet, warm in sleep. He lifted the dipper to his lips. The metal was cool — he drank it empty, refilled then drank another. Now the dipper clanked softly against the bucket. He turned and stood a moment on the back steps, still stiff with sleep, his joints and bones complaining of the chill. He stretched out his arms, yawned, then strode down the steps toward the team.

Taking the reins, he nudged the horses forward. They moved gently, knowing that this was not the place to start their work. He tipped the plow onto its side, guiding it by its upper handle, as they dragged it along through the dirt of the drive. Crossing the road, they went up the field a hundred paces. He turned then and halted.

There was less than an acre to be done for the early potatoes. It would be a good breaking-in for the team and for himself. He judged his distance from the fence line, faced down the field toward the glimmer of dawn. His job now, by which his skill as a ploughman — a *rolnik* — would be judged, was to plough this first furrow straight as an arrow and unswervingly parallel to the fence along the road.

Talking low, he steadied the team. The reins he tied into a knot, then passed them under his arms to fit snugly behind his back. This was dangerous; men had been dragged to their death by a team which had bolted. But he trusted Molly and Dewey, and they trusted him. Gripping the handles of the plow, he knew he held sway over the horses' wills.

At the far end of the field, in the grey morning light, he found a tree to serve as a guide, toward which he would drive the horses. All was quiet now, except for the chink of the traces and a solitary mourning dove cooing quietly away down in the hollow. Frank judged the distance from the fence, resighted his guide tree.

"Hyah!" he shouted, and the team sprang forward, the point of the plow digging into the dark earth. He held it steady and level. Not yet used to the drag of the collar against their shoulders, they pulled somewhat uneasily. Their heavy feet beat against the earth, the clevis clanked, and the ground itself made a faint tearing sound as it turned. Now in the chill dawn rose that familiar smell, comforting as the breath of a lover, from the new-turned furrow.

Frank held the plow straight and had only now and then to turn the horses a little this way or that. At the end of the furrow he pushed the handles down, and the plow lifted itself. He balanced it on the beam wheel and turned to follow the first furrow back. Sighting it, it seemed satisfyingly straight and clean. His feet kept a steady swing across the turned earth, the plow clinking now and then against stones it found deep in the ground.

The back furrow done, he plowed another furrow fifty feet on either side of the first. On this side of the road his soil was heavy, which meant his lands had to be narrower, to allow for better drainage. As he pulled he talked to the horses, steadily comforting them, his tone changing to reprimand when Dewey, the more independent of the two, would pull at an angle or not as steadily as he ought.

Resting on a headland, Frank caught his breath. The wide swath of turned soil was black in the morning light, its slick skin shining darkly; perhaps, he thought, just a bit too wet. But it was time for the early potatoes to go in, and disking and harrowing would dry the soil. So he started again, the horses with each furrow catching better the pace of the work. For two hours more they worked, until the day was well begun, and the rest of the family was long at work on the morning chores. But he had to be careful not to overwork the team — their untried muscles and tendons might easily strain. So he would stop for breakfast, and feed and give the horses a break.

The plow they left in the field. Frank bent to scour off the share, then plodded behind the team across the road, to a bucket of oats and a good draught of water for them and breakfast for himself.

***

After breakfast it was back to work. The children started to prepare the seed potatoes. Set up just outside the woodshed was the razor-sharp knife which their father had fashioned from an old scythe blade and mounted on a board. In the shed were seven big gunny sacks full of certified seed potatoes which Frank had ordered weeks before. In previous years, cutting potato seed also meant hauling it, bucket by heavy bucket, up from the basement. But this year they had set the entire operation up outside.

The Triumph spuds were big, firm and scab-free. Knowing how much each cost, they were handled with special care. Bruno, seated on an unsplit log of elm, opened a bag. He picked the spuds from the sack, one by one, and broke off any sprouts which might get in the way. One end, called the rose end, had the most sprouts — it would be the most fertile and give the best yield. He dropped the cleaned spuds into a bucket, the sprouts at his feet piled together like a tangle of pale witch's fingers.

Angie, meanwhile, ferried the bucket as it filled to Mary, who worked the knife. Carefully turning each potato to find just the right angle, she pushed it through the knife, leaving each piece with two or three eyes. Their mother would be out, they knew, to make an inspection, and if any of the pieces were found without eyes, or with too many, they would be in for it. Mary worked quietly, but carefully; the knife was sharp, and a wrong move could result in a badly cut finger.

Beneath her another bucket was filling with pieces, which Sophie carried into the granary to spread out where they could heal. It was tedious work. It seemed like it would take forever to finish all seven sacks. But working outside was better than working in the cold and dark basement. And watching their father across the road, making his way slowly up and down the field, they were constantly reminded that they had the easier job.

***

Stash, meanwhile, had started on the new garage. It was his first building. He was a bit nervous: he might measure wrong, cut a board he wasn't supposed to, or miscalculate his rafters. But he was proud his father had trusted him with the work. You don't ask a boy to build a garage.

A site had been selected just across the drive from the house. Most of the morning he spent hacking brush and weeds down, leveling the dirt, and with ropes and stakes squaring off the building site. By lunchtime he had holes dug for the corner posts. His father, coming in to eat, stopped for a minute to talk. He said it looked fine.

After lunch Stash got Bruno to help mix the cement and pour the posts. Then it was a matter of hauling lumber from the granary to the building site. The hardwood boards were heavy; especially the four-inch posts and the two-by-six rafters. But they were all straight and clear-grained, and just handling them, the faint odor of fresh wood they gave off, was something Stash loved. Within a few days he would have the walls framed and, with his father's help erected and braced. Then he could give the framing square a try. Roman Gruba had showed him how to use it, for everything from cutting your rafters to calculating the area of a triangle, to multiplying two numbers. Roof up, the walls would be sided, and the windows and doors set in.

As they stacked the lumber beside the stakes, Stash could see in his mind the finished garage: painted a snappy red, with a wood-shingled roof, trimmed in white. When it was finally done he could at last call himself a carpenter and could show it off. And it might just be his ticket to other jobs — paying jobs — from friends and neighbors. Then, perhaps, he could really think about a wedding.

In the days ahead, as the young man went about his work, carefully selecting just the right board, cutting it square and clean, the sawdust smelling so fresh and sharp, driving each nail straight so as not to split the wood, as he worked along, Stash felt himself growing with the work. As much as a garage, he was framing up a part of himself. Hour by hour he gained self-assurance. Mary and Lotti and the other girls, going about their work, watched him and felt proud, too.

To Stash this was an even larger step out of the family than going off to the service. And though he might not say it just this way, while his father walked the long and hard miles behind the plow, repeating each day an annual ritual, Stash was granted instead the gift of starting something completely new. Not just a building, not even just a profession, but a new life: a step outside the cycle of things.

✻✻✻

A few days later, Father Nowak, seated in the living room, was on the edge of his chair. Across the room, by the window through which he could see a light snow falling, sat Berenice. She held her embroidery ring, concentrated on needle and thread as though he weren't even there. It was only out of a sense of respect for the priesthood that she'd offered him coffee and cake.

The girls were in the haymow, cleaning oat seed with the fanning mill. When the oats were done, when they'd filled a dozen sacks with seed, they had the corn and beans to do. But that was handwork, done at the table, each seed handled one by one. In the mow, the door closed against the chill wind, they didn't even know the priest had stopped in.

Through the window Father could see Frank driving the team back and forth through the field, pulling a single riding disk in spite of the cold and the flurries of snow. It was almost as though the window were the glass of an aquarium, and Frank were out there in some alien environment. Or as though he were merely the celluloid image on a movie film, he seemed that distant. Too distant, for the priest.

He had second thoughts about his visit. Just the mention of the girl's name had put the mother off. And now they faced each other like cats defending their own territory. Every move, every rustle of dress or clink of cup on plate was magnified, in the charged air, a hundredfold.

She was not a pretty woman. Her steel-rim glasses sat near the end of her nose, through which she squinted at her embroidery. Mostly, she let his questions fall unanswered into the silence. Was there someone other than Joe planned for Mary's future? He had to be careful — he was not supposed to know about the letters. She touched her glasses. She was on edge as much as he.

"Do you think someone would marry her now?" She spoke as though to herself. "After she's broken the banns?"

So, he thought, you mean to keep her unmarried? Indentured into the household business. Yes, it certainly was a stigma. But the whole parish knew it wasn't the girl's fault.

"Joe will," he said.

The needle moved through the linen without a sound. She didn't break the pace of her work — only her lips moved. "Never," she said.

Father breathed in abruptly, set down his cup. "But my dear Pani Topolska, in God's name why? Why not Joe?"

She preferred not to answer.

"Instead of Joe, someone else?" She looked up at him. Was he pressing too hard? Could she guess that he knew? "Who else, Pani Topolska? A drunkard, perhaps, who will beat her?"

Now she went back to her work, and spoke the words of the proverb mechanically, as though he didn't deserve a more exact response. "Better," she said, "to make a bad marriage than no marriage at all."

He stared out the window. Again Frank came into and moved across the field of vision, the steady gait of the horses so easy, so natural, and Frank behind them as though part of them. He stood. He was angry now; real anger flared up inside him of the kind he would have to ask God's forgiveness for. Only the dignity of his office restrained him from lashing out against her. But beneath his words there was no mistaking the contempt.

"She is the one who will have to live with him," he said, his hands tightened into fists, "not you."

She shrugged her shoulders, ran a thread through her lips. "If they want to live here, I won't turn them out."

***

It had grown colder. Father felt sorry for the man and the team who had to drive through the flurries of snow. Stash, on the roof of the new garage, continued to drive nails in spite of the weather. Father waved up to him.

Pulling his horse to the side of the road, he wrapped his scarf tight around his neck and trudged through the freshly disked field toward the man and his team, who had stopped at the far end. Frank was bent over the disk, unhitching it to hitch instead the harrow for the final smoothing of the field. Not seeing the priest approach, he was startled to find a man suddenly standing beside him.

"Winter has come back again to haunt us," the priest said, holding out his hand.

Frank brushed his hands clean and took the priest's. "Yes," he said, "but it won't last." There was an innocent faith in the farmer's eyes which lifted the priest's spirit. Only he wondered: is it too trusting a faith?

"I've stopped to talk with your wife," he said. Frank stood still, obedient, respectful. "About Mary." Little piles of snow were building on the men's shoulders. Molly edged to one side, and Frank stepped back to steady her. "I didn't get anywhere," the priest said, stepping forward. "Can you reason with her?"

Frank stared off into the slicing snow. Already in spots it was building on the field. Much more and he would have to quit. He had hoped to be able to plant in the morning. At least to the west the clouds were thinning.

"I can reason with Molly," Frank said, patting the horse. "And Dewey, too; though sometimes he has a mind of his own. And Shep, and the cows." The men were both aware that Berenice was likely to be watching them from inside the house; and as they spoke it was almost as though she were able to overhear them. "You don't know my wife," Frank said. "When she makes up her mind, even God cannot change it." Their eyes met. "She knew nothing of America, yet she came. She knew nothing about me, yet she married me. She knew nothing of farming, yet she followed me, first to Necedah, then to here. She is that kind of woman." Frank sighed. "Without her, you know, I could never have done it." His eyes swept across the farm. The priest knew how proud he was of the place.

"Yes," the priest granted. "She is a strong woman."

A smile came over Frank's eyes. "Strong? Yes."

Father smiled.

Molly shivered the snowflakes off her coat. It wasn't good for the horses, who'd worked themselves up to a heat, to be standing in the cold. Father's hand came out of his pocket and pulled the collar tight around his neck. "So," he asked, "have you given up?"

"No," Frank answered, staring at the dark earth, frosted with delicate crystals of white. "No, not yet."

Father's eyebrows lifted. "But what will you do?"

Frank clapped his boots together, knocking dirt off the soles. "I don't know. Finish this field, start another." There was an apology in his eyes. He stared at their house. From the chimney came a white smoke which quickly disappeared into the slanting snowflakes. "I do what I know how to do, and pray that God will do the rest."

Father Nowak stared at him. Suddenly he felt very sorry for his friend and put his arm around his shoulder. "Don't give up, my friend. If we pray, surely God will help us. Come to me, any time. If you love your daughter, together we can help her, God willing." Frank, uncomfortable with that kind of intimacy, held the horse from moving. The priest offered his hand. "Well now, you'd better get back to work."

"Yes."

Father Nowak patted Molly on the flank and headed off toward the road. Frank stood for a few moments watching him and behind him the house in which Berenice sat unseen. He wondered, for a moment — less than a moment, an instant, only — if it had been worth it, all the days and months and years of hard work. What, after all, did he really have? A piece of ground, not big enough to use a tractor on, about a dozen dumb animals always ready to get sick or unexpectedly die, some boards and posts nailed up into a barn and house which ten years from now would be too big for them.

But the thought was like a sudden gust of wind from across the field, which swirled the snow and had no effect, ultimately, on the season of things. Spring, with its striving sprouts and chirping nestlings, and summer in its full bloom, would come in spite of any doubts.

He bent over the harrow, hooked the chain through the clevis. The break in the western clouds grew wider and wider. The snow had stopped. He would finish the fields.

18

The rain means something to mankind beyond better crops, greater stream flow, the cooling of the atmosphere and the laying of dust. Rocks mean more than building materials. Trees mean more than timber, more even than shade and refreshment. The animals that man has domesticated and befriended mean more than meat and milk and clothing...
    — from *The Harvest*, by Liberty Hyde Bailey

They'd each brought a friend, as he'd asked them to. That made fourteen, counting Father Nowak, who said a prayer at the start and at the end of the meeting. It was too bad about Joe not being there. They got into some pretty warm discussions about the resolutions. The one on the Voight Bill to make interstate transport of substitute milk products illegal, that one they supported. And rural electrification. Chester said they'd never live to see it, but there was no harm in passing a resolution. But when Frank himself proposed they support statewide testing of herds for tuberculosis, he ran head on into opposition. They didn't want government inspectors nosing around their farms. Frank gave in. They tabled it.

Frank and Roman were appointed as delegates to the June County convention. Frank didn't want to go — it was such a busy time. But, after all, he'd started the whole thing; it was up to him to keep it going.

He wondered, again, if they could make any difference. Were they just growing old and clinging to outmoded ideals while the world changed around them? Well, he had to try, before the whole neighborhood fell apart and went belly up. Maybe with real economic security they could keep men like Joe Stelmach from running off to the city.

Back in the old country, after all, people helped one another. Like a big family, the village worked together. Not to say there weren't arguments. But they knew that if they didn't help each other, no one else would. Frank missed that. Here, in America, it was everyone for themselves, the devil take the hindmost.

Money, money, money. That's what it all came down to.

And he thought to himself, if the Union falls apart, Berenice will only say "I told you so." That in itself was reason enough to keep fighting.

✳✳✳

And then it was back to work again. There was no stopping now, unless the weather should turn really bad. But the weather held. He plowed ten acres of oats, disked, harrowed, and planted it. That took a week, measured out moment by moment, hour by hour, step by single step behind the plodding team. They did take off the afternoon of St. Mark's day, to go to church. There Father Nowak, as he had at the Union meeting, prayed for good crops, and from the church led a procession outside to ask God's blessing on the new seed.

✳✳✳

Stash had the garage almost done. It was roofed and sided, and he was busy on the two big front doors which would swing wide to let in the Overland and the Ford. By the end of the week he would have it painted, and like his picture in uniform, it would become a depository of family pride.

Mary secretly wrote u letter to Joe. A short letter, because she was afraid of being caught. She told of the fieldwork her father was busy at, and the garage Stash had made. But why would her hand not write what her heart suffered?

And then she waited, and waited, each day seeming a hundred years long, for a reply.

***

Frank was up at dawn each morning — which came earlier and earlier now. He would have an hour or two of fieldwork done before chores. By evening his shoulders and legs — his whole body, sometimes — would be sore and tired. And he would sleep, most nights, the undisturbed sleep of the weary.

But one night, as though there had been some loud noise in the house, he was startled out of his sleep. He lay awake, listening, wondering if his mind had played a trick on him. The house was still, and dark. Only now and then would the fire in the woodstove crackle quietly. In the winter, when the temperature outside dropped to twenty or thirty below, he would sometimes wake like this, feeling the cold draw round him, and get up to put more wood in the stove. But now it was warm in the house. Knowing nothing better to do, he padded out into the living room and put another stick on the fire.

He stood a moment, uneasy. He was like a caged animal which had suddenly realized there was a world beyond the bars — and after this realization, the enclosed world would never be the same. From outside something was tugging at him. He glanced at the clock in their room. Three-thirty. Pulling the curtain aside, to see if the morning would bring a workday or rain, he saw a black earth slumbering peacefully beneath an ebony sky studded with uncountable sparkling stars. To the east, between the two tall pines which marked the limits of his land, he saw a big, bright silver-white point which outshone all the others. He stood a moment watching it. Somehow it was that star which tugged at him, pulling him away from this world.

He crawled back into bed. Lying on his back, through the curtain lace he could see that bright shining star. He closed his eyes, tried to sleep, but something he couldn't see or touch, something he could hardly even feel, was keeping him awake. And strangely, through his mind like bubbles rising through murky water came those peculiar phrases from the Novenas: *Virgin most faithful, seat of wisdom, mystical rose, tower of ivory, house of gold, gate of heaven, queen of peace.*

Mystical Rose. Tower of Ivory. Queen of Peace.

They haunted him, these names of someone he had known. And then it all had to do with Joe Stelmach. Why? How? It had only the logic of dreams behind it, and all he knew was this overpowering urge to see Joe, to talk to him. It was all mixed up. But for a moment there was nothing more important in the world than finding out exactly why Joe had gone off to the city.

Then a dream he hadn't had for years drifted across his mind. It was when he was blasting the well, just behind the house. The night afterwards he'd awakened, like now, in the middle of the night, from a terrible nightmare. He looked up, in that dream, from the blast and had seen, through the weirdly dancing smoke, that where the house had stood was nothing but a huge, gaping hole. That was the kind of hole he felt now, in the quiet dark: a big, deep, empty, terrifying abyss — all the more frightening because he felt it was his fault.

He closed his eyes. But still he could feel it, like a grave opening for himself or some close friend. He opened his eyes. The bright star shone through the curtain, accusingly. Beside him Berenice slept on, and her presence seemed unbearable to him, a great darkness trying to snuff out that white light which pulled at him.

At last he rose quietly and slipped into his clothes. In the kitchen he found a lamp. Around him the house was still and dead as a tomb, in which the dead slept unwaking. He lit the lamp, and in its light slipped into his boots and coat. Pushing the door open, he went outside. Shep, asleep on the back porch, woke with a short grunt, then growled for a moment. Recognizing his master, the dog stood stiffly up and wandered to his side, confused by the hour.

They walked together across the farmyard, the kerosene light pushing the darkness aside as they went. Frank's breath puffed in the night air. It would be a good morning, clear and cool, perfect for putting in the oats. But that seemed such a long way off, as though he faced the day's work from across some wide and raging river, as yet to be crossed. Half asleep, half awake, he was just entering the current, driven away from something and toward something else — but impotent to name either.

The hinge on the barn door squeaked as he opened it. The dog scurried in before him; he followed, then closed the door. The air inside was warm and moist, full of the breath of the cows and horses, spiced with the smells of hay and manure. Suddenly he felt as though he'd been sick and someone had wrapped him in a blanket. He shivered slightly, stood a long unmeasured moment holding the lantern high, its yellow light revealing the nearer cows, all standing, their eyes shining to him as their mouths slowly, patiently, worked the cud. Beyond the nearest — White Star, Brownie, and Duchess — the others blurred off into the darkness. But even in the dark or with his eyes shut Frank could have found each, and named them, and told you how well they milked and recited their life histories: when and how they were born (because he'd been there), whether they were a strong or weak calf, when each had first freshened, and like a doctor with a familiar patient, could count out the litany of their illnesses.

He was embarrassed, the way they stared at him. He felt suddenly foolish. What nonsense was this, his coming out to the barn in the middle of the night? Even at summer's height chores didn't start till after five — and that was more than an hour away. He wondered if he'd frightened them. But they didn't seem frightened. From White Star's eyes came that same quiet acceptance with which she faced a sudden summer thunderstorm with its terrifying lightning; or the first snowfall of October. Alone in the pasture on a moonlit night, she seemed to be saying, there are things far stranger than you.

Shep turned and lay down in the aisle where he most often lay during milking. He had decided, as dogs would, that it was his clock, not his master's, that was wrong; and so it must be time for chores.

But Frank had not come to milk the cows. He hung the lantern on a post and stepped between White Star and Duchess, who sniffed in his direction as though anxious for his touch. He lay one arm over each of their backs. Duchess moved farther toward him, leaning her rear so that he had to pat her gently lest she crush him.

And so he stood, his mind slipping back into darkness, slipping toward home at last. Home? But where was home? Certainly not this barn in Marathon County, Wisconsin, nor another five thousand miles away in Poland. No, not any particular barn, but all barns: a stable in Pennsylvania, a station in the outback, a byre in Germany or Ecuador. He was slipping out of his skin into that shared by all farmers who were at home with their cattle. Not Polish any more, nor yet ever to be American.

He stood for a long time between the two cows, absorbing their warmth, secure in the touch of their skin. And when he found himself slowly nodding away into sleep, he patted Duchess lightly on the rump and stepped across the gutter out into the aisle. Shep's tail wagged. Frank reached up and turned the lamp out and felt his way toward the pile of hay he'd thrown down for the morning's fodder. Pulling his coat around him, he lay down in the hay. Enfolded in its rich, clear smell, he was soon asleep.

Outside the morning star faded under the brilliance of the rising sun, until like the last breath of life in a dying man, it flickered out. The sun's rays, shining into the barn, woke Frank. Astonished at first, he shook his head, wondering where he was. Then, realizing, he rose stiffly and brushed the hay off his coat and pants. He stooped and gave the faithful Shep, who'd slept beside him, a good scratch behind the ear, then still thick with sleep trudged to the milk house for his pail. The night's foolishness was over. Tiny white drops fell from Duchess' udder. Everything mysterious and unknown dimmed, faded away. It was milking time.

***

The furniture was all pushed back in the living room. There was tea for Gertrude and Berenice, and beer for Frank and Henryk. How Henry loved his beer. The Victrola, turned up full volume, was playing a mazurka. And the dancers were dancing, swirling around and around. Just two couples, in a little farm house on a long-ago Saturday night.

But from above, where the children knelt at the register in the boys' bedroom, it looked like the Grand Ballroom in the Crown Prince's Palace. From below they could feel the stomping of the dancers' boots on the wooden floor, which sounded like a crowd of a thousand; and the scratchy Victrola blared out like the world's biggest, and best, dance band.

But then the record ended, and all was quiet. Henry put an oberek on so Gertrude could dance with Frank. He and Berenice, meanwhile, stood aside clapping hands and tapping their feet as the other two turned and swung around. How strange it was for the children to see their mother smiling so — she seemed another woman, twenty years younger. She had insisted that the children go to bed — was it because she didn't want them to see that part of her?

All four were waltzing now, weaving between each other, staying clear of the sofa and chairs, skirts flying out, their father laughing lightly, Henryk more serious, not so natural a dancer. And then a polka, and when it started they were all flying around the room, their boots stomping out the beat of the dance. It was too much for the girls; Angie and Lotti took hands and twirled round and round. Oh how they wished they knew how to dance! But it didn't matter, really, that they stumbled and stepped on each other's toes. No one was watching. While the floor rocked below and the music blared out, they whirled and whirled, Anna and Sophie and Mary sitting on the bed laughing and clapping their hands.

And when the music ended, it was over, and they fell on the floor exhausted.

They had asked their mother, time and again, to teach them to dance. But in reply she would tell them the story from the old country, the one about the wedding dance. When everyone was enjoying themselves, who should appear but a tall stranger, dressed in black coat and tails and sporting a tall stovepipe hat. From girl to girl he went, dancing with them all. He was so handsome, so debonair, they wondered who he was. At last fixing on the prettiest of them all, he was about to escort her out the door when someone noticed a tail sticking out from his pant-leg. The stranger and the girl ran toward the river. The other dancers all chased after them and grabbed the girl's arm just as he was about to pull her into the river.

The music started again. Below the dancers danced. Above they knelt once more and watched, the memory of that story like a grey smoked glass between them and the world. And it went beyond that night, beyond simply dancing or not dancing: whenever they enjoyed themselves, ten, twenty, even fifty years thereafter, they would keep watch, out of the corner of their eyes, for a movement there, like a shadow in the night, come to take them away.

19

Before school Anna and Sophie each picked a handful of trilliums, little pink and white trumpets announcing the full arrival of spring. The other girls took time in the morning to scour the woods for the last of the spring beauties, the first timid yellow wood violets, cowslips and bright dandelions. Lotti, who had a knack for such things, made the final arrangements. She and Angie set out across the road to lay the little basket full of blossoms on the Tomczak's porch. They knocked, a rapid burst of timid raps, then ran as fast as their legs would go straight across the pasture to their own house.

And there, on their own front porch, as if by magic, was a May basket every bit as overflowing with glorious color and tender blossoms as the one they'd just left the Tomczak daughters with.

✳✳✳

There was church that evening, after chores. On the night of May first little St. Francis of Xavier was aglow with glory, a triumph of song and color and fragrance. The altar and statues were all festooned with flowers; but especially the gentle, blue-robed Mary, crowned today with a crown of glory and carried in procession around the churchyard in the warm evening light, Father Nowak swinging the thurible, which clanged against its chain and gave to the sky rich sweet clouds of holy incense.

It was for Her they'd come, to Her they prayed, from Her they took their joy in the season: the Blessed Mary, ever Virgin, Queen of Queens, Queen of May, Queen of Poland, Stella Maris. It was a festival of the return of spring, the rebirth of the earth, and tasted to them like a gasp of air after the long suffocation which was winter.

But it was to be the passing of an age. Not many more years would see those grand processions around the church, with Holy Mary at their head. Already the schools were renaming such faith as superstition; and with scalpel and forceps would tease apart those blossoms lain so devoutedly at her feet. Calyx and corolla, sepal and anther would no longer be offered to Her — and jealously would she then turn her back on them.

✳✳✳

He drew the shears to a razor edge, steel against stone, stone against steel. Lumbermen huddled in their shanties on a Saturday night would set their axes to skin and tolerably well shave; mowers, relaxing in the shade would take the hair off their arms with their scythes; and so Frank, effortlessly, neatly, drew the shears across his arm. Satisfied, he sat to finish his coffee.

He would need Stash's help, and Stash was in the barn helping Bruno. From the floor of the calf pens the matted straw and dung had to be lifted, forkful at a time, out of the pen and then thrown into the great swinging bucket which ran on tracks out the end of the barn. Thick with manure from the young calves, so often bothered with scours, the straw was heavy and gave off a powerful, gagging smell. And the calves, which had huddled together at the far end of the pen, curiously watching the goings-on, were now overtaken with a fit of excitement, dashing this way and that, tripping over the fork and stepping on Bruno's boots.

Stash dumped the manure where he and his father had so recently hauled off the old pile, then trudged in with the empty wheelbarrow and picking up his fork, began again to fill it. His father came into the barn, and called out to him to come to the sheep pen. Bruno, who was scattering fresh straw around the frisky calves, would have to finish loading the last load.

Frank had taken his jacket off and hung it over one of the rails of the pen. He opened the gate and moved slowly inside, trying not to frighten the animals. Stash sneaked silently in behind and closed the gate.

There were in the pen six ewes and one ram, all Suffolks, their long faces and short legs black, their grey coats thick, although matted with manure and overlain with a fine dust. Beside one ewe the twin lambs born more than a month ago stood distrustfully eyeing the man.

Frank nodded to one of the ewes, a little separate from the others. Stash moved cautiously between her and the others and bending, kept her cornered. His father grabbed her by the forelegs and in a motion so sudden it startled even Stash, had her onto her tail with her back up against his chest. Slipping the shears out of his back pocket he began snipping quickly and adroitly, starting at the neck, then down around the belly, where the wool was short and especially dirty. The razor-sharp shears, pumped by his hands, powerful from milking so many cows, worked easily through the wool. Now he worked her sides, where the best wool was to be found, thick and long and relatively clean. One last snip and the whole fleece fell from her, unbroken. He flopped her onto her feet and she ran to the others, shaking herself, her nose skimming the straw. Nearly naked, she bleated as though for her life.

Frank bent to fold and roll the fleece into a tight bundle. He tied it with a piece of twine; Stash lay it just outside the pen. Selecting another ewe, Frank had her shorn in no time. Then he rested his back and arms while Stash did the next animal, working slower, the fleece not cut so evenly and coming off the animal in three pieces rather than one. Bruno, meanwhile, had come over to lean on the pen and watch.

When they were done, all the sheep stood forlornly in the pen, shivering though it was warm, bleating pitifully. The men's shirts were dirtied in front, greasy from the wool and smeared with manure. They locked the gate shut and lifted the bulky wool, which came, Frank guessed, to thirty or thirty-five pounds. Bruno was drafted into carrying one of the bundles up to the porch.

Already at the edge of the *dompki*, the girls had fires going under the big iron kettles. As the men went in for their lunch, the water was beginning to steam. In a light misty drizzle Angie and Lotti stood above the kettles, tending the fires and feeding them with wood dragged from the *dompki* and drier pieces out of the woodshed.

Mary, Sophie, and Anna pushed themselves away from the table as the men came in. Slipping into their jackets, each girl lifted a fleece off the back porch and set it beside the steaming water. Mary untied the one she'd brought and slipped it into the largest vat. The water had to be warm enough to clean the wool but not too hot or it would ruin it. She sprinkled soap over the wool and she and Angie, using long sticks, poked the fleece apart. By pushing, kneading, and turning it, large pieces of matted dirt broke free and came floating to the top of the water. Anna, using a shovel, skimmed the dirt off and threw it into the woods behind her.

Now the water was a tepid brown, in which floated bits of straw and hay, wool and manure. With the steam came a strong, earthy smell, heavy almost to the point of being nauseating. The girls had to hold their breath as they leaned over the water to push on the sticks; and it seemed that the steam and the smoke from the fires, like spoiled children, followed them around no matter on what side they stood.

For half an hour they worked the fleece, until most of the dirt was free. Carried then on the end of a stick, heavy now that it was wet, they dropped it into a second vat, where two of them began working it all over again. The worst dirt, meanwhile, was skimmed off the first vat and another fleece dropped in, with a little more soap. Each of the six fleeces had to go through both vats, then the water was replaced in the kettles with clean water, which had to be heated and the fleeces run through one more time yet before being rinsed with clean, cold water. It would be dark before they were done and the wool hung on the clothesline to drip dry. By then the girls would be worn-out and sick of the heavy smell of the lanolin-rich wool. And their skin and hair would be greasy for days, with the oil carried up by the steam.

Once dry, the wool would have to be teased and carded — both long and tedious jobs — before their mother could draw it out on her wheel into yarn for stockings, sweater, mittens or hats. But there was, anyway, one member of the family who rather enjoyed the whole process: Bruno, who'd been forced that morning to clean the calf-pens, stopped by the smelly vats now and again all day, expressly to point out to the girls what miserable work they had.

***

This first week of May was warm, but it was wet: perfect for pasture and hay. One evening the bats returned, careening above the barnyard just as darkness set in. And by the end of the week the first yellow rocket came into bloom; this provided still another chore for the family, walking through the wet hay fields and oats, pulling up the weed and carrying it in soggy bunches to piles along the road.

And now the cows were let out to pasture the fresh grass. It was Bruno's job to follow the herd down the path, across the marsh, and onto the forty acres which their father rented from Ganthers. The boy had to take along a lunch and sit all day watching them, as there were no fences around that pasture. He didn't mind really — he liked being off by himself. And when the mosquitoes got bad, in a few weeks, school would be out and it would be Anna's job.

The lead cow, with a big heavy bell which clanked noisily as she walked, was a husky red and white guernsey named by Mary for the star-shaped blotch on her forehead. White Star was born a puny calf, the first spring on the Dancy farm. Though they all thought she wouldn't survive, all the attention lavished on her pulled her through. But she was a runt, who grew so slowly their father threatened to sell or butcher her. Only now the girls had grown attached to her, and made him promise to keep her. As she grew, it became apparent she was retarded. She exhibited none of the normal curiosity of a calf, none of the natural spunkiness when taking the nipple. Instead she spent long hours just standing inside the calf pen staring out into seemingly nowhere, run down and bumped into by her friskier brothers and sisters. And when she did move, it was with clumsy little jerks, as though her rear legs were too far from her brain to bother with obeying.

She was slow to come into heat, and her first two calves,

a heifer and a bull, were stillborn. On top of that, once let out for the summer, she could never learn to find her own stanchion. Patiently she would stand waiting in the lane while the rest of the herd filed into the barn and found their places to munch the hay left for them in the manger. Then in would trudge White Star, her back legs sometimes getting lost along the way, to walk up and down behind the others, looking more and more anxious lest there be no hay left for her. While it would take less than a week, in early summer, for the others to learn their stanchions, White Star would never quite manage it. Someone — usually Bruno — would have to go around and show her where she belonged.

What saved her, poor White Star, besides the insistence of the girls who knew just how to manage their father, was the fact that when she milked she milked easily and copiously — was one of their very best milkers, in fact, filling at her best both morning and night an entire twelve-quart milking pail.

But now White Star was dry, for she was heavy with calf, due to freshen any day. The girls were happy for her, anxiously awaiting the birth of her first live calf.

That afternoon it was drizzling lightly, and Bruno, out with the cows, had taken shelter in the tumble-down shack, not lived in for many years, which stood at the edge of the pasture. He sat for a while, watching the herd, until that grew tedious. Taking up an old wagon axle left in a corner of the building, he began prying the floorboards up, one by one, hoping to find some buried treasure. He kept at it a long time, though all he found was old spider webs and moist and clammy rocks and the dried and bleached skeleton of a rat. He sat down to rest, then suddenly realized he could no longer hear White Star's clanging bell. He ran out to look. The herd was there, placidly grazing, but no White Star. He yelled at Shep, lying under a hawthorn tree just breaking into bloom.

"White Star! Where's White Star?" he shouted. But the dog did not understand. Bruno cursed himself. He looked all over, wandered down along the edge of the marsh, calling her, searched for a track or a glimpse of her big, splotched back somewhere out in the low hardwoods. But he could find no sign of her.

He brought the cows in that afternoon trembling with anxiety. He was sure his father would be mad as a hornet's nest. But, to his surprise, he was told not to worry. She'd gone off to calf, that was all, his father assured him.

"But won't the wolves get her or her calf?" Bruno asked, helping his father throw hay into the manger.

"There aren't any wolves around here," his father chided him.

"But Chester says..."

"I know what Chester says," he was told. "You don't have to believe everything you hear."

Bruno was going to ask his father why he should believe *that*; but it was time to start milking.

So they waited for White Star to return.

A day passed.

Two days passed; the sun broke through the clouds.

Now, on the afternoon of the third day, even their father began to worry. But then, just as Bruno, with Shep's help, was rounding up the herd to bring them in, there she was, as if by magic, right in the middle of the herd, grazing peacefully away as though nothing had happened. She was thin now, and her swollen udder dripped as she grazed. Bruno walked up to her. At first he wanted to hit her or kick her for all the trouble she'd caused. But instead he patted her on the side and shook his head. She acted as though he wasn't even there, busily cropping the thick green grass, her lips and teeth taking it in by the mouthful. When it was time to go in, she led the herd back as though her daily routine had never been interrupted.

They milked her out that evening, saved the rich colostrum for the calf. Before it was dark they went out and searched for it. They looked and looked until their eyes could see no more; and afraid of getting lost themselves, they had to give up and go back to the barn and let the cows out.

"We'll follow her, in the morning," Frank said.

Let out after morning milking, White Star moved slowly, clumsily down the muddy trail through the marsh and to the pasture. And as though she didn't care any more whether or not they followed her, she headed straight across the pasture and into an alder thicket. They kept a fair distance, but did not lose sight of her. At first she headed off at an angle, deep into the alder. Bruno wondered if she was heading straight out into the swamp; but his father said this was probably a diversion. And sure enough, she then turned sharply to her left to skirt behind a low hill. Stash said he'd stood on that hill the evening before but hadn't seen a thing.

White Star turned again, leading them through a maze of underbrush and low oak branches. She wended her way through a grove of birch, and disappeared at last behind the roots of a great elm which had fallen over. There, behind those roots, they found her nest, and in it a fine, healthy heifer calf, more white than red, which seemed overjoyed to see her mother. White Star licked the calf; it hurried around to her bloated, dripping udder.

They stood in silence and watched. White Star seemed to be the proudest mother there ever was, turning to lick the calf's side as it eased the milk from her bag, then looking up at them as though to say: Well, what do you think? Pretty nice calf, huh?

They gave the calf time to finish its meal. Then Frank walked up to her and her mother and gently lifted the calf. It was heavier than he'd expected. He turned carefully and headed straight out to the pasture, having to duck between and under branches and brush. White Star seemed confused by all this, anxiously looking around her nest, lowing mournfully, searching the nearby underbrush. Frank turned and hollered to her; the bleat of the calf brought her to him.

Frank carried the calf as far as the pasture but then, tired out, he let Stash heft it and carry it the rest of the way to the barn. White Star followed obediently. And when they put her calf in the pen and tied White Star into her stanchion, she bellowed forlornly all through the day, staring over toward the calf as though they were separated for life. At last, during evening milking, when they let the calf out to suck, she quieted down. The girls stood around watching; their wish had been granted.

They kept the cow inside for several days, and with each passing day she seemed less and less interested in the calf, which Lotti had named Blotches. By week's end, when they let White Star out with the rest of the herd, she plodded out the path, her bell clanking away, headed for the fresh grass of the pasture, as though she'd completely forgotten that she'd just become a mother.

20

"This afternoon," Father Nowak proudly announced, "many of us will be going to St. Stan's for their annual festival. There will be, I am sure, a glorious table set in God's name, and no shortage of friends to keep us company.

"And we should remember, those of us who go and those who will not or cannot, what this day is, this seventh day of May, this feast-day of St. Stanislaus." He paused, scanned the congregation. "There is in Kracòw a cathedral — some of you, I am sure, like myself, have knelt and prayed in the sanctuary of its spacious vaults. I'm speaking, of course, of the cathedral of St. Stanislaus, after which the smaller church in Stevens Point takes its name. The altar of that venerable cathedral in Poland's most beautiful city stands precisely on the spot," and here the good priest pointed to the floor beside his lectern, "at which the Holy Saint was martyred, nearly nine hundred years ago. In a crypt below that altar are the mortal remains of Sobieski, Kosciusko, Mickiewicz, and the Saint himself — all the great stars of the constellation which is Polish history.

"How did this man, this Bishop, this courageous patriot, come to be canonized by the Church? Through his Holy martyrdom, a story much like that of another Bishop of the Church, another Saint martryed by the hand of the very King who appointed him. I speak, in the latter case, of course, of St. Thomas à Becket, whose name and history we read so often in literature, a man so much better known than our own great Saint.

"Remember, my children, that Thomas à Becket was martyred a hundred years after our own patron, and yet it is he, not Stanislaus, who receives all the glory. So it must be. We Poles are destined, it seems, to be overlooked by the writers of history. Ours is a drama no less tragic, no less heroic, no less overflowing with the courage and conflict which makes martyrs and literature. But Stanislaus is forgotten, while the name of Beckett lies on the lips of every schoolchild from Maine to Madagascar.

"So be it. We Poles must then share our joys and sorrows

together — as today we will gather in our very own, national, holy festival. And should the world shut their eyes and turn their backs it is they who suffer for it, not us."

The feast day of St. Stanislaus was one of Father Nowak's favorite days, surpassed perhaps only by Christmas and Easter. Every year at this time he worked himself up to an enthused and excited fervor compounded of equal parts of patriotism and religious devotion. The food — which, admittedly was no small part of it — and the good talk with other priests from Mill City, Polonia, Milladora, Stevens Point, all over the diocese, why that made it really something.

But favorite day or not, the good priest was faced with a problem. The thought of commanding a ton of cold steel at breakneck speeds of forty or more miles an hour sent him, as always, into spasms of anxiety. A team and buggy he would drive. He had yet to meet the horse which would run full speed into a tree the way automobiles were wont to do. Driving would require far too much concentration for his mind, which had a habit of gliding away into more interesting and important theoretical considerations. He should not, he could not, by all that was great and holy he would not, place himself behind the wheel of one of Mr. Ford's cantankerous Tin Lizzies.

So it was that to get to St. Stan's that afternoon he would need a car and chauffeur. It had, in fact, already been arranged. A phone call to Berenice Topolska, a few kind words, and he had the services of her oldest daughter, Mary, who in other years had driven him into town to shop for religious supplies, clothing and even groceries. This time, Father was rather surprised that her mother acquiesced. But, he thought, she probably feels bad for not letting Mary come that week when Verna was off.

That morning before Mass, Mary climbed somewhat nervously into Stash's Ford, its top and isinglass windows up against a light spring drizzle, and sat a moment, her hands gripping the wheel. It would be the first time this year she'd driven.

Stash stood beside the car, overseeing her sister's technique. He watched as she set the handbrake, pushed the spark up to retard, pulled the throttle open a little, and switched the ignition to "mag." Everything was ready. Stash went around to the front of the car, put the crank into its slot, pulled on the choke ring, lightly turned the engine over, then gave it a sharp crank.

The motor fired off. Mary opened the throttle a little more, pulled the spark down, as Stash had reminded her, to the sixth notch, and sat back to let the engine warm.

"There's plenty of gas," Stash shouted to her over the throb of the motor. "And don't forget that the bands are a little worn so she won't stop the way she should." He stood back, gave the rear fender a little slap, the way he would to get a horse going.

Mary gave it more gas, set one foot on the brake, pushed the clutch in halfway, and struggled for several long minutes with the hand brake until she got the latch loose; pushing it forward, she put the car in gear.

Grimacing nervously out at Stash, she pushed the clutch all the way to the floor, and the car jerked ahead, the clutch clattering noisily. At the end of the drive, she turned and waved good-bye to Stash, then let the clutch all the way out, putting the car into high gear. But her foot hovered over the brake pedal, as a mother might hover over a child playing at the edge of a river. The rest of the family pulled out of the drive, following her in the Overland.

***

Mass over, Father had to wait for all the parishioners to leave before he could crank the car over for Mary, then climb inside. As they pulled out onto the highway and headed south, the slow drizzle made it hard to see out of the windshield, only adding to Mary's anxiety.

There was heavy traffic on the road, many parishioners from miles around headed down to the festival. Father had his prayer book with him; there was never a priest more devout than Father Nowak. For the first few minutes of the trip he sat reading from his book, but then he closed it and stared silently ahead through the rain-slicked windshield.

There was a car ahead of them and a car behind, all following in a line along the river, the low grey sky continuing to drizzle on the asphalt highway. On their right the river flats were carpeted with white and pink trilliums, looking somewhat soggy in the dim light. And on their left they were just passing the cemetery, its granite stones slicked with rain, nestled in the slope of a little hill beneath the towering pines.

"God's own acre," Father said, crossing himself. "It means 'dormitory.'" He spoke to the clouded window in front of him, through which Mary strained to see. "Did you know that?" he asked. "Cemetery, it means 'dormitory.' Where we sleep, where we all shall sleep, awaiting the resurrection."

He was nervous, being alone with the girl, riding in the car, and he was excited. It all made him talkative. "I wanted to go to solemn High Mass this morning," he confessed, "but I had my own to say. There's nothing like a real Mass, Pontifical, in cathedra." And his mind went back to St. Peter's, the focus of the Church, the center of the City of God.

"Ah, St. Peter's!" he exclaimed, from a fullness of heart, speaking to himself as much as to the girl so tightly gripping the steering wheel. "In June, at the feast of Saints Peter and Paul, the square will be thronged with pilgrims. His Holiness will come out onto the balcony and bless them. I have seen him, you know, with my own eyes, Leo, the Lion of God, as he stood to bless us all. And some day I will go for a coronation, or a canonization. Rome, the Eternal City," he daydreamed.

The Pantheon, the Colosseum, Hadrian's Wall. And exploring the catacombs, stealing away with Andreus and that little French boy, what was his name? Guy, they called him. William. Like St. Jerome a thousand years before they would wander deep into the bowels of the earth. How dark they were, the catacombs, how fetidly close, yet on all sides nothing but the glory of God; as though the early martyrs had taken it upon themselves to carry His light into the very depths of Hell. And yes, it was true, the first Eucharistic feasts were shared there with the dead.

"*La bella lingua,*" he said, suddenly, turning to Mary. He put his hand on her arm. "*Ciao, Maria,*" he said. "*Ciao, signorina.*" He clapped his hands lightly, laughing to himself. "It's how they say good-bye. Say it, Mary."

But she drove on, clinging to the wheel.

"Oh come on, say it. *Ciao!*"

She glanced at him from the corner of her eye. "*Djaow,*" she said, shyly. It sounded like a cat begging for milk.

He giggled. "*Si, signorina, la bella lingua.*"

She had no idea what he was talking about.

It seemed to Father Nowak, as he thought of those long-gone days, that he had already led three quite distinct lives. First, of course, as a child in Posnan, in the embrace of his family. Son of a poor shopkeeper, he remembered those days with mixed emotions — how he loved his mother, her soups and dumplings and the occasional *ponchki* with which she would treat him and his brothers and sisters. And how he'd loved his father's shop, where they sold harnesses and leather goods. Then he did not see it for what it was — a dead-end corner of a dead-end and dreary city. It was all the world to him, then, and how he'd loved it.

But he was a bright and studious boy, and through the almost miraculous charity of an uncle, was sent to Rome, to study for the priesthood. He knew it when he boarded the train taking him south through the night: a whole new world was opening for him.

The seminary life! He was on his own now. It was all up to him. Those long wonderful arguments about the meaning of life and death and our role in God's plan. The glorious Masses at St. Peter's, the very stones you walked on speaking of the great ones who'd come before — the doctors of the church, its Bishops, and Popes.

And the city, out there, the eternal city, with its hot lascivious nights; the brothels — a pornocracy, they called it, a city ruled by prostitutes. Its smells, in the night: the overripe fruit, the fountains smelling of the sea. And always the cats.

"Cats!" he said suddenly, startling Mary, whose foot went for the brakes. "No, no," he laughed. "Not here. In Rome. Infested with cats." She looked at him warily. But he was lost again in thought.

Ever since he'd hated cats. As though they were the souls of the lost women of Rome, beckoning him toward sins of the flesh. That had been the most difficult, all those days in the seminary, knowing what waited for them out there in the city.

Goodness, he had learned, can only be measured by the evil it overcomes.

He sighed. What a struggle that makes of life.

His studies were nearly complete when an uncle in California sent money and asked him to come for a visit. What was meant to be a month's vacation turned instead, because of the intervening War, into a lifetime emigration. He stayed in Chicago for a few months, then reentered the seminary, at St. Francis in Milwaukee. Out of the LaCrosse diocese he was first appointed to Thorp, then to Necedah — where he'd first met the Topolskis — and now, here.

Had anyone suggested, when he was a poor schoolboy in Posnan, grubbing around in the back room of his father's shop, that some day he would end up driving along this quiet river in central Wisconsin, lined with budding elms and a carpet of wildflowers, he would have laughed and called them crazy. He would never have imagined it.

But God's plan was God's plan.

And now, as they came into the edge of Stevens Point, its shabby houses and grimy warehouses, at this edge of town, dreary enough in the slow drizzle, he felt quiet resignation about his life; a resignation which lay heavy on him, which threatened to smother those incredible hopes he'd held for himself as a seminarian. The world lay all in front of him, then. Now he seemed to be passing it by, and more and more it was behind him. He felt now so very much middle-aged, and just a little too comfortable with his station in life. Was that all he would ever be, then, a middle-aged, affable, slightly excitable parish priest in some backwater country village?

"Do you know," he asked Mary, "how far it is from Rome to Stevens Point?"

The girl shook her head, pushed the clutch in a little to slip it as she rounded a corner into Jordan Road. Stash was right. The bands were worn. Now the tall red spires of St. Stan's were straight ahead of them. Cars were parked up and down the street, interspersed with teams and buggies. A steady stream of people flowed toward the church, whose wide-open portals, colorfully decorated with banners and ribbons, seemed to greet them warmly, then swallow them up into its dark interior.

Mary slowed to park.

"A long way," Father mused, straightening his collar. "A very, very long way."

***

Down the steps they went, part of the crowd, into the basement filled with chattering people and tables already laden with food. Father had to pull the shy Mary along behind him. As they passed the tables, he smiled and nodded to friends and acquaintances all along the way. It seemed to Mary that he knew everyone.

"Where would you like to sit?" he asked her. He would be sitting with the other priests at a special table.

Scanning the milling faces, Mary wished she hadn't come. She didn't recognize a soul. But Father suddenly tugged her and dragged her to the far wall where — of all people — sat Alex and Sophie Stelmach. Her heart leaped. Was Joe with them? No, of course not. But next to them was an empty chair.

"Would you mind some company?" Father asked, nodding to Mary.

Alex pulled the chair out. "Sit down, Mary!" She sat, next to him. They were as friendly as ever. Father waded through the crowd to join his priest friends. Laughing and joking with Mary, Alex made the girl feel right at home. They were such nice people. She clung to them now like a life raft in a tossing sea of strangers.

The food was brought out, more than they could ever eat, while a small orchestra played Polish music. Several of the priests got up and made speeches about Polish culture and Poles in America. Everyone clapped, went back to coffee and desserts. After a while, people began to leave.

Sophie leaned across toward Mary. "Our Joe always asks about you in his letters," she said. "He's not happy you know, away from home. He belongs with us."

To Mary, it was as though Sophie were blaming her. Sensing that she'd been misunderstood, Sophie reached out and held Mary's hand. "He'll come back, don't you worry," she said reassuringly.

Then Father came up behind them, along the wall, and put his hands on Mary's shoulders. He leaned over, flushed with the fun he'd been having, and suggested, sadly, that perhaps it was time to go. Yes, Alex agreed, there were cows to be milked. So they all stood and went out into the fine drizzle. On the steps of the church Father and his chauffeur said good-bye to the Stelmachs and turned to leave just as an ambulance rushed into the emergency entrance of St. Michael's Hospital across the street. They crossed themselves.

✳✳✳

Father, still buoyant from the festivities, laughed and joked as the car headed out of town. He talked nonstop, relating news and gossip about friends Mary didn't even know.

But when they'd left the town and the wet fields, freshly green or black from plowing, moved past the car, he stopped suddenly and stared outside, as quiet and thoughtful as he had just been loquacious and frivolous.

Mary slowed to let a herd of cows, on their way home for milking, cross the road. Father pulled his breviary from his pocket. They drove along the river, the sky to the west growing lighter, the drizzle thinning to a light mist. But in the air there was still a sense of a long, interminable greyness — it seemed like weeks since the sun had shone.

Father closed his prayer book, wiped his round-rimmed

glasses. "The Stelmachs, they're good people, aren't they?"

Mary nodded. "Yes."

"It's too bad about Joe. I mean, about his going off to work. Really, he's needed at home."

Only the sound of the motor, turning easily over, and the splash of the wheels on the wet pavement. Then, after a few moments, Father, who seemed to be struggling with himself, put his hand on Mary's arm. "What will you do, my child?"

She steered the car, tight-lipped, frightened. Now they passed the cemetery again, then the bridge over Peplin Creek. Soon they would be back to the rectory.

"Does Joe write to you?" Father asked. "I hope you don't mind my asking."

Mary thought a moment. "I wrote to him, but maybe mother..."

"Intercepts your letters?" He considered. "Yes, yes, she might do that. And tell me, Mary, this person you write to, do you expect him to come here?"

Mary swallowed. "Next week," she said, coldly.

Father inhaled sharply. "Yes?"

The church was visible ahead, its white tower standing above the trees, the wide expanse of its yard turning a pale but promising green. "Could you give up Joe for him, my child?"

But Mary could not find an answer.

"I can't advise you, in good conscience, to disobey your mother," Father said. It sounded to her as though he was saying something he'd been waiting all day to say. "I know it's not easy," he added. "If it were a sin to marry someone you don't love, then most of us would be the children of sin. But you must do as your conscience tells you. We priests, you know, we haven't so much freedom as you might think. I mean, in advising others. Canon Law tells us exactly what we're supposed to do, during the Liturgy, when administering the Sacraments, and when we're offering counsel. Sometimes," he sighed, "I think that if we could only know all those rules by heart, then it would be impossible to fail. But it's not that easy. So there are times when I, too, pray for someone older and wiser to advise me. Then, as I kneel in prayer, I listen as clearly as I can to the voice of my conscience, and pray again that I am hearing it right. Yet one can never be sure... Do you understand?"

She did, and she didn't.

"If God were not merciful," he said, staring out the window, "we would all of us be damned."

The car squeaked to a stop. Mary left the motor running. Idling, it turned over roughly. It was near suppertime, she would have to drive straight home.

Father stared at her, but made no move to get out. It was as though he had to look deeply inside her, inside her soul. "Do you love Joe?" he asked, quietly, but the words rolled through the car like sudden heavy thunder.

Mary would not look at him. "Yes," she said, the word catching in her throat.

"Then promise me one thing, child," Father said, laying his hand on hers. She turned to face him. "Promise me that if you have any doubts at all, any serious doubts, about giving yourself to this stranger, first you will come to me." They looked into each other's eyes. "Perhaps then I will be willing to sin for your sake."

Mary felt a sudden compassion for this man who was struggling so hard for her sake; this priest who was more than a priest, friend who was more than a friend. Her lips moved, her eyes clouded over. "Yes," she said at last. "Yes, but..."

He raised his hand to place his finger over her lips. "Shh!" he said. "That's enough."

Then suddenly he was gone, out into the rain. His door slammed shut and she saw him run up the steps into the rectory. Alone in the car, she felt suddenly lost, as though she didn't know where she was or why. Her foot moved across the pedals, searching for reverse. But she had forgotten how to drive, and afraid of stalling the car, she sat instead only staring ahead at the door to the rectory, from which she saw, at last, no help would come.

✳✳✳

There was a letter, next day. Something about a delay in being mustered out. Walerych wouldn't be coming until early June. It was at least a reprieve. But no matter. He was coming. And already Berenice envisioned a summer wedding.

She told Frank that he was coming, in a few weeks. Frank took it quietly. She pointed out that they would then have another hand on the farm, just in time for haying. Frank only shook his head and said nothing.

After lunch he usually took an hour's break from fieldwork, lying on the floor in the dining room, resting, while Berenice read to him from *Rolnik*. There was that day a long article

which made him burn inside, about a national Ku Klux Klan
meeting. And in a small Texas town a Catholic priest had been
tarred and feathered.

As she was reading, he interrupted her suddenly, his voice
tight with anger, as though weeks and weeks of frustration were
about to burst free. "Where will he stay?" he asked.

"Who? Where will who stay?"

"This soldier friend of yours."

Berenice looked over her reading glasses at him. He was
on the floor, his head on a small pillow, eyes closed, hands clasped
on his chest. "The guest room is empty," she said.

"But Edward's coming." Frank's friend Edward Ciepalek
had just written that he was soon to make his usual pilgrimage
up from Chicago.

"That's next week. The other one, he won't come till later."

Frank sighed. Only half the fieldwork was done. Almost
a month of it left; and then, without a break, he would have to
start haying, followed by cutting oats, threshing, digging potatoes. There would be no real rest now until, well, Thanksgiving.
And then the firewood to be cut. Already he was worn out.
Maybe she was right. Another hand could make things a whole
lot easier. He was feeling his age, feeling older than he really
was.

"And how long will he be staying?"

Frank and his wife had been slipping apart, these past
months. It had to do with this thing about Mary and Joe, and
now the stranger from Texas. The whole family could sense it,
but it was especially apparent to Mary. With few other models
to judge what marriage meant, she wondered sometimes if that
was what she really wanted for Joe and her. Could she marry Joe
and still love him?

Maybe, she sometimes thought — especially when she'd
seen a bull, big enough to break the poor cow's back, mount and
thrust himself into her — maybe it's better to marry someone
you don't love.

Berenice realized that Frank was trying to corner her. "Who
knows?" she shrugged, setting the newspaper aside. "We'll have
to see."

"To ask a guest into the house," Frank said, sitting up and
rubbing his aching muscles, "is to ask God into the house." It
was an old proverb. "Could you ask God to leave?" he asked,
standing up.

Berenice had no reply. She let him stand and walk out of the house, his question unanswered.

✳✳✳

A heat wave came upon them, in the next days. The temperature soared into the eighties. A wild flurry of activity followed, planting late potatoes, plowing, disking, hoeing the garden and the berries. On Wednesday it got even warmer, up into the nineties. Frank was out plowing for corn. The horses needed frequent rests. So did he. Their bodies just weren't accustomed to the heat.

The children were running around barefoot already, as they would all summer long. Mosquitoes breeding in the puddles hatched quickly in the heat and kept everyone inside after dark. A few made their way through the screens and buzzed around the beds all night. It was as though they would have to forgo spring and jump instead straight into summer.

On Friday morning Frank drove Anna and Sophie into Mosinee where they were to take their matriculation exams. Of the entire family only Stash and Mary had completed elementary school. Mary even had three years of high school, would have finished but for the move from Necedah. She insisted on staying, for her final year, with her godparents in Mauston, as she had done the previous years. But her mother would not have her so far away, and demanded instead she stay with the Klebas — at that time little more than strangers — in Stevens Point. Mary was too shy for strangers, so she never finished her last year.

Lotti and Angie hated school, and both quit in their fifth year. Walter, too, had quit to help with chores, and Bruno. But Frank had high hopes for the youngest girls. Though Sophie was a year older than Anna, she had already tried the exams once and failed. Now she went again, feeling at the bottom of her heart that she would fail once more. But Anna, who liked school, and talked of becoming a teacher, beamed confidently on the way into town.

Frank shopped around a while, stopped at the bank, sat in the park in the shade, until it was time to drive back to the high school — brand new that year — to pick the girls up. He parked and waited, smoked a cigar he'd bought uptown. Out of the doors they streamed, their futures just left behind. Seeing Anna and her sister run down the walk toward him, he could already guess how each had done.

21

It is a beautiful thing to know that the
wealthiest among us have often felt to have
remained voluntarily poor would have been a
higher state for them. That you cannot serve
God and Mammon is an economic truth of the
highest value. We have to make our choice.
　　　　　— Mahatma Gandhi, in a speech
　　　　　　　at Allahabad, 1916

For seven summers now Edward Ciepalek had visited his friend on the farm. But this year was special. He was not coming alone. Edward Ciepalek was married in September. The Topolskis wondered what Angela was like. They were sure of only one thing, which in letters to them Edward told and retold, and then told again. She was young, and she was beautiful.

Now they had only to wait a matter of hours to see for themselves. After a weekend at Lake Geneva, Edward and Angela were driving up to arrive before supper.

Their visit had meant a complete housecleaning, and this only a month after the traditional spring cleaning. The girls had spent several days scrubbing, sweeping, dusting, laundering, and now were putting the final touches on the house. It was always exciting to get company; but especially so for this big, jolly man who never failed to bring each of them a special present.

In the early morning light Frank had taken the team across the road to work the last few acres to be plowed for corn. If the weather held, by week's end he would have it planted. Then remained only the soybeans and he could begin cultivating the potatoes. With plowing and planting nearly behind him, he was in a good mood, sharing with the girls a simple excitement over Edward's arrival.

The team pulled smoothly through the dark clay, the plow neatly turning the sod onto the near furrow. It was a delicious morning. As Frank turned on the headland, he stopped a moment for a breath. Across the road he caught a glimpse of his cows headed out to pasture. White Star led them, the others strung along in single file, and Bruno sulking along at the rear. As they followed the path down into the marsh, one by one they disappeared over the slope. Frank was glad to see them out of the barn — it meant less work, when work was one thing there was already too much of. Fed by the fresh green grass, the cows had produced buckets of creamy rich milk as they hadn't since last summer.

Stash pulled out of the driveway on his way to the sawmill for the morning. After lunch he would drive down to Rybarczyks to help with the farm work. The garage, all finished, was something to show off to Edward. But Stash had to go out — it was as though, after spending nearly three weeks at home working on the garage, he had lost time to make up.

Anna and Sophie walked down the road toward school, waving to their father as they passed. Frank was sure Anna had passed her exams, and was proud of that. Yet underneath he had a strong current of distrust for public schools. In Prussian Poland, where he'd grown up, the schools were German schools, effectively used by the Germans to force their culture and language onto the Poles. So his father had taught him that schooling was to be avoided. And here, in America, education was secular. The teacher was as likely to be a Norwegian Lutheran as a Catholic. Who could say what heresies she might teach the unsuspecting children. So in Frank there arose that conflict again, between the old and the new.

Eddie was having his own problems with education that morning, though his conflict was somewhat less theoretical. It was for him just too exciting a day to waste at school. Feigning a sore throat, he'd managed to finagle from his mother permission to stay home. But he could not restrain himself, as ordered, to staying in bed. When he slipped downstairs in the middle of the morning and began, as was his habit, to get in everyone's way, his mother led him outside to the garden where she handed him a dibble and three flats of cabbage plants, already too big for the cold frame.

Lotti and Angie were given the most important chore: to air out and clean and dust the guest bedroom. After breakfast their father took a minute to peek in at them and caution them to do an especially good job. Then as he pulled his boots on at the back door, he spoke to his wife. "The old days are gone," he said, with a little smile. She looked at him, uncomprehending. "The bedroom," he said, "has replaced the barn." Then he was out the door and could be seen striding eagerly across the yard toward the team and the rest of the day's work.

Berenice had Mary helping her in the kitchen. A big batch of dough was rising behind the cook stove. Supper was all planned out. The day before Stash had butchered three chickens. These would be fried and served with leftover Easter ham — a favorite with Edward. And from the chicken backs and necks would come a kettle of soup, floating with big, chewy egg dumplings. *Kapusta,* potatoes, canned beans, and applesauce would finish off the menu. It would be a Sunday dinner, served on a Monday.

First working in the garden, then cooking, then supervising the girls used up every moment of Berenice's time. A year before — how long ago it seemed now — she'd turned over to Rose the task of supervising the girls. But now Rose was gone, and Mary didn't have the heart for the job. So once again it was the mother's chore. She seemed that morning especially irritable; they did their work to perfection and simply tried to stay out of her way.

So the morning went, and lunchtime had come and gone. Instead of taking his usual break, Frank headed right out to the field. And even Berenice passed up her afternoon nap, choosing instead to give the house a good looking-over. In the dining room she found an unironed doily and dust on a picture frame. She could find no fault with either the living room or the guest room. She told the girls it was time to change into their Sunday best, then went into the kitchen and slid the bread and rolls into the oven.

She checked on Eddie's progress in the garden. In two hours he'd planted a total of eleven young cabbages. The rest of his time was spent in throwing rocks at the bobolinks who'd set up housekeeping in the nearby pasture. Shaking her head and mildly rebuking him, she told him to get in the house to clean up and change.

Getting all dressed up in the middle of the afternoon made the day seem like a holiday. To the girls the extra work was now paying off. They fluttered about their room, slipping into their best dresses and stockings. Lotti, pulling on a shoe, turned to tease Angie. "We should go over to Steven's," she said, "all dressed up on a Monday afternoon!"

Angie, who'd begun to show some interest in the youngest Wolniak boy, rather liked the idea. Carefully arranging a ribbon in her hair, she answered her sister smartly. "It's no sin," she said, admiring herself in the mirror.

And now Lotti turned to Mary, who was lacing her high boots. "And Joe ought to see you!" But Mary only blushed.

Bright ribbons in their hair, shoes shined to a high gloss, dresses straightened and smoothed, the girls hurried downstairs and stood in line by the dining room table like a trio of servants obediently awaiting their orders. Just then Sophie and Anna burst in from school, panting from the run up the hill. And at last, as the girls stood nervously fidgeting, Eddie came down the stairs, buttoning his shirt, his hair uncombed, shoes in hand. But with his best navy blue, store-bought suit, for which the girls were deeply jealous, he looked, all in all, the real Lord Fauntleroy.

Wiping her hands on her apron, Berenice stood before them. She smoothed Eddie's hair as he bent to tie his shoes. "You two go upstairs and change," she said to Anna and Sophie. The two girls hurried for the stairs. Berenice grabbed Anna by the arm. "Anna, I expect you to keep Edward's wife company. Her name is Angela. Pani Ciepalek, to you. And if she speaks to you in English, answer in English. That goes for all of you." Anna, though the youngest, had been given the job of entertaining Edward's wife because her English was best, because she'd read the most, and because her manners were, all in all, the most refined. "Understand?" her mother asked. Anna nodded. "Well, go on then."

"There's to be no arguing tonight," Berenice said to the remaining girls. Sweat was still pearled on her forehead from the heat of the kitchen. "Mary and Stash will eat with us. Lotti and Angie, you help serve. The others, in the kitchen. But quietly, you hear?" She stopped a moment, wiped her face with a dish towel. "Mary," she asked, "did you give the outhouse a good cleaning?"

Mary nodded.

"Extra ashes?"

Another nod.

"Before they arrive, I want you to put a good handful of mint in one corner, and bruise the leaves. Eddie can bring us a nice bunch of cowslips to set inside the door. But mind you, take your shoes off and keep your pants clean, young man." Eddie nodded obediently. The girls admired their mother at times such as these; there seemed not to be a single detail that she would forget. "As soon as Anna's changed, she can take a jar of cold water out to your father. But we don't have a moment to waste. They could be here at any time."

So they scattered. Eddie ran for the marsh behind the barn, Mary to the garden to pick the mint, the other girls busily setting the supper table, as nervous as if it was their wedding day. As they worked, they listened anxiously for the sound of a car pulling in the drive.

Anna was just coming back from the field when the big Buick, its top down in the warm sun, pulled into the yard, a ton and a half of shiny, black steel and chrome. Edward gave the horn three long loud toots, which sent chickens flying in chaos out of his path. Mary, on her way into the house, quickly disappeared. For an instant, as he stopped the car, setting the hand brake and shutting the motor off, it appeared to Edward he'd stopped at a deserted farm. But then, suddenly, from out of the house they came, all in line, led nervously by the timid but obedient Mary.

Edward sat in the car, admiring the spectacle. Berenice, at the end of the parade, lined them up by the back steps, fussing and whispering under her breath. "Where's Eddie?" she asked. They all shrugged.

Edward Ciepalek got down from the car. He paused a moment to throw his driving goggles onto the back seat, then hurried around to open the door for his wife. Arm in arm they came toward the girls.

On a crowded street in bustling Chicago, Edward Ciepalek and his wife would have been a striking couple, to which eyes would enviously turn. But here, in a common farmyard, with its dirt and mud and rusting machinery, they were absolutely, undeniably, breathtaking. Standing tall and massive as a pine tree, Edward seemed to the girls to be a miraculous materialization from their dreams of a prince from a far-off fairy-tale kingdom. Dressed immaculately in white shirt and black tie, his dark pants pushed inside elegant high boots, sporting a jaunty straw hat, which he whisked off his head, he hurried straight toward their mother.

And his new wife, this Angela of his was a vision to behold. Granted the choice, each of the Topolski girls, from oldest to youngest, would probably at that moment have given up their souls to trade places with her. Almost twenty years younger than her husband — exactly Mary's age, in fact — Angela seemed to have stepped right off the cover of a movie magazine. She wore perfectly a silken, silver, day dress, straight-lined, above the

ankle revealing sheer stockings. Her shoes were of finely cut
alligator. Her hair was bobbed and mostly tucked beneath a tiny
robin's egg blue pillbox hat. But it was her face which caught
their eyes, in spite of all this finery: a perfect childish vamp's
face, the fine almost insolent mouth, the blue eyes behind their
long lashes, the cheeks lightly rouged. There was something in
her which meant to intimidate the world: especially this world,
this homely, rural world.

At last Edward broke away from his wife and wrapped
Berenice in a warm, prolonged hug. *"Jak sie mas, matka?"* he said,
his voice full of emotion. He called her mother, because his own
mother had died, back in the old country.

"Dobrze, dobrze," Berenice answered. "And you?"

He held Berenice at arm's length. "How do you manage it,
dear *matka*? Every year I see you, you seem two years younger!"
Berenice looked away, embarrassed. Now his face grew serious.
"I'm sorry," he said, "about not coming to Rose's funeral. You
know how much I thought of her." Berenice looked down.
"Well!" Edward said with a full, confident voice. "I want you to
meet my Angel!"

Angela stepped forward, cautiously, held out one perfect,
soft hand. Berenice reached out, enveloped it between her own
dark, aged hands. The two women looked in each other's eyes
a moment, while the girls in line witnessed the sudden transformation of their mother, whom they thought they knew as part
of themselves, into a wrinkled, frumpy old woman, beside the
gloriously beaming stranger. For Lotti the contrast was too
much: she looked away, stared at the shiny black Buick, its
radiator popping as it cooled, on its shiny fenders a fine layer of
dust.

Berenice greeted the young Angela. "Welcome," she said,
"welcome to our house."

Angela smiled. Edward beamed. Taking his wife in his
right arm and Berenice in the other, he planted on each a kiss
on the cheek. Suddenly, as though it had been conjured out of
nothing, he saw the new garage, bright red with its white trim,
and like a child discovering a Christmas tree, broke away and
hurried toward it. "A new garage!" he said. "You didn't tell me,"
he was saying when he realized, to his own surprise, that he was
walking right past the line of girls. He stopped. The garage, as
suddenly as it had caught his attention, was now forgotten.

"What do we have here?" he said happily. "A general inspection? Am I to be Kosciusko inspecting his troops?" The girls blushed and backed away, like a row of corn bending in a sudden wind. Edward stepped to the head of the line, where Mary stood nervously holding Lotti's hand. He looked her in the eye, could almost feel her trembling from shyness. "Mary!" he said, simply, warmly, kissing her forehead. Then he turned to pinch Lotti on the cheek. He held Angie's hand, squeezed it affectionately, clicking his tongue; ruffled Sophie's hair and bent to place yet another kiss on Anna's head. He turned to their mother. "Berenice," he said, winking at the girls, "these flowers of yours grow bigger — and prettier — every year. Why, if I weren't already a married man..."

Angela, standing beside Berenice, as though her husband's naive enthusiasm had embarrassed her, looked away to the small figure of Frank walking slowly behind the plow far across the road. Berenice had the unmistakable impression, just then, that Angela did not understand her husband. And suddenly she thought: she's not Polish! Edward's married a girl who isn't Polish!

Little Eddie, just then, came scurrying out from behind the barn and ran straight across the yard to hand his mother a big bouquet of yellow blossoms and then retreated, awkwardly, behind her skirt.

"Eddie!" his mother scolded, tugging him out into view. "What have you done?" His brightly shined shoes were covered with black, oozing mud, his best pants wet all along the cuffs and spattered with mud and water.

Edward bent down. "Come here," he said to the boy. "I won't hurt you." Eddie moved cautiously forward, prodded by his mother. The big man scooped him up and twirled him around, laughing and tickling the boy into a fit of giggles. And when he set Eddie down, the boy dizzily but shyly smiled back.

"You get in the house and clean up," his mother scolded, "before you catch cold."

Eddie turned, and with one last furtive glance at their guest, ran onto the porch. Berenice held the flowers he'd picked at such cost. There was a moment of awkward silence. Behind them, the screen door slammed shut. Berenice stepped toward Angela and offered her the big yellow bouquet.

"I... Why, thank you," Angela answered. It was the first she'd spoken; her voice was a fine, unaccented English. She held the flowers rather hesitantly, out away from herself. And as a sunflower might pale in comparison to the sun itself, suddenly next to the bright bouquet in her hand, she seemed terribly pale. Awkwardly she watched a tiny gold and black sweat bee crawl slowly out of one of the yellow blossoms; watched it, holding the flowers at a safe distance, until it had launched itself away into the brilliant air.

"We can put them in a vase?" Berenice asked, speaking in English.

"Please." Angela's voice was thin and quiet. She handed the flowers to Berenice, who turned to pass them on to Sophie, reminding her to put them in the guest room.

Sophie ran inside with the flowers.

"Well, you must be very tired," Berenice remarked, "from the long trip, no? Come inside where you can rest and feel at home." She guided her guests onto the back steps, and on into the house, the bevy of girls following behind. In the dining room Angie and Lotti were directed, above Edward's sincere objections, to bring the bags in from the car. Eddie, changed into different socks and shoes, followed his sisters out and stood in the driveway admiring the big, powerful roadster.

Edward was in his glory. First he vociferously admired the new tablecloth which Berenice had recently finished embroidering. Then he noticed the new clock on the mantel, which Frank had bought the family for Christmas, and went on to compliment each of the girls, one at a time, on their beautiful dresses. And of course he had to point out how clean and tidy everything looked. He was the center of attention, like a whirlwind drawing everything into his eye and throwing it back out again. And all the while poor Angela, out of her element, stood forlornly in the shelter of a corner.

In the living room Edward pulled back the delicate lace curtain covering the big bay window. "Frank's plowing?" he asked Berenice. "I'll go out and say hello." He was talking a mile a minute.

"He'll be in in a few minutes," Berenice said. She sniffed the air. "Jesus Marya!" she cried. "The bread!"

She rushed into the kitchen just in time to avert a disaster. While she was knocking the loaves out of their pans, Angie and Lotti came in with the luggage. Edward took it in hand, placing a rather large box on the kitchen table, winking meaningfully. Mary showed him and Angela where they would be sleeping. Edward set the bags on the floor. The three of them stood for a moment, in front of the big double bed. And suddenly there was nothing any of them could say — even Edward was caught wordless. Mary backed quietly out, leaving the guests alone.

The kitchen was a beehive of activity. Frank would be in from the field soon. A moment later Edward appeared, combing back his hair, and announced that while Angela took a little nap, he would go for a walk outside. "You don't mind, do you?" he asked, sniffing the steaming fresh bread. But they were far too busy to mind. He stepped out onto the back porch, stood a moment breathing deeply the fresh country air.

In the yard, Eddie still stood admiring the big Buick. The boy had actually gotten up the nerve to walk up to the car and run his hand down its warm, smooth fender. "Get in!" Edward told him. The boy turned, embarrassed. "Well, go ahead. Get in!" Eddie climbed in over the door, on the driver's side. "Would you like to drive it?" Edward asked, leaning on the opposite door.

Eddie put his hands on the steering wheel. It seemed so big.

"We can take her out for a spin in the morning and maybe you can handle the wheel a bit, okay?" Eddie beamed incredulously. "That is, if your pa gives us any time away from all the work."

Eddie turned the wheel from side to side, pretending to drive at reckless speeds down curving country roads. Their guest, meanwhile, strolled nonchalantly into the milk house. The air inside was cool and damp. As he'd expected, he found all the utensils, the milk pails and cans, spotlessly clean and in their proper place.

He passed into the barn and peered up into the silo, which was empty of silage. From its top came the gentle coo of pigeons, which he tried to imitate, but only managed in the process to cause a sudden flutter of wings as the birds poured out into the open air. He turned around again and surveyed the barn. The mangers were clean, the gutters empty, the calves in their pens well-fed. He was drawn to White Star's calf, Blotcheo, who'd poked her head through the stall and was curiously eyeing him. He gave the calf his thumb to suck. Her tongue was rough, her mouth wet and warm. She jerked her head back, again and again. He pulled his thumb free, wiping it on his pants, only then realizing that these were not his work pants.

As he crossed the aisle he glanced out through one of the

flyspecked windows and caught sight of the herd just then plodding its way back home. He recognized White Star, and Blackie and Short-Tail. And there at the rear came Bruno, with Shep. Edward walked through the barn and out the west door, past where the chickens were kept. He paused to look in the nests, but someone had already gathered the eggs. Once outside the barn, he carefully maneuvered around cowpies and mudholes and rounded the corner just as Bruno sat down on a low wall. The boy was lazily watching the cows, tapping the wall on which he sat with a long hickory stick.

Edward sneaked up behind and wrapped the boy in a hearty bear-hug. "Gotcha!" he shouted. Bruno pretended to be surprised. Edward sat down next to him on the wall, his right leg dangling loosely down, the shoe cocked away at a strange angle. Bruno tried to imagine what it was like walking on a wooden leg.

Shep came up and sniffed Edward, not quite sure if he recognized the smell or not. Edward coaxed the dog nearer and patted his head. A small flock of swallows, twenty or twenty-five, were busy carrying mud up from the cowpath to their nests under the eaves. The air was filled with their busy twittering.

"Look how hard they work," Edward observed. "From dawn to dusk. Like your father. You know," he turned to the boy, "my mother used to say that the swallows know where to find a plant that can bring the dead back to life." Bruno squinted at him. "You don't believe it?" The boy shrugged. They watched the graceful birds flying back and forth, back and forth. After a moment Edward spoke, quietly, as though to himself. "I do."

The sun was behind the *dompki,* and here on the north side of the barn the air was chilly. A dragonfly, one of the year's first, rose from a little puddle in the grass and like a sharp blue needle darted to the wall alongside Edward. Its wings twitched nervously as it and the humans regarded one another; then, when it zoomed away toward the marsh they kept it in sight as long as they could.

"Aren't you going in for supper?" Edward asked.

"Is pa home?" Bruno asked. He didn't like company. He had hoped to hide out behind the barn until everyone else was done eating.

"He'll be in soon." Edward slid down off the wall, his shoes making a wet noise in the dirt. He brushed his pants off in back, but felt where two small wet circles had formed. "Don't you want to meet my Angel?" he asked, ruffling the boy's hair.

Bruno shrugged.

"You just wait," Edward teased. "In a year or two you'll be running after the girls." Bruno looked back at him as though he thought the idea was absurd. "Well, come on anyway," Edward said, pulling the boy by one arm.

Having left the team in Eddie's care, Frank was already in the house. Stash, too, had returned and was cleaning up with his father. As Edward came in, Frank was splashing his face clean with water. Grabbing a towel, he dried himself, then took Edward's hand in his own. The two men looked in each other's eyes. There was a deep friendship between them, a kind of intuitive understanding. Frank had worked for Edward's uncle Antek, almost thirty years before. It was during the panic of '93 when work was so hard to find that he'd hired Frank on as a groom. Antek had stood up for their wedding a year later. But when Frank decided to try his hand at farming, and had to quit his job, Edward's uncle had confessed he'd never seen anyone so good with animals: it almost looked, for a while, like the old man would cry.

And now Edward had the business, wholesaling coal for most of north Chicago. Frank remembered how as a boy Edward would hang around the stables, asking a thousand and one questions about the horses, some of which even Frank couldn't answer. Next to his uncle, Edward loved Frank most. Now that Uncle Antek was dead, Frank was his closest link to that generation.

"Come on," Frank said, an arm around his friend, "let's go eat. Or have you given that up?"

"Me?" Edward laughed. "As likely for the devil to give up tempting us."

The two men walked into the dining room. The table was already loaded down with platters of food. Frank showed Edward where to sit. But their guest stood looking around.

"Where's the Angel?" he asked, anxious to show his wife off.

Berenice nodded toward the bedroom. Edward disappeared a moment, then reappeared, leading Angela out by the hand. Frank stood up to be introduced, smiled and nodded to her lightly, but was too frightened by her good looks to get any closer.

They all sat down to eat. Frank said the grace. Edward ate

as heartily as they'd hoped: three big helpings of chicken and more than his share of ham and potatoes. He managed, too, to get his foot caught in his mouth when he suggested that this was the first time since last year that he'd had a chance to taste real home cooking.

Berenice spoke over her spoon, in Polish. "But Angela must be a fine cook," she said.

Angela, suddenly realizing they were talking of her, looked curiously to her husband. Edward took her hand and squeezed it affectionately. "Yes, of course she is," he said.

But Berenice was not convinced. A painted doll in a queen's costume wasn't likely to be found standing over a hot stove. The girl's hands were too smooth and clear, her nails too long for that. Berenice doubted she even knew how to sew. And it didn't help her opinion of Edward's wife when Angie came by to take the plates away and on Angela's dish was still half a drumstick and a big serving of uneaten *kapusta*.

Edward sipped his coffee, bit deeply into his third *ponchki*. "Well, young man," he addressed Stash, wiping his lips with his napkin, "are you still courting that Rybarczyk girl? Josie, wasn't it?"

"Helen," his mother answered for him.

"You'll invite us to the wedding? And you, Mary, I seem to recall a certain tall and handsome farmer stopping by last summer. We wouldn't be having two June weddings, would we?"

But Mary only looked down at her plate. Berenice called out for more coffee. Edward sensed he'd touched on the wrong subject; patting his stomach, he found something else to talk about. "It's a good thing I only come once a year," he confessed, putting his hand over his cup as Angie paused to fill it. He slid his chair back and with a slight groan stood. "If you don't mind, I'm going to change into my work clothes. If they still fit, that is," he said with a wink to Berenice.

Guests were not normally allowed to help with the chores. But an exception was made for Edward, for whom a stay at the farm was a chance to assure himself he hadn't lost his touch with the old ways. All winter long he looked forward to these few days, bending under the warm, soft cows, filling the bucket with rapid squirts from the dripping teats. He was, as he loved to confess to his city friends, a farmer at heart.

Out in the barn he sent Lotti packing. "You're too pretty for the barn," he teased, commandeering her stool. "This is work for ugly old toads like me. And your father." He whistled and sang short snatches of old folk songs while he milked. Mary and Angie couldn't help but giggle over his antics.

Berenice and the other girls were still busy with the dishes. Watching a kettle warm with rinse water, Berenice remembered Edward's last visit, the year before. He'd shown an honest interest in Rose then; had taken her to a movie and bought her a new hat. To Berenice, he was a wealthy man. On the basis of those few innocent days, she had built high hopes for her oldest — and prettiest — girl. It was these hopes, unknown to anyone else, which had set her against the Derkowski boy.

Yet Edward had married, last fall, without consulting her. And this even before Rose had died. Well, she thought, that was water over the dam, which could not be put back in.

Anna was sent into the living room to keep Angela happy. Desperately she tried to think of something worth talking about. But her nervousness was like a gag through which she could not speak. Their guest, meanwhile, had placed herself in their father's favorite chair and lit by the golden glow of the setting sun, sat like a tintype of herself, oblivious to the world. Only now and then did her hand move, to turn the page of a magazine.

But at last Anna's anxious stares touched her, and she set the magazine aside, with her long nails teasing a single hair from an eyelash. "Have you ever been to Chicago?" she asked, sincerely trying to be friendly.

The girl, thankful for something to talk about, answered rather abruptly. "Yes. Two years ago. For my grandmother's funeral."

A look slipped over Angela's face as for a moment she wasn't sure if the right thing would be to express sympathy, or maintain a sophisticated reserve. She overcame the indecision, out of habit, with a cool detachment. Now her hand twirled slowly a curl at the side of her head. "Did you like it? I mean, Chicago?"

The question caught Anna off guard. She'd never considered Chicago as something one liked or didn't like. She had quite simply been overwhelmed by it. But she thought a moment and answered, rather tentatively, that yes, she thought she liked it.

"Did you go to the movies? Edward and I go to the Congress." Angela turned the magazine she'd been leafing through to show Anna the cover. Some unnamed starlet smiled vampishly out, and to Anna the resemblance was startling. "Valentino's my favorite," Angela said, paging through the magazine until she'd found a picture of her idol as a gallant young sheik. "Ain't he something?" She handed the magazine to Anna, who took it gingerly, afraid at any moment that her mother might come in. Movie magazines were not allowed in the house. But she had to agree with Angela that Valentino really was something.

"No. I've never been to a movie," she said, handing the magazine back. "We stayed at Aunt Mary's. We call her Big Mary because Mary, that's my sister, is Little Mary."

Angela wasn't sure about all that. At such times the best thing to do was act bored. So she gave a petulant sigh. "Didn't you go anywhere else?" she asked, picking her little silver purse, which perfectly matched her dress, off the table and taking from it a cigarette. Anna watched in shock as Angela struck a match and lit it. Except in Madison, Anna had never before seen a woman smoke. After the shock, she began to think it was terribly brave, and rather liked Angela for it.

"Aunt Mary has a candy store. She let us pick out a different penny candy every day. They had lots and lots of different kinds. I liked the licorice best. One day Sophie and I went up on the porch, on the top floor, and looked out over the houses. We couldn't see the end of the city, in any direction!"

Angela blew a lazy puff of smoke, holding the cigarette beside her head most elegantly. "It's a big city," she said.

"I'd love to go to the movies," Anna confessed. "Rose, she's my sister who died last fall, she went with Edward..." But before she'd finished the sentence she realized she probably ought not to have said anything about that. "Joe, that's Mary's boyfriend, he took her to the Majestic once in Stevens Point. She said it was very nice." Anna didn't mention about the people kissing in the back that Mary had told her sisters about.

"Are Mary and Joe getting married?" Angela asked innocently.

Anna stared at her shoes. "Oh, I don't know."

"Do you have a boyfriend, Anna?"

"No. I'm too young."

"How old are you?"

"I'm thirteen. I'll be fourteen this fall."

"I had a boyfriend when I was your age," Angela said, somewhat nostalgically. It would take time for Anna to absorb that. "You know," Angela said, "you really haven't seen Chicago until you've been down to the Loop. State Street, Michigan Avenue, Marshall Fields. I just love Navy Pier and Lake Shore Drive. It's pretty grand. And to think it was all burned down in the fire of '71."

"Seventy-four," Anna corrected her. And suddenly the tenuous warmth which had been building between them dimmed, and Angela resumed her pose of easy boredom.

"But the real money, it's out East," she said. "Edward took me to Philly last month, when he was shopping for coal. Some day," she announced, "I'll walk down Fifth Avenue in the Easter Parade. Wouldn't that be swell?" She smoothed her magnificent dress down over her knees, with a certain dissatisfaction, as though it wasn't good enough for her. "Edward's promised me a plane ride. Maybe in Florida, next winter. I hate Chicago winters. I think they're absolutely unbearable."

Anna was enthralled. To think of riding in an airplane! As likely as eating watermelon for Christmas. Once, while they were picking potatoes, that was the first year they'd moved here, a noisy warplane had flown over the farm, quite low, shying the horses hitched to the digger. Their father had held onto the reins, shouting to calm Molly and Dewey, while the rest of them stopped their work to stand and stare up at the shrieking monster. When it disappeared over the horizon, headed, they guessed, for Wausau, they went back to their work, which seemed for the rest of the afternoon to have taken on a new and heavy insignificance.

✳✳✳

Milking was done, and the long May evening promised at least an hour more of twilight. Frank and his friend set off on a walk. Across the road, through the strawberries whose buds were swelling to open, and down the many rows of early potatoes, their soft green leaves, so large and coarse, just pushing up through the soil, ready in a few days for the first cultivating. Soon they were striking across the new plowing. Frank adjusted himself to his friend — whose pace was hindered by the rough furrows — by bending to pick a rock here and there which the plow had turned up. He cradled the stones in his arms as they walked toward the stone fence which marked the south boundary of the field. Edward too found a stone, then another, and at the big pile the men clanked them onto the others. Soon they were bent over, cleaning that end of the field of rocks.

Frank stopped and stood a moment, silently watching Edward. "Say," he said, "you didn't come all this way to pick rock, did you?"

Edward dropped his load and turned. "Why not?" he smiled. "Maybe we'll find some coal."

He put his arm around Frank, then the two men set off together, following along the edge of the dead furrow. As they walked they flushed several bobolinks who fluttered away over the fence, introducing themselves by name as they went. And lower down, in the marsh, the plaintive notes of a solitary veery were already putting that corner of the world to sleep.

"It looks real good, Frank," Edward said, his voice just touched with envy.

"It's a load off my back, having it paid for," Frank admitted. "Only now there's too much work. I'm getting old, my friend. Every year it gets harder."

"Nonsense."

They crossed the road and were into the east hay field, where the new planting of alfalfa was coming up thick and green, scattered with brilliant dandelion blossoms. Bees, busy bringing in the day's last loads, hummed happily around them.

"And I don't get much help from the boys," Frank confessed. "Stash is over to Rybarczyks when he's not at the sawmill... Well, he did build the garage. Walter's in Milwaukee. We won't get him back. Bruno's not made for the work, and Eddie's too young."

They were walking straight north now, down a slight slope, toward the marsh on that side. Edward paused to pull a young shoot of timothy from its sheath and stick the fresh juicy stem between his teeth.

"I'm sorry about Rose," he said quietly.

"It took Berenice real hard. They weren't getting along at the time," Frank admitted. "Rose had a boyfriend."

"Oh?"

"Only Berenice didn't approve of it. God knows why. So Rose went away for a while, to visit Berenice's sister in Chicago. It was there she caught the flu; they brought her home in a box." They walked more slowly now, in a brooding silence. "And now with Mary..."

"Berenice doesn't like the farmer friend?"

Frank shrugged. "No. I think she's plotting a match with some soldier from Texas."

"You mean a stranger?"

"Yeah. I guess."

Edward shook his head. "Women!"

"One thing for sure," Frank said, "I couldn't get along without the girls." They stopped abruptly as Frank pointed off to their right, at the edge of the woods, where a yearling doe, its rust-colored coat silken in the low sun, was nibbling the young alfalfa. Seeing the men it turned — though not in a hurry — and bounded into the woods, where it hid among the young poplar leaves shimmering silver in the light breeze.

It was a perfect spring evening. The air was heavy with the smell of the earth and fresh grass; filled almost to overflowing with a kind of delicious serenity. The two men stopped again, at the north edge of the hay field, where the cowpath headed across the marsh into Ganther's pasture. Behind the barn, they could see the cows, settling in for the night. Only now, near the edge of the marsh, a few mosquitoes found the men and buzzed sluggishly around their heads and necks.

"You know I've got work for you anytime," Edward remarked, his voice soft, as though in a church, the air was so quiet and holy.

Frank turned to look at his friend. "How many teams do you still have?" Edward looked down. "That's what I thought. I'm too old to learn mechanics. I'll leave that to my boys." Frank held up his right hand. "Anyway, I can't hardly read, I can't hardly speak English, and look at these hands. They're too big, too clumsy to hold a pencil or wrench all day. No, I'll stick it out." He paused, surveyed the marsh to the north. "Thanks anyway," he said, reaching out to put his hand on Edward's shoulder.

Then, as though an unspoken signal had passed between them, they were walking silently back toward the house. In the gathering darkness, the birds had stopped singing, and the air had grown a little chilly. Walking next to Frank, Edward realized for the first time the profound loneliness which, like the soil beneath the fresh grass, was hidden just under the surface. And he knew the incredible work, from daylight to dusk, that farming meant, and how uncertain were the returns. So now instead of envy he felt toward his friend a deep admiration — and, surprisingly, a poignant sympathy.

The lamps were already glowing when they came in the house. Edward hurried into the living room where his young wife sat alone, quietly scanning her magazine. He bent and kissed her forehead, then sat down across from her. Now, in her presence, he returned to English.

"The farm looks great!" he said; like a child, he was one moment serene and contemplative, the next bubbling over with enthusiasm. "It's so nice out here, my Angel, we ought to find a little piece along the river and build a cottage. Somewhere nearby so we can visit our wonderful friends. I'll spend my weekends cutting wood for the fireplace while you putter in the garden."

But Angela simply looked up from her reading, her face set in exasperation. "Edward. What would I do in a garden? I don't know lettuce from... well, from anything."

"But you can learn! It's wonderful, I tell you. The fresh air, the smell of the earth, the good food." He leaned back and patted his stomach. Frank, who'd gone into the bedroom to change out of his barn clothes, appeared. "You don't know how lucky you are, Frank. This is what life's about, I tell you. None of that selling yourself to the devil. God, sometimes how I hate Chicago. I tell you, I have half a mind to trade you, even up, my business for your farm..."

Angela, startled, almost dropped her magazine, as though Edward might be speaking seriously.

Frank stood beside his friend. "We can go into town to-morrow and draw up the papers," he said, smiling.

"Well, I only meant..."

Lotti walked into the room with another lamp, and set it by the bay window.

"My God!" Edward said, jumping up. "I almost forgot!" He hurried into the guest room and brought out a large box, which he placed on the dining room table. As he opened it, he bellowed out everyone's name, one by one, and they came around him from every direction, to surround him and accept their gifts. For each of the girls there was a long silk ribbon: yellow for Lotti, Sophie's a pale blue, Mary's purple, Angie's white, and for Anna a beautiful deep rose. "Put them on, put them on," he insisted, then stood back and like Paris tried to judge the prettiest. Berenice insisted they each give him a kiss. Once again he was in his glory.

For the boys there were double-bladed pocketknives, with real horn handles; though for Stash he'd gotten a beautifully balanced 20-ounce claw hammer. Berenice was presented with dress kid gloves, elegantly black. And Frank, shaking his head, held his present up: a velvet-lined jewel box cradling a shiny gold watch chain.

"Edward!" he said, as though scolding his friend. It must have cost ten dollars. But Edward was smiling from ear to ear. And for the family itself there were three brand new records. Polish records. And a shiny stainless teakettle for the kitchen.

Lotti hurried into the living room and dropped one of the records onto the Victrola. The house came alive with a lively polka. Angela, who'd sat quietly through all this, set her magazine down and listened. Even she was becoming infected with her husband's enthusiasm. Until, that is, he tried to pull her out of her chair to dance. She refused; refused again. So he turned and grabbed Lotti, nearest to him, and whirled her around the floor. Though he was an excellent dancer, the poor girl didn't have the slightest idea what she was supposed to do. They traversed the living room, whirling and laughing, while their audience clapped hands to the music. At last it stopped, and the couple stood, panting and smiling.

Sophie lifted the record to turn it over, but Angela stood at that moment, and stretching her arms wide, yawned. Edward went to her. "Tired?" he asked.

She straightened her dress, picked up her purse. "I'll go to bed," she said, then stood still, waiting for a response.

But he only pecked her on the cheek and gave her a little hug. "Go on. I'll stay a bit."

Looking somewhat displeased, Angela disappeared into her room. A moment later she reappeared, to whisper in Edward's ear. He found a lamp and followed her out to the outhouse, where he stood in the darkness until she was done, then escorted her back to the house. By then Frank was sitting at the dining table, the last of the homemade whiskey in front of him. The children were all upstairs; Berenice was just visible in the living room, sitting and embroidering.

Edward sat next to his friend, accepted a glass of liquor. "Na zdrawia!" the two men toasted, clanking their glasses. They sat and talked. Frank told his friend about the Union. But Edward had little use for "Bolsheviks and Anarchists," as he called them. He reminded Frank that only a week before, two policemen had been killed in labor riots in Chicago. And as for LaFollette, of whom Frank spoke rather glowingly, Edward labelled the little Senator "That Damned Socialist!"

And though their views on politics were so far apart, they never let it come between their friendship. They turned, instead, to the old country, a favorite topic for both. When they spoke of Poland, it was with a certain reverence — in the same way they spoke of the Church.

"We've each left two mothers behind," Edward said. "The mothers who gave us birth and the country on whose soil we first set foot." They drank to Poland, which as they soon remarked, needed all the support it could get. Poland had returned as an independent nation, for the first time in more than a century. But inflation was rampant, the government changed hands every year, and the question on every Pole's mind was whether or not they could prove themselves worthy of self-government.

Frank let himself be drawn out in the company of his friend. As though this one time of the year he allowed himself to say the things he only thought about all the other months.

Time flew past. The clock above them struck the half-hour, then the hour. Eleven o'clock. Berenice was already in bed. And though Frank wanted to stay up longer, he'd been working since five in the morning, had allowed himself no rest until after chores, and now with the liquor inside him, had to fight to stay awake. So they emptied their glasses and set them on the table.

Edward was the first to rise. "Good night, my friend," he said, pushing his chair back in its place. "We've work to do in the morning." He stood a moment, Frank sitting there clutching his glass, as though he were trying to keep the past from crashing into the future, on his face a look of weariness and futility.

Edward's hand came to rest on his friend's shoulder; then he slipped into the kitchen and outside. It was a calm, beautiful night, clear and cool. When he came back in, Frank had already gone to bed.

The house was quiet, unnaturally quiet to one used to the city. His footsteps seemed strangely loud as he passed through the house on his way to his room.

Frank, not quite asleep, could just hear what Edward and Angela were saying. First there was Angela's voice, heavy with sleep, then overlain with astonishment. Then Edward, soothing her. A moment of silence, the rustle of sheets, and the bed creaking. Angela's voice again, louder. "Edward!" she said.

Frank heard the guest room door open.

"Edward!" she said again.

"Shh! You'll wake them up," Edward admonished her.

The door clicked shut, and Frank strained to hear. All was silent for a moment. Then Edward's steps padding through the darkness, the uneven gait of his wooden leg a little out of time. The back door opened, then shut, and all was quiet.

Frank turned in his bed, the faintest tired smile growing on his lips. "He's going out to the barn!" he whispered to Berenice, who was asleep and didn't hear him.

✳✳✳

High over the barn's tall roof hung a quarter moon, giving a faint ivory sheen to that part of the otherwise ebony sky, from which the stars sparkled like old friends gathered for a wedding. Edward walked slowly up the ramp leading to the mow, in no particular hurry. The corn liquor warmed him from within, fueled his innate sentimentality. He pushed back the big doors, stepped inside, and turned around. Beyond the darkened house lay the road, and past it the fields which faded away into a quiet obscurity.

Just inside the mow he found a big armful of straw, which he laid by the doorway. He sat down. A single mosquito found him; he let it sink its sting into his cheek, then crushed it. His nose, accustomed to the bite of truck exhaust and coal dust, opened to search and find in the air the old familiar smells: the hay in the mow behind him, the cows below and their manure, the sharp smell of the sheep who'd huddled along the barn's stone wall and were quietly talking to one another in a language he'd not yet forgotten.

Edward unfastened his leg, lay it carefully beside him, and rubbed the stump below his knee where it itched. He lay back in the straw, his hands behind his head. From far to the south, over the new plowing and the early potatoes, the stone fence and the marsh, came the distant hoot of an owl. Far as it was, it made him shiver. He closed his eyes. The stars went out. He said a silent Our Father.

Edward Ciepalek came to this farm in Wisconsin once each year as a kind of pilgrimage to the ancient and sacred ruins of his past. Here, in the quiet, he could forget the office, his desk with its blasted ledger books full of interminable debits and credits, forget the irate customers — always right, always right — and the petty, self-centered salesmen on whose greed the

business depended. Instead of all that, which by the way was a
game he played very well, here he could go back to the days
when he was a young man. A youth, just only becoming a man,
just discovering himself and the world, which was for him no
more than a few square miles of some of Creation's most breathtaking handiwork, the north slopes of the Galician Tatras.

Eyes closed, half asleep, he would let himself drift far from
the here and now, and once again be alone in a shepherd's hut,
the sheep baying complacently on the steep stony meadow; a
young man alone with the stars and the wind and the night,
leaning over his campfire, staring into the flames and seeing
there God's face, and the face of death. Remembering all that,
his strength would come back to him and his faith in God and
himself would refresh him like air to a man drowning in the
murky depths of some foreign sea — and he could survive another year.

He would remember, too, those reckless nights in the village, the fine young men in their long sukmanas and white felt
trousers, all his friends, he could remember them by name —
Antek and Karol, Stash, Janek, Tomas — the peacock feathers
sprouting insolently from their hats. The noise, the shouting,
the vodka and dancing! The squealing goatskin pipes and the
squawking fiddles; and the wide-skirted women, rainbows of
ribbons flying through a Krakowiak. Live! they used to shout.
Live today and forget tomorrow!

All this would come back to him, find him somehow from
far across the world, here, just inside the door of the mow, just
once each year. And then, lastly, just before he fell asleep, his
mother would bend over him, running her gentle hand across his
hair, and his father, straight and tall and long-moustached, poor
as hell but proud as the devil. And Jashu would be there, too,
his little brother, who'd taken over the farm. And the two brothers would embrace and throw back each a glassful of vodka.

"*Pskiakrew!*" they'd say. "What men we were!"

But it was only allowed of him once a year, here on the
farm, alone in the barn. As though those ghosts from the rustic
past would have nothing to do with busy, broad-shouldered
Chicago.

And so tonight he would sleep in the barn.

Married, or not.

***

And, as usual, he slept well into the morning. Until, that

is, a hungry sheep wandered up the ramp and into the opened doors and started poking at his foot, searching with its nose through the straw. Startled awake, Edward shooed the animal away and rolled over to sleep again. But now there were two, then three of them. And they would not go away, wanted to walk right over him into the mow with its delicious hay.

Exasperated, he picked up and threw his leg at them, and they ran, bleating noisily, out the door and down the slope, the wooden leg bouncing after. He laughed at them and what they must have thought. Sitting up, he rubbed his eyes. The sun was high in the sky. And the air, fresh and clean, was full of birdsong. Below, in the barn, he could hear voices.

"Anna!" he shouted. "Anna!"

After a few moments, the girl appeared bashfully at the bottom of the ramp. She looked up at him warily.

"Oh come here," he said, brushing the straw out of his hair. "I won't bite you, girl."

She started slowly up the ramp.

"Wait! Bring my leg!" he shouted.

She stopped.

"My leg. Bring it here," he said, sitting helplessly in the straw.

Sure enough, there in the weeds lay his leg. Anna bent and lifted it, shivering just to touch its wood and leather. It seemed somehow an unholy mockery of a thing. Holding it far away from her, she carried it up to Edward.

"Thank you, thank you," he said, fastening the leg into place. "Now I suppose you're wondering how it got there in the first place?" The girl kept her distance, staring silently. "Well I'll tell you anyway. It was those blasted sheep!" The animals had moved to the edge of the *dompki*, were innocently cropping grass along the drive. "They were pestering me, so I threw it at them."

He looked up at the girl with such a childishly silly grin that she giggled. He reached out and took her into his arms for a big hug. "Thatta girl," he said. Then he stood up and stretched, walked slowly to the doorway. Straw was stuck here and there on his pants. "What a night I've had!" he said, peering out into the morning light, which made his eyes squint. "I was back home, in the old country, looking after my flock. And my mother and father and Jashu, they all came to see me." He turned to the girl. "You think I'm crazy, don't you? Well, I'm not." He looked outside again. "At least, I don't think so."

He stepped out onto the ramp. "Well, is milking done already?"

"No," Anna answered. "Almost."

"You better get down and finish up. We don't want your father getting mad at us, do we?"

"Father's plowing," Anna answered.

Edward peered to the south, over the house. There he saw his friend, patiently following the team through the field, the plow slowly but surely turning the soil. Edward clicked his tongue and shook his head. As Anna walked past him, he put his arm around the girl's shoulder and leaned lightly on her as they went down the ramp. "Is Angela up?" he asked.

"No," Anna answered, turning at the bottom of the ramp to go in the barn. "And mother told us we must be very quiet so as not to waken her."

Edward laughed. "And that you must! And that you must! Waking a young bride, that's a privilege that belongs to the husband, isn't it?" Anna smiled, then disappeared into the barn.

A flock of chickens and four white ducks followed Edward toward the house, as though expecting feed from him. He turned and swung his empty hand toward them, clicking his tongue. They hurried around him. "Silly birds," he said, opening his hand. "I don't have anything for you."

As he strode into the kitchen, heavy with the smell of bacon and coffee, he hugged Berenice from behind and warned her that he was so hungry she'd better go out and butcher another pig.

Then, as quietly as he could, he entered the dimness of their bedroom. On the bed, Angela was still asleep, her back to him. The covers had fallen off her, lay partly on the floor. Under her soft chemise he could see the gentle curves of her figure. And whether it was the country air, the time away from his work, or the influence of his night's dreams, he wasn't sure, but suddenly he felt a great rush of tenderness overtake him for this young woman, only so recently a stranger, who allowed him now to share her bed. And suddenly he knew how much, how very much, he really loved her.

He bent to straighten the covers, carefully covering Angela, still asleep. Then he went round to the other side of the bed, and sat on its edge, where her soft hair brushed lightly against the pillow. He kissed her lightly on the temple, then the cheek.

But still she slept. He bent lower and kissed her lips. She woke with a start, her eyes jerking open with fear. His hand on her shoulder, he reassured her. Recognizing him, she relaxed, turned away, buried her head in the soft feather pillow.

Edward stood and threw back the curtains, flooding the room in strong morning light. Angela blinked, covered her eyes with her forearm.

"Well my sleeping beauty, my little Angel," he said, standing above her, "did you sleep well? I slept like a bull."

Her mouth was dry, her lips stuck together. "I'm not surprised," she said, clearing her throat. "Bulls do sleep in barns."

He bent and kissed the back of her neck. "Oh, but aren't we clever?"

"I hardly slept an hour," she complained.

"But why?"

She grunted lightly, edged away from him as he knelt beside her.

"I should have stayed with you, I know," he confessed, running his hand along the curve of her waist and the rise of her hip.

She spoke away from him, to the other side of the room, giving him only her back. "I was afraid, after you left."

"You silly goose. A house full of friends and you're afraid."

"It was so quiet, quiet as a coffin." Now she turned onto her back and looked up at him. Her eyes, pleading, reflected her fear. "And so dark. Pitch dark." She glanced toward the door, spoke more quietly. "And sometimes I could hear them in their room. Snoring. Terribly, like... like monsters of some kind."

Edward laughed.

But she looked up at him sharply. "It's not funny!"

"I'm sorry," he said.

"And then, in the middle of the night, I heard something scratching at the window, like it was trying to get in. I was so scared I didn't know what to do. I just stuck my head under the pillow and prayed. Any moment I was expecting... something... to reach out and touch me."

Edward stood up and went to the window, pulled the curtain farther back. "Look," he said, pointing. "It's just a lilac branch that the wind blew against the glass. And such a pretty thing, too." Its first few blossoms were already open, steeples of deep blue in the holy light.

"I'm not spending another night in this house," Angela

said, turning onto her side.

"Dear, dear Angel," he said, running his hand down her hair. "I'll stay with you, tonight."

"Not here."

"Then you can come out to the barn with me," he offered, putting his hand under the covers. But she moved away.

"Can't we go back to the lake?" she asked, using all her feminine appeal. "It was so nice there, in the hotel."

Edward turned to look out the window. A little mother wren, cascading whole paragraphs into one feverish phrase, glided onto the lawn. "What would they say? They expect us to stay two or three days. What will they think?"

Angela kicked the covers back onto the floor. "I don't care what they think," she said. "They ain't nothing but... but country rubes, anyway. And they smell!"

Edward turned as though she had slapped his face. "Don't you dare talk about my friends like that!" Angela cringed. She'd never seen him so angry before.

She reached a hand up toward him. "Oh, Edward, I'm sorry."

But he backed away from her, looking at her as though she were a perfect stranger. "You forget," he said, "it's what I was, in the old country. A smelly old rube."

"I said I'm sorry. Oh Edward, let's not argue about it. If you must stay here another night, at least take me to town so I can stay in a hotel." She had risen on her elbow, revealing the curve of her breast. She was thinking as fast as she could. "They're kind of cute, really. Oh Edward, I'm just not used to the country." She looked up at him, her eyes and perfect lips beseeching him. "Couldn't I stay in a hotel?"

"There's no hotel in Dancy," he said, coldly.

"No, no. That bigger town."

"Stevens Point?" Angela nodded. "You want to stay by yourself in Stevens Point?"

She glanced up at him seductively. "Oh, I think I could find some company," she teased.

"I'm sure you could!" Edward strode past her to the door.

"Edward! I was only joking!"

"Get up and get dressed!" he said. "I'm going to have some breakfast." He turned to her, forcing the words out. "A country rube breakfast, if you don't mind."

Angela raised herself on the bed. But he whirled around

and slammed the door shut.

Morosely wolfing down his breakfast, Edward was for some reason unknown to Berenice in a bad mood. As he finished his coffee, he found the courage to explain that since Angela wasn't feeling well, they'd have to be leaving as soon as possible. He apologized.

Berenice tried to brush the whole thing aside; but it hurt her, really.

Edward was ashamed. He hurried out the door and into the field where Frank was still plowing. Frank unhitched the team and followed his friend back to the house. As much as he viewed company — even Edward's — as an interruption of his work schedule, he was profoundly disappointed.

Angela picked at a little breakfast, gathered up her things, and let Bruno carry them out to the car. Now she was polite, almost repentantly effusive. Edward cranked the Buick, let it idle a bit. While Frank and Berenice stood by, he kissed the girls who'd come out to see him off. Then, while shaking Frank's hand, he tried to press into it a ten dollar bill. But the money was firmly refused.

"*Dzienkuje*," Edward said, embracing his friend. He turned and once again hugged Berenice, then climbed in behind the wheel. "See you next year," he announced, pulling his goggles on. But they all knew that a cycle had been broken, that the past was now buried — and they all wondered, to themselves, if they would ever see each other again.

Frank slammed the car door for his friend. "You're welcome here any time," he said. "And you, Angela." He nodded to the woman in the other seat, who thanked him and nodded back.

"Good-bye then!" Edward shouted, revving the car up. Little Eddie stood watching with great disappointment — now he would never get to drive the massive Buick. Edward let out the clutch and wheeled the big car around the yard and out the drive, waving to the children as he went past. As the car turned onto the road he shifted into high, and they could all see that Angela, so beautiful and nicely dressed, was once again happy. And she looked so fine, going down the road in the big black touring car, her hair blowing in the breeze, that even Berenice couldn't help but admire her.

Only Bruno insisted on the last word. Jerking his head in the direction of the receding car, he ran his foot through the gravel. "What a *panusha*," he said.

His mother was shocked at his disrespect, for Bruno was calling Angela a fussy, demanding woman. She put a finger to her lips to shush him, but then broke into laughter with the rest of the family.

22

E dward had come, Edward had gone. Frank knew the time would some day arrive. There was no one to blame. It would just take getting used to — not having his visit to look forward to each year. It would just take getting used to.

But in the breaking of that ritual a thin thread — though only time could tell how vital a thread — snapped inside Frank Topolski. If having friends and celebrating their companionship was a way to grow into life, then something like this was just advancing the book one page closer to its final chapter. A thread snapped, and inside Frank reacted to it. Usually so easygoing, he became instead tight-lipped and surly, ready to take out his frustration on team or family. He controlled it, for the most part. But underneath he was suffering; underneath it smoldered, that ultimate sense of futility.

Mary still awaited her letter from Joe. Twice she'd written, to no avail. She was hanging up laundry one morning when the mailman's Ford sputtered up the hill. She dropped the bag of clothespins and ran to meet him. But all he had was the latest newspaper and some tragic gossip. Coming home on the Soo Line the night before, after a ball game at Stevens Point, one of the Walkowski lads — Tom, the oldest — had jumped off the train at Junction City and been run over.

Mary knew the boy — he was only a year or two older than she.

"They say he'd been drinking," George added, shaking his head. "Musta been. Almost cut him in half." Mary's hand was on her mouth. "Well I guess I gotta be going. Gonna be a beautiful day, that's for sure."

As she walked back to the house, without the letter she'd hoped to find, she carried instead the dreadful weight of the young man's death. And she realized, suddenly, that this was a tragedy wrapped inside a tragedy. In July of last year John Klips had lost three of his boys who, with a Peltzer lad — Mary knew them all — had drowned in the Big Eau Pleine. All four were in their late teens or early twenties. It had been terrible; was carried in all the state newspapers. So John Klips, broken-hearted, sold his farm in the fall to Ed Walkowski. And now Ed's boy was dead. It was almost unbelievable — as though some malign destiny hovered over that farm.

She repeated to her mother what George had said. As she spoke, she was on the verge of tears. But her mother, darning socks at the kitchen table, only muttered something about the wages of drinking. Mary went out to finish hanging clothes; but in the warmth of the morning sun she found herself shivering.

***

As school got out Eddie's mother and father stopped to pick the boy up so he could ride to town with them. Sophie and Anna, meanwhile, walked cheerfully up the hill, elated by the wonderful spring weather. Quickly they changed clothes then ran outside to enjoy a few minutes of freedom until their parents came home. Anna found Eddie's bike leaning against the granary. The girls weren't allowed to ride bikes — just as they weren't allowed to swim, or dance, or even whistle. But last summer Anna had stolen away once or twice on Eddie's old two-wheeler. It was great fun, balancing yourself, moving along so swiftly.

She could go for a little ride and no one would ever know. She swung a leg onto the bike and pushed away, out the drive. The seat bounced as she tottered around the biggest ruts in the dirt. Turning onto the road, she almost tipped over. But now she pedaled hard, picked up speed on the gravel. When the road turned to blacktop she was really going. At the top of the long hill toward town she had to decide: should she coast down it, or stop and go back? It seemed a shame to waste the speed she'd already picked up. So she started down the hill, with each passing foot going faster and faster. She felt free, like a bird in the air, the steady click of the bike's chain telling her just how fast she really was going. The trees and bushes seemed to blur past. A wrong move now and she would tumble down the road at twenty miles an hour; she might not walk away from such an accident. It was dangerous, it was exciting, it was all those things her life had not enough of.

Clutching the handlebars she sped past the school. But here where the road leveled her long glide was already beginning to slow. Almost to town, she put her foot down to steady herself, then turned the bike around and faced the long hill back home. Her heart was still racing. In town, just beyond the tracks, she could hear Altenburg's one cylinder Chore-Boy: putt, putt, putt, putt, putt, click! Otherwise the afternoon was absolutely silent.

There wasn't time to rest. She had to have the bike back home before her mother returned. So she pushed herself away, pedaling faster and faster to get speed up before the hill. Only halfway up, she already had to stand to get enough power. It was hard work. But she was testing herself, had promised herself not to get off and walk the bike.

She was within twenty yards of the top, breathing hard, her legs sore and almost turned to rubber, when the car came up from behind. As she turned to look, the bike nearly tipped over into the ditch. Staring out at her was Eddie's face, and her mother's. The car went on ahead, turned into the driveway. For an instant she thought of turning around and racing away downhill. The bike came to a standstill. She knew what she faced at home — but there was no where else to go.

By the time she'd leaned the bike where she'd found it and timidly approached the house, her mother was already on the back porch with the *pida*, gripping its handle imperiously, the long leather thongs, knotted at the end, ready to snap righteously at her legs.

She didn't cry out. The sting was bad; she could bear that. But worse was the sight of Eddie gloating in the kitchen. And knowing that her father, still in his own bad mood, would not that evening console her.

✳✳✳

With the next morning's mail came affirmation that Anna had, indeed, passed her exams and so could go on to high school in the fall. Another day it would have made her jubilant, and the sincere congratulations of her sisters might have meant more. But her legs still stung; and her father, behind the barn with Alex Stelmach, was still too irritable to give her the hug and kiss she'd hoped she would get. So instead of reveling in her own glory, she turned instead to consoling Sophie, who would not be returning to school.

Alex had come to look at an extra harrow that Frank had picked up last fall in exchange for some animal doctoring. The two men were leaning on the fence, and as was the custom spending a good deal of time on other topics before getting down to business. Shep's barking, from out in the pasture, got Alex talking cow dogs.

"You remember the little white dog I had a few years back?" he asked, spitting into the grass. Frank wasn't sure. "Might've been before you got here. Smartest damned dog I've ever seen. Picked him up from some city folk over near Rozellville. Paid two dollars for him."

Frank stared at the harrow, let his body settle in for a long talk.

"I don't think that pup had so much as seen a cow before I brought him home. I took him with me that first evening out to get the herd. He followed real close, and when he got back to the barn, just sat and watched me take them in. Same thing for the next two days. I started to think I'd been took, that he was too dumb to herd cows. But the next day after that, when we started out for the cows he ran on ahead, all on his own, like he knew just what he was supposed to do. So I thought, we'll see, we'll see. I tell you, Frank, he rounded them up and brought them right back to the barn. I didn't have to say a word. Never had to train him a bit. He even took them inside. Just figured it all out on his own."

They could hear the roar of a tractor from down by the river. Somebody was out plowing with a Fordson; you could recognize it by the high-pitched whine of the gearbox. Frank didn't like it. If everybody had one, there'd be no peace and quiet left at all.

"Friendly dog, too," Alex went on. "Kids would climb all over him. He used to pull the gloves out of my back pocket, just playing like. I was working on something by the barn one afternoon and stuffed my gloves back there and he come up and swiped one. Well, I didn't pay any mind, I was too busy, and after a bit I headed back to the house. He was laying there under that big elm beside the porch, so I says to him, where'd you put my glove? Huh? Where'd you put it?"

Alex paused, and the image formed in his mind, the light afternoon haze, the dog's head on its paws, glancing up at him with those bright, playful eyes. "And I'll be damned," he went on, "if he didn't jump right up and run off to the granary and in a minute he was back with that glove in his mouth. Understood every word you said to him," Alex emphasized. "Just like a person. More than some."

"What ever became of him?" Frank asked.

Alex looked down, spit again: in the dirt, a circle of tobacco juice. "Had to shoot him."

Frank's eyebrows went up, then he looked away again.

"I liked that dog so much I thought I'd pamper him over
winter by letting him stay in the basement. It was just exactly
the wrong thing to do. In the dampness down there he picked
up some kind of disease, on his feet. Some kind of growth,
smelly grey stuff between his paws. By spring he had it so bad
he couldn't hardly walk. Just lay around, never complaining or
nothing, just looking like it was all his own fault and he was the
sorriest thing in the world for letting me down that way. But he
was getting kinda touchy from it, and the nephew's kids were
coming around in the summer. I was afraid maybe they'd catch
what he had, or maybe he'd snap at them. Lord, how I hated to
shoot that dog. And George and Joe, they were both younger,
they both cried about it."

There was a long moment of silence, through which Shep's
insistent barking arose once again. "I know one thing," Alex
said with finality, "I'll never see another dog like that one in my
life."

That was the way it was and always would be: you could
never tell what tomorrow would bring. All you could do was do
your best and at any moment be ready for the ground to break
open under your feet. They shared that, Alex and Frank, that
knowledge learned the hard way, firsthand. It put Frank in mind
of Mary and Joe. They'd looked forward together, he and Alex,
to binding the families together. And then along came Berenice.

Out of the quiet he asked how Joe was doing in the city.

"Don't know," Alex confessed. "Haven't heard from him
since Easter. Mary get any letters?"

"No," Frank said and shrugged. "Don't think so."

"Sure be nice to have him back on the farm," Alex remarked. "You know, Frank, if he could marry your daughter he'd
be home tomorrow."

"Yeah," Frank said quietly. "I know."

"It isn't that he's lazy or drinks too much..."

"No, of course not. Not Joe."

"Then why?"

"I don't know." Frank was looking out over the marsh to
the woods. The morning air was serenely indifferent. "It's got
something to do with Rose, I think."

"Rose? But I don't see..."

"I don't either," Frank interrupted. "But Rose went off to Chicago, to get away from her mother. Berenice figures, I guess, that if she'd been stricter she wouldn't have let her go. And if she wouldn't have gone, she'd be alive today. So I guess it's a mistake she doesn't mean to make a second time."

"She's still living in the old country," Alex said. "And Mary and Joe, they're the ones have to pay the price."

"That's right."

"That's it, then, Frank?"

Frank didn't move for a long time. It hardly looked like he was even breathing. "I don't know," he said at last. "I just don't know."

That seemed to be all there was to say about that. At last Alex sighed and stood away from the fence. "Well, I've got plenty of work to do," he said. "How much you want for it?"

Frank slipped his hands in his pockets. He figured he could get twelve dollars for the extra harrow if he advertised it in the paper. Less the quarter for the ad. But Alex was a friend. "How about eight dollars?" he asked.

"Now Frank," Alex scolded. "I don't want to steal it from you."

"I didn't give a penny for it," Frank replied.

"You worked for it. I'll give you ten."

"Eight's all I want."

Alex pushed a ten dollar bill into his friend's hand. "I'll bring the wagon over in the morning."

✳✳✳

When Frank came in the house he handed the ten dollars to Berenice. "I thought you said it was worth twelve or fifteen," she observed, sliding the money into her apron.

"Might be, in the paper," he answered, taking a long drink from the dipper.

"I thought you'd learned by now," Berenice said, "not to mix business with friends."

Frank went out to the barn to throw a little hay down. He was back to feeling bad again. But he had to admit he couldn't hold it against her. She was the one who had to look after the money. If the girls couldn't buy shoes or they all had to get along without sugar or coffee, that was Berenice's fault. He just did the work. That was the easy part. He didn't have to squeeze every last dime for all it was worth. And if she wasn't the way she was, but instead like some wives he knew who spent the money even before it came in, why they'd never have made it. Never.

✳✳✳

The next day Frank was at Chester Tomczak's, checking on a newborn calf, and Chester told him that Adam Laska's horse had been sick for days now. Adam had hardly even started on his plowing. From what Frank had seen of the animal two months before, he wasn't the least bit surprised.

"He should have let me know," Frank said. "I'd have gone down and had a look at it."

"Probably doesn't have any money and he's too proud to take charity," Chester observed somewhat bitterly.

"How you doing with the field work?" Frank asked, letting the calf go. It scurried into the pen and turned to eye them suspiciously.

"Just the beans left."

"Me too," Frank said. "What do you say we get over to Adam's tomorrow and do his plowing for him? If he doesn't get at it pretty soon, it'll be too late. Then he'll be in trouble for sure."

Chester didn't look very enthusiastic. As long as the weather held, he wanted to get his own crops in.

"Come on," Frank urged him. "If you run into any trouble, I'll come over and give you a hand."

"I can manage," Chester said.

"Well, then."

"Oh, all right."

So the next morning Frank hitched Molly and Dewey to the wagon and threw on a couple sacks of oats, a bag of carrots and a bucket of molasses and told Berenice not to expect him home til evening chores.

"Don't you have enough work to do around here?" she asked as he headed out the door.

It pained Frank just to look at Kurt. The poor animal's ribs stuck out like the teeth of a dump rake. Anybody could see what was wrong. The horse was starving to death. Last year's crop of oats had been the worst in many; and the potatoes hadn't been anything to brag about either. Adam had to use every penny he had just to keep himself and his family alive. Now that there was pasture, Kurt, as always, had been given the second-rate land, while the best was kept for the cows. Wiry old marsh grass would fill the animal's belly but did not go very far toward putting meat on his bones.

Frank carried a bucket of oats, fortified with molasses, and set it under Kurt's nose. Listlessly he chewed it. "Don't give him too much at first," Frank said, throwing a handful of carrots into the pen. "But don't worry, Adam, we'll have him up and around before haying time. Now, where do you keep your plow?"

"Well, it's behind the barn." Adam nodded toward it. "Why?"

Frank headed out to the plow. It wasn't very sharp. He wished he'd brought his own. But he got the team hitched to it — with Adam's help — and headed out to the field. Adam was just plain too thunderstruck to protest.

Chester pulled up with his own plow on the wagon. The men got his team hitched up and Chester and Frank went to work. By lunch they had almost two acres of the peaty black soil turned. Helen fixed a big meal for them, and cold barley water to drink. Frank held little Franchek on his lap, teased him till he cried and Helen had to take him back.

In the afternoon Adam spent some time with Frank's team while the older man rested. Walking over behind the barn, Frank found a big burdock plant which had been bent over, the top of it held to the ground with a stone. Frank shook his head and had to restrain himself from kicking the stone off the plant. It was an old country remedy Frank had almost forgotten. You bent a big plant over, telling it that you would let it free only when your animal was healthy again. Adam could have bent all the plants on his forty acres over, Frank thought, even the big hemlocks along the drive, and Kurt wouldn't get any better.

By the time, late in the afternoon, when Frank and Chester were hitching their teams to the wagons, sweaty and tired, they'd done five acres. Chester could finish up in the morning and Frank would stop by to do the disking.

Chester pulled down the drive, taking with him Adam's sincere thanks. Frank sat in his wagon. In the doorway of the house Helen stood, the children huddled behind her apron.

"We got her plowed," Frank said. "But you got any seed?"

Adam looked down at his worn and cracked boots. "I had to feed all the oats. Got a few potatoes left."

"I've got some oats and some corn," Frank said.

"Now Frank..."

"Will they give you credit down at the feed store?"

Adam shook his head, embarrassed.

Frank thought that this was a perfect opportunity to say a few words about how a cooperative would pull together at times like this, that a cooperative could extend a hand to those who needed it. But he kept his mouth shut. "Just don't worry," he said. "We'll scrape some up for you."

"Frank," Adam said, reaching out with his hand, "I don't know how to thank you."

"Then don't."

***

By Saturday afternoon Adam's fields were planted. Roman Gruba, who'd been contacted by Frank, had brought over three bushels of seed corn along with some oats. There was even a little of each left over. Only the potatoes needed putting in.

As Frank left, he saw the whole family standing in the yard, Helen and the children waving cheerfully. Adam put his arm around his wife's shoulder. Before Frank was all the way to the end of the drive, he saw his friend lift the sack of seed potatoes and carry it out to the field, to finish the last of the work.

***

Every morning the cows, after milking, were let out to pasture, and again in the evening. They spent most nights huddled behind the barn, lazily cropping the fresh grass, and were always standing waiting when morning milking came. But that next morning, Sunday morning, when Mary went out to let them in, they all came in but White Star. Mary tied the others in and looked around out back, but the big friendly guernsey with only half a brain and a big bell around her neck was nowhere to be seen.

Frank had the girls start milking while he and Stash set off in search of her. They could find no sign. He told Stash to head back into the brush behind the barn while he checked the rented pasture. Walking down the cowpath he was getting more and more worried. There was no explanation for her disappearance this time: no calf for her to run off and hide with.

She wasn't in the pasture. He stood a few moments, trying to think, worry getting the best of him. As a last resort he decided to head off into the woods, in the direction of where she'd had her calf. Maybe she'd forgotten, and gone off there to look for it.

He walked across the pasture to the heavy alder thicket. In the brush the mosquitoes were thick around him. But he pushed the alder back, walked in farther. There, in the mud, he saw her track. Then he knew where she would be.

But he was wrong.

She hadn't made it that far. Fifty feet short of the nest she'd fallen on her side. He hurried to her. She was alive, but her eyes stared up at him with a glazed kind of indifference. The way she was breathing so heavily, he knew she was in terrible pain.

He hurried back to the farm, brought his bag of medicines and Stash. But there was nothing they could do. Already in the five minutes he was gone she'd slipped closer to death. Frank knelt beside her, stroked her thick, heaving neck. He did not move for a long, long time. The mosquitoes filled themselves, one after another, on the back of his neck and hands. Stash stood by, swatting and fidgeting.

At last her body stiffened, she breathed a long, heavy breath, and she was dead. When his father stood up, Stash had to look away, the print of pain was so deep on his father's face.

They brought the team and dragged her out. The children came round to see. No one said a word. When Frank cut her open he found she'd been bleeding internally, probably since the calving. And now that he thought of it, he realized she'd not looked well these past days.

But who would have guessed?

And as she was dying she'd headed out to the nest — to find what?

***

That morning they were late for church. They rode all the way in a gloomy silence. Even the weather, which was beautiful, and the fact that the fieldwork was almost done, could not cheer them up. That evening during milking her empty stanchion stood accusing them of something they somehow felt responsible for. And each of them, on their own, went over to Blotches, in her pen, to soothe the calf who, though she didn't know it, was now an orphan.

Frank, though he realized it was blasphemous, thought to himself that if he governed the world, the way they said God did, White Star would still be alive. And the Walkowski lad. And Alex's best ever cow dog. And Edward's wife would have been someone else. And Mary and Joe, they'd be planning a wedding now.

But that was all nonsense. How could he run the world

when just taking care of himself, and those around him, seemed now too hard for him, much too hard?

That night, lying in bed, for the first time ever he wished, earnestly, reverently, for the peace of the grave.

23

The three days before Ascension were called Rogation Days. Each day there was a mass, in the evening, and a procession asking the Lord for his blessing on the crops. Frank, still brooding over the death of White Star, elected not to go. Instead he made his own processions around the fields, riding the cultivator back and forth between the rows of potatoes. For horse and rider this, compared to plowing, was easy work. Only to keep the cultivator knives in the ground Frank had to bear down on the pedals, and by the end of the day his legs were cramped. Stash would have to do his part.

But Stash, with Frank's approval, was busy starting the mash. They had decided that now with the warm weather was a good time to run some whiskey through the still. So the mash tub was set up in the granary. Stash malted a bushel of corn and half a bushel of barley, ground them, then he and the girls carried nearly fifty gallons of water to mix with the grain, to which they added some oatmeal and yeast. Now that the mash was set, it would be left to ferment till the end of the week.

✳✳✳

Frank, meanwhile, started the last of the plowing, just two acres for soybeans. Grey clouds blew in from the southeast, threatening rain. Stash used Prince on the cultivator. The perky little Morgan, though not accustomed to field work, seemed to like the variety it provided, and pulled the cultivator through the potatoes much more rapidly than would have Molly or Dewey. But Stash had to rest him. While doing so, he broke the mash cap and stirred the now-bubbling mash, then spent an hour or two gathering and cutting ash — which gave little smoke, hence little signal to the agents — to be used under the still.

The next day Stash was called to work at the sawmill. Frank was finishing up the potatoes. Berenice, after lunch, went to her room for a nap. The girls were in the kitchen, cleaning up, when they heard a clomping racket on the back porch and turned, frightened, just in time to see the screen door pull open.

Half expecting some kind of terrible monster, whom should they see sticking her head in through the open door but the beautiful bay Queen. Looking from side to side, she surveyed them comically, lowered her head to sniff the hardwood floor, then snorted lightly as though to reassure herself of her right to explore this foreign territory. Around her back there wheeled a dozen flies. When one settled, her skin would twitch and her tail bang up against the screen.

The girls, too astounded even to move, simply stood staring. But Lotti, seeing the flies and the open door, came at last to her senses. "Close the door!" she said to the horse. "What's the matter, were you born in the barn?"

They all giggled. Queen stared back at them. Then, as though understanding Lotti's request, she clomped right on into the kitchen. The door slammed shut behind her. She seemed so big in the room, so out of proportion to everything else. And now, inside, her smell which in the yard might have been pleasant, seemed almost overpowering.

On the table was a bowl of potatoes, left over from lunch. Queen, looking around, caught sight of the food and, carefully with her big, curled lips, picked one potato out of the bowl, chewed it, and swallowed. Oblivious to the complaints of the girls, she picked one potato up after another, until she'd cleaned the bowl completely. Her tongue chased the bowl around the table, threatening to push it off the edge. Angie grabbed it away from her. She looked, to the girls' surprise, somewhat insulted by their lack of hospitality.

But enough was enough. If their mother should wake up now, would they be in for it! So Lotti and Mary moved the table alongside the cream separator into the corner, giving Queen room enough to be turned around. Angie held her by the bridle and as gently as she could stepped her around to face the way she'd come, then out through the open door and one foot at a time down the porch steps. Somehow she'd come untethered. Angie made sure she was tied properly this time. Back in the kitchen the girls couldn't seem to settle down after this marvelous break in their daily routine.

***

The next day the mail brought a package from Walter, addressed to Anna and Sophie. When they came home from school, the girls eagerly tore it open. There was a new pair of slippers for each one, and for Anna, because she'd passed the exams, a pen and pencil set, a very nice powder blue. Anna, holding the pen, imagined herself as a teacher, and carried the set upstairs onto her dresser, promising herself not to use them until high school in the fall.

On Wednesday there were light showers. The potatoes were all cultivated. Only the bean field needed disking and harrowing. But because of the rain, that would have to wait. So Frank and Stash spent the afternoon setting the still up far back in the woods behind the barn. They hauled it as close as they could in the wagon — the big copper still, the barrel it set on, the heavy boiler plate, thump keg and coiled condenser. Here in the woods the mosquitoes were bad, but they wanted to be near enough to the creek so they could haul cool water for the condenser.

After evening chores Stash went to see Helen. He stayed late, driving home in the Ford after dark. It was near ten when he was coming up the hill and, looking off to his left over the potatoes, saw a movement out in the dark. A little nervous, just then, about nosy agents, he slowed the car to have a better look. There, above the stone pile which marked the edge of the property, he saw a diffuse, faint light, hovering in one spot, then moving a little this way and that. He stopped the car, stepped out onto the road. Was someone out there with a lantern? No. The light was more like a cloud. As he walked out into the field, it grew dim, as though afraid of him. At last it went out, and he was left to stand there in the dark.

When he came in the house his father was in his chair reading, his mother weaving her incessant needlework. Stash, all excited, told them about the light in the field, pulled back the curtain to show exactly where it had been. Berenice called it a will-o-the-wisp. She'd seen one in Necedah, and before that in the old country. Then she remembered Sophie Tomczak saying there was a rumor that an infant child — perhaps unwanted, perhaps unbaptized — had been buried somewhere in that stone pile. Berenice suggested it might have been the soul of the child hovering over its grave.

Frank had never seen a will-o'-the-wisp. But he told Stash that back in the old country it was claimed such lights were the soul of a surveyor returned to correct a mistake he'd made while surveying the land. Since the stone pile was supposedly the south boundary of the field, that explanation seemed to fit best. The men wondered to themselves if it meant they had more or less land than they thought.

Stash went quietly up to bed, but he couldn't sleep. It wasn't that he was frightened. He had, he knew, a kind of clairvoyance which he seemed to have gotten from his mother. His dream of Rose drowning, the night she died, was just one example. Such things happened. There was no reason to be afraid. But there was a mystery to it, that fascinated him. From his bed he could just see out the window across the road to where the stone pile lay in the darkness. Long into the night he stared, half asleep, over the field, half expecting the strange light to appear. It never did. At last, near dawn, he fell asleep.

✳✳✳

St. Augustine asked himself the question: "Who are the feet of the Lord?"

And he answered it himself: "The Apostles of the Church."

But he asked himself again: "Who are the feet of the Lord?"

All the Church's clergy, he replied, through whom He travels across the world. St. Francis Xavier, Missionary to the East, was one of the Lord's feet. And preacher of the Gospel, ordained minister of the Holy Sacraments, Father Nowak, too, celebrating Mass on Ascension Thursday, he was a foot of the Lord, carrying His message to the faithful gathered to hear.

The church was filled; but Father's sermon seemed diffuse, without focus, shifting this way and that. Somehow he seemed unable to concentrate, his mind on something he couldn't quite grasp, some theological dust devil which just as he approached the lectern whirled through his mind and left his sermon in utter disarray. It had something to do, this unsettled state of mind, with his ongoing concern for Mary Topolski. But there was much more to it than that. It was the opening scene of a long and powerful drama, which the priest, just entering middle age, would be playing for years to come.

In the end he found his way through the sermon, using the beacon lights of the liturgical cycle: the close of the Easter season, for Christ Who'd come among us now returned to the side of His Father. And would only reappear at the end of the world. So we wait, Father Nowak said, going about our daily business. And there was no sense in standing like an idiot to stare up at the sky from whence He would come. The hour and the day we did not know. Only we knew it would happen.

On the way home from church, Frank stopped at the mailbox. Mary stepped out of the car and opened the box. Inside she found two letters. With her back to the car, she turned them over. One was from Ohio. The other, in Joe's forthright but clumsy hand, she slipped quickly inside her coat pocket.

Back in the car she handed the letter from Ohio to her mother, her heart racing. But Berenice, seeing who the Ohio letter was from, put it into her own pocket, apparently having no clue there was another letter.

Frank changed into his barn clothes and went out to work. The girls were left to prepare lunch. Berenice sat alone in the living room reading the letter. It was short but courteous, confirming Walerych's arrival in early June. He was already out of the Army, staying with his brother in Cleveland. He was anxious, as he put it, "to meet the wonderful Topolskis."

Mary had slipped upstairs to open her own, infinitely more important correspondence. She fumbled with the envelope, tore it in her haste. She unfolded the single-page letter and her eyes rested on Joe's rough script, pressed onto the page with a soft, dull pencil. The letter, dated May 23, had been written only two days earlier.

My dear Mary, he wrote, *I sit in my little room thinking why am I here at all and so I had to write because I thought of you again like I always do when the sun goes down and I get lonely for ma and pa. You know it was the way your mother schemed against us, it was too much for me to stand by and take and I didn't want to hurt you so I had to go.*

A guy next to me this afternoon caught a log in the shin, I guess it broke the bones so he won't be back for a while. They say it happens like that pretty often. I don't tell you this to make you worry but just to show it's not all cream in your coffee here. I think sometimes I'm crazy and if the War was still on I'd join up.

The other guys they spend their pay on drink and talk all the time about women. They don't bother me though once I had to slug a smart-aleck mick who wouldn't leave me alone. What's the sense of working all week just to drink it up on Saturday night and wake up with a sore head to boot? I'm saving a little, but it isn't much.

I'm not much for writing, as you know pa had me out of school when I was big enough to give a hand around the farm. I don't blame him, he needed all the help he could get. Youse guys got plenty to learn right here, he used to say. But I want you to know I haven't forgot you and thanks for the letter and I wear the scapular day and night and hope you haven't forgot me too and pray for us like I do so maybe someday your ma will see it different and I suppose I haven't got a right to expect it but I thought we could be real happy together, you and me.

Mary's hand trembled, her eyes clouded. She found a handkerchief. She turned the paper over to the back side.

I been thinking about maybe I'd come home this weekend. There's a Union meeting isn't there and I don't want your pa to think I'm a slacker. I don't believe I have a better friend in all the world. And if I get there, I don't know yet, I'll stop by to see you if that's okay or like a fish out of water I won't last very long.
Mary, you take care of yourself.
Joe.

Slowly she folded the coarse paper and slipped it inside the torn envelope. She breathed in quickly several times, holding back the tears. Then she just sat, gripping the letter, overcome, staring at the pale blue wall with its flaking plaster and the rough pine chest of drawers with Anna's new pen and pencil set on top. And she felt utterly, terribly, alone.

But she thanked God for the letter. And that he was coming. And she thanked the Lord for letting her, and not her mother, get the mail today.

But then like a hawk which in soaring flight is suddenly struck by an unseen bullet, her heart fell. If only, she thought, she'd had strength enough to stand up against her mother, or to run away with him, they'd be together right now. She hated herself for that, for letting Joe down, for those other letters she wrote, for not being strong enough. Not strong enough to sin.

But if he loved her, if he really did, he wouldn't ask her to sin.

And he hadn't, either, so he really must love her.

For her, it was too much. Too much.

Below, her mother called out her name. She slipped the letter into her drawer of the chest, far to the back where she kept the picture of Joe and her which Stash had taken last summer: standing in front of the house, Joe's arm casually around her shoulder, her face timidly turned from the camera, as though even that much intimacy was too much. And there, under the picture, was the holy picture from Rose's funeral. She remembered then just how much Rose and Joe used to have fun, laughing and teasing, so that she even got jealous of Rose, God forgive her, because Rose was so much prettier. And at the funeral Joe, so strong, yet how he had even cried.

The drawer slid quietly shut. She wiped her eyes again, straightened her hair, then walked down the stairs, step by step in the dim stairway, her knees weak, her hand running along the plaster wall, just for something to touch, to bring her back. The voices below grew louder and louder, and with each step that brought her closer, she felt more remote, irrelevant, insignificant. So that when she stepped into the kitchen and mechanically picked up the paring knife and a potato, she was shocked to realize where she was — as though she'd just awakened from a momentary amnesia.

✷✷✷

The stars were fading, though many could still be named in the sky when Frank led Molly out from the barn and in the chill morning walked beside her, muttering low encouragements. He hitched her to the harrow, lifted the reins, and they began the slow, steady shuttle back and forth across the open land, like spiders weaving a web of time in which they meant to catch their own survival.

High cumulus clouds streamed away from some point a hundred miles beyond the western horizon. From the east a breeze picked up, as though running from the sun, just at that moment peeking, a rich gold, over the trees. The roosters were crowing in the barn, competing for prizes they'd most likely already won. The air was cool, and following beside the harrow, smelled of freshly turned earth and that indefinable vitality, that fullness of life, that rises from new-grown grass. Above the clank of the harrow and the harnesses Frank could hear the full chorus of blackbirds, robins, phoebes, bluebirds and a dozen other unnamed songsters who filled the morning with song.

There was plenty to be done. He hoped to have the field done by lunchtime. Then he would have to take Anna to town for the school picnic. So they worked the field from east to west, smoothing it and breaking up clods left by the disk. Then back, from west to east, and as they walked he spoke to Molly, short expressive phrases. "*Tja*, so," he would say as they turned up a rock, and have her stand and wait while he threw it on the pile or out into the ditch, then quietly complain to her that the rocks seemed to grow up like weeds and multiply just as rapidly.

When the sun was up from the horizon, far north now of due east, he muttered to her, "Well girl, look, the sun's come to see us again, to watch us work another day."

When she lifted her tail and fouled the whippletree, he chided her for dirtying it and not waiting till she was unhitched.

There was a resemblance between them, the cadence of their gait and the compact, efficient motion of their muscles. Seven long years now they'd worked together. Each considered the other a close friend. Each would rather share the other's company than just about anyone else they knew.

Frank's limbs loosened, the stiffness worked out of them like leather worked with oil. Now his feet rose and fell of their own, with no apparent effort. Only now and then when his boot would fall on an unbroken clod or into a hole left by the disk would he lose his pace. Otherwise they moved as fluently and rhythmically across the field as the very top of a pine might wave in a wind.

They had covered half the field already, when Frank pulled Molly to and unhitched her. He walked beside her, holding the bridle, to the yard. There he tethered her, bringing a bucket of fresh water to dip her nose into and slobber over the ground, and a short bucket of oats. Having served her, he went in to his own breakfast.

The kitchen was empty, but for Berenice. Eddie was still asleep — everyone else was out in the barn. Berenice was planted solidly in front of the stove, mixing dough for bread and *pierogi* for lunch. It was Friday, a meatless day. Working the long wooden spoon through the big bowl of dough, she uttered low unconscious grunts. There was a tension between them, man and wife, which they had over the years adjusted themselves to and hardly noticed, as Molly hardly noticed the pull of the bit in her mouth. Only sometimes, when they ran up against a hard spot, it would jerk, and then it would hurt.

Frank ate the oatmeal, kept lukewarm over the stove, smothered with milk and sugar, and drank two cups of his favorite chicory coffee. In a few days the beans would be planted. Then, until haying began there would be only cultivating. Things had gone well, very well. Only there was that thing about Mary and Joe. It nagged at him, like a sin he'd forgotten to confess.

He asked for more coffee. Berenice poured it silently, then turned again to her work. He wanted to bring up again the man from Texas. He felt ashamed of himself for not facing it. But there was the morning's work to do, and he didn't have the energy to waste on a quarrel. Maybe at lunch, he thought, when he could take more time.

Molly and he worked through the morning. The horse was easier to get along with than his wife. So he could relax here, forget everything but the work at hand. But the clear morning air had given way to broken clouds, and the air had an eerie unease to it, as though beyond the horizon storm clouds were brewing. It made Molly restless, whatever it was, so that when the sound of a Fordson started up, from far away, she twitched and jumped and for a moment Frank thought she might bolt. He pulled her to, stroked her head and reassured her. Just a tractor, he said. Just a tractor. But for the rest of the morning he had to keep a close rein on her, and her own restlessness translated in him into a mild indigestion.

At lunch the kitchen was hot and busy, the delicious smell of frying *pierogi* and *kapusta* rising from off the stove. He sat down in the dining room. Mary brought him a plateful of *pierogi* and the sweet-sour cabbage. Their eyes met. To Mary, he looked older than she'd ever seen him before. She knew how he suffered for her sake and somehow she wanted to make things even between them. But the chance never arose.

He ate, as he usually did at lunchtime, hurriedly, biting off big chunks of *pierogi* and drinking big swigs of milk. Berenice sat with him, picking at her own plate, sipping tea, while the girls worked in the kitchen.

Now Frank was too tired to start an argument about Mary. He would just finish his lunch and then drive Anna down to the picnic. Suddenly he stopped chewing, set down his fork. Berenice looked up at him to see him grasp his stomach, and grimace. He held onto the edge of the table, the pain gripping him from deep inside.

"What's wrong?" his wife asked.

He was breathing in short gasps now, still gripping his belly with one hand while the other held the table.

"You eat too fast," Berenice said, then went back to eating. But there was something compelling about the way he just sat there, staring forward. She knew how much pain he could stand without showing it.

She set her fork aside and stood up. "Why don't you lay down?" she suggested, and from the living room brought his favorite pillow, which she lay on the rug beside the table. She helped him to stand. As he tried to straighten himself, the pain tugged at him, pulled him over. He slid to the floor. There, knees drawn up, his head beside the pillow, he held his gut with both hands, moaning low. Abruptly he began to hiccup, each spasm tearing through the taut muscles of his abdomen like a knife cutting flesh.

Berenice slipped the pillow under his head and hurried into the kitchen. "Your father's swallowed too big a piece of *pierogi*," she said, anxiously searching through the cupboard. "Where's the stomach drops?" She seemed almost out of control. They hadn't seen her that way in many years.

Mary found the bottle on top of the cupboard. Her mother took it and a spoon and scurried off into the dining room. The girls stood in the doorway to watch their mother as she bent over their father. He lay on the floor as though hit in the belly with a bullet, convulsed with rapid hiccups, his face pale and tight with pain.

Berenice poured syrup into the spoon and led it to his mouth. But when she tipped it, half ran down the side of his chin, the other, which he swallowed, set him to coughing terribly. Now her face reflected his. She muttered sudden silent prayers.

The wave of fear and helplessness hit the girls. They stood there, staring, while the *kapusta* on the stove began to burn, and saw only that man on the floor, still moaning, and the woman leaning over him, hovering, futile to protect him from the pain, tenderly running her hand through his hair, her voice half fear, half soothing.

"What's the matter, Frank? What's the matter?"

But his eyes were closed, his lips tight as he fought the pain, his only movement those sudden spasms as he hiccuped again and again.

"Call Stash!" their mother demanded.

At first they wondered whom she was talking to. But at last Mary stepped forward, picked up the telephone, cranking its handle hastily. When the operator came on and asked the number, she stood a moment staring at the wall, its faded floral wallpaper so familiar and yet as though she'd never seen it before. Who was it she was trying to call?

Who? Stash!

Where was he? Where was he?

24

When Stash arrived he and Mary carried Frank, step by painful step, to his room and onto his bed. He lay quietly, then, his body adjusting itself to the pain. But still the corners of his eyes and lips were drawn up, his face strangely taut. The children left him to rest. Berenice closed the door. The room was quiet, warm in the spring afternoon. She unlaced his boots and pulled them off, unloosened his belt. Though she moved slowly, meticulously, at every touch of her hand along his stomach he winced with pain. Her lips moved through prayer after prayer as she stood above him. She lay her hand on his forehead. His eyes opened, thankfully. Now there was no one to turn to. It was up to her.

She covered Frank with a light blanket, then turned to leave. She pulled the door almost shut. The house was quiet. Their minds were not on their work, but on him. Words were superfluous, irreverent. All they could manage was to go about their chores — thank God for their chores — beating against the anxiety like moths against a windowpane.

Berenice told Stash to call the sawmill. He'd have to stay home to finish the field work. He made the call, then stopped in the kitchen for a drink of water, and quietly slipped outside. Expecting Frank, Molly shied at his approach. He calmed her, ran his hand down her long neck and over her side. But still she was on edge. He talked to her low. His voice, so like his father's, at last settled her down. He untethered her and led her across the yard out to the field where he bent and hitched the harrow.

Berenice, enlisting Mary's help, sat at the table skimming through their seldom-used copy of *The People's Medical Advisor*. But it only confused them. How could they know if it was acute indigestion, stomach neuralgia, liver trouble, or as Berenice secretly feared, appendicitis? The symptoms were so much alike. Nowhere in the book could they find mention of those strange hiccups, which still at frequent intervals racked his body.

Berenice left Mary to make sense out of the book and called the Bolloms. She prayed as she waited for them to answer. But no one was at home. So she tried the Tomczaks.

Sophie, detecting the fear in her neighbor's voice, became worried herself. No, Berenice answered, there was no fever. Yes, he was vomiting, and sometimes it was dark and awful-looking. The pain seemed all over his stomach, not in any one spot. Berenice at least was relieved when Sophie advised her that it didn't sound like appendicitis, something she herself had suffered not so many years before.

When Berenice hung up, she was left to wonder what was wrong with Frank. A doctor could say. But a doctor's visit was twenty-five dollars, perhaps more. Not that she begrudged Frank the money. Only her mind clung to the hope that it was nothing more than indigestion from eating too fast. If she was right, when Frank got better he would blame her for throwing money away on a doctor.

But at least she could talk to Doctor Hess. She called him on the phone, described as best she could the symptoms to the nurse, and then the doctor himself. He recommended getting Frank to the hospital immediately. Now she hung up, worse off than if she'd not called him at all. She decided she would have to ask Frank.

But Frank was resting now, his body only occasionally jerking with a hiccup. She thought it best not to wake him. So it was, for now at least, her decision. Doctors, of course, always wanted you to come to the hospital. That was how they made their money. And so many people died in hospitals, in spite of the doctors. It was as though just by taking him there, she would be making his condition worse than it really was.

Anna, of course, would not go to the school picnic to which she'd so looked forward. Instead she was sent out to relieve Bruno in the pasture. When the boy came in he asked quietly how his father was, drank some water, then went out to the barn to feed the calves and lay hay in the mangers. It seemed strange to him, working in the barn while his father lay in the house. And stranger still when Stash came in from the field, the harrowing finished, and stopped to help him.

Frank, in the coming hours, got no better or no worse. Still every so often a terrible vomiting, and still the hiccups, though less frequent and less severe. Mary sat with him while the others were out milking. She held his hand, kept a damp cloth on his forehead. He spoke a little, asking now and then for a sip of water, apologizing for keeping the girl from her work.

The family ate their supper in silence. The food was taste-less, had almost to be forced down. In the quiet evening hours Berenice tried first cold then hot compresses on Frank's stom-ach, but neither seemed to help. She urged onto him chamomile tea and more of the stomach drops. But he could keep nothing down. They went to bed in silence, all but the youngest lying in the darkness all night, with their eyes wide open, listening, hoping, praying.

When the morning came, it came with all the beauty of a spring morning, which seemed so out of place. The girls, weary from lack of sleep, went to their milking. Bruno and Stash cleaned the barn after milking. Anna followed the herd out to pasture. Stash filled the planter with soybeans and started plant-ing the field his father had been working on when taken ill.

In the granary the still-beer was going sour. At lunch Berenice told the girls to carry it in buckets to the pigs. Bucket after bucket they poured into the trough. It smelled strong, gave off a grainy, yeasty smell. The pigs loved it, slopped it up almost as quickly as it was brought to them. The foam from the yeast gave the animals moustaches and beards around their slobbering mouths. By the time the entire barrel had been carried to them, they were getting drunk, the five fat sows and the big boar, all teetering this way and that, lunging clumsily at one another, staggering as they stood, until at last their legs gave out and they lay down in the dirt and closed their eyes, sighing and grunting peacefully. It would have been hilarious, the way they acted. Only no one was laughing.

***

There was a Union meeting scheduled for that evening. Stash called Roman Gruba to tell him of Frank's illness. Roman said he'd call the Stelmachs to find out if Joe was home. Maybe they could have the meeting without Frank. But he called back in a few minutes to say that though Joe was at home everyone else was in the middle of field work and thought it would be best to wait till Frank got better.

Roman asked if there was anything he could do. He rec-ommended to Stash that they get Frank to the hospital.

That evening Roman, Chester, and Alex Stelmach stopped in, to see for themselves how their friend was. They stood at the end of his bed, hats in hand, nervously trying not to look wor-ried. Frank seemed to appreciate their visit, asked about their fieldwork, apologized over the Union meeting and thanked them as they left, telling them not to worry about him. But in the kitchen they stopped to urge Berenice to get him to a doctor. Roman offered to take him right then. But she said no, he seemed a little better.

It was a second long night, seemed to go on forever. When morning came Frank was the same, still deep in pain, unable to eat or drink. Only he smiled a little when Berenice opened the curtains and he could see out across the field to the big pine trees to the east; for a moment he thought he saw that glowing white star which had tugged him out of bed a few nights before. But it couldn't have been. The sun was already bright.

It was Sunday. Mary and Lotti were left behind to stay with him while the rest of the family went to Mass. It was strange, to the two girls, watching the others get dressed, combing their hair, shining their shoes. It was a new perspective on a Sunday morning — one they'd rather not have seen. Mary heard Alex telling her father that Joe was home. She had hoped, this morning at church, to at least see him. But that was selfish of her. Her father needed her now. When the family hurried out the door, and Stash drove them off in the Overland, the house seemed painfully quiet, painfully empty.

Lotti worked in the kitchen while Mary sat with her father. The minutes dragged on. Most of the time he was only half conscious, moaning and sighing in his sleep. She wished there was something she could do — anything. She prayed. That, at least, was something.

There was a knock on the door. Mary heard Lotti open the door and suddenly could hardly breathe as she recognized the voice. She stared at her father's pale, drawn face. She stood and looked at herself in the mirror, combed back her hair and straightened her dress. She had just turned toward the door when he appeared before her, like an apparition.

"Mary," he said, all dressed up, straw hat in hand. "How is he?" He was whispering, for the sake of Frank, at whom he stared in deep concern.

Her hands flitted around her pockets, then found a handkerchief to hold and twist. She turned to see her father, his dark hair matted on his head, his skin pale, his big hands joined on his chest, which rose and fell in even waves. "Sleeping," she whispered.

Joe stood a moment looking at him, and she could feel the life go out of him as he stared at her father. "Come out here," he said, backing half a step so Mary could pass him in the doorway.

She hesitated.

He reached out, held her by the arm. "Come on. We'll leave the door open."

She passed by him so close she could smell the soap he'd used that morning to shave with, a smell so familiar and so full of the conflict — the need to get closer, and the fear of getting closer — he always brought with him. They could hear Lotti, in the kitchen, now turning the separator.

Joe stood beside her. Both felt how trivial their own needs had suddenly become. Seeing the strength in Joe's eyes, the pain and worry so apparent there, Mary wanted to fall into his arms and let herself go. But instead she stood straight and stiff, futilely twisting and untwisting the worn-out handkerchief.

"I wanted to come last night," Joe said quietly, "with pa. But we had a cow with milk fever so I had to stay. I wanted to talk to your pa, to ask him what to do with the cow. You know..." He was going to say more, but it seemed unimportant. "Can I sit down?" Mary shrugged. He gestured toward the chair across from him, but she remained standing.

"I should be in church," he went on. He knew she was blaming him for coming when her mother was gone. "I'll go tonight, in Point, and pray for your father." Now his voice changed. "Listen, Mary, why don't we take him to the hospital right now? My father said..."

"But..."

"He's very sick, Mary. Too sick to be at home." She looked away, did not want to hear what her heart already knew.

"But mother..."

"To hell with..." But he stopped himself, held his anger within. Suddenly he stood and wrapped her in his arms. "I'm sorry," he said. She put her head on his shoulder, releasing in quick sobs the topmost part of the feeling she'd pent up inside. He held her close, one hand on the back of her head. He stroked her hair, gently.

There came a soft groan from the other room.

She broke away and hurried to her father. He was waking now. She bent above him, ran her hand through his hair, hurriedly wiping her own eyes dry. His body, strong as it was, seemed worn out from the two sleepless nights and the ever-present pain. He seemed to have lost the battle. His will was broken.

When his eyes fluttered open he turned to look at her, and smiled weakly. "Mary," he said, raising one hand a little. Then he caught sight of a movement in the doorway. His head turned.

"Joe's come to see you," Mary whispered.

Frank turned his head more. Joe stepped forward, took his friend's hand and held it tight. "Frank," the younger man said.

A spasm of pain shot through the prone man's body. He closed his eyes, let it pass. They stood like that a long moment, Joe trying with all the power he could gather to pass his own strength down through his hand and into his friend. But it was as though Frank cared no longer to trouble them. He was breathing deeply now, slipping back away, his breathing loud and steady. Mary slipped a chair to Joe. He sat down and she sat across the bed from him, each gently cradling one of Frank's hands.

Now he woke again, smiled lightly, seemed glad to see them there. Staring up at Joe, he saw himself, thirty years before: a young man with his wife, their future stretching out before them like a great unplowed field. Only now he had plowed that field and planted it, had gathered its harvest to him. His work was done.

Yet Joe and Mary's future, it was different. It was not their own, like his had been. Through all his pain came that guilt which these past weeks had nagged at him. He'd learned to milk, to tend the sheep, to care for the horses, when to cultivate or plow. But no one had ever told him how to deal with a woman like Berenice.

"I'm sorry Joe," he said, concentrating his strength.

"Shh!" Joe said. "It's okay."

"No," Frank replied. "It's not..." His body shook. Mary reached for the white porcelain pan. But he did not vomit, only coughed a little.

"You better rest," Joe said. "Frank," he asked, almost as an afterthought. "Can we take you to the hospital?"

"Yes," Frank said, not because he wanted to go or thought he needed to go, but because it would make them happier. But then a shadow passed over his eyes. "Maybe not. Maybe I'll get better."

Joe patted his hand, gently, then stood and disappeared into the living room, by the big bay window, waiting for Mary. Wiping her father's forehead, she pulled the blanket up to his shoulders, waited for his eyes to close peacefully, then left him to rest.

Silently she came beside Joe. They stood, unspeaking, looking out the window. The day was growing into another warm and gentle May morning. From the kitchen they heard Lotti cleaning the separator, the bang of its cups and disks in the hot sudsy water. Joe was wrestling with something inside him. Frank coughed. Mary turned quickly, but he was still again.

"We could have him halfway to Point before your mother came home," Joe said, his voice flat and monotonous, as even he knew the futility in it.

Mary said nothing for a long time. At last she breathed out a resigned "No." He looked at her. But she had to turn to look away.

Now he was angry, smelled the smell of her mother in the girl's eyes. "Would you rather he die?" he asked suddenly. But Mary winced. And sorry to his core he'd said it, he softened. "Could you convince your mother?"

"I think so. I think we'll take him, tomorrow," Mary answered. "If he's not any better."

Joe looked again out the window. That would have to be good enough. As much as he was worried about Frank, he had to think of Mary, too. It was wrong to push her so hard, to blame her for something she could not help. He turned and took her shoulders in his hands, held for a moment as he looked into her eyes. He kissed her on the forehead. "Mary," he said. His voice was half sigh of resignation, half hymn to the love he felt for her. "Mary. I'm not going back to the mill," he said. She blinked, her forehead furrowed. "No. You need me now. Your father needs me. I won't go back." A deep tenderness passed between them. "Now, I'd better go."

He turned abruptly and walked out the front door. Mary stood by the window, saw his car pull out the drive. When he glanced in her direction, she raised her hand lightly and waved.

Then his car was gone, and there was only her father behind her, the world and the future and everything else was gone. Only her father was left, who needed her. She would offer to him the last dregs of her strength and her courage. In him she would lay up all her hopes.

25

The Overland idled roughly at the back steps. Slowly, carefully, for each movement caused him terrible pain, they brought Frank out the door and laid him on the back seat. Berenice went round and cradled his head on her lap. Stash got in behind the wheel; Mary, tight with worry, beside him. It was Monday morning. He had not gotten better.

The rest of the family crowded around the back porch, bleakly watching the car begin to roll away and head out the drive, drifted along its edges with white fluff blown down from the popples.

His head propped up, Frank could just see out the opposite window. He watched, fondly, the apple orchard slide past, with its trees he had pruned and grafted now in the full flush of their bloom, their white blossoms glorious in the morning sun. From high on one tree, a gaudy oriole warbled. He could just hear it over the sound of the car.

Though Stash drove as slowly and carefully as he could, each small bump sent shivers of pain up from Frank's gut. He fought it away, the pain, concentrating to see the fields, there, where the corn he'd planted was coming up, three black crows in the far corner busy pulling up the seedlings. And the bean field, next, which Stash had been working on.

"Tomorrow you'll finish the beans," he said weakly.

Stash cocked his head back, not having heard.

Berenice repeated. "He said for you to finish the beans tomorrow."

Stash nodded his head. Yes, of course.

The countryside had made that subtle transformation, within the last week, from spring to summer. Not long before all trees but the popples were as bare as winter, but now the woods flowed past the car in many different shades of green: the bright maples, the yellow-gold oaks, only just leaved out, the silver and green popples shimmering in the morning breeze, and there the two tall pines which marked the boundary of the farm, from this distance almost black, though, up close, a rich full green.

The wheels of the car mounted the macadam on the hill and now Stash could shift up on the smoother road. Looking out, Frank caught a glimpse of the school tower. No sounds came from the school yard. Today was the first day of summer vacation. He wished Anna was with him. She knew more than anyone else how to cheer him up. Because of him, she had missed the school picnic, and today would miss the graduation exercises in Mosinee. He knew how much that meant to her. He tried to remember her face, as she stood on the back porch to watch him go. But the pain blurred it all.

They crossed the tracks, Stash nudging the car over slowly, and turned south to take the shortcut to Stevens Point. Treetops skimmed past the window. Closing his eyes, Frank knew by the rise and swing of the road when they were just passing the Stelmachs. He wanted to ask if Joe was home or had gone back to the city. But with Mary and Berenice there, it was best not to ask.

Now, past the Stelmachs, he rested. When they'd turned onto the highway, its concrete expansion joints ticking rhythmically along underneath, he could hear trucks zoom past, and the train on the tracks. He looked to guess how far they'd gone, but could see no familiar landmarks.

At the edge of town the car slowed, rose over the bridge. The top of Carley's Potato Warehouse moved slowly past, its ownership emblazoned in broad white letters, the only English, really, that Frank could read. He raised his head, then, to catch a glimpse of Rynek, as always busy, the bustling public square. Then the big brick Northern Motor Supply, where he'd bought the Overland.

Berenice glanced down at him, ran her hand across his forehead. There was something troubling him. He was chasing a memory he'd somehow misplaced. There was something he was supposed to tell Stash. About the car. Yes. About the miss in the car, the hesitation you could feel on accelerating. He'd first noticed it just after Edward left — how long ago it seemed — and meant to mention it to the boy. But with White Star's dying, and all the work, and now this, he'd forgotten.

It didn't matter. They could take care of it some other time. He relaxed, letting it go, and feeling a certain pride in how well the car had held up, in having chosen so well-made a machine.

They came into the peaceful residential section. He could

see the tops of the many elms lining the street. Here he'd often turned to visit the Klebas. The car stopped, sat idling as Stash waited for traffic on Division, a busy highway, to clear. Then they moved ahead again, turned north. Frank caught a glimpse of the tall tower of Old Main, its big white cupola standing high above the trees. That would be the Normal School.

The hospital was only a few blocks more. Stash slowed, turned the car, then stopped. They were at the back, the emergency entrance, to St. Michael's. All Frank could see now was the big square walls of the building, broken regularly by the windows. It looked so institutional, so foreboding to him, he was overcome with a sense of finality, and had to come to terms with the real gravity of his situation. For an instant, while the others sat in the car wondering what they should do next, he wanted to tell them to take him back home. No matter what, that was where he wanted to be. Just take me home, he thought. Home.

Then suddenly a nurse was helping him out of the car. With Stash and Berenice they got him onto a trundle cart. Lying back, as the nurse wheeled him into the building, he looked up into her unfamiliar but friendly face. She seemed efficient, yet sincerely concerned for him. He wanted to thank her. The cart bumped as it went into the building. He winced from the pain. The pale green antiseptic walls of what he thought was probably the emergency room passed by, then a long echoing hallway. He closed his eyes.

He was wheeled into an elevator, with room only for the nurse and Berenice crowded in alongside the cart. He felt the car rising, slowly, swaying lightly from one side to the other. That was his sharpest sense now, as his gut responded to every little movement. The tiny wheels of the cart got stuck trying to exit the elevator. The nurse pushed, Berenice pulled, someone else came to help, and at last they were on their way once again. In a few moments they'd turned into a room.

He opened his eyes, saw Stash and Mary, who'd come up the stairs, standing so solemnly waiting for him. Berenice backed away. The nurse and another man lifted him onto the bed. He groaned from the hurt. He looked up to see his wife and children. It seemed so strange, they were so grave, so serious. He wanted to tell them not to worry so much. God will take care of me, he would tell them.

But taking the trip in the car and up into the room had

jarred his insides. All he could do now was close his eyes and fight the pain which had been brought on. And again, though he knew his gut was empty, the nagging urge to vomit.

Another man, dressed in white — a doctor, he supposed — came in, held his wrist, then probed at his stomach, hurting him terribly. But he would not show it. The man seemed so serious. What was he thinking? Did he know what was wrong, what caused this terrific pain? Frank heard Stash mutter the word "appendix" and saw the doctor shake his head from side to side.

The doctor was gone, and a different nurse rushed in. She slipped a needle into Frank's arm. Slowly, minute by minute, the pain grew less insistent, and he grew tired, unable to keep the fires of consciousness alive. He tried to focus on his wife, then on Stash's familiar face, so like his own. Was that himself he was looking at, when he was younger? But how could he be looking at himself? The face slowly disappeared, Berenice's returned, blurred, went out, came back, then there was only a calm and restful darkness.

✳✳✳

Alone in the refuge of St. Stanislaus', its smell of incense and its thick light stained by the colored window, the wife, the daughter, the son, knelt side by side in silent prayer. Across the street was an alien world. They had left him in it. Now that he was out of their hands, it was up to God to care for him. So they prayed: Dear God, watch over and cherish and protect him. He has ever been your kind and just servant. Reward him now, with renewed health.

For long, long moments they prayed. At last Berenice rose, slipped a coin into the coffer, and lit a votive candle in Frank's name. She stood before it, head bent, then knelt to pray, the candle's flame flickering weakly into the air. Without weight or substance the tiny flame soothed and consoled her as she invoked the Blessed Mary's help and St. Francis and Peter and Paul, and all the others she could think of to name for his sake.

Mary, kneeling and praying to the other Mary, Christ's Holy Mother, could not help but feel it was her own selfishness, her love of Joe, which had brought this on. Sickness and death, she had been taught, are the result of original sin. Thinking of her own needs, she had turned away from her father. She begged God to forgive her. It doesn't matter, she prayed, about me. Only save him. Please, God, only save him.

It was nearly ten that night before they left the hospital.

Frank had not changed. Stash drove the Overland to the Kleba's, where he dropped off his mother and sister, then drove home in the dark. The children were still up, awaiting the news. There was little he could tell them. They told him of all the many calls inquiring about their father's health. Adam Laska had come by with a cake. Father Nowak would mention Frank in the morning Mass.

***

John and Marie Kleba welcomed their friends into the house, only wishing they'd come under happier circumstances. They peppered Berenice with questions about Frank's condition, but got few satisfying answers. Then they tried to reassure her and Mary. "My uncle, in Chicago," John said as they all sat nervously around the table, "had an attack of indigestion like that. He was in the hospital four days, and all of a sudden he was better."

Berenice looked up into John's eyes. "Do you really think...?"

Marie reached across the table to hold her hand. "It's in God's hands now, Berenice. We must trust in Him."

Mary sat on into the night hardly saying a word. Her rosary wrapped around her hands, she prayed silently. She was trying to get away from the terrible guilt which hung over her. She was not convinced that it was so. But neither was she convinced that it was not so. And if it was, it needed a great penance to right it.

It was hard to understand God's ways. Berenice needed a priest to counsel her. She wished now she hadn't brought Frank. That had been a mistake. She'd been weak to let the others convince her. He belonged at home. She never should have brought him. She could see that now. But it was too late.

***

They sat up late, the four of them, around the dining room table lit by the single electric bulb hanging above. They sat and waited for the call they hoped would never come. It was nearly three o'clock when they'd got so tired they could no longer stay awake. Berenice and Mary crept upstairs to sleep. They did rest u little, but it provided scant relief.

The morning light coming in the window woke them, like a bad dream from restless sleep. Below they heard John Kleba dressing, he and Maria talking quietly as they had their breakfast. Then John left. Berenice went downstairs, then Mary. After coffee and bread, they walked the few blocks to the hospital. The air was warm and quiet, hung peacefully in the tall trees from which birds sang their morning prayers. A few cars sputtered past on the road. The city around them was beginning to go about its morning duties. Though they were in it, it seemed a world away.

Frank was awake when they walked into his room. Through the morphine he managed a smile, gently gripping his wife's hand. All morning they sat by his side, as nurses came and doctors went, checking his pulse, his temperature. At home, Stash was finished with the chores and, as his father had reminded him, out planting the last of the beans. The whole family knew what work they had to do, but they went through it mechanically, all their thoughts centered on their father, just twenty miles away.

For the rest of the nation it was a pleasantly warm Memorial Day. The hospital was staffed with a minimum staff. They would perform only emergency operations. In the afternoon, through the slightly opened window in Frank's room they could hear the blare of trumpets and the steady beat of drums as bands marched up Main Street, lined with crowds and goggling children, the veterans of the Civil, Spanish-American and First World Wars stiffly carrying their flags in a quiet but deep patriotism. Far away in Washington, President Harding was just at that moment dedicating the recently completed Lincoln Memorial.

To Berenice and Mary it was almost a blasphemy, these celebrations: like dancing in church.

That evening John and Marie came to visit Frank. But Frank would not wake to see them. Now they knew just how serious it was. Before Berenice and Mary left, the doctor stopped in to tell them they would operate the next day, when they had a full staff. They suspected, but could not be sure, that the problem was an impacted bowel. Only by operating could they be sure.

But it was a dangerous procedure. Though surgery had come a long way in the past twenty years — had, admittedly, learned a lot during the War — such major operations were touch and go. At every step there were serious hazards: from the anesthesia itself to the hemorrhaging to the sepsis possible here in the intestine. But, the doctor told her, an operation was essential.

✳✳✳

That night John Kleba phoned Stash and told him of the

operation and that he should come to town first thing in the morning. It was another night for all of them with hardly any sleep. Only Frank himself, with the aid of morphine, rested peacefully.

John left his store to the care of his help that morning and walked with Berenice and Mary to the hospital. Frank was still asleep. Stash arrived a few minutes later. The nurse asked Berenice if Frank had made out a will. It seemed like a nightmare to Mary, this talk of a will. Did it mean he was going to die? No. Such a strong man, you could see it, the strength in his body even through the hospital sheet. No. He would not die. It was only a precaution.

John Kleba phoned a lawyer he knew, who came to the hospital just as Frank was rising slowly out of his sleep. The lawyer had a standard form to be filled out. Though still drugged, Frank was perfectly aware of what he was doing. He left everything to his wife. John Kleba and two of the doctors put their signatures on the document as witnesses. The lawyer said he'd send Berenice the bill.

There was still some time yet before the operation. They went across the street to the church. They would need all the help they could get.

When they came back, the doctor was waiting for them in the room. Frank was resting, half awake, half drifting into a hazy sleep. There was another way, the doctor said, which might save Frank from an operation. He'd consulted with his colleagues, and thought he should mention it. Sometimes, he said, the bowel obstruction could be forced from below with water pressure. It might work, and it might not. There was a danger, too, of rupturing the bowel. But in some cases the procedure was a success. Would she agree to try it?

Berenice's sole thought for the past two days had been to get Frank out of the hospital. An operation had a spiritual significance to her — this cutting open of the body. As though it might allow the soul to escape. To her any alternative was better. But she didn't know. And Frank, they could hardly ask him.

John Kleba tried to learn from the doctor what the chances were of the bowel rupturing, and what the consequences if it did. But the young intern was noncommittal. Rupture of the bowel, he said, was certainly a serious trauma. There was something in his voice which frightened John. But who could tell?

the doctor said. It depended on what was causing the blockage in the first place.

John and Berenice walked up and down the harsh, echoing halls of the hospital, past the other patients in their rooms, smiling and nodding to the nuns and nurses who scurried past. John did not want to influence her decision. It was, after all, up to her. It was, in the end, Berenice's profound distrust of doctors in the first place and operations in the last which made the decision for her.

***

Now the room seemed crowded. Berenice held Frank's hand. Stash and Mary were at his other side, John and Marie standing back a bit. At the foot of the bed, two nurses and a doctor. Frank was awake, feverish and in growing pain. Five days without eating; five days of terrible suffering; five days of little sleep, had turned him into a remnant of what he had been — like a cornstalk after a heavy frost, rustling in the cold winds of autumn.

They began with the water. He moaned. They waited, hoping the pressure would break loose whatever was bound inside. More, the doctor said. The nurse pumped more. Frank moaned again. It hurt, he said. They stopped, waited. It was absolutely silent in the room, but for the low moaning of the patient and the muttering of prayers from his wife, daughter and friends.

Stash stared silently.

More, the doctor said. More.

Berenice looked at him, as though asking: Do you know what you're doing?

But already the nurse was pumping. They stared at Frank, watching.

Suddenly a high scream escaped his lips. His eyes rolled back, his face turned white as he passed out from the pain of it. Below the blood came gushing out.

Mary leapt forward, to grab his hand. The doctor pushed Berenice aside and slapped Frank's face to bring him to. John held onto Berenice, who struggled to get back to her husband. Already they had him onto a cart and were wheeling him away, down to the operating room, leaving behind a trail of blood, like a wounded animal in the forest.

The doctor tried to talk to Berenice; but in her hysteria she could understand none of his English. John Kleba translated for her. The bowel had burst. Now only an operation could save his life. And she must not set her hopes too high.

"Franchek, Franchek," Berenice crooned as they took her down the stairs to sit just outside the emergency room. Frank was already inside. The two children sat one on either side of their mother, the Klebas across from them. Mary and Berenice clung to their rosaries. Marie handed Berenice a handkerchief to dry her eyes. Through the door they could hear occasional clanks of metal and muffled commands. The air was afire with a sense of urgency, of imminent disaster.

Mary felt, for the first time in her life, that God had deserted them. She looked up at the clock, hardly able to think. Four-fifteen.

Time passed slowly, ever so slowly. She prayed to God that they would find the trouble and fix it. In a few days — even if it were weeks, she would not complain — her father would be home again, and they could look out across the fields to see him steadily treading behind his beloved Molly. Or in the barn, bending over the cows; driving the family to church; or in his chair, reading. It wasn't much to ask. God would certainly grant her that.

But there was all that blood. And who could scream as he had screamed unless the injury was mortal?

They waited. Half an hour went past, forty-five minutes. It seemed a year, a lifetime. John Kleba rose to go to the bathroom. He had just disappeared when one of the doctors, smoking a cigarette and wiping his hands on a towel, came out of the door.

His eyes told all. "Come with me," he said, quietly.

They followed. Only Marie stayed behind, to wait for John.

There on the operating table they saw a man, covered to his neck with a sheet. The closer half of him and the table and the sheets and even the floor around him were covered with blood. Stash held onto his mother, who seemed ready to faint. Mary looked away, her stomach uneasy.

Supported by Stash, Berenice was led to Frank's side. He was pale, his breathing slow and shallow. His eyes closed, he was still under the effects of the anaesthetic. The doctor stood behind Berenice. "There's nothing we can do," he said, his voice cold, matter-of-fact. "The bowel had burst. Loss of blood, sepsis of the cavity..." He paused, realized she was not listening.

He turned to Stash. "You are Catholic?"

Stash nodded.

"We've called a priest."

Mary looked out the window. There, across the street, the door of the rectory beside the church flew open and a young priest came running out, with one hand carrying his sickroom case, the other holding up his cassock as he hurried across the street. He disappeared and in less than a breath — it seemed impossible — he was beside them in the room, panting, with his hand combing back his hair.

He set his case beside the table on which Frank lay. He put his hand on Berenice's shoulder. "Are you the wife?" He asked once more, this time in Polish. She would not respond. Her hands were clasped on Frank's, her eyes staring into his pale, grey-tinged face. "Please," he said, "I must administer the last rites."

Berenice turned and looked at him as though she did not understand.

"Please," he said again, taking her by the arm. Stash came round to help. She yielded, at last, to the priest's authority, allowed herself to be backed away from her husband.

Quickly the priest opened the sickroom case. His movements were practiced, yet reverent. He placed two small candles beside Frank's head, lay a white crucifix in Frank's hands, which were folded on his breast. Holding the vials of oil and chrism, the priest began intoning the prayers of parting, beseeching the Lord to accept the soul of His faithful servant.

"Let us pray," he said, kneeling. Mary and Stash helped their mother to her knees. Together they prayed. Only the doctor remained standing. The priest rose again, turned to the doctor. "Is he conscious?" he asked. "Can he understand me?"

The doctor shrugged.

The priest bent to Frank's ear, whispered, in Polish. "I am Father Malkowski. Can you hear me?"

They watched, from the edge of sanity they saw his eyes flutter open, focus on the priest's near face.

"Can you hear me?" the priest repeated. "Do you have any sins to confess?"

Frank's lips moved. The priest bent his ear close. But what the man said to the priest was heard only by God and his ordained servant.

"Is that all?" the priest asked.

Frank's eyes fluttered shut, then open again. It was all.

With holy oil on his thumb, the priest anointed Frank's eyes, lips, ears, hands, feet, cleansing the dying man's senses of all sins and weakness. He wiped his hands on a small, soft towel which he lifted from the sickroom case.

"Let us pray," he said again, and they all knelt, all but the doctor, who stood watching from one corner. "Lord have mercy," they chanted, "Christ have mercy, Lord have mercy. Holy Mary," the priest intoned, and they responded, as they knew the prayer from their hearts, "pray for him." One by one through the litany for the dying they moved, invoking all the angels and the archangels, the saints, martyrs, virgins, and widows, not to save this kind and gentle man from death, but to save his soul from eternal damnation.

They prayed, then, the Our Father, aloud, ominously, yet in those familiar words Berenice and Mary found some consolation. Even Mary, trembling with fear, felt as though she might be able to bear what she now knew was coming.

The priest rose, turned to help Berenice to her feet. "I'll wait outside," he said. "We have done all we can do. Now it is between God and him."

The priest left. Sobbing quietly, she moved to her husband's side. His eyes were open. He smiled to see her there. She held his hand.

The doctor moved toward the door, to slip out behind the priest. But Berenice, seeing him go, turned and shouted in a language he did not understand. "Wait!" she cried. "Why is he dying? You haven't told me why he is dying!"

The doctor stopped, looked at Stash.

"Why?" she shouted, the rage and despair pent up inside her.

Stash spoke, his own voice cracking. "Why? She wants to know why he is dying."

The doctor stared at the boy a moment, then blinking and with a slight shrug of his shoulders moved to the operating table and bent slowly on the far side where they could not see him When he reappeared, he held high a stainless bucket, big almost as a milk bucket, half full with dark clotted blood and bile. He held it up for Berenice to see.

"This is why he's dying," he said, slowly, quietly, then put the pail back under the table.

Staring at him from over the body of her husband Berenice

was sure — and would swear it to her dying day — she smelled the odor of liquor on the doctor's breath.

But he only turned and walked out of the room, Berenice's futile curses following him out.

Frank's face was grey now, seemed setting, his lips drawn taut, his breathing labored and irregular. Mary and Stash stood at the end of the table, where the sheets were stained with blood, while Berenice stayed at his side, her hand running through his hair. "Franchek," she muttered, trying to call him back.

His eyes closed. He was almost gone.

But then his eyes opened, his lips moved. He stared at Berenice. "Take care of the children," he said to her, his voice weak but distinct. It seemed he was suddenly more lucid than he had been in days.

Berenice nodded.

He moved his hand, gesturing his children to come beside him.

"Stash, you be good, help around," he said. "Be good with Molly." Now his eyes turned to his daughter. He paused a moment. They thought he might slip away. But then, almost miraculously, he smiled, to see her there. Suddenly a pain or some thought carried the smile away and his brows wrinkled together.

"Mary," he said. "Obey your mother, Mary."

Their eyes held for a moment. Mary nodded, whispered. "Yes." She held back her tears. "Yes." His hand fluttered toward her, this big, strong hand which seemed hardly now able to move. She took it, squeezed it in her own.

These were the longest moments of Mary's life, waiting almost breathlessly for the miracle which would never come. Each second seemed an eternity, as though the agony of it had to be drawn out beyond the point of bearing. And yet, when months or years later she would look back on it, as she often did, then it would seem that the whole terrible week had happened in the blinking of an eye — one moment her father had been home, happy, milking and plowing, and the next...

His eyes were closed. He seemed asleep. They held him as long as they could. He was a strong man, with work in life yet to be done. He did not go easily. But he had struggled so hard these last days. The point had come now in which the instinct for life — to stay and finish his work — had given way to the instinct for death. The need, now, the utter, final and implacable need for rest. And beyond that point, there was no returning.

His eyes opened; but they were glazed, unseeing.

Berenice bent above him. "Franchek!" she whispered, urgently.

A thin shudder shook his body, as though the soul were shaking itself loose. He breathed a long, weary, final breath.

They waited. The silence screamed in their ears. Berenice's eyes flew from Stash to Mary, to the face of her husband, resting, at last, on he who in life had known so little rest.

> *Siwy kon, siwy kon,*
> *Malowany sankie*
> *Poja dem, poja dem,*
> *Do twoja kochankie.*

> *Little grey horse, little grey horse,*
> *Brightly painted sleigh,*
> *Take me with, take me with,*
> *To my little darling.*

26

> *The Virgin Mary walked among the stars,*
> *cooling the souls that smolder...*
> — from *Idyllic Dreams,* by Josef Czechowicz

"I was out in the garden, setting in tomato plants," Sophie Tomczak said to her friend Mrs. Stelmach, "when we heard the bells. And I said to Chester, Jesus Marya, not Frank!"

The room, though wall to wall with friends and neighbors and family, collapsed as they were into a shared but solitary emptiness, was quiet: too quiet, unnaturally quiet, deathly quiet. He for whom they had gathered would rest in peace. But they would know neither rest nor peace — all their everyday chores, set aside now to be soon enough taken up again, all their everyday chatter, all had been stunned into this bewildered soundlessness, from which it seemed only Sophie Tomczak found it necessary, for her own sufficient reasons, to talk circles around the central mystery they now so unwillingly confronted.

"They said she fainted," Sophie asserted, "when he died. Jesus Marya, who wouldn't! With all those children. Of course they're not as young as ours, but..."

Her neighbor's incessant whispering was an affliction Joe's mother preferred not to suffer. Bending to find in her purse the ever-present rosary, she quietly crossed herself with its tiny silver crucifix, and began the Creed. Sophie would not interrupt her prayers.

Alex Stelmach sat hands on knees, his body shaken with occasional, uncontrollable tremors. He had no rosary to turn to, no miracle of faith which might explain this the inexplicable. His, therefore, was a burden never in his life to be completely shed. Beside him an even darker, more wounded figure, slumped in his chair like a marionette whose strings had suddenly been cut. Those who had watched Roman Gruba sink into the depths and then pull himself up from his mother's death wondered, silently, if he had the strength to do it all over again.

And what but this could bring so many children — twenty, almost, counting the Wolniaks, Ganthers, Laskas, Tomczaks, Rybarczyks — what a mighty thing it must be to bring so many children to such a terrible quiet. Their silence, though, was blessed with ignorance. What was death to young Julia Tomczak? There was in her eyes a certain skepticism, a certain fundamental doubt that what was happening was in fact real. How could someone, she asked herself, as big and strong and full of laughter as Frank just suddenly die? It was not possible. There was something make-believe about it. Death, to a child her age, was hardly more real than life was, at that moment, to Frank Topolski.

Only through her mother she knew of its reality. Her mother, at supper the night before, suddenly recalling, her hand to her mouth, that today, the day they were to bring his body home, it was Angie's birthday. And the day he died, that was Bruno's. That had meaning to Julia, when her mother shook her head and said to her father, who was poking away at a supper he usually gobbled down, how cruel it was to bring such a present.

They sat, the Topolski children, in a broken half-circle, up front by the casket. With them was Walter, who'd come home from the city. And all, from Stash down to little Anna, seemed only half alive. Lotti and Mary held hands, and Anna and Sophie. Eddie, next to his mother, sat staring straight ahead. She seemed so different now, so far away. But he would stay at her side, in case she should need him.

And Bruno. How he'd surprised them all, how he'd cried, out in the barn, in the house, once even collapsing halfway between, sitting in the drive and sobbing into his hands. As though they expected, just because he liked to tease and have his fun, that he couldn't feel the same hurt they felt. No one was more alone in all the world these past two days than Bruno Topolski. He was a child no more. The rogue had been tricked out of him. Now he would be a man, a sullen, sulky, isolated man, whose finest days would still taste the taste of death.

***

That evening two nights before when they'd heard the bells ringing from St. Francis, when Anna, Sophie and Angie were out in the corn hoeing, they stopped and stared into each other's eyes. But no, they thought. No.

And until they saw the car pull in the drive and Mary and Stash help their mother onto the porch, there was that last fragment of hope, that the bells had tolled for someone else. They hoed. Stash came out to them then, just stood standing there unable to find the right words. And they just kept on hoeing, as though by working impossibly hard they could make the impossible happen. The incessant scratching of their hoes in the rocky soil was like the sound of membranes tearing deep inside them, tearing and tearing until they could stand it no longer. Anna was the first to stop, then the others. There was an instant then of nothing — of neither grief nor joy, of work nor rest, an empty, resonating instant; and they felt themselves falling, falling, and their only hope was to go back a week, a month, a year, to have him with them again. From that emptiness came that: that burning need to turn time around, that wanting only the impossible. Wanting only, him.

Stash turned and shuffled desolately toward the house, left the girls standing each in her own row, each leaning silently on her hoe, until suddenly Anna was in Sophie's arms and Angie, dropping her hoe, ran to the house, where she knew her mother would need her.

It was Berenice's sister, Mary, who rode the train all that night to be at her side, who had held the family together. She'd cared for her sister as though she were a child, sat beside her, always, fed her her meals, helped her dress and undress, even slept with her, Mary's body filling the emptiness where Frank till then had lain. Not for a single moment would she leave Berenice alone. She was waiting, waiting like a peasant in his hut who hears the snow break loose on the mountain above him and waits, hardly breathing, for the inevitable to engulf him.

For Berenice had not yet broken down. Only now and then, sitting in the chair beside the casket, a light moan might break free from inside her. Otherwise she sat staring dumbly, her eyes swollen with tears. But the reckoning was yet to come. And her sister would be with her when it did come.

Now, in the quiet room, next to Aunt Mary sat her niece, the one they called Little Mary, whose hands squeezed the brown beads of her own rosary, as though the short string might hold her from the long fall she too was facing. Her lips moved in little spasms, the wells of her eyes gone dry, for three days having lavished their balm onto the indifferent world. Still she felt it was her fault, that selfishly she'd petitioned the Virgin for her own needs, and when it came time to help him, the Holy Mother was tired of hearing that timid voice from down below, and turned Her back.

To her had been given the task of ironing, for the last time, her father's best shirt and pants. She had slipped the handle into the hottest iron, and between the tears, forgot to test the iron on the paper. Laying it against his shirt, a faint sickly smell rose up, and there, when she jerked the iron up, was a small brown scorch mark, a pale burnt triangle. How she suffered over that. Don't cry, my child, don't cry, Aunt Mary had said, taking her in her arms. No one will ever know. No one will ever see it.

But he would see it. He would know. And how could he ever forgive her?

Joe's presence, now, was like a burning brand in her side. She could not find it in herself to hate him. How he'd cried that first night when he came over to help with the chores. How he'd found the strength, from the depths of his own grief, to reach out to them. No. She could never hate him. She could pity him, for the pain he so obviously suffered. And she could sit with him, those long nights side by side, staying up with the body, here in these chairs they now filled. Though they were allowed that at last, being together again, it was too late. Too much had changed.

***

Father Nowak quietly laid his hat on the pump organ, beside a vase of begonias. The organ had been Rose's, and since her death a short six months earlier, had been silent. Hands folded together, he walked to and stood beside the casket. This was not his first, nor certainly would it be his last; yet it would undeniably be one of his hardest funerals. He searched the cold grey face of his friend for answers: but answers were not given. These hands, folded now so peacefully, so strong, so made for work — and made by work — would work no more. He recalled a phrase, from some poem or saying he'd learned while in the seminary: some men, it is said, are born for the fields, others for the cross. But this man, this kind and gentle man, had borne them both, the heavy drudgery of the field and the agony of the cross.

God grant me, the priest prayed silently, the strength to bear my own so silently, so selflessly.

He knelt and bowed his head. "Let us pray," he intoned, one hand on the oiled walnut of the casket. The room, which had been so quiet, filled now with murmured prayers. They prayed the rosary, together, prayer after prayer, and litanies and novenas for his sake. And as they prayed, on and on, endlessly it seemed, the room grew darker, as evening slowly turned to night. The casket seemed almost black now, black as the draperies hung beneath it to conceal the big tubs of ice giving off a faint clamminess to the air — but which could not hide the smell of death.

It was time — past time — to light a lamp. But the prayers went on, and no one would rise to break their continuity. They had gathered to pray, those who had worked together, and laughed together, danced and planned for the future together — to pray for him whose future had ceased to be. The light faded, and looking up, Mary saw the lilies at his head grow suddenly bright as though glowing from within. And the light from them, shining off his face, showed a line of red where it was bleeding again. All night he'd bled, a thin stream down his cheek from the cold marble lips. Her handkerchief was blotched with it. She wanted to reach now, and blot it off. But still the prayers went on.

And all she could think was: still he hangs on, still he won't let go completely.

***

The house was full. He had so many friends: you could almost say everyone he knew was his friend. And there was all the family, all except those still in the old country. They'd sent the telegram, the day before. Stash had gone down to the depot. Leaping the broad Atlantic, that miracle of modern science had brought yet another family to their knees.

When the praying was done, Father stood, to lead them in song. *Witaj Krolowo!* they sang. *Welcome, Queen of Heaven, welcome to our house. Come, oh Blessed Virgin, to soothe our souls; come to take him with you, who ever thought of you in his life.*

Their voices were strained, weirdly blending in a kind of common moan, rising out into the darkened yard where even the animals could hear, where a cooing mourning dove at first added its sad notes to the chorus, then stopped to cock its head and listen. And the horses, in the barn, stood still, ears cocked, wondering what wind or storm that eerie noise portended.

Uncle John's voice rose the clearest and the loudest. Frank's older brother, the one who'd talked him into farming, had come the night before with his wife Anastasia and their little girl Pearl, who alone of twelve siblings had survived beyond infancy. John, though just four years older than Frank, had never expected to live to see his brother's funeral. So now his voice carried the others through the hymns, these slow solemn songs which had served their grandparents and their grandparents' grandparents to the same end: songs which they knew by heart, and sung from the bitterness of the heart. Prayers were to be prayed in silence, but in these wailing hymns they let themselves go. And to the children it was frightening and unforgettable, the pain and the sorrow filling the hymns.

✳✳✳

It was nearly ten o'clock when the singing was done. One by one the families left. The house was empty, almost: but filled, too, with an unwelcome stranger, who had stolen in and would not leave. At last Aunt Mary put Berenice to bed, who now actually slept, deeply, deeply almost as death itself.

The children, too, went off to bed, weary and sorrowful. Joe went home to get some sleep himself. Only Stash and Mary and Uncle John stayed up. But before settling in for the long night, the two men brought ice in from the icehouse to replenish that which had melted in the tubs. Then they sat, the three of them, sharing with Frank his last night at home. The hours slipped past. Twice Mary rose to pat dry with her handkerchief the blood on his cheek. But for three nights now she had hardly slept. By midnight she was dozing in her chair. And Stash, too, his eyes slowly shut, his chest rising and falling quietly.

Seeing them asleep John rose carefully and went into the guest room, where his wife and daughter lay asleep. Quietly he opened the suitcase they'd so hurriedly packed and took out to hold in his hand a small ring box, covered in soft velvet. Walking as quietly as he could he carried the box to his brother's side, then carefully lifted the pillow on which Frank's head lay. He slipped the box beneath, let Frank's head rest again. He smoothed his brother's hair, his hand lingering on the cold flesh, then quickly turned and disappeared into his room.

Almost forty years before, when Frank and he had set out from Poland's shores, he'd secretly slipped that little ring box into his pocket. In it was a tiny handful of soil, dug reverently from the farm his father worked but did not own. He'd told Stasia, and reminded her every year or so, that if he should die, it was to be placed under his pillow. So that forever his head would rest on Polish soil.

But now, instead, it was for Frank.

27

They took his body and walked in a silent line.
Toil still lingered about him, a sense of wrong...
Should his anger now flow into the anger of others?
It was maturing in him through its own truth and love.
Should he be used by those who come after,
Deprived of substance, unique and deeply his own?
— from *In Memory of a Fellow Worker,* by Karol Wojtyla

To the sky was given a depth which allowed of no movement, which humiliated even the thought of any attempt at reaching it. So clear, so blue, so perfectly serene it seemed to alter time itself, to prolong beyond belief each single moment. As though within an hour a lifetime — a dozen lifetimes — could be played out,

But beneath that sky the earth went its way, its natural way, ignorant of such things, covering itself joyfully with the fresh green grass as bright and impermanent as the last of the clear yellow dandelions already giving way to the more somber and moody hawkweed. From across the river came the impertinent rattle of a kingfisher, angry at the morning for not providing fish and minnows enough for its young. And a lone, lugubrious heron soared toward its clumsy nest hidden in the flats along the Big Eau Pleine. It soared so slowly, there above the river, its wings scarcely seeming to move; as though it were suspended there by some mysterious levitation or thin, invisible filament.

Beside the church, where the dark cars and trucks had gathered in their own expectant silence, a single horse, lean, spavined, dropping its head, beyond hope of grain or anything more than second-rate marsh grass, its perpetual hunger only made more poignant by the sight of fresh grass growing on the church lawn. But it had come so close to death that even hunger, even the hardest pavement on its tender feet and the squeaking axle of the buggy were something to be thankful for.

The church inside is almost full, but the usual ordering of the congregation is disturbed. In the front pews today sit the immediate family: Berenice and beside her Aunt Mary, then the children, one by one, somber, dark, inconsolable. Uncle John. Across the aisle the pallbearers, staring erect at the dark coffin on which lies a single spray of white lilies. Farther back, others of the family, and friends. Then, self-arranged according to how well they felt they knew him, neighbors, shopkeepers, some from as far as Mosinee and Stevens Point. The Topolski pew is empty.

Vested in black Father intones the Sequence of the day: *"Day of wrath, dreadful day..."* And the Requiem Mass goes on, according to its own precise logic, remote, unfathomable by those gathered to reap from it what comfort they might. There is something in the depth of its drama and the incessant recurrence of its themes which like the sky outside frames an immobility, a profound serenity, which even the most poignant grief is impotent to jar.

Dimly they give themselves to the incomprehensible. Hovering around them is that mystery to which they all bow — and before which not one of them dare stand up and demand what in no way can be given. So they sit, dim in their grief, with faith their only consolation.

"Thy will be done..."

Who was this man who stood before them, bowed in prayer? Whose this face which, so ravaged in the course of four days had found, ultimately, so profound a peace, a peace reflected almost as off the face of the dead man himself, or He there on the cross. It seemed that they knew him. But who they'd known had undergone such a transfiguration that he was now a stranger to them.

The Gospel he read mechanically, then closed the book, as though it was not in liturgy that truth or love were to be found. Those four simple words... *Thy will be done...* This was the treasure he'd found, having traversed the desert and arrived at last, weak and weary, at the gates of the City of God. Fervidly he offered them, as one lover whispering to another.

"There are no more profound words in all our prayer, in all our manifold liturgy," he said, eyes closed, hands clasped at his lips. Each word followed the other in exact aptness, astonishing even himself.

***

He'd been fussing over parish accounts — a dreadful, tedious task — that evening when Berenice walked in — no, stumbled in. Ring the bells, she'd said, her words slurred, scarcely intelligible. Ring the bells, for Frank has died. Ring the bells and tell the world. For an instant the world went dark. Surely there was some mistake. Frank dead?

But there was no mistaking her grief. Dutifully he rose and walked across the yard, into the vestibule, and let the bells peal the pain he was only just beginning to feel. Their sad, steady knell, as though calling him to Matins, began for him a long retreat. Verna, his housekeeper, worried over him. Days and nights he knelt and prayed, searching for an answer, a justification of this good man's untimely death. Death, of course, was not new to him. He'd stood helplessly watching young children perish of the flu; had anointed young mothers for whom childbirth was a mortal injury; had agonized over the death of his own father, communicated to him in the cold lucidity of a telegram. But this, this had bent him nearly to breaking.

As though, in worrying over Mary's marriage and his collaboration in it, he'd been carrying a full arm load of firewood; and suddenly a heavy oak log was dropped on the others. It was too much. No longer could he concentrate on the daily liturgy. No longer could he even sleep, or taste the food Verna so solicitously urged onto him. Until, just the night before, on his knees in his room, at the little altar, the crucifix and the vigil light his only company, to the east the day already crawling out of its sepulcher, at last it had come to him.

"*Thy will be done,*" he repeated, his lips caressing the syllables as they formed. "Four simple words, but like four walls so gigantic, so impenetrable, so inviolable, they can contain within them all the joy and all the agony ever endured in man's long, sorry history. In the end, in the dark of night facing that which we all must come to face, we come to know that our hearts are — and forever must be — empty. Like sieves our lives pass through them. Our souls, insubstantial as air. And even our minds, with which we can rise to such heights, are impotent against the darkness of life, which is the shadow of an infinity no mind can ever touch. But, my friends," he spoke the words out of habit, for he was speaking now to himself, "in abandoning ourselves to these four, these simple words, our hearts, our souls, our minds are extinguished: but with a flash so brilliant it throws light into the deepest recesses of those other, unseen worlds."

For the first time since he'd taken upon himself the yoke of Ordination, Father Nowak spoke heedless of his audience. These words were not taken from prayer book or Canon, were not organized by the severe logic of dogma, carefully thought out, intellectually precise. This sermon, this first sermon like those of Jerome's, of Thomas Aquinas, Loyola, Francis of Xavier, was a conversation between his soul and the Lord Himself.

Slowly, surely, he continued, bringing to bear those lovely images shaped by the winds of two thousand years usage. He spoke of life's twin baptisms, in the waters of infancy and again at the flood tides of death. They did not understand. And of Christ's reconciliation with the Father, from the perspective of the Cross, they did not understand. Of the miracle which renewed the Resurrection in the lives of good men like Frank Topolski, they believed, but did not understand. And when he spoke of the soul judging itself at the moment of death, they did not understand. Nor of the enthusiasm of the souls in purgatory who, like the martyrs of old, welcome the tormenting fires which will burn away all but the Divine Vision. And they wondered, too, what he might mean when he spoke of the Christian miracle which transforms pain and death into mighty weapons by which we can each of us be victorious over our own mortality.

After so many years these images had once again taken on, for the good priest, a real meaning. As though the death of his friend had torn aside the veil woven of everyday custom, revealing the ultimate spirituality at the center of life itself. Perhaps only once in a person's life — if even that — are we granted a glimpse of naked divinity. And for this devout priest, so far from home, and with such a long, lonely journey still ahead of

him, that hour had come. The doubt, the agony, the sorrow had
all given way in that morning's growing light into a flood of
tears, not of sorrow, but of thankfulness. Trembling, he had
arisen and begun the preparations for the Mass, in each quiet
movement thanking his friend, Frank, for granting him this.
And marveling at how much more he had received than ever he
had given or could hope to give to that simple man and his
family.

So he tried to tell them. But his words passed over their
heads. Only a few — that suddenly aged man there among the
pallbearers who in these past days had gone through his own
Gethsemane — might have caught a blurred reflection of their
true meaning, before like the thin incense rising from the thurible,
they rose unhindered to He from Whom they had so miraculously come.

✳✳✳

The mass was ended. In the sacristy, Father slipped into
a dull black cope. He reappeared. The congregation stood. It
was almost over now. Flanked by his servers, he stood at the
foot of the casket, muttering low prayers of absolution. Now he
circled the body, shaking holy water and praying silently, *Our
Father Who art in heaven*, tiny drops like beads of sweat upon the
box's skin. Taking the thurible, he circled again, *hallowed be Thy
Name*, the cold chains clanking, *Thy kingdom come*, blessing them
all with the sweet smoke of holy sacrifice, *Thy will be done*.

He handed away the smoldering thurible, stepped solemnly
back as the pallbearers, one by one, slid quietly out of their pew
to arrange themselves beside the coffin. Chester Tomczak and
Henry Bollom; John Kleba and Roman Gruba; Alex Stelmach
and his boy, Joe. Lifting gently, their shuffling feet followed the
priest and servers down the short aisle of the little church —
Frank's last passage under this familiar roof — while the choir
sang the antiphon:

May the angels lead you into Paradise...

Abruptly they are in the morning sun, the clear and glorious morning sun. Down the steps, carefully — he was a big man
— crowded from behind by the dark widow and her inconsolable
children. And suddenly it leaps up at them, the ungracious idle
of the waiting truck. They pause, all but the six. The clunk of
wood on wood, then scrape and burr as the casket, shiny in the

morning light, spattered as with tears, slides into its bed.

One after another the cars are cranked to life: the air is no longer still. The truck moves out, and the others pull in behind — first Stash driving the Overland with Mary and Walter beside him; his mother and her sister in the back, with Lotti. Then Uncle John, with Stash's Ford, and the rest of the children. His wife Stasia and Pearl ride in Edward Ciepalek's big Buick. Behind them Joe Stelmach at the wheel of his father's Chevy, with the other pallbearers. Then the rest, Joe Carley up from Point, Ben Lang representing the Farmer's Union, all the friends and neighbors moving noisily out onto the highway and down along the river. At the end of the long, slow line, Adam Laska with Helen and the children, Kurt's feet noisy as he plods on the hard pavement.

Across the river, not far from where three months before Frank had warmed himself in cutting the ice which these last days had instead cooled him, a lone fisherman sits morosely in a big green punt, the tedium of the morning broken by this sudden line of cars sputtering across the Peplin.

They take the little rise before the cemetery, on their left, and pull to a stop. There, under the remnant pines, the grey stones are many of them already more than Frank's allotted age.

Carefully off the truck they slide their burden and heft it laboriously up the narrow path into the shade of the trees. To one side of that deep hole in the alien earth lies a pile of rich brown clay. They stand in a half-circle before it — the circle has been broken — the sound of low sobs drifting over the cheerful birdsong and the low incantation of Latin. Again the casket is sprinkled and the grave.

"Eternal rest grant unto him, O Lord."

And they respond, through their tears:

"And let perpetual light shine upon Him."

"May he rest in peace, and may his soul and the soul of all the faithful departed through the mercy of God rest in peace."

And finally, finally, amen.

The ropes creak through the pulleys as the body is lowered, hand over hand, into the darkness, where resting at last it seems so terribly near yet so impossibly distant.

A spider, black, small as a penny, scurries across the upturned earth as Berenice, scarcely conscious, bends to throw a handful of soil. Aunt Mary leads her away, faint, inconsolable, to the stern reality of an empty car.

They trickle back to their cars and trucks, ones and twos and little knots of friends and family, and crank the vehicles to life. Sputtering, they go down the short steep drive to turn around, to face for an instant the emptiness of their own futures before backing out and heading home again or stopping at Frank's place — but not Frank's, anymore — for that one last meal together. What had been so solemn, so orchestrated, now suddenly unravels, as they each go their separate ways.

Little Pearl, standing and looking out the back window, watches the hillside disappear. "Mommy," she asks, her voice framed in wonder and fear, "why do people die?"

Her mother draws her to her, lightly embraced. "So they can be with God," unthinking, her mother answers.

To be with the quiet of the morning light, the sighing pines, to be alone held in the bosom of that peace not granted the living.

Father Nowak and the altar boys follow behind, chauffeured by Henry Ganther's father, a little annoyed for having to take the morning off from cutting hay. As they accelerate down the hill toward the bridge, behind them now is only the Laska buggy, beginning its slow plod homeward.

And then it is empty and quiet, and he calls them back. But they do not hear. Instead, in reply, a solitary veery, down along the flats, cheerlessly dismantles the summer air. And he calls them back, but they do not hear.

✲✲✲

Suddenly there is a stirring, there, in the grass over the rise. Two men stand, hesitantly, and stretch themselves. The taller, older one, coughs, lights a cigarette, swears low and mutters of cold beer for lunch. They bend, quietly, to lift their shovels and wearily step into the bright calm beside the grave, their work yet to be done.

28

The old world is dead, the new not yet begun.
— from *The Eve of Spring*, by Julius Slowacki

Stash, Mary and Lotti sat with Walter around the kitchen table. They were trying to convince him to stay. It was nearing ten. Berenice and the other children were in bed already. None of them knew anything about making these kinds of decisions. Like a body without a head, they thrashed about, sometimes bumping into and hurting one another.

"I wish I could," Walter said, his hands clasped on the slick checkered oilcloth. "I really do." No one moved. Only Mary's fingers, speeding though the needlework, and the incessant buzz of a June bug trying to break through the screen door broke the silence. "But after all that schooling," Walter said, "I can't quit a thirty-dollar-a-week job."

"Just for a while," Lotti argued, "until things straighten out."

"If I quit, they won't take me back," Walter replied.

Stash lifted a cigarette to his lips, drew on it. It was the first time he'd smoked in the house. He knew, and they all knew, that as oldest boy the farm was really his responsibility. He wasn't running away from it, but neither was he stepping toward it. Like his father before him, he would take things as they came.

But that wasn't Lotti. She knew things her father never knew. "You're needed here," she said to Walter.

He understood. But it wasn't his responsibility. He turned to Stash, whom he admired deeply — there were pictures of Walter squeezed like a sausage into the casing of his brother's Army uniform. But Stash was no farmer. There was too much of the child in him, too much feeling, not enough drive. No, he would be a carpenter, taking work when he needed it, turning it down when he didn't. With that he would be happy.

He held the cigarette rather awkwardly, had only begun to smoke the year before. His voice was quiet as he answered Walter's unasked question. "Sure," he said, "I'll do what I can."

Walter enumerated on his fingers. "You know the horses,

you know the land, you know how pa used to do things. Can you handle it by yourself?" Stash was noncommittal. "It'll mean quitting up at the mill. And less time down to Helen's."

Stash bent to drop the long ash from his cigarette into the cuff of his pant leg. Already, through the long week of his father's illness and death, he missed Helen. So it was something he didn't look forward to.

"We'll help," Lotti volunteered, before realizing that she was now taking Walter's side, and helping him back out.

"Maybe we could hire someone, for haying or threshing," he suggested. "Whenever there's extra fieldwork." He leaned far back in his chair, catching the table legs with the tips of his shoes. "How about Joe?" he asked, addressing Mary. "He's helped out around here before." No one replied. He dropped the chair back onto its legs and stood up. "We've got to do something," he declared. "I'll give Joe a call right now."

"No!" Mary barked. The sound surprised them all. It was so unlike her.

She turned back to her sewing. Walter edged back to his chair, sat down again. There was a long silence.

At last Lotti tried to explain. "Mother," she said.

"Ah," Walter said, his voice touched with sarcasm. "So mother and Joe don't get along?" He read their silence as affirmation. "Is that why the wedding was canceled?"

Stash sat smoking. Mary worked faster than ever on her embroidery. Again it was left to Lotti. She stood up and turned up the lamp on the shelf. But it was running low on oil — another job neglected in the turmoil of the past days. "Mother changed her mind about Joe," she said.

This was the first visit Walter had made since the banns were canceled. No one had explained to him why it had happened. He was beginning, now, to understand. "Did *you* change your mind?" he asked Mary.

But she would not answer, would not even look at him.

"No," Lotti answered for her. "Not her. Not Joe. Only mother."

"And pa?" Walter asked.

Lotti sat down again. There was a moment of silence. Stash turned to drop the butt of his smoke into the cook stove. Upstairs they could hear Anna and Sophie tossing in their beds, and talking.

Walter shook his head. Clearly being away from the family

had given him a different perspective. "Mary," he said, "I could find work for you in Milwaukee. Why don't you come back with me?"

For an instant his sister broke the rhythm of her sewing, as though she might embrace the idea. But then she shook her head, only, once, and began again.

"She's writing to someone else," Lotti said. Mary looked up at her reproachfully.

Walter's eyebrows lifted. "Someone else?" You mean she's got two boyfriends?" He pulled a toothpick from his pocket and chewed it. "Who is it?" he insisted. "Who's the other lucky guy?" He was making fun of her.

Stash looked on curiously. He knew nothing about another man.

Walter knew his sister well enough to know it wasn't a laughing matter. If there was another man, it wasn't by her choice. "Did mother put you up to this?" he guessed, narrowing his eyes and studying his sister. "What's the matter, cat got your tongue?"

At the end of a thread, Mary stopped to tie a knot. Pushing a new length into the needle, she spoke very quietly. "He's coming, this week."

Even Lotti knew nothing of that. It astonished them all.

"Who? Who is he?" Walter demanded.

"A soldier, from Texas," Lotti answered. "Mother's made her write to him."

"So you knew all about this?" he turned now against Lotti.

"I didn't know he was coming," she said.

"Well that's that then, isn't it?" Walter said, flipping his toothpick into the woodbox. "There's your hired hand."

He was only half serious, but they took him at face value. So, he thought, I'm not leaving the farm in Stash's hands, but I'm leaving Mary in the grip of her mother. Even if I stay, he had to admit, the best I could do would not be nearly enough.

They sat gloomily around the table, seeing no way out of Mary's predicament. Just when the farm needed another hand, that hand was on his way, in the form of a man her mother meant to replace Joe. Her only salvation now was the chance that her father's death might have softened her mother. That was possible. But so was the other.

Walter leaned forward, put his hands on Mary's. "Would you marry him?" he asked. "This stranger?"

Mary, too close to tears to respond, only jerked her hand from his. Walter looked to his older brother, whose eyes drifted away, and then to Lotti, herself near to tears. At last he sighed, shaking his head from side to side.

***

He wanted to get away before his mother was up. But Aunt Mary insisted he go in to say good-bye. He slipped into the darkened bedroom, bent to kiss her forehead.

"*Tja, Wladek*," she said, "you be good."

Already in her eyes he could see the strength returning, the will to live coming back to her. She held his hand. Aunt Mary bustled in with hot tea, giving Walter a chance to make his escape.

Bruno was busy feeding cows. He was the only one, now, who knew just how much hay, just how much grain to give to each. He was working with a resolution uncommon to him, as though trying to prove something to himself, or to someone who wasn't even there. Walter reached out and shook the boy's hand. It made Bruno feel grown-up. He wasn't sure he liked it.

Stash, Mary, Angie, and Lotti were on their stools busily milking. Walter went from one to the next, saying good-bye, still self-conscious about the decision he'd felt himself forced to make. He knew by the old ways, his place was at home. But he no longer lived by the old ways.

He took Stash's hand, wished him luck with the farm. "You've got a big job," he said. "But you can handle it."

Then he turned and walked out the door into the cool, quiet morning. Shep followed him to the car. Walter bent to pet him, lifted his paw and shook it and rubbed behind the grinning dog's ear. He pulled a fat tick from the dog's head, and when he threw it on the ground Shep pounced on it and ate it. But when Walter bent to crank the car over, the dog hurried back to his sanctuary under the porch.

In the barn they heard the car sputter to life, then smooth out. And, a moment later, Lotti looked out through the dust-layered window to see him turn out of the drive and disappear down the road.

Stash and Mary were busy with Brownie. Since White Star's death, the big, gentle jersey whose calving had given Frank and Joe so much trouble, was their best milker. But two weeks before, slipping in the mud, she'd stepped on her udder. The rear quarter was infected. Frank had been treating it with camphor and sweet oil. She'd begun to mend, when he himself was taken ill. Since then no one had thought to rub her down, and there'd been a relapse. Now milk from that teat was flaky, specked with blood. Her whole udder was sensitive, as though the infection might be spreading. And when Mary sat to milk her, the poor cow fidgeted, lowed pitifully, and sometimes tried to kick Mary's hand away, no matter how gently the girl squeezed the teats. So Stash had to set his own pail aside and stand with one arm over the cow's back, reassuring her, holding her tail away from Mary's face. Even then, as Mary milked her, Brownie's skin shuddered, and she leaned away.

"You'll have to milk her more often," Bruno suggested, passing by with a bucketful of oats for the horses.

Mary stopped, looked up at Stash. "How often?" she asked. But Bruno only shrugged. "He was here four, five times a day," the lad said, unable yet to speak his father's name.

And Lotti thought: we should get Joe over here. He'd fix her up.

***

That afternoon John Kleba drove into the yard. He'd come for Berenice, to take her to a lawyer he knew in Wausau. They had to get probate started, and at the courthouse register Frank's will. As she came down the back steps, humped over, dressed in black, Berenice rather frightened the children. She seemed so self-contained, more than ever unreachable. Yet hour by hour she was regaining her sense of the world. She was well enough now that Aunt Mary had decided to leave the next day.

Bruno cleaned the barn, after milking, and Stash drove down to the sawmill to turn in his resignation. They'd expected it, knowing he was the oldest Topolski boy. It was no loss to them. There were plenty of young men around willing to work for thirty cents an hour.

When he got home, Stash took Molly out of her stall. She hadn't been worked for over a week — when Stash and she had planted the last of the beans — and now she seemed diffident, obeying him only begrudgingly. She jerked and fidgeted as he fastened the harness, skittishly, as though her skin was hypersensitive. Stash knew that she expected Frank's familiar voice, smell and touch. He knew, too, that she would give to him only what he could take from her.

But at last he got her harnessed and hitched to the mower, and as she pulled it toward the yard from behind the granary, he put it in gear. It rattled away in the grass, cutting some and missing some here and there. The machine, he realized, would need a good oiling, adjusting, and sharpening. Unhitching Molly again he bent above the mower to remove the sickle, forgetting exactly how his father had done it. Then he sat at the big round stone, its surface already worn by years of use, and pedaled steadily away, wishing he had someone looking over his shoulder to tell him just how far the edge needed drawing out. By the time he'd finished, he had two deep cuts in the fingers of his left hand.

✳✳✳

Aunt Mary was leaving in the morning. That evening, there was last counsel to give, final reassurances to her sister that things would, in the end, work out. She and Berenice sat in the kitchen, sipping tea. Mary's bags were already by the back door, packed and ready to go. The rest of the family was in bed.

"It will be hard," Mary said to her sister. "But time will heal your wounds. You have your family to think of, your children. And the farm. Only try to do as Frank would have wanted."

Berenice seemed very distant. It was Anna she wanted with her now; Anna and she'd always been the closest. But Anna was in another world. And Mary had done all she could, and done it well, there was no denying that.

"They say," Berenice said, quietly, holding her tea cup on the table, letting the warmth of it seep into her hands, "they say in time the dead forget the living." Her eyes turned to her sister. They were sharp, clear, pleading. "Has he forgotten me, already?"

Aunt Mary shook her head, her eyes closed. She rested her hand on Berenice's. "No. He hasn't forgotten you."

"When he thinks of me, what does he think of?" Mary had no answer. "Of his life," Berenice said quietly, her voice almost prayer-like, "he will remember the fields, the corn seed going into the ground and the little plants you have to keep the crows from. And hay, just cut and on the wagon; the sun, warm as it is now, and in the winter bright but cold. Molly, he will remember Molly, and the plow, walking behind the plow" She thought a moment, searching for some part of herself in all that. "And dancing."

Mary nodded. "Yes. Dancing."

"He held me so close, at our wedding, so gently, as though he did not trust his own strength. He was... He was such a man. And how he loved to dance." She turned to her sister. "You remember, the wedding?"

"Yes. I remember."

"Dancing. Yes, he will remember me dancing." She was trying, as hard as she could, to convince herself. But as she stared out the door, into the darkness gathered around them, there was only, like a great beetle trying to break in, that hovering uncertainty.

✳✳✳

The two sisters stood in the dusty barnyard and embraced. Mary had given all she could to bring Berenice back to health. Now she had her own family to worry about. Over the idling Ford, Stash could not hear their words, only the meaning... the short, reassuring phrases, calm and sorrowful, understanding.

When they broke apart and Mary climbed in, Stash put the car in gear and drove out the drive. Looking back, once on the road, they could see Berenice standing there, twisting her handkerchief in her hands, staring after them.

✳✳✳

The train had arrived on time and taken Aunt Mary away on time. He was walking back to the car when Albert ran out of the depot. "Stash!" he shouted, waving a piece of paper. "Telegram!" Stash turned and accepted the paper. "An old Army buddy?" Albert asked.

Arriving Friday, was all it said. *Signed, Anton.*

"No," Stash said. "Never met him," and left Albert to stand and wonder whatever was going on. Stash set the telegram on the seat beside him, backed up and started up the long hill home. It didn't seem right, a stranger coming into the house, not now. It was an insult to his father.

He handed the paper to his mother. She read it, sighed, as though she felt the same as he did. She sat at the table, staring at the telegram a long time, trying to fit it into a world in which there was no longer room for so much.

Friday. That was tomorrow. It meant he was already on the train, and there was no calling him back.

That afternoon the girls were once again put to cleaning the house. It was like cleaning a sepulcher, to them, the pictures and mirrors still draped with black, his absence the strongest presence of all.

But it gave Berenice something to do, just when that was what she needed. And now, with sister Mary and Walter gone, she was once again back in charge. In the kitchen she began to act the mother hen, clucking and pecking, shoving, warning, hovering. As though her eyes, just opened after a long sleep, suddenly discovered how untidy the hen house had become, and so she set about cleaning it up.

***

Anna was out in the pasture, watching cows. She'd missed the school picnic — that was the day her father got sick — missed graduation — that, the day he died — and now she was sure there would be no high school for her. She had all of that to deal with, but most of all, her father's sudden death. It had been hard on her, they'd been so close. There was no hiding she was his favorite. Now it would have been better to have something active to do, like her sisters in the house; instead, she could only sit and crochet and watch the cows, mulling over what no child her age should ever have to face.

Even Berenice's favorite, Eddie, seemed unable to get involved in life again, in work or play. He moped around the house all day, sitting quietly in a chair, or on the front porch stripping bark off a willow stick and throwing it heedlessly into the tall grass. Berenice would try to fill that emptiness in him; but no matter how hard she tried, it was not hers to fill.

Stash, out in the alfalfa, was getting a start on the haying, riding the noisy mower. Molly, with Prince next to her, still wasn't used to Stash, was constantly balking and refusing to back properly on the corners. The machine itself seemed devilishly rebellious. Twice that first day it broke down — once when a bolt shook itself loose from one of the pitmans and he had to spend twenty frustrating minutes wandering up and down the field, kicking the hay aside, until he found it. And again when the outboard wheel fell off. He'd forgotten to check the cotter pin; it must have slipped out. That he never did find, and had to walk back to the shop and search in the old sugar tin of nuts and bolts until he found another. In the whole day's work he'd cut less than half an acre of hay — might have done as well, he realized, with a scythe.

***

Walerych would either arrive on the 6:35 morning train, or the 7:07 in the evening. He hadn't said. Only Friday.

At morning milking, Mary was all worked up. She squeezed Brownie's sore teat too hard and received for it a kick in the arm, almost upsetting the full bucket. Lotti and Angie wanted to calm their sister but didn't know what to do. They suffered almost as much as she, as each long minute went past. Carrying her bucket of milk to the house, Mary heard, down the hill, the sharp blast of the morning train, whistling as it left the station.

It was like waiting for the sun to come up on her execution day, wondering what faced her on the other side.

She set her bucket on the counter. Lotti, cranking the separator, looked up sympathetically. Mary lifted two buckets of the skim milk to carry out to the pigs. Her nerves were taut, the slightest sound made her jump. As she walked out to the barn, she wondered if he would call for them to pick him up, or walk. By the time she was back in the house, she saw that ten minutes had passed since the train had left. He would have called by now, she thought. He must be walking.

Lotti finished with the cream. Mary washed the buckets with scalding sudsy water. She tried to concentrate on her work. The clang of buckets against one another hurt her ears. But when the clock in the dining room chimed seven o'clock, it was like a reprieve from the governor. It wouldn't take him more than fifteen minutes to walk up the hill. So he hadn't come on the morning train.

Her heart slowed, her senses relaxed. She would have one more day to herself. But it only prolonged the inevitable. She began to think: perhaps there will be a train wreck. Then, realizing what she was wishing, she crossed herself and asked the Lord's forgiveness. Maybe he had changed his mind, and wasn't coming at all. All day long she reached out for any reason she could find to keep him from coming.

Her mother was on edge, too, and terribly demanding, the perfectionist in her coming out beyond all reason. She lashed out at Mary for spilling some tea, and for not watching the oven full of *ponchki* closely enough. When she looked around, but could not find Mary, Lotti had to say she'd gone to the bathroom.

But Mary was upstairs, crying. On the edge of her bed, handkerchief in hand, she was at the very end of her wits. She prayed to the Virgin, prayed for her father, who was in heaven now. Then, full of remorse, she remembered how she'd promised him, on his deathbed, to obey her mother. That meant going through with it. Wiping her eyes, she started down the stairs, weak-kneed as she was, toward the sound of her mother's grumbling chatter. But halfway down she stopped, and leaned on the railing, to catch her breath.

✳✳✳

The day drew out forever. Only those days waiting at the hospital seemed longer. After lunch, her mother took a nap. Mary was left at the dining room table, her hands usually so deft seeming twice their normal size and only half as agile. She had to rip the doily she was crocheting, begin it again. Above her the clock noisily dragged out the minutes. She thought she might suffocate.

But then it was suppertime, and Stash had come in from cutting hay, like his father before him, hungry and thirsty. There was the evening milking yet to do. By then she was exhausted from the tension, had resigned herself to whatever fate had to offer. Hauling the buckets of milk into the house, the evening settling in around the yard, her knees were weak. The air was still and cool; rich with the smell of new-cut hay. It should have been a perfect evening, one of those quiet June twilights one dreams of all the rest of the year. Instead, to her, the robins putting the *dompki* to sleep and the fresh, sweet breeze seemed only that much more cruel.

It was her turn to work the separator. She poured in the milk, then started it cranking, round and round, a steady fifty turns a minute, no more nor less. The thick cream flowed into its bucket on one side, the thin faintly blue skim milk out the other. She thought: I'll finish, and let Lotti clean it while I go out for a walk. And there was a voice inside her she'd kept muffled till then, whispering: and not come back!

It scared her. But she thought: I'll just go for a walk, and then decide.

Lotti brought in the last two buckets, returned to the barn to rub Brownie down. Mary cranked, the familiar noise of the separator lulling her bare nerves to a relative calm. Only half a bucket left, she thought. And if I have to run away, then run I will.

Above the clink and whir of the separator she thought she heard Shep barking, and the sound of footsteps on the porch. But she'd been imagining noises all day long, had confronted shadows and faces where there was only empty air. She no longer trusted her senses, her mind, even her heart. There was nothing left to trust. So certainly she had just imagined that knocking at the door.

And was she imagining her mother, now, hurrying out from the living room to see who was at the door?

She would not look, she promised herself, cranking the separator with all the energy she could muster. She would not look. Now no more cream came into the bucket, and no more milk. She'd finished. Now she could get away. Now she could run across the field, and never stop running...

She turned to escape.

"Jesus Marya!" she muttered, low, leaning suddenly on the cold metal of the separator.

29

Gosc w dom, Bog w dom.
(A guest in the house, God in the house.)
— Traditional Polish proverb.

He stepped in, dragging with him a rather ponderous and well-worn canvas duffel bag, which he set beside the door. The walk up from the depot had apparently been more than he'd expected. He might have been more comfortable but for his uniform, with its heavy wool jacket, bulging woolen pants and high-laced spats, which, though it was wrinkled and soiled here and there from the long journey, he wore to provide what effect it might of authority. The first thing, however, which Mary noticed about this Anton Walerych was not his uniform, but his size. He was shorter than Mary. Shorter even than her mother, by almost half a head. Mary could not believe it. She stared at him, as though mesmerized — then glanced down at his legs, half expecting to see them sunken from ankle down into the floor. But no, his boots — dry, cracked, covered with dust, turned up at the toes — were firmly planted right there on the linoleum. It was no mistake. He had to look up to her mother, and to her. He, whose fundamental goal in life was to get others to look up to him, instead had to look up to everyone else.

"Mary!" her mother barked. Then, louder, "Mary!"

She pretended not to hear. Now her mother took her hand, pulled her forcefully away from the separator. Reluctantly she followed, her eyes averted.

"This is Mary," she heard her mother say. But to the girl, it was as though the voice came from a stranger. And the Mary she spoke of, where was she?

He stepped forward, offered his hand. Her hand, by another, was attached to his. Now she had to look.

She looked at him — looked down at him — to see his jet-black hair, thin and wiry. Self-consciously his hand rose, ran across his head. But still, in back, his hair stood up. His dark eyes were placed rather narrowly on either side of a rather prominent and bulbous nose. His face, though not fat, was fleshy and blotched with veins here and there, Texas-tanned, but not healthy. In his mouth he held a dark cigarette holder, which twitched somewhat nervously, and from which the short butt of a cigarette was smoldering.

Stash used to say that the Army made two sizes of uniform: too big and too small. Though undoubtedly issued what for everyone else would have been the latter, Walerych's erect posture, shoulders back and chin high, was given a comic relief by the four enormous pockets of his jacket and by the way the sleeves seemed to creep down and cover his hands. The oversized jacket, the stiff and formal pose, his face itself, all might have made her titter to herself, under different circumstances.

His handshake, at least, was gentle. Yet he held it beyond the point of courtesy; beyond the point when she wanted her hand back. She knew what he was doing, and inside, she fought it. I am master, he was saying, like it or not. Like me or not.

He bowed slightly; she could see little white flakes sprinkled through the ebony of his hair. She shivered involuntarily.

"*Dzien dobre,*" he said, politely. His Polish had a strange inflection to it. She stared at him, and suddenly she realized — as her mother had long ago suspected — that this Anton Walerych was no Pole at all. Though their letters had been exchanged in Polish, she suddenly realized he was, God forgive him, a Russian.

He let go her hand, smiled. How she wanted to run! But he blocked the door. He turned and extracted the short cigarette from its holder, pushed the screen door ajar and tossed the butt out into the driveway. She watched it there, as though entranced, as though it were her soul tossed out into the dirt to smolder and then go out. But suddenly, from toward the barn, a big red hen came running and pecked at it, picked it up, shook it, and when its smoke drifted into her eyes, dropped it and made a quick retreat.

"Well, I," Walerych said, slipping the cigarette holder into his pocket and clearing his throat, "Well..." He turned to Berenice. "Would you have for me a drink of water, please?"

Now Mary could see the sweat pearled on his forehead. Berenice nodded to the bucket and dipper behind him. Her mother was not as cordial to the young man as Mary had expected. There was a chance, buoyed up with the growing certainty they were dealing with a Russian, that her mother would send him on his way. Mary said a silent prayer of thanks. God had inspected His legions and sent the least acceptable candidate He could find. Certain of this now, that fate had at last taken a turn on her side, Mary could view Walerych with some ironic detachment.

"Come in, please, and sit down," her mother offered when he'd set the dipper back into the bucket, wiping his mouth on his sleeve.

Berenice directed him into the dining room, and let it be known Mary was to follow, too. He stood beside the table. Here, in the house, he looked more droll than ever. Mary almost felt sorry for him. He was scrutinizing the room, his hands resting on the tabletop. His eyes fixed on the wedding picture hung on the far wall, draped with black cloth.

"You are in mourning?" he asked.

"My husband," Berenice replied, finding it difficult yet to say the words, "passed on. Only last week."

Now Mary watched Walerych closely. He stood a moment staring at the wedding picture, all his attention drawn to the figure of the groom, then so young, so masculine, a big cigar in his fist. Her husband had been a handsome man. And the bride handsome, too. He could see the resemblance to the darkly sagging woman beside him, but he had to look closely. He stared at the picture a long time, reacting to this unforeseen turn of events. At last he turned to Berenice. "I'm sorry," he said, with true feeling. He glanced at Mary, who had to look away. "It was sudden, then?" he asked.

"Yes, sudden," Berenice repeated. "One day healthy, four days later he was gone." She pulled a chair out. "Please, sit down. Would you like some tea? Or coffee?"

"I've been sitting on the train for two days," he said. "Thank you. But tea, yes."

"Mary, some tea," her mother commanded. Mary hurried into the kitchen. There she found she'd suddenly forgotten where the cups were, and opened instead the canned-goods cupboard.

She wondered if she were losing her mind entirely. At last she got a cup and was just pouring the water into it when Lotti and Angie appeared at the door, their chores in the barn all finished. Seeing the canvas bag on the floor, and the way Mary's hand trembled as she held the steaming kettle, they stopped halfway through the door.

"He's here?" Lotti asked. Mary nodded. Lotti turned to Angie: then both backed out the door and went for a long walk out in the field. They were no more ready to meet him than Mary had been.

"Dzienkuje," Walerych said, as Mary set the cup and saucer in front of him. He lifted the tea bag to dunk it in the water, quietly watching it soak and the clear water slowly turn a faintly reddish brown.

Again the back door opened. Now it was Stash and Bruno who came in. Mary could just see them in the kitchen, washing up. Walerych, as though their entrance made him nervous, pulled a cigarette from his pocket. "Do you mind?" he asked Berenice, but fit it into the holder and lit it before she had time to reply. He held the extinguished match until it cooled, then slipped it into his pocket. The cigarette holder grasped firmly between his teeth, he lifted the tea bag out of the cup, wrapped it around the spoon, squeezed it and lay it beside the cup. He knew how closely they were watching him; every move he made was deliberate and cautious.

Suddenly Bruno was standing in the doorway, confronting his mother, his sister, and this rather eccentric stranger with a kind of cool and deliberate aloofness. As he stepped into the room, he was astonished to see that this apparent forgery of a man, who depended for his dignity on an ivory cigarette holder, who stood unnaturally erect, whose brows scowled out at the world, was not an inch — not a hair, nor even a quarter of a hair — taller than himself. As they peremptorily shook hands, it rather pleased the boy to recognize that the stranger was at the moment as uncomfortable as he was.

It was not a question, with Bruno, of liking or not liking the man. He'd never met anyone — his father and Joe Stelmach excepted — he really, fundamentally liked. No, for him it was a matter of whether or not he could bear the man's faults. Holding Walerych's hand for just a moment — it seemed to him rather small and weak — Bruno nodded, then excused himself and hurried off to the living room.

Walerych just had time for a sip of tea when Stash appeared from the kitchen. He stepped up to the stranger. There was a commonality, in the uniform; though Stash had within a week of being mustered in come to realize that the simple act of draping a uniform on a man doesn't change him any more than giving him a haircut or polishing his shoes. They faced one another, the tall farm lad still in his barn clothes, broad shouldered, his limbs weary from the day's work, and the short, nervous stranger, and instantly and intuitively, each recognized his opposite.

"This is Stash," Berenice introduced, "our oldest boy. And now, the man of the house."

Stash, always uncomfortable with formalities, smiled, shook hands, and slipped away to join his younger brother.

Mary, meanwhile, had been sitting at the table in a kind of unconsciousness. She was not unaware of Walerych's furtive glances in her direction. He was sizing her up; of course, he would. She felt — and smiled to herself at devising the image — rather like a duck her mother had brought to market for sale. And she thought, if that's their game, then I'll look my worst.

But it went no farther than that. She was not used to playing parts, or games — or anything, really, other than herself. That, of course, she suddenly realized, would be her downfall.

"Would you like something to eat?" Berenice asked the stranger.

"That would be all right," he answered, sipping his tea. He sat down, then: and Mary was sent into the kitchen to bring the cabbage and potatoes, kept warm on the stove, and the big heap of *ponchki* baked especially for him. She obeyed willingly and silently, only angry at herself that she knew no other way.

Walerych sat at the table and ate with a slow elegance they were all unaccustomed to. He even asked for a napkin. With her mother's permission, Mary pulled one from the chest of drawers. Silently, carefully, he chewed each mouthful, Berenice standing beside him, and Mary, towel in hand, as though awaiting his next command.

Lotti and Angie came in at last from outside, and busied themselves in the kitchen. Mary could hear them complaining that the separator had not been cleaned. Gladly would she have gone to clean it.

When Walerych was finished eating, and had carefully wiped, then blotted his mouth with the napkin, which he dropped indecorously onto the plate, he thanked Berenice for the food, complimenting her on her cooking. He seemed so polite now. Someone so courteous, Mary thought, certainly cannot be dangerous.

"Aha!" he said suddenly, frightening both Mary and her mother. "I have almost forgot!" He stood and hurried into the kitchen, paying no attention to the sisters busy there. In a moment he hurried back into the dining room to present Mary with a small box, wrapped carefully in deep blue wrapping paper and tied with a yellow ribbon.

"For you, Mary," he said, setting it on the table before her. "Go on, open it."

Mary glanced at her mother, whose eyes urged her on. Nervously she tore aside the thin paper and held a flat black box. When she opened it she saw a fine bracelet, of artificial pearls, which sparkled with a colorful sheen. She looked again at her mother, then to the stranger who stood beside her, beaming joyously.

"Please, put it on," he said. The bracelet was beautiful, its pearls shone with an incandescence. It had not been cheap. But Mary set the box back on the table.

Walerych appealed to her mother. "She wouldn't feel right," Berenice explained, "so soon after her father's death."

"Of course," he replied.

"Now what do you say, Mary?" Berenice demanded.

Not looking up, she muttered, *"Dzienkuje."*

"And for you, Pani Topolska." He produced another box from his coat pocket, which Berenice accepted and opened. It was a religious cameo, nicely worked in ivory on a cerulean ground, of the Sacred Heart. She was quite surprised by this unexpected generosity.

"I had something too for her father," Walerych muttered.

"Yes," Berenice said. "It was nice of you."

Mary was left to clean the table off while Berenice and Walerych made their way into the living room. There he had the chance to meet the younger girls, Sophie and Anna, and Eddie. He seemed to take to the younger children with an honest affection, held Eddie's hand warmly: perhaps because, smaller than him, he saw them as no threat.

But when Berenice asked him to please sit, he looked around the room and found the chair their father used to sit in. Unknowingly, when he sat down, he managed to extinguish what little good will he'd established with the children.

Mary came into the room. Her mother gestured her to sit opposite Walerych. She brought her crocheting, turned inward, using her work as an escape from his presence. A long, awkward silence ensued. Noticing Stash's picture on the table where only a week before had lain Frank's casket, Walerych asked what unit he'd been in. It turned out that Stash, who had been a cook's assistant, had been stationed only a hundred miles from Walerych's Depot Battalion.

Again there was a silence. Smoking calmly on his cigarette, Walerych was reappraising his position in light of what he'd learned so far. The death of the girl's father, that had made it rather awkward, his arriving when he did. They should have let him know. He might have waited a week or two; it would have been the proper thing to do.

But of course there was the other side of it. He remembered Mary writing that the farm was held in free title. So now it was her mother's. Yes, it was hers to dispense with as she saw fit. From what he'd seen of the place, coming up the road and now from inside the house, it was well-managed. A place to be proud of. And a new garage, yes, he remembered that, too.

It was a good farm. And now someone would have to take over where the girl's father had left off. Funny, he thought, I don't even know what his name was. But it would be awkward to ask. He knew as little of farming as he knew of, say, cooking or sewing. But they couldn't know that. For all they knew he'd been sent by God just in time to keep the farm from falling apart.

And the girl, he had to admit he could have done far worse. She was quiet — and how he hated brash, big-mouthed women! She was obedient, that he could see. And really quite good looking. There was nothing to be ashamed of there. No stranger to work, either. He could see that just then, the way her hands, though they trembled, moved through the needlework. No, he thought, he could have done much worse.

He imagined a wedding. Yes.

He imagined a wedding night.

Relaxing back into the big, comfortable chair, he held the cigarette holder complacently in his hand. It was the mother who held the title to the farm, and to the girl. It would be the mother he would have to win over. Properly played, it was a hand he could not lose.

He smiled to himself, began to feel at home.

***

Upstairs in bed Sophie was passing to her younger sister, like a precious heirloom, what she'd learned through overhearing Lotti and Angie about Walerych's visit. "He's come to marry our Mary," she said.

It took Anna some time to absorb this. "But," she whispered, "I thought Mary and Joe were getting married."

"Mother won't let them," Sophie answered.

Anna turned in the bed, to face her sister. "Why not?"

"Well, because," Sophie began to answer with all the wisdom of fourteen, "because... well, just because."

Anna lay back. "I don't like him. I hope he goes away, tomorrow. I want Mary and Joe to get married." Then quietly, her voice hardly more than a sigh, "I wish father was here."

***

In the morning, they went out to the barn already tired. Bruno, shaking a forkful of hay to each of the cows, stopped in front of Brownie. She looked feverish, her eyes listless and glazed. Now and then she was racked with deep coughs. He called Stash to have a look at her. He bent to feel her udder; it was apparent now that all four quarters were infected. If the infection spread to her lungs, it would be pneumonia, and then, the end.

During breakfast Stash brought up Brownie's infection with his mother. She'd already noticed that their milk was down. It could have been because Frank wasn't doing the milking, it could have been because the first flush of fresh pasture was already over. Or it could have been some sickness spreading through the herd. There was no way of knowing.

They spoke quietly at the kitchen table. Their guest was still in bed, though his just being there was like a shadow over the house, or like a too-tight collar making it hard to breathe. Stash went out to hitch up the dump rake and get ready for the first load of hay. If things went right he could drive over to see Helen after chores.

***

It was nearly nine when Walerych appeared out of his room. He stood a moment in the dining room, seemed pleased with himself, yawned. He was dressed now in civilian cloths: a blue cotton shirt and dark pants. And instead of his oversize Army boots he had black shoes on, slick patent-leather shoes of little use on the farm.

The sleep had made him more amiable. Coming among the girls who were busy in the kitchen, he wished them all a hearty good morning. But they stayed away from him as though he were carrying some kind of disease.

He opened the back door to look out into the warm summer morning. He coughed, spat and closed the door. He stood a moment watching all the bustling around him: as though this were an infantryman's dream, a kitchen full of girls.

He ran his hand across his cheek and down over his chin, was clearly in need of a shave. "Could I ask you for a little hot water?" he spoke to no one in general. Mary, already peeling potatoes for lunch, ignored his request. Berenice herself carefully poured a pint of scalding water into Frank's shaving bowl and handed it to Walerych. Fetching a razor from his pack, he returned to the kitchen in his undershirt. He stropped the razor on the leather hanging on the wall. He stood at the counter, all lathered up and scraping the blade across his skin. The girls were accustomed to their father shaving in their presence, and Stash: but this was almost repulsive.

Rinsed and dried, Walerych slipped back into his shirt and sat at the table. Mary brought him a cup of coffee. Berenice slid onto the table the plate of *ponchki*. He drank the coffee down. Mary refilled his cup, then he attacked the pile of *ponchki*.

Finished, he lit a cigarette, sat smugly sipping his coffee while everyone else was already three hours into the day's work. Mary felt the life being drawn out of her. Her skin crept whenever she moved near him. She clung desperately to the hope that her mother would feel the same about this man as she did.

Outside there was the sound of a car. Berenice peered out through the curtains. It was Verna Las, Father Nowak's housekeeper, at the wheel. The car had barely stopped when Father himself stepped out of the car. Berenice did not want Father coming in the house: but already it was too late.

"*Dzien dobre*," he said to Mary, who opened the door for him. "God be with you." He stepped inside, removed his hat. "I was passing by," he explained, "and thought I'd stop in. Do you mind?" There was a moment of silence. Father found himself staring at the stranger seated at the table.

"Ah, Father," Berenice was forced to introduce them, "this is Anton Walerych." The priest held out his hand. "Father Nowak, our priest," Berenice explained to Walerych, who stood and nodded. When they'd dropped hands, Father turned to Mary. He put his arm around her shoulder. "And you, my little Mary, how are you?"

It was clear to Walerych, already, that he'd just met a man he would in time have to deal with.

Berenice slid a chair back. "Sit down," she asked the priest, though her voice was clearly lacking in conviction.

"Just for a moment, perhaps," he answered, setting his hat on the table. He was about to sit when a movement outside caught his eye. He turned, looked out the screen door. There, waddling across the yard was a proud mother duck, followed by a dozen bright yellow young, not more than two days old. "Look!" he said. The girls and their mother glanced outside. Angie, who was standing by the car talking with Verna, stopped to watch the pretty little parade.

Father sat. Mary brought him a cup of tea. No sugar, a little cream, just as he always liked it. She moved the plate of *ponchki* to his end of the table. "Thank you," he said, smiling up at the girl. "And how are we getting along?"

Walerych's cigarette burned perilously close to the holder. But he seemed self-absorbed, defensive, as though plotting strategies against the deference they showed the priest.

"Oh, we're managing," Berenice answered, standing beside the table. "Sophie," she turned to her daughter, "you and Anna go up and clean your room. Right now." Then she sat, the two men opposite one another, she between.

"Yes, yes," the priest said, chewing the doughy *ponchek.* "I'm sure you're managing." He wanted to feel sorry for Berenice, who had to carry the burden of the farm on her own back now. But Mary's presence in the room stood to accuse him. He turned to the other man. "You arrived recently?"

"Last night," Walerych answered, at last carefully extracting the butt from the holder. He stood and threw it into the cook stove, then sat once again.

"There wasn't time," Berenice explained, "for us to tell him. About Frank."

"No, I suppose not." The priest seemed, in his answers, to be asking further questions. He was in an impossible position. His heart told him to join in the girl's revulsion for the stranger. But he knew, too, that he must try to love and care for all of God's children. There was no room, in Christ's heart, for hatred, so there must be no room in his. "I see that Stash is out haying," he observed.

"They'll bring in the first load today," Berenice explained.

The priest sipped his tea, the breakfast dishes clanked on the bench. Walerych sat quietly, then coughed.

Berenice had something she wanted to say. Her hands, on the tabletop, massaged her fingers. At last she came out with it. "Would you bless our animals, Father?"

"Well of course. Are you having trouble?"

"Our milk is down, our best milker has a fever."

"Ah." He had seen it so often before. With the master gone from a farm, diseases of all imaginable sorts hopped out of nowhere. He ran his hand through his hair, finished his tea. "Now?" he asked.

Berenice shrugged. "If you like."

"Well, why not?" He stood. He had come to see how the family was getting along without Frank. What he found did not reassure him. The stranger Mary had spoken of was already here. The herd was suffering — how badly, he could not say. Berenice, of course, would keep from him the worst of her problems. But this blessing of the animals, at least it was something he could do to help. "I'll go, then," he said, picking up his hat. Berenice stood and reached into her apron, brought out her coin purse. She flipped it open discreetly and extracted a half dollar which she offered to the priest. "No, Pani Topolska," he objected. But she insisted. So he took it, with a rather formal slight bow. He slipped the coin inside his pocket. "Will you come to the barn?"

"Bruno's out there. He'll have to let them out to pasture soon."

"Ah." He waited for Walerych to make his move. But the man had a perfect poker face.

"Why don't you go and see the barn?" Berenice urged him.

"Of course," Walerych replied, as though she were his commanding officer.

Father reached into his car to get his black traveling case. Opening it, he paged through his breviary, then took out the aspersor. "I'll be back in a few minutes," he told Verna, still chatting with Angie.

Walerych, no taller than the priest's shoulders, followed into the barn. Bruno, who was standing on the railing of the calf pen, whistling to himself while he waited for the cows to finish their grain, was taken by surprise. Shyly he jumped off the railing and stood before the priest.

"Well young man," the priest said cordially, "you've twice the work now, haven't you? Your mother tells me the stock aren't doing very well."

Walerych stood just inside the door looking the barn over, uncertain if he was quite ready to step any closer. Bruno, who could just see him behind the priest's robe, would at the moment have liked to take the fork to him.

"Which one's the sickest?" Father asked, moving along the aisle. "This one?" He stopped behind Short-Tail, who though carrying little flesh, was perfectly healthy. The boy shook his head, nodded toward Brownie.

"Ah." Father rather timidly patted her haunch. He could see drops of clotted milk on the floor beneath her. "Poor thing," he said. He closed his eyes, and with his hand resting lightly on her back, muttered a silent prayer. Bruno bent his head. Walerych looked on unaffected.

"And the others?" Father asked, stepping back across the gutter.

"Mostly not too good," the boy shrugged.

Father's tongue clicked against his teeth. He liked the smell of the barn: the hay, the fresh manure, the rich warm smell of the cows themselves. "Well then, we'll have to do something about that, won't we?" He held the aspersorium in his left hand, raised his right in a gesture of blessing.

"Oh God," he spoke, quietly but with feeling, "who has lightened man's toil by the creation of dumb animals, do not let us be deprived of their use, upon which we depend for our livelihood. And especially now, in this time of great sorrow, grant this family the ease of good health for themselves and all their livestock. We ask this in Christ's name. Amen."

Bruno stood absolutely still, wondering if there was something special he was supposed to do. When the priest was finished, the boy crossed himself. Now Father held the aspersorium high, shook water from it onto the backs of the nearest cows, then turned to bless the calves behind. He walked slowly up the aisle, blessing the animals in their turn. He stopped to study the horses, then turned again to Bruno.

"There now," he said. "That's done."

Suddenly he turned to face Walerych, who flinched unconsciously. "And you," the priest asked, "you are a farmer?"

The man's dark eyes studied the priest coldly. It was time

to make a decision. Quickly he spoke the single syllable. "No."

The priest drew in a long, meaningful breath, let it out slowly. "It's terrible," he said, "Frank's going so quickly. Who would ever have guessed. Such a strong man! And such a farmer!" Then he remembered the boy, put his hand on his shoulder. "They're a good family, all of them good hard workers." Bruno hung his head shyly. Father pulled the boy's cap down over his eyes. "Well now," the priest said. "I've more visits to make yet before lunch. God's work, like the farmer's, is never done."

He stopped in at the house to say good-bye to Berenice and the girls, expressing his opinion that the animals would soon begin to pick up. Angie, still standing next to the car, he kissed on the forehead. Bruno cranked the engine over for them. As Verna pulled out of the drive, Father allowed himself to pity Berenice. The rest of the family, too. And he allowed himself the luxury of a moment's animosity toward the stranger who stood beside the barn door, legs far apart, hands behind his back, as though sentinel over his own private treasury.

***

But the sentinel stayed at his post only until the car was out of sight, then slipped into the barn to silently watch Bruno let out the cows. When they were gone, the boy and his sister following them out to pasture, he walked slowly down the aisle, scrutinizing, calculating. Yes, it was a fine farm. It showed the work and pride which the girl's father had put into it. He could not have come into a better situation.

He stopped to study the horses in their stalls. He had learned, in the Army, a little about horses. He knew you could tell a lot about them by the condition of their teeth. He patted Molly on her nose, tried to open her mouth. But the animal pulled away, whinnying and kicking the side of her stall.

He swore at her and marched out of the barn.

That evening Walerych asked Berenice if he could have a look around the farm. Stash, who with the help of the girls had brought in the first load of hay, was just cleaning up to go over to Helen's. But instead he was drafted into giving Walerych a tour. They walked in silence through the fields, keeping their distance from each other. There were a hundred questions Walerych might have asked, about soils, drainage, crop rotation, fertilizers, frost dates, had he known enough to ask them. Stash volunteered only to show him the boundaries of the property.

They had not spoken a dozen words. They headed back to the house, shuffling through the stubble of alfalfa which Stash had taken off that afternoon. Passing then into the orchard, whose trees had already lost their blooms and were bedecked instead with tiny green apples, hardly larger than peas, Stash stopped beside his beehives. Coming in by the hundreds, the bees had their regular line of flight, which he was careful to stand away from. Four or five landed on the bottom board of the hive every second. He could see, by the way they fell clumsily onto the board or the nearby ground, that they must be heavily laden with pollen and nectar. He stepped beside the nearest hive, lifted its top and cautiously pulled out a single frame. It was heavy, half full with thin, clear nectar: it and the warm wax gave off a sweet, delicious smell. The bees were too busy to bother him. He held it high for Walerych to see. But the other man had backed away, afraid of the buzzing bees which seemed to surround him now from every direction. Wide-eyed he stared at Stash, astounded that the young man could stand so calmly as the bees buzzed all around him.

Then Walerych did just the wrong thing. He began to swat at the bees near him, and in so doing, angered one to the point of stinging him. So when Stash slid the frame back into place, very carefully so as not to harm any bees, and turned to rejoin his guest, Walerych was already halfway to the house, nursing a growing welt on his neck. He had seen enough of the farm.

30

*It seems not to be the case that there
is a Power in the universe which watches
over the well-being of individuals with
parental care and brings all their affairs
to a happy ending.*
> — from *New Introductory Lectures on
> Psychology*, by Sigmund Freud

L otti stood at the telephone, anxiously peering out the window. Her mother, Angie and Sophie were still busily planting peas. "Four nine three," she said. "Thank you."

Though she was alone in the house, she spoke quietly. "Sophie? *Ya.* Is Joe around? Can I talk to him?" There was a long silence on the phone. "Joe! Lotti. Yes... Yes... Say, Joe, our cows ain't doing too well. Yeah. Brownie's all feverish. No, she stepped on her udder and it's all infected. Yeah. No, they ain't been milking too good either. I don't think so. Bruno's feeding them just fine. Listen, would you? I'll tell him to bring them in early... Say, Joe, mother doesn't know I'm calling. Yeah... Oh, she's okay."

Berenice had woven a blanket of ignorance over the family. No one knew how much anyone else knew about almost anything — especially about this fellow from Texas. Had Joe even heard of him? Lotti wasn't sure. But if he was coming over, he'd better know ahead of time.

"That guy from Texas, did Mary tell you about him? Yeah? Well, he's here. Three days ago. He's... Well, you'll have to see for yourself. Joe, there won't be any trouble, will there? Thanks. Okay. Right."

She hung up the receiver quickly and hurried out to rejoin her mother, praying to God she'd done the right thing.

After lunch they all went back out to the garden. The planting was all finished now, but there was weeding to do, and in the strawberries, too. By midafternoon Mary and Angie were sent into the house to start supper. They'd just gotten inside when the Stelmach's Chevy pulled into the yard. Mary, recognizing it, stared out the window. She saw her mother, bent over hoeing, straighten up and peer at Joe as though he were the devil himself. But Joe jumped easily out of the car and walked right up to her. Mary could see his lips moving but could not hear what he was saying.

"I heard your cows were sick," Joe informed Berenice.

A coarse babushka over her head, the billowing uneven folds of her heavy skirt making her seem as wide as she was tall, Berenice swung her hoe and sliced a young pigweed in half. "Oh?" she asked. "And who told you that?"

But Joe only stood facing up to her with the same silence she'd so often used on others.

"Father Nowak's come and blessed them," Berenice said, turning back to her work. Did Joe know about Walerych? she thought. He seemed to know more than he should.

"That was nice of him," Joe answered, his hands on his hips. "Are they any better?"

Lotti glanced up at him guiltily. He winked at her, smiled.

"Anyway they're out to pasture," was Berenice's answer. But just then, as if by signal, they heard the bell of the lead-cow, saw them coming in a line up the lane. Berenice, confused, looked up at the sun. "Now what's the boy up to?"

Again Joe winked at Lotti. "In Frank's name, Pani Topolska," he said, "let me have a look at them."

She stared at him coldly. Far out in the field, behind him, she could see Stash and Walerych, tedding the hay. The taller man moved gracefully, steadily, his fork swinging up and over with an easy rhythm. In his row, Stash was far ahead of the other man, who was every few steps stopping to catch his breath.

If I keep them apart, she thought, and keep Joe out of the house.

She nodded curtly.

Joe turned quickly and picked up his medicine, all of which had been selected for him by Frank himself, out of the car. He hurried into the barn, arrived just as the cows came lumbering in. He helped tie them into their stanchions. Bruno, seeing him, smiled and waved.

"Brownie doesn't look so good," Joe said. "What you been giving her, whiskey instead of water?" Bruno smiled, beat the mud loose from his boots with a stick.

Joe moved carefully behind Brownie, bent to squeeze milk from her udder. Her foot lifted to push his hand away. He crooned to her; it was a familiar voice. She turned, her eyes clouded with fever. He reached up and scratched behind her ear.

"Don't worry, girl," he said, "we'll have you better in no time." He shouted to Bruno, locking in the last of the cows. "Bring me some oats, will you?" Bruno disappeared and in a moment had half a bucket of oats at Joe's feet.

Joe opened his bag of medicine, twisted the top of a small bottle and sprinkled a dozen drops onto the oats, then did the same from another bottle. He mixed the oats around and set them under Brownie's nose. She sniffed at them, licked fussily a few of the grains.

"Some water," Joe said. After she'd drunk a half bucket of fresh water, she took to the oats with more appetite.

Joe looked each cow over carefully, one by one, and gave to some the same medicine, to others different drops. He handed one bottle to Bruno with instructions on how to use it. Bruno, holding the bottle in his hand, tried to read the label. "Sulph...sulphate of..."

"Quinine," Joe said. "It's for the fever. But just to those four. I'll be back in a day or two. If they aren't better by then we'll have to try something else." He gave Brownie a reassuring slap on the rump, then went over to the calf pen to see her calf. It was growing well, looked strong and healthy. It brought back memories, to both Bruno and him, of the terrible time they'd had, working alongside Frank, getting the calf out. Joe reached out and scratched the calf's head. It was the way life was. Some are born, some must die.

By the time he'd left the barn to put his medicine case back into the car, the garden was empty — they'd retreated into the house. It was near suppertime. As he went around to crank the car over, he saw Stash and the new man coming in from the field. Joe could not pass up the opportunity of meeting this man whose relationship to Mary — at least according to the girl's mother — was meant to supplant his own. He promised himself to control his anger. He could save all that for a later date.

So, instead of cranking the car over, he put one foot up on the bumper and stood chewing a succulent timothy stem, watching the two men grow slowly larger and larger as they neared the yard.

Stash, coming around the woodshed, was the first to see him; he held his hand out and smiled. "Joe!" he said.

"I stopped by to treat your herd," Joe said in way of explanation, shaking his head and clicking his tongue.

"Yeah," Stash replied. "If pa was here..."

"I know," Joe agreed. "I know."

The other man, sensing Joe's intimacy with the family, kept back. Leaning on his fork, he wiped his forehead with an old handkerchief already wet with sweat and stuck with dust. Joe gave him a good looking over; swore to himself that he would keep Mary from having to marry this man.

Stash turned. "Anton, this is Joe Stelmach."

Walerych stepped forward to shake hands. He alone did not know that he was meeting, in the cold glare of this young farmer, his arch-rival, who would fight for Mary to the end.

Joe couldn't believe that Berenice would actually be serious about this man, who seemed so out of place on the farm. "Getting some hay in?" Joe commented, nodding to the open doors of the mow.

"Just three loads so far," Stash confessed, and from the tone of his voice spoke eloquently of what little help he was getting from the man beside him. Walerych, sensing himself the outsider, dropped his fork on the ground, turned and walked over to the pump, where he stood pumping cold water over his head.

"How's he doing?" Joe asked quietly.

Stash shook his head. "Gets in the way as much as anything." Walerych had pulled a cigarette from his pocket, was lighting it. "Say, come on in for a drink of something," Stash said.

Joe glanced at the house. He really did long to see Mary. But his guess was that she was already hidden away somewhere — or else, right at her mother's side, like a chick under wing. "No, I'd better not," he said wistfully. "Say," he turned to Stash, "we're having a Union meeting Saturday night. Eight o'clock, my place. You'll come?" Stash shrugged. He'd never been as enthusiastic about the Union as his father had. Or Joe.

Angie stuck her head out the back door. "Suppertime!" she shouted, then waved to Joe.

"Come in for a few minutes," Stash urged.

Walerych was already headed for the door. His going in there with Mary, it snapped something in Joe. He'd been Frank's best friend. Berenice couldn't keep him out of the house. "Just for a minute," he said.

"Good." Stash walked over and picked up Walerych's fork and leaned the two together against the porch.

When they came in the door, Berenice turned. Her eyes burned at Joe; even he was intimidated by the power they held. Angie and Lotti were carrying plates into the dining room. Mary was nowhere to be seen.

Stash drank from the dipper, filled it again and handed it to Joe. Joe emptied it, set it back into the bucket. "I gave them some tonic," he explained to Berenice, "and left some for Bruno. It should help."

Berenice wheeled and picked a big bowl of potatoes off the table, carried them into the other room. "Time to eat," she announced coldly. Stash hesitated, then went in to sit down, leaving Joe alone in the kitchen. Suddenly Berenice reappeared, lifted the milk jug.

"I'd like to see Mary for a minute," Joe asked, politely.

But Berenice swept into the dining room. Joe followed her, to stand in the doorway between the two rooms. They were all seated at the big table, passing plates among them. There was an extra setting. It was for Mary. Joe felt out of place, watching them settle into their meal.

The new man gulped down a glass of milk and stuck his fork into the pile of bread halfway across the table. Joe figured the little stranger must not have known about him and Mary. Well, he thought, it's about time he found out. He turned suddenly and shouted up the stairs. "Mary!"

There was no answer.

Berenice approached. "We're eating, Joe," she said, as politely as she could force herself. But Joe did not move.

Walerych set his fork down, was looking back and forth from Joe to Berenice. A light was dawning behind his narrow dark eyes. All the others at the table had turned inward, were eating quietly, pretending not to notice what was going on. Lotti was wishing she hadn't called Joe.

Joe turned, toward the stairs, as though he was about to go up them. Berenice's hand caught him, like a cat springing on a mouse. "Joe!" she said.

Walerych stood up. "What do you want here?" he said to Joe.

What right did this stranger have to suddenly take the position of head of the family? Scorn flickered out from the edges of Joe's lips. Then his eyes broke away from the stranger, turned to Berenice, who still had him by the arm. "You won't get away with this," he said, "if I have to burn in hell for it, I'll stop you."

Walerych pushed his chair back, stepped around the table toward them. Now Stash stood, too, uncertain what was going to happen. Berenice's arm went out, held Walerych back.

"Go!" she said to Joe. "Go on home!"

He fixed the stranger with a contemptuous stare. Joe was almost twice his size, strong, quick, agile. It seemed a ludicrous contest. "Mary!" Joe shouted. "It's Joe, Mary!" The house was absolutely quiet, still as a tomb. A long moment passed. A car went by on the road. Shep barked at it.

Joe pulled his arm free from Berenice's hand and turned suddenly to hurry out the door. No one moved until they'd heard his car cough to life and roar with defiance out the drive.

Stash was the first to sit down, then Walerych. They went back to their meal. Berenice pulled the curtain back in the living room; satisfied that Joe was indeed gone, she went to open the door to her bedroom.

Mary followed her to the table. But when she sat to eat, the girl's hand was trembling so she could not hold the fork. She could feel Walerych's eyes on her. She sat staring at her empty plate, her hand beside it, palm up, limply lying like a flower just cut but thrown aside in favor of some more perfect bloom.

31

How sad and still tonight
by the old distillery!
And how the cobwebs cob
in its old machinery!
But in the mountaintops,
far from the eyes of cops
Oh! how the moon shines on the moonshine
so merrily!
How sad and merrily!

— *The Moon Shines on the Moonshine*
from *Broadway Brevities*, 1920

The wagon was already half loaded, and they'd not gone the length of the field. Stash urged the team forward to a new windrow. He'd never seen alfalfa as heavy as this. A warm May, some rain in June; and the lime his father had insisted on pouring on, even at three dollars a barrel. He remembered Henry Bollom, so grave, so pale, at the funeral remarking on how heavy the hay looked. "He was a farmer," Henry had said. "Your father was a farmer, *stimmt?*"

And Stash had learned from his father. Learned just when to cut the hay, how to handle it to cure it up to a nice light green, neither limp nor brittle, but to a good, sweet-smelling forage. His father had told him, time and again, that you had to be especially careful to get alfalfa — and clover, too — at just the right stage or the leaves, which dried first, would shatter and you'd lose all your protein. At a time when nine out of ten farmers didn't even know there was such a thing as protein.

Molly and Queen stood still while Stash tramped the hay. On one side Walerych pitched forkfuls up, and on the other side Lotti. Only it seemed Walerych could never put them where Stash wanted them. He was so consistently bad at it Stash figured he was doing it on purpose. It meant extra work, kicking it around, leveling it, before tramping it down. Under his feet the bruised leaves and stems gave off a warm, sweet smell. The hay was at its prime.

He remembered how that morning Walerych had tried to talk him into gathering it before lunch. "It's the same hay, isn't it?" he'd asked. "Why work out in the afternoon sun if you don't have to?"

But Stash would have none of that. Hay put up damp could smolder in the mow and catch the whole barn on fire. It happened often enough. Maybe Stash wasn't at heart a farmer, but he had learned a thing or two from his father.

He held the horses, waiting for Walerych to pitch up the last of his windrow. The short man had paused to wipe the sweat off his forehead. Lotti stood watching, waiting. Now Walerych scraped his fork along the ground, lifted it, turned the hay onto the wagon. Stash was just ready to move ahead when he caught sight of Sophie coming out through the windrows. He held the horses. Walerych, who could not see the girl coming through the field, looked up at him curiously.

Sophie passed a jar of cold lemonade up onto the wagon. Stash drank deeply, paused, drank again. While Lotti drank, then Walerych, he took time to wipe the fine, itchy dust off his face.

"Second load?" Sophie asked.

"Third."

Sophie turned to Lotti, who was leaning against the wagon. "Mary's coming out, soon as the wash is hung." Lotti nodded. It was a hot afternoon. She'd worked as hard as a man. Harder than some. She'd be more than glad to go in and do housework.

They started again, the wagon jerking ahead beside two more heaps of hay, where the dump rake had dropped them. Then the steady rhythm, up with the hay on one side, Stash swishing it across, tramping it down; up with a big forkful from the other side, swish, tramp, and back again to the first. The hay was a yard deep all across the wagon, and when the horses leaned against their harnesses you could see their powerful muscles bear down against the load.

But before the load was finished, Mary was suddenly there beside Lotti, taking her fork, the rhythm of the work not broken. And as she bent to tease the hay together, then steadied herself to lift the big forkful onto the wagon, Walerych watched the strength in her legs. And knowing he was watching, she blushed, angry with the possessiveness she felt in his eyes.

"Hey!" he called, half seriously up to Stash, "Isn't someone going to come and give me a break?"

Stash, kicking hay about, yelled back. "You're a man, aren't you?"

Walerych swore under his breath; Mary turned and smiled to herself.

Three, four, five loads were hauled in, pulled slowly up the ramp into the mow, the wagon creaking, the horses straining against the weight. And there, in the still, dark heat, the dust heavy in the air, each load was thrown off onto the growing stack.

The wagon unloaded, they would stop at the pump for a drink, then ride back out to the field, Stash standing against the front end, reins in hand, Walerych and Mary sitting, on opposite sides, their weary legs swung over the edge. Up and down they'd bump, over the field, their bodies swaying with the wagon's jog and jerk. It was a little cooler now, the sun gone lower in the sky and hazed over with thin clouds. They'd barely started the last load when Stash, atop the wagon, could see Anna coming home with the cows.

But Stash insisted on getting this load in, in case it should rain. So they worked on, until the wagon was heaped high, and Walerych and Mary climbed up the back rack to ride the load to the barn. It seemed so high, on top of the load, you had to be careful not to fall. The wagon creaked and moaned, complaining of the weight. Stash, carefully balanced on the wagon tongue, waved to the Tomczaks, whose new pickup was raising dust on the road. Mary lifted her hand and waved. The back of the truck, loaded down with cement blocks for a new milkhouse, seemed perilously close to the ground.

Walerych watched the truck disappear. He wanted to crawl over to sit beside Mary, to steal a kiss perhaps. But surely they could be seen from the house; and it seemed the girl's mother missed absolutely nothing that went on around the place. Besides, he was too tired, too itchy with hay dust, too hot for that kind of foolishness. A cold glass of beer, now that would be something else.

They parked the wagon in the mow. Stash told them to leave it loaded. It would give them something to do in the morning while he was out raking. Walerych helped Mary off the wagon. They walked together to the pump and stood waiting while Stash splashed the dust off his head and arms.

"I think it's going to rain," Walerych observed, gesturing to the clouds gathering in the west. "It would be nice to have a day off," he remarked.

"It wouldn't be off," Mary said. "There's always house-work."

He was ready to ask her why they all worked so hard and never took time off for rest — except Sunday afternoon, of course. Between coming home from church and evening chores that meant no more than five hours; five hours rest during the whole week. But then, Stash was done at the pump. So Walerych grabbed the handle and worked it rapidly up and down while Mary splashed her own face, drank from cupped hands, the water running down her tanned and dust-covered arms and splashing noisily into the stock tank. When she was done, had wiped her face with the back of her hand, straightened the hair which she'd gotten wet, she took the handle and pumped for him.

They walked together, back to the house. He opened the door so she could go in. Berenice, seeing them, smiled to her-self. They have that in common now, so she thought, that day working in the sun, that growing tired together which was, after all, half of what Frank and I shared.

✳✳✳

Walerych would have nothing to do with the milking. He'd never tried it, he said, and had no desire to learn. The others were surprised at how Berenice shrugged it off. He'd come round in time, she thought. But now, while the rest were in the barn bent beneath the heat of the cows' bodies which only deep-ened the heat of the evening, he wandered aimlessly about the yard, poking into this and that. During supper Anna had said she'd found a hen's nest under the granary. Walerych decided to try to locate it.

He took the cigarette out of his mouth and stuck his head between two boards. There, in the cool dampness under the granary he found not only a hen's nest but two full sacks of corn and what looked like a mashing tub. He stared at it. How in the world did it get there? Of course, the door on the other side. Backing out and going round, he opened the door and crawled in, the earth damp and cool, staining the knees of his trousers. Inside the tub he found a measuring cup, and inside that, a scribbled recipe for mash beer. His heart accelerated.

He replaced the paper in the cup, the cup in the tub, and backed carefully out. Brushing off his pants, he marched straight to the barn, pausing only to stamp out his cigarette. Stash, seated beside Brownie, whose udder, thanks to the medicine Joe had left, could now at least be milked out, looked up curiously. Walerych seldom came into the barn at milking time.

"Do you have a still?" the little man asked. He seemed excited, and for the first time ever, enthusiastic. Almost a different man. He stepped aside to let Lotti pass with a bucketful of milk.

Stash continued milking. He wasn't sure what he should say. He milked Brownie a minute, then merely nodded.

"Where?" Walerych asked, his voice demanding a reply.

"In the woods," Stash answered, picking up his stool to move around to the other side of the cow. Brownie's tail — affectionately, almost — caught him in the face. He arranged his stool and pail, sat down to begin again the steady squirt of milk into milk.

"Where in the woods?"

Stash shrugged. There seemed only one way to get rid of him. So he told him. Behind the barn, between the two big oaks, until you get to a lone cedar, leaning north. Go left there another fifty feet or so and you can see it down in a hollow.

"Does it work?"

Stash was getting tired of this. "It should."

Walerych spun round and was out the door.

Before they were even done milking, Walerych had dragged the tub and sack of corn out from under the granary, talked Berenice out of a bag of sugar and a little yeast. Setting these aside, he wet about five pounds of the corn and laid it back under the granary, in the cool shade, with damp burlap bags on it. And he went into the workshop — for the first time — to find the grain mill which he'd need in a few days to grind the unmalted corn.

While the others were cleaning up in the house, sitting in the living room to take a few minutes rest before bed, he wandered out to the still. When he came back in, the girls already in bed, only Stash and his mother still up, in spite of all the mosquito bites, he was buoyant. You could say that for the first time since he'd arrived, he was actually, visibly, inarguably happy about something.

He sat down, lit another cigarette. Stash watched him a moment, then stood and stretched. "Better get some rest," he said, "four or five loads to haul in tomorrow." He said it all for

Walerych's sake, to remind him there was work to be done.

But Stash was wrong, Walerych right. Before dawn the
clouds had blown in, and they woke to a slow drizzle. There
would be no haying. Walerych slept in. At breakfast he collared
Stash and pumped him for all he knew about making the still
beer and using the still. Though the drizzle had not let up, he
went out into the woods where he studied, adjusted, caressed the
still, till he knew it by heart. He dragged windfalls into a pile
beside it. Stash had told him only to use ash, which gave little
smoke, so he crashed through the woods searching for more. He
wanted to have enough.

He was out there all day. When he came in for supper, he
was wet to the bones. But he whistled as he came in, then after
devouring his supper hummed an old Russian melody, and joked
with Sophie while he tried to get Anna to sit on his knee.

The grain was malting. Meanwhile they'd begun haying
again, after giving the wet hay two days to dry out. Walerych
found time in the evening to grind the sacks of corn and mix it
with some cooked cornmeal and yeast, to set the mash to working. Now he only had to stir it twice a day. During milking he
would go out into the woods and come in only after the others
were already in bed. And so he would sleep in, past when
morning chores were done, only appearing in the kitchen in time
for breakfast.

One evening Stash and Berenice sat in the living room.
The house was quiet. Walerych was, as usual, out at the still.
Stash set his *Rolnik* aside. "I hope he doesn't get caught," he
said, reaching into his pocket for his knife. He sat cleaning his
fingernails.

"You'll have to tell him to use it only at night," his mother
said. Every week there were articles in the paper about local
folk who'd been charged with revenue offenses.

It wasn't getting caught so much which bothered Berenice,
but the way Walerych, since discovering the still, had ignored
Mary. And just when she'd thought there was some feeling
growing between them. "He's picked it all up pretty fast," she
observed. "I mean, the brewing and distilling."

"Oh, he's clever all right," Stash replied. "But its backs and
arms we need now, not his head."

Yes, Berenice thought, that's true. But anyone who could
pick something up that fast — anyone that clever — could make
a way for himself in the world. For himself, that is, and a family.

✻✻✻

On Friday the mash cap sank. It was ready. Bucket by bucket Walerych brought it out into the woods, thinking to himself: next time I'll brew it right out there beside the still.

He'd already filled three milk cans with cold water from the creek. He poured the big copper pot full with still-beer and dumped the rest into a barrel, handy for when he needed it.

Now came the moment. He pulled a match from his pocket and rather anxiously set some papers to fire; on this he piled dry leaves and bark until it flared, then put on larger and larger kindling. At last he laid on the ash branches, thick as his arm. The darkness was gathering around him, the mosquitoes tormenting him. The smoke from the fire kept them away; and as the light around him dimmed the fire seemed cheerful, friendly. The beer began to heat. He stood above it, stirring it to prevent scorching. At last steam began to rise, wet, rich-smelling steam.

He was excited. It was just a beginning. And if it worked!

Now it was time to put the top on. He reached for the bag of rye flour he'd gotten from Berenice, stirred up a thick paste of it and sealed the joint where the top fit onto the still.

Anxiously he waited, his ear to the thump keg straining to hear the first bubbles come over. At last he heard one — a single, spirited *burp*! Then another. And another. Faster they came, faster. He poured cold water into the coiled condenser, and set a cup under its spout. Watching the fire now, to keep it going but not too high, listening to the thump keg bump away, he was in another world.

The first drop dripped out of the condenser. Then another. Soon almost a stream. These were the foreshots. He let a drop fall onto his finger, smelled it and tasted it on the tip of his tongue. These bitter fusel oils would have to be discarded. It was dark in the woods now. And even the lights in the house had gone out. He was alone with the night, the slender moon, the owls, bats and mosquitoes.

Carefully he smelled and tasted the clear liquid now dripping from the condensers. Yes, there was no mistaking it now — it had the sharp bite of alcohol. He slipped a whiskey bottle under the condenser to catch the drippings and stood back to watch in the flickering light as drop by drop the bottle filled.

But there was plenty to do — which was well enough, because standing still the mosquitoes almost ate up what little there was of him. He had to keep adding cold water to the condenser, keep the fire going at just the right degree; once he let it get too hot, and the beer boiled over into the thump keg. And best of all, he had to watch the bottles as they filled, slipping empty ones in to replace full ones.

He banked the fire, spreading it a little to cool it, broke the still open, scooped out the dregs and refilled it from the barrel. He built the fire up and stirred the beer before, as it began to steam, sealing the top shut again. Working as he was, he was not aware of the passage of time. He wasn't even tired, though midnight had long come and gone.

✳✳✳

He stumbled into the barnyard, awkward from crouching by the fire all night and from lack of sleep. Stash and Mary, headed for the barn, caught sight of him coming out of the woods. By the way he walked, they thought he was drunk. Stash waited outside the barn for him. Walerych, half asleep, walked right past.

"How'd it go?" Stash asked.

Walerych jumped, surprised. He hadn't even seen the other man. "Okay," he said. His clothes smelled of smoke and sweet malt. If there's a revenue agent within five miles with any kind of a nose, Stash thought, he'll be here like a hound after a coon.

Walerych stopped in the kitchen only long enough for a hot cup of coffee and some *ponchki*. Berenice was curt with him. That was all right with Walerych — he was too tired to be friendly, anyway. He threw his clothes on the floor in his room and crawled into bed. He slept right through lunch.

When he came out of the room, bleary-eyed, his voice raw, he ate some leftovers and wandered out into the field with his fork to help load the day's last hay. Stash was astonished to see him at all. Though he could tell Walerych was still tired, stiff from the long night in the woods, he worked harder than ever before, pitching the hay just where told, not once complaining about the heat of the sun.

This is the last field, Stash thought, and he wants to impress mother.

✳✳✳

That night, a Saturday night, Stash went over to Helen's. Walerych, as they'd expected, wandered out into the woods again, to fire the still and rework the low wines. It would be a pleasure, compared to the night before. Just one firing and he'd be done.

The temptation, of course, was too much. As the low

wines dripped out into the catching bottle, he dug up one of the jugs from the night before, sat sipping it, at first wincing from its bite, but then little by little getting used to it, taking whole mouthfuls at a time. The alcohol made him nostalgic, and he began to think of the old country. Here, alone in the woods, he might really have been out on a bivouac in the forests of Lithuania, on the lookout for Bolsheviks.

But in the end the liquor confused him, made him tired. He caught the last of the alcohol from the condenser and instead of putting the fire out, lay back to watch it flicker and send up into the night little flares of orange and red. His eyes closed. The pot-still boiled empty, the dregs on the bottom burned and charred; but he was oblivious to the mess he'd made and would have to clean up in the morning.

When they called for him, for breakfast, he wasn't in his room. No one could recall hearing him come in during the night. So they dressed and went to church without him. When they came home and started on dinner, he was still nowhere to be seen. Berenice sent Bruno out to look for him. Not particularly interested in finding him, Bruno began looking in all the places he knew Walerych wouldn't be: in the silo, under the granary, up in the hay mow. But at last he thought for his own good he'd better go out to the still.

And there, of course, he found Walerych. Asleep, leaning against a tree, a half-empty bottle of whiskey between his legs. Bruno could see where the mosquitoes had feasted on him — there were welts all over his face, which was smudged with smoke and badly in need of a shave. Bruno turned around and walked back to the house to tell his mother that yes, he'd found Walerych.

"Well, go back and wake him up," Berenice said, as though the boy were a complete fool. When he left, Bruno slammed the door behind him.

He rambled out into the woods, slapping the mosquitoes and swinging a big stick against the underbrush. Standing above the sleeping man, he wasn't sure how to go about this waking him up, which his mother thought was so important.

He bent closer. "Anton!" he said, rather timidly at first, then louder. "Anton!" But there was no response. For an instant Bruno was afraid the man had died. But no, his lungs were rising and falling in a steady, peaceful rhythm.

He set his stick aside, shook Walerych's shoulder. To no effect. He shook harder. In a flash an arm came up and gripped him, squeezing tight; two dark eyes sprung open and peered out at him from a deep, deep distance, like the eyes of a steppe wolf surprised in its den. Walerych, seeing who it was, grunted and pushed Bruno's hand away.

Bruno was shaken by the cold-blooded depths he'd glimpsed in the man's eyes. "Dinnertime," the boy said, backing away. He turned and hurried out of the woods — and all the way out he could hear the crack of twigs and low guttural grunts of Walerych at his heels.

32

T he tumbler of whiskey clumped onto the table. Only a week old, it was far too raw to drink. But there was another batch started in the woods — so why wait? "But Pani Topolska," Walerych crooned, leaning towards her, his breath heavy with smoke and liquor, "all your wonderful children, all these strong and healthy children, wonderful children all of them, so why would you want to sell the farm?"

Berenice looked up from the peas she was deftly shelling. "I'm only getting a mortgage."

Walerych chewed thoughtfully on the cigarette holder. What good was a mortgaged farm to him? "A mortgage, yes, I see. A mortgage." He leaned even closer, so close that from the end of his cigarette the long ash could have fallen into the bowl of cleaned peas she cradled in her lap. "A mortgage. Yes, I understand. But why?"

Berenice spoke without looking up. "To pay for the hospital bills, and the funeral."

He retreated, leaned back in his chair, in thought again. "Too bad, eh, there was no insurance?"

"Frank never believed in insurance."

"Of course not. It's only a swindle." He picked a single pod out of the pile, opened it, ran the peas one by one into his mouth, chewed thoughtfully. "But Pani Topolska, you wouldn't sell the farm?"

She did not answer. Why should she answer? He was too nosey for his own good. Even Frank had kept his nose out of her business.

From the living room came a polka, scratching its way out of the Victrola. It was another Saturday night, and the children

— except for Stash who'd gone to Helen's — had gathered around the record player, trying to find what little pleasure they could in a world gone dreary and somehow senseless.

She was tiring of him. She could boot him out in the morning — not one of the others would miss him. He was lazy, he drank; but without him Joe would be back. And somehow he fascinated her — though she wasn't aware of it, it was the way he flattered her. She wasn't used to that, being flattered.

Walerych had long since realized that the letters supposedly written by Mary were really authored by her mother. It was the mother's hand that moved the family. It was the mother who'd invited him. It would be she who'd have to ask him to leave. So he played his cards, one by one, carefully. Flattering her, that was easy: about the children, the house, the farm, her cooking. And reminding her, too, of how far he'd come, because of her invitation.

"My brother Leo," he said, "he could have got me a job in Cleveland. In the factory, pretty good job." Berenice was suspicious, but could not disprove him. "And the girls, too, lots of them, just waiting for me to leave the army." He sat back with his cigarette. Did she believe him? Better not push it too far.

His glass was empty now, his cigarette burned down. His hand on the oilcloth tapped along with the music. Little orphan peas rolled out of the pile and bounced up and down on the table. It irritated Berenice; but what did he care?

He would make himself at home. The more at home he was... well, the more it was his home.

"Would you dance?" he asked abruptly.

Berenice, somewhat flustered, swept the pile of empty pods into a bucket, bent to pick several peas off the floor. "No," she said. Now, so soon since Frank's gone? It would be a sin. To herself, then, she made an unspoken promise never in her life to dance again.

Walerych shrugged, pretending he didn't care. He had been foolish to ask. Embarrassed, he pushed his chair back, filled his glass, and wandered as nonchalantly as he could into the living room to join the children. Standing in the doorway he leaned beside the Victrola. He was happy, envied the children their quiet domestic life. His foot tapped with the beat from the record player. He stood like that a long time, lost in the music, touching the edge of their little family circle. When the record ended and Sophie rose to turn it over, he disappeared into his room.

He reappeared in a few moments, cradling in his hands a small concertina. He smiled self-consciously, took his place within the doorway. The record began; his fingers searched for its melody, though only found here and there a few right notes. They stared up at him. It made him nervous. When the record was over, he kept right on playing, and now it sounded better. He alternately frowned and smiled, swayed his body back and forth, his foot going up and down with a steady beat.

"I'm not so good," he said, pulling one hand free of the squeezebox and running it through his hair. "My brother Leo, he's a lot better." He set the instrument on the floor, nervously lit a cigarette. "Won't someone dance?" he asked. Sophie held another record in her hands, uncertain what to do with it. "Put it on," he urged her. "Go on."

She set the needle in place and after a few scratches it began a lively polka. Walerych stepped forward and seized hold of Sophie and swung her around. She stumbled around with him, trying to break free. Though he was a good dancer, the drink had made him clumsy. So he let Sophie go, stood flushed and embarrassed beside the Victrola.

He looked rather dizzily down; and there he saw Mary, on her knees on the floor. He reached down to pull her up, then twirled her around the room. She tried neither to get away nor to follow his steps; only not to fall or to trip him. At first they were all shocked; but after a bit, the boys found themselves smiling. Lotti even clapped with the music. For an instant they all really did forget about their father, and there was only the music and the whirling bodies, the magic of the dance.

But when Berenice appeared in the doorway, to see what the commotion was, reflexively they went serious again. The mourning crepe found its place on the pictures; Frank's chair once again seemed intolerably empty. They expected their mother to bring a sudden halt to their fun. But instead she smiled, seeing Mary dancing with Walerych. And even she began clapping her hands. The younger children were completely confused.

At last he let Mary go, and heated up by the dancing, broke into a wild Russian dance, kicking his feet out from under him while his arms were folded, lowering his body lower and lower. They watched, amazed. Sophie and Anna crept away from him, afraid of his flying boots. Bruno was delighted. It seemed so wild, so free.

But after only a few minutes he was tired and had to sit to catch his breath. Berenice told the younger children to get up to bed, then followed them up the stairs to be sure they said their prayers. Stash came in then, and sat down in the living room. The rest of them were reading, or doing needlework. Walerych lit another cigarette.

"So you were a cook's helper, eh?" he asked of Stash, his voice tainted with disdain. "I was the Sergeant Pawlak's Private Secretary!" He inhaled from his cigarette, waiting for the import of this announcement to sink in. But its effect was less than he'd hoped. "Everybody, they liked me," he said, "because I stood up for them. Everybody but Stipek, that is. He was the Captain. He couldn't stand me, because, you see, I had more schooling than him." Walerych paused a moment. They were listening, rather against their will; he'd never spoken of himself so much.

"We had to go to school, you know, the four of us. We had to pass a test." He turned to Bruno. "What's six times twenty-five?" The boy sat flabbergasted. "Hundred fifty," Walerych crowed. "Ask me another... Well, I got ten out of ten right. It never happened before, so the Captain was mad. But there wasn't a damned thing he could do about it!"

Berenice scowled. Words like that were not welcome in her house. The clock in the dining room struck ten. He waited for it to finish. "We were in school five months," he said, "learning the regulations and the Army bookkeeping. We had textbooks to read, but I never opened them. They gathered dust under my bed. All I did was listen to the teacher and I knew what to do. The rest of the time I read, novels. English novels. Charles Dickens, have any of you read his books? I got them from the town library. When the officers walked around in the classroom, I'd have a novel hidden inside my textbook."

"Stipek caught me one day. 'What, reading novels?' he shouted. 'We'll see how much you know!' So he drilled me up and down and across the day's lesson. And I knew more than he did. After that, he couldn't stand me. But he respected me. So when I asked for something, like a weekend leave for my buddies, we usually got it. I was pretty popular, I tell you."

Stash listened skeptically. He knew the type from his own service experience, but doubted the story was true. Walerych, Stash was guessing, probably had known someone like the man he was describing and was putting himself in his place. But one could never be sure.

"Sometimes," Walerych went on, "I would spend all afternoon with the officers, talking about God and heaven and hell and the eternal soul, and even they were amazed. Even they were amazed, I tell you! There was a sergeant had spent two years in the seminary. 'Where did you learn these things?' he would ask me, and pat me on the back and beg me to come see him again the next day so we could talk some more."

Bruno believed every word of it. As much as he distrusted Walerych, he admired him. Because he was so much cleverer than all the others, had seen so much more, had done so many things. And for the wildness he had seen under the surface.

Walerych raised his hand. "But the real stories, they are when I was in the Czar's service. That was the life! They didn't know what they were doing, I tell you, so we were free to come and go as we liked. Huh! It's no wonder the Bolsheviks came out on top." He brought with him, into the little farmhouse, a certain exotic flavor, with his Russian accent, his army ways, the elegant cigarette holder. And now he was using it all for effect. "We'd taken a train from Minsk to Wilno and were going to spend the time wandering in the countryside. It's beautiful, really beautiful. Of course, we had hardly any money. So we begged our way around and just, well..." Here he tapped his head. "It's wild country, Lithuania, beautiful and wild, like walking straight back in history. Places where they still grub the soil with sticks. We were sleeping nights in the open, hiking around, having a great time of it. But a storm came up. A big one. We got drenched, needed shelter for the night. So we asked a farmer if we could stay in his barn."

Walerych stood up and imitated a clumsy peasant's gestures. "Come in the house," he said, his hand sweeping the air. "They made the Christ child sleep in the barn but my guests stay in the house!"

Walerych sat again. "So in we went. It was a little shack, no bigger than your woodshed. Mud and sticks, a dirt floor, nothing more. No chimney, even, so the smoke had to run around the room and find its own way out the doors and windows and cracks in the walls. Everything was black. Everything! What there was, that is. A table, three chairs, all hand-made, no bed, just two shelves — the top one for the parents, the bottom for the children, all four of them.

"He asked me to sit down for supper. Well, we didn't like the place but sometimes your stomach's bigger than your head, if you know what I mean. When they brought it out, I lost all my appetite. Some kind of raw cucumber soup, with yellow pus floating in it."

The girls shuddered.

"We were all eating out of the same bowl. And the children would hit their filthy cats with their spoons, to keep them away from the food, then dip them in the soup. I almost got sick.

"Then when it got dark they didn't have any light. When they wanted to see something they would lift up a burning stick and carry it around. It made your eyes sting! We had to go out for fresh air. It would have been better to sleep in the barn. But he'd invited us in. We couldn't say no.

"I didn't sleep all night. Never have I been happier to see the sun! As we tramped down the road, away from that hell-hole, the sun breaking out of the clouds, and we knew we could spend the next night in the clean open air, with soft moss for our beds, we started singing."

Walerych sang a few notes of an old Russian folk song. Though they couldn't understand it, it sounded sad — no, not sad, but it made you think of times before, that were happier. But he didn't remember much of it — after a few lines, he took to humming it instead.

He stopped suddenly, opened his eyes. "It's true. It's a big world, I tell you. They say in parts of Africa they still eat human flesh."

✳✳✳

After their mother had left them with their prayers, and Walerych's voice began to drone through his stories, like ghosts let loose from the past, two silent figures glided, unheard and unseen, down the stairs and quickly out the back door: possessed, defiant, and not a little frightened. Once outside, they ran quickly across the moonlit yard to the security of the barn, with its cow smells and the creak of horse flesh against wood. The lantern they found where expected. Out back they hurried, the dew shockingly cold on their bare feet.

At the edge of the woods they stopped. Was it too late already to turn back? The taller one stepped boldly into the shadows, and the younger hurried to catch up and find her hand.

Now, out of sight of house and road, they stopped, ran a

match across a rock; flaring up it seemed an old friend whose language they could understand. Now, with the lantern glowing, they could see each other's faces, and found new courage. But the darkness seemed blacker, and at the edge of the light their fears drew together. It was almost better to have no light at all.

The taller, in front, held the lantern high; with her other hand she held her sister's. Startled at the slightest sound or movement from the woods around them, they made their way down the path until before them suddenly it loomed: an alien, menacing apparatus, a medieval torture machine from some terrible nightmare, an incomprehensible fragment of evil. They stopped, facing the enormity of their purpose.

"Sophie," the smaller whispered. "Let's go back."

But Sophie only squeezed her sister's hand the harder and dragged her forward, into the clearing. They stood a moment, half expecting at any moment some unseen, unknown justice to sweep out from the trees and carry them away. Sophie set the lantern on an old stump whose half-rotted surface still bore the imprint of a man's seat. She glanced quickly around. There stood the barrel; she lifted its cover and smelled the sharp still-beer. The cover slipped, suddenly, from her hands and clunked loudly against the barrel. They stood perfectly still, staring into the darkness, as though startled out of a dream.

Sophie bent and lifted a bucket, dipped it into the barrel and emptied the beer onto the ground. Anna, timidly, found an old kettle, and helped her sister. Now the smell rose so thick around them it made them almost dizzy. They hurried to finish, splashed the rancid liquor in their hair and spattered their dresses. The barrel almost empty, they tipped it over, the thick settlings oozing over the earth.

Then made bolder by their success, they attacked the still. In no time their work was done. And when they stopped, out of breath, spattered with mud, smeared with ashes, heavy with the stench of beer, the whole crushing weight of what they'd done fell down on them. And they stared at one another, in the glimmer of the lantern, each wondering if it was her sister standing there, eyes wide, hair dishevelled, hands and arms covered with dirt; or some devil in disguise.

Afraid almost to tears they grabbed up the lantern and hurried out of the woods. But they had to detour, after snuffing out and hanging up the lantern, to the pump where they ran water, as cold as the moonlight, over their arms and legs, rinsing their smocks and skirts where spattered with beer. But it was no use — they would never get themselves spotless again. Suddenly from the darkness they heard a low, deep-throated rasp, like the sound of a dragon creeping up from the dark. Their hearts stopped.

Anna smiled, suddenly. "It's only Molly," she whispered, "snoring in her sleep."

Tiptoeing they made their way onto the porch, eased the screen door open. They stopped in the kitchen, little streams of water running down their legs. Anna reached for a towel to wipe up the floor, but her sister put her finger to her lips. "Shh!"

Walerych's gravelly voice was still running on, spilling its stories, slurred with liquor. Under the cover of his voice they made their way back up the stairs, one step at a time, hung their smocks to dry, and slid at last, breathlessly, under the blanket.

Outside the moon, no longer pure white, but with every moment muttering incriminations, slipped sadly down the sky. It grew quiet downstairs, after a bit, but still the sisters did not sleep. They lay, long into the night, hugging each other, surrounded by visions of the swift and ruthless wages of their sin the morning light would surely bring.

33

Woman, what have I to do with thee?
— Christ, to his mother, at the
marriage of Cana. John 2:14

Already, only halfway into the woods, he knew something was wrong. He stopped. Vaguely it rose into his mind and gathered. The smell. The smell of the still-beer: sharp, rancid, it overlay the faintly rich wood smells like a foretaste of death on a summer afternoon. He stood by the cedar tree, where the path veered to his left. He took the cigarette from his mouth, sniffed the air. Yes, the still-beer.

Had it boiled over? Fermented so strongly that it had boiled over? But it wasn't that full. An animal, then, during the night. Yes. A raccoon, probably, had knocked off the lid and now, exposed to the warming rays of the sun, the smell pervaded the woods. Vaguely anxious, unconvinced, he started again on his way.

Ducking under a branch, he pushed back the thick young maples which enclosed the little clearing. What met his eyes made him stop dead, holding the branches back, staring, his heart gone on a race. There, just in front of him, the big wooden barrel was on its side, empty, the beer long since soaked into the earth. Around it flies had swarmed, and delicate white moths, their wings fluttering as they padded the ground with their tongues. And behind the barrel his eyes caught the still: this creature he had felt was his own, which he'd studied, caressed, urged on in its work, now no more than a scattered chaos of parts.

He stepped into the clearing. The moths fluttered up into the air. Some landed on nearby branches, others waited, hovering, for him to leave. The buzzing of the bloated flies which filled the air rose above the beat of blood rushing through his ears. His first reaction, of nothing less than disbelief, was giving way to the next which, when worked up, would be a heady, frantic anger. He lifted the condenser coil, a twisted tangle of thin copper tubing. It was beyond repair — beyond, anyway, his ability to repair it. He let it fall from his hands. The pot still, no longer a carefully-shaped cylinder, had been bashed in on all sides. He kicked it. Kicked it again, harder, adding to it the imprint of his own boot. The thump keg, knocked off its barrel, lie on its side, half full of dirt.

He was like a sergeant who'd sent his troops out on an ordinary detail only to come abruptly upon their ambushed, mutilated bodies. And now primary in his mind was a single question: who? Who could have done it? The thought of revenge rushed through his body like a fire over the prairie. He had to find out who. His first thought: revenue agents. But revenue agents would have hauled the still away as evidence, not merely destroyed it. And surely they would have stopped at the farm to make an arrest. No, not agents.

He sat on the stump which in recent weeks had come to be his favorite chair. The flies and moths settled around him, tentatively, still skeptical of this uninvited intruder. He sat and fought his own mind, struggling to keep a sense of reality. Who, he wondered, even knew of the still? The family. No, that was absurd. They were too stingy to destroy their own property. And what would have been their motive? No. Not the family.

One of the neighbors? But he'd not met a half dozen people since he'd come.

That young man, Joe what's-his-name. Yes. Or no, the priest. Either one — yes, either one — could have done it. Or turned him in and left the dirty work to some local vigilantes. Yes. He remembered the old woman telling him that the priest was an avid prohibitionist. If he knew about it, he could have done it. But who told him?

He stood up, vented his rage by kicking the pot still across the clearing. The priest would pay. By God he would pay for this. Walerych tried to calm his mind to focus on some scheme of revenge. But only hatred and anger would come. All this crap about heaven and hell, he was thinking, and treating your neighbor like yourself and then turn around and pull something like this.

He stopped. The bottles!

He hurried to his cache, beside the big rotted log, tore back the leaves. He breathed out a sigh of relief to see them still there, all four, nestled in the leaves.

By the time he'd pushed the brush aside and begun the slow, desperate journey out of the woods, leaving the beer to the flies and the still to the slow rot of time, he'd resolved to keep his mouth shut about the whole thing. In time he would get even. Meanwhile no one needed to know.

At the edge of the woods he brushed the mosquitoes away from his face. There in front of him stood the barn, the granary, the bright new garage, behind them the house. Suddenly it came to him that with the still gone he'd lost his last refuge from the insufferable family he was forced to live with and their miserable chores which day after day ate up any chance of a future. Hidden in the woods he'd left his bottles of whiskey. When they were gone, without money or a job, he was a prisoner who'd lost all hope of escape.

***

He slunk past the girls, busy in the strawberries, headed for the house tight with anger, that old familiar desperation coming over him. Not enough, he was thinking, to be born with this body no man should be made to inhabit. Not enough that his father was a drunkard and that his mother would ignore him and give everything instead to Leo. No. Not enough, damn you. We'll hound you clear across the ocean, through the Army — no, they hadn't left him alone there either — and find you here on this miserable farm in the middle of nowhere; and finding you, work on you once again our unrelenting mischief.

As he stepped onto the porch a big black sedan pulled into the drive. Customers from town buying fresh berries. He slammed the door in their faces, then stood alone in the house: the utensils, the cupboards, the potatoes and ham coming to a boil on the stove, the table and chairs which he was just beginning to feel familiar with, seemed now instead to be secretly laughing at him, mocking him.

He turned and searched above the cupboard and found the bottle. Pouring a tumbler full, he sensed now that even the whiskey could mock him: at last something he could do, and do well. And now that too had been taken from him.

He ran the liquor down his throat, quenched his anger. It sat like a hot coal in his stomach. The empty glass he set on the table, then stepped outside onto the back porch. He sat on the steps, smoking his cigarette, the whiskey working at him from within.

The girls were busy. They were always busy. What a life they led; and yet it seemed not to occur to them to be unhappy. Their mother was carefully pouring quarts of berries into the customers' pails. How he despised her, the tightfisted pettiness of the old woman, the way she counted strawberries or pennies like they were souls in need of saving. He had the urge, then — and he was barely able to control it — to stroll right out and hit her, to knock her to the ground.

And the younger girl, Sophie, the way she stared at him, just now: as though he were a ghost or a monster of some kind. Unconsciously a low growl rose from his throat — and the girl turned quickly back to her work. None of them had even once shown him the respect he deserved. It was all he wanted: to be treated like a man. And it seemed the more he wanted it, the less chance he had of getting it.

The way he sat on the porch now, staring out at them with the cigarette clenched between his teeth, it put them all on edge. They could sense that something was wrong, some storm brewing over the horizon. And the old woman, he knew without asking what she was thinking. She had nagged him often enough before. Stash needs help, she would say, afraid to look in his eyes but not to tell him what to do, Stash needs help out in the field. Bruno needs help in the barn. Bruno needs help in the silo. Stash needs help... He knew what she was thinking: as she counted out her pennies and smiled and bowed to the customers who couldn't have cared less for her groveling whimpers, she was all the while looking out of the corner of her eye at him and thinking, Stash needs help in the field and Bruno needs help in the barn. So why are you just sitting there, you little Russki, useless as a dead toad on a log.

Because, woman, he growled to himself: because I choose to.

✳✳✳

After a lunch in an uneasy silence, they scattered back to their work. Sophie ran out to the pasture to confer with Anna. Panting from the run, she tried to tell her sister how things seemed. Yes, he knew, she said; he came back from the woods looking like he'd seen the devil himself. But he must not have told their mother, not yet anyway.

They sat staring at the cows, and now they felt sorry for him. They hadn't, after all, wanted to hurt him, only to make him leave. If only they hadn't done it! But it was too late for that. And what they faced, it was the worst of all; this not knowing when the punishment would come.

Berenice was on her way to a nap when Walerych cornered her in the living room. He pretended, on the basis of recent newspaper reports, to be worried about being caught. "How about the Tomczaks?" he asked her. "Would they turn me in?"

"Chester?" Berenice asked scornfully. "He's got his own still!"

"Well then, who should I worry about?"

"Don't tell anyone and you won't have to worry at all," Berenice chided him. She wished he would go away. It was time for her nap.

"What about that priest?" Walerych stood by the window, his hands clasped behind his back.

"Does he know?" Berenice stared at him. There were rumors, from reliable sources, that Father had spoken of turning people in.

The suspicion in her voice did not go unnoticed. "I didn't tell him," Walerych defended himself.

"Then he doesn't know."

"Did your husband have any... enemies who might try to get even with the family?"

"You never met my husband," Berenice asserted. "The only enemy Frank had in the world was the devil, who hated Frank because over him he had no power."

He would have to let it go at that. She was getting suspicious. So he shrugged, wandered outside, while Berenice lay on her bed, in the quiet heat of the afternoon wondering what the man was up to. It was all they needed, she thought, for him to get caught. Well, if he did, he'd have to sit it out in jail. Unless his brother — if he even had a brother — would come up and bail him out.

But she could sense that there was something which either was happening or had happened that was beyond the edge of her knowing. And it was the first time she could remember, since Frank had gone off and signed the papers on this place, that she felt left out of what was going on in the household. As she fell asleep, she took with her forebodings and anxieties: and her first substantial doubts of her ability to carry on. And she thought: it was easier when you were here, Frank. The Lord knows we didn't always see eye to eye. But it was easier. Yes, easier.

***

Walerych, meanwhile could not contain himself. Here he was, alone in the midst of this family with a terrible secret. He needed to share it. He needed an ally. There was only one he could really trust. He wandered out to the strawberry patch where she was working, by herself, busily hoeing weeds from around the plants. For a long time he stood watching her. At last when she stood to wipe the sweat from her forehead and took off the broad-brimmed hat to dry her hair, he spoke up.

"Why don't you rest," he said. "It's hot."

Mary squinted at him through the heat. "Not much left."

He struggled with the decision. But then it was out of his lips. "The still's been wrecked," he said suddenly, and quietly, so no one else might overhear.

She stood holding her hat, wondering what he was muttering about.

"During the night," he went on, "someone came and wrecked the still."

She found it hard to believe. Was he drunk? People didn't just wreck other people's property. She stared at him as though he were mad.

"Who could have done it?" he asked. He coughed, then spat into the grass.

She shrugged. How would she know?

"Stash maybe?" he asked. She shook her head slowly from

side to side. "Bruno then?" She squinted at him. "Who?" he demanded, as though it was her duty to answer. Her hair, wet with sweat, was coming out of its bun. She lay the hat on the ground, pulled out her hairpins, put them one by one into her mouth, and smoothed the hair out behind her. She wound it into a bun and fastened it again.

And now he was thinking: she doesn't even believe me. "You don't believe me, do you? Well come with me then, you'll see for yourself."

But that was impossible, going out into the woods with him. "Did you tell mother?" she asked.

"No. I haven't told anyone but you. What about your priest? Would he have done it?"

She stared at him. Father Nowak was a man of high principles. But he would never stoop to vandalism.

As though reading her mind, Walerych added, "But he might have told someone and they could have done it for him."

"No," Mary said, but her voice was not convincing. There was something there in his eyes she hadn't seen before; the look of the dog who'd just been given a good beating.

"If I'm not wanted here," he said, pulling the cigarette from its holder and tossing it into the grass, "then perhaps I should go somewhere else."

He turned and walked away. She was astonished, then, to realize that he might not have known, all along, how unwanted he really was. She tied her hat back on and bent again with the hoe, hacking gingerly around the plants, careful where she set her feet so as not to crush any of the berries which hung in heavy clusters. For the first time, she was seeing things from his point of view — he'd forced her into that. And she thought, how strange it must be for him, so far from home but just as dependent on their mother as they were.

And she realized, from this totally new perspective, how hard it must have been for him. How badly they were treating him. But he'd come at the wrong time. How could he expect them to welcome him in, their father not cold yet in his grave?

But that wasn't his fault. He didn't know. The image kept coming back to her, of Walerych standing there, his hands in his pockets, a little boy really, an orphan. "If I'm not wanted here," he was saying.

It was her nature, like her father's, to sympathize with the underdog. So now she began to feel sorry for him. It surprised her, that that would happen. But she saw him as a victim now, no less than she, no less than the goose about to be slaughtered.

How could she feel sorry for him? He disgusted her, the very thought of why he'd come made her almost physically sick; the way he moped around, half drunk most of the time. He wasn't even a man. Like a moving shadow at the edge of her vision, the thought of Joe came into her mind, of what he was and what he stood for, and for an instant reproached her. But it was there only an instant: and again in her heart all she could feel was pity. And then she realized the full horror of it — if they stumbled ahead into what her mother had in mind, and even Walerych himself had second thoughts about it, how terrible that would be. How miserable it could make him. And he in turn would share that misery. That, she decided, would be beyond bearing.

She continued to work away, but her mind was elsewhere. As she hacked with her hoe, she cut off two, then three, strawberry plants. She closed her eyes, swore at herself. There would be no hiding it. Though she threw the plants far off into the weeds, her mother would see the bare spots.

Her back was sore from the bending. She straightened herself up, stared across the field, where the oats were already heading out, to the far horizon, where a light haze shimmered in the heat. She was tired and she was thirsty. But the time had come. The time had come to see if Father Nowak would, as he had hinted on St. Stanislaus Day, be prepared to sin for her sake.

She dropped her hoe beside the berries and hurried into the house. Her mother, thank God, was still asleep. Nervously she spoke into the phone, asked for the rectory in Knowlton. Verna, Father's housekeeper, answered. Mary asked for Father himself. In a low, tremulous voice she asked if she could come to see him after supper.

It was arranged. He would be waiting for her in the church.

***

Stash started the Ford in the middle of evening chores and backed it out of the garage. Mary sneaked out to the car and drove away. As she shifted up on the road she could feel her mother's eyes on her. There would be plenty of explaining to do when she got back. But she had other bridges to cross before that.

Now, late in June, the warm summer evenings stretched out long past nine. There would be plenty of time before darkness settled over the countryside. She drove slowly along the river. The business of driving, which she was still not quite comfortable with, kept her mind off what she faced. This, she knew, would be the moment of truth; it would be on the basis of Father's advice that she would have to make a decision. And the finality of that, its ultimate meaning to the rest of her life, made her shake with anxiety.

She parked the car, turned off the engine. It was quiet in the churchyard; only some swallows dove low over the river, twittering, carrying food back to their ravenous young, and from treetops around the church a few robins had begun their evening song. The light, coming obliquely across the water, gave the trees and buildings long shadows. But the sun was still warm, and the light wrapped her in its embrace.

Nervously she walked up the steps, pulled open the church door. At the font she dipped her fingers and crossed herself.

The church was empty, except for Father himself, who was kneeling at prayer in a front pew. She slipped quietly into place. It was strange, being in the church when it was so empty. It made her feel so alone. As the kneeler bumped against the floor, Father turned. She bowed her head, her hands clasped together, open thumbs on her temples. She prayed a Hail Mary, an Our Father, then asked the Lord, in her own words, to come to her assistance.

Father rose, genuflected and came down the aisle past her. At the rear of the church he waited quietly until she rose out of the pew; he stepped forward to meet her. He took her by the arm, led her into the vestibule; and as she reached for the font, as they passed, firmly he guided her away. How many times he had preached to them not to cross themselves as they leave the church. It is a ritual of cleansing, he would say. You don't wipe your feet when you're leaving a house, do you? And he would notice, that day, most would heed his advice. But within a week they were all back to their old habits.

The two of them stood now on the top step, Father holding Mary's arm, facing across the water to the sun whose rays were already turning from faint yellow to a deeper, richer gold. It was so calm, so quiet, it almost took their breath away. "Come, Mary," he urged her down the steps, "let's walk a while."

As they came down the stairs a sedan pulled into the Knowlton House just across the road. Another carful of tourists. Like a rock thrown into calm water, the roughly idling motor rippled the evening air. When it was at last turned off, the silence descended like a gift from God. On the river, far out, they could see two small motionless punts, in which fishermen, from this distance hardly more than tiny smudges against the water, would quietly sit out the end of the light. Father turned the girl toward the rectory. They would stroll, slowly, up and down the path between it and the church — a path Father had so often strolled himself on such evenings, deep in prayer.

"I'm so glad you've come," he said. "I've been thinking about you a lot, lately." They made small steps, tiny careful steps, their feet shuffling in the gravel. "I went into the church to pray," he said, "to pray for guidance." She waited for him to go on. He was silent. He knew what he wanted to say; knew also what he must say; but knew not how to begin.

"Mother is already talking of the wedding," Mary volunteered.

Father Nowak sighed. "Yes?" He clasped his prayer book close to him, as though it would keep him afloat. "How the days get away from us. It seems like just yesterday it was Easter, and your father was there, with everyone else, on the church steps..."

"Yes."

"It's not easy, you know," he said, his voice warm but strangely distant, "this life as a priest." He turned his head slightly to watch her. Her eyes were straight ahead. "They don't know how hard it can be. No, not in the Mass, I know that by heart, even recite it sometimes in my sleep. And the sermons, they come easy. But at times like when your father died. And now, too, when I have to reach down within my own soul and offer what I find there, and in the end live with what I've found and what I've given, it's not easy."

"Father..."

But he would not let her interrupt him. "Remember, Mary," he said, leaning his head toward her, "that I am only a man. I can tell you what in good conscience I think is best for you, but it is your life and you will have to live it."

She glanced quickly at him. He looked away. She wanted more than that. She wanted him to speak with the authority of God. And she realized it was more than he could give — was more even than she had a right to ask. But then for an instant she thought: why then have I come?

He turned her around, near the door into the rectory, and they walked back toward the church. "I was in love once," he confessed, so quietly she could hardly hear. He was speaking to her as a friend now, not as a priest. "Or thought I was. When I was younger than you, before the seminary. I thought then that breaking our love would break me." He smiled, remembering. "So you see, I know what love, what infatuation, can be. How foolish we are, Mary, in our youth."

They stopped a moment, under the spreading branches of a tall pine. Mary had the feeling he'd rehearsed every word he was saying, was now just being sure he had it all right. Then he stepped on again, and she followed. "You are young yet, Mary, so very young. I've seen fifteen years more of life than you, and the one thing I've learned, if I've learned anything, is that a long and tolerant patience is the best we can give to life."

She knew now what he meant to say, but doubted he could come right out and say it. How much, she realized, she had overestimated him!

"At your age," he went on, "it is only natural to search for complete fulfillment. We think we can find it in love, in the one we love. But there is no complete fulfillment in this life, Mary. There are only isolated moments of satisfaction, little flashing gems of happiness. All the rest, the setting, so to speak, for those gems, is our trial, which we must learn to bear. I know this may sound untrue to you and you may rebel against it, but I tell you that ten years from now you will understand what I am saying and say to yourself: he was right. That old chatterbox was right."

It was not an easy thing for him, sifting through his feelings to find what was best not for him, but for her. He'd spent hours — days — going over and over again in his mind how he really stood in regard to her. He wondered if he had taken her side secretly, hoping her success would make up for his own failure, of which he'd just hinted to her. Yes, that was possible. And it was possible, too, that the unspoken but ever-present conflict with her mother had only reinforced that stand: Berenice Topolska, the Untouchable, Unfathomable, Unconquerable Mother, the same mother he'd himself left behind in Poland. There was, complicating all this, his admiration for Joe, his immediate dislike of this fellow from Texas, and Frank's sudden death, which left him, as he saw it, as the girl's last hope.

On the other hand was he only trying to prove to himself that he could love anyone — even the Unconquerable Berenice — and would he therefore be willing to sacrifice Mary, for his

own sake? As for Church doctrine, it spoke to him too, in a
voice not easily understood, but the direction was plainly there.
He had all this to deal with. But he kept it to himself. In the
end he was sure he'd found the way out. It contradicted half his
feelings — the stronger half — but it was what he would have
to tell her. And now there was only the nagging doubt, the
vague, tantalizing suspicion that he might have chosen this path
because it was, in the end, the easiest way out.

But there was really no easy way out. "Our love and loyalty
for God and His church," he went on, "must persist beyond all
reason. Beyond all reason, my child! That, then, becomes our
own crucifixion, becomes the real meaning of Christ's death."
He turned to look at her. But as they walked she caught sight
of Verna staring out the rectory window at them. It embarrassed
her, he could see that — and suddenly he was overcome with an
urgent sense of failure. No, he thought, she does not understand.

His hand let go of her arm. He slipped his prayer book
into the sleeve of his cassock and held his hands flat against one
another, the tips of his fingers at his lips. "Christ was God," he
said, concentrating as hard as he could. He slowed to barely a
shuffle, she slowed to stay beside him. "We know that. Or
rather, we believe that, if we as Catholics believe anything. And,"
his fingers folded, his thumbs crossed, "if Christ was God, then
there was no reason, no reason within our understanding, for
Him to die on the Cross. Do you understand?" He stopped.
She nodded, hesitantly. Yes, she understood. Not all. But some.
Enough. "It was out of love, beyond all reason, that He saved
us, you and me and all of us."

She stared at him. He was lost in another world. She
struggled with what he was saying. He spoke of love beyond all
reason. Did he mean that the love she felt for Joe, that there
was nothing more important than that?

"If you understand this," he said, taking her arm and beginning again to walk down the path, "then the crucifix which
hangs over your bed or above the altar there in the church can
never be only an ornament. It will signify instead that nothing
is hopeless, no matter how hopeless it may seem, as long as an
effort to love has been made."

Now she saw. But how it seemed to twist everything around.
Was the effort to love more important than the love itself? In
a way, that was how she felt about Joe: her love from a distance

was purer, more real, than when he was actually there. But it seemed so tangled up.

"Reason may throw light upon our world," the priest went on, and she had the impression he was beginning now to speak to himself, "but the world it lights is a cold, uninhabitable place. Without faith it is like Wisconsin," he said, with a sweeping gesture, "in the middle of winter. It needs faith to warm it. It is faith that brings into our souls the warmth of a summer evening, such as this."

They stopped, halfway between church and rectory, turned to face each other. Were it not for his clerical robes someone glancing out of the Knowlton House and seeing them there, under the branches of the big pine tree, might have mistaken them for a pair of lovers quietly reassuring one another.

"Think of it, Mary. A hundred years from now, what will you and I and Joe be? Can you say your love will endure beyond the grave?"

And she thought that moment, not of Joe, but of her father. And her answer, which came like a flash of lightning illuminating the darkest recesses of her soul, was: Yes!

"A hundred years from now we will all of us be no more than ashes. But in a hundred years God will not have changed a single iota. Better it is to love Him, then, isn't it? You know how much your father's death meant to me, my child. It came at an important time, at a time when I was, well, when I was susceptible. I learned, one night, shortly after your father's death, in a dark night of the soul but which also brought a great light to my life, that it is God's will we must bow down to. *Thy will be done*, we pray. It means we must, in the end, depend on Him. Even if we do, we'll still sin, we'll still make mistakes. After all, only the dead are truly innocent. But God is merciful. And when we give ourselves, beyond all reason, then God is with us. Is within us! Do you understand, Mary?"

She understood. And she felt sorry for him. After all was said and done, he was still afraid to come right out and say what he meant. Yes, he was just a man. She'd never seen him that way before. She'd learned so much, really; though it wasn't what she'd expected to learn. And she felt a great upswelling warmth go out toward him, toward this man who suffered so the recognition of his own mortality and yet could, in the middle of all that, reach out to help her.

They turned again and walked toward the church. She

found it hard to breathe. She shivered, had given him all her warmth and faced now the growing darkness utterly alone. And she knew now what road lay ahead of her; already, she knew, they'd set off down it. And she had the vaguest of senses that from the moment of her birth this was the road she was destined to take.

The car was just ahead. His words washed through her like cool water. He was explaining to her the grounds on which a marriage can be annulled. First, he said, if there is an existing marriage bond. If, for example, this other man is already married, then though in outward form their marriage had transpired, it would in the eyes of the church and in the eyes of God be as though nonexistent. If either man or woman were not of age. This, he explained, did not apply in their case. If they were connected by too close a blood relationship. If, in the end, either proved to be physically impotent — he used the word delicately — for to the church, the only valid justification for marriage is the creation of a family. And finally, he said, the marriage cannot be considered binding if there is in it an overriding element of compulsion or fear.

"Your marriage," he said, "could at any time be annulled, if you and if I, too, are convinced that you have been compelled into it against your will."

He stopped. She looked at him, but could not read in his eyes the answer to that further riddle. He took her hands, held them warmly. He was struggling for something to say, for just the right thing to say. His lips moved silently, his tongue making nervous excursions around their edges. "Mary, I..." he said at last.

"What?"

He seemed paralyzed, unable to speak. "Nothing. There's nothing more to say," he blurted out. Suddenly he dropped her hands, turned and walked away, slowly, heavily, toward the rectory.

In a daze she watched him go. He slowed. Would he stop and come back? Instead he pulled from his sleeve the little prayer book, opened it, and continued on his way.

She moved mechanically to the car and inserted the crank. She turned the engine over. It failed to fire. She jerked it over again, as hard as she could, and now it took. She climbed in, smoothed the engine out. Her hands found the controls. She put it in reverse. One last time she stared at him. He held the breviary folded open, his black cassock skimming over the gravel as he moved slowly on his way, muttering the Divine Praises.

34

*Nothing exerts a stronger psychic effect
upon the human environment, and especially
children, than the life which the parents
have not lived.*
— Carl Jung, from *The Spirit in Man,
Art and Literature*

The days slipped past. From a later perspective they would be the days most easily forgotten — marked neither by moments of great joy nor signal grief. They were, like most days, the tablature for better designs, or worse. There was, then as always, more than enough to be done. And so it was done. Only Walerych never broke, after losing the still, out of his daily despondency. Mornings he slept in, refusing to lift as much as a finger to help with the work. Only the two girls — and Mary, separately — knew why he no longer tramped out into the woods to spend his day; the others, wonder as they might, didn't have the nerve to ask.

Berenice was becoming impatient. It wasn't her way to feed and care for unproductive stock. Yet she had to admit getting rid of him wouldn't be easy. Fate, she decided, had dealt her a bad hand: the Good Lord might have sent anyone else on the earth and it would have worked out. A favorite aphorism, which she often used on the girls, came back these days to haunt her. *You've made your bed*, she used to say, *and now you'll have to sleep in it.*

Evenings Berenice spent by the big bay window in the living room, her needlework on her lap. Lotti was the first to notice, and whisper to her sisters, that each evening their mother picked up the same piece of work, yet seemed no closer to finishing it. After a few perfunctory stitches, her work would drop to her lap as she stared out the window into the summer evening. In her mind's eye she was seeing Frank again, with his short but steady gait headed out to the barn, or following behind Molly around and around the field; at the kitchen table with a steaming cup of coffee — half chicory, the way he liked it — already exhausted from work but getting excited about some new tool or plant variety he'd just read about. Or here, in this very room, relaxing in his chair, his stockinged feet up on the stool, in the warmth of the stove his eyes fluttering shut. And the smell of him, too, would come to her; the sweat and barn-smell, which for so long was so much a part of her she took it for granted. It seemed impossible that all those days, those many days which while they lived them seemed they'd never end were gone now, gone forever.

She would sit in her rocker as the evening drew itself out and the light dimmed around her and Lotti, or Angie, would light the lamps, then one by one they would all go off to bed, leaving her alone or sometimes with Anton, sitting in the quiet of the gathering night, which each day came earlier now. Most evenings after ten o'clock he would rise and slip into his room, the whiskey taking him into sleep; and just as he was drifting off, he would hear Berenice as she stiffly stood, snuffed out the light, and headed off to bed.

But one evening he sat finishing a last cigarette. The rest of the family was in bed; he and Berenice shared the room like strangers sharing a waiting room. He moved, shifted his weight, crossed and recrossed his legs. He had something to say. But she sat, indifferent to whether he said it or not. At last he spoke up, slowly and carefully, yet in his Polish that intrinsic accent. "Maybe," he said, his voice low and gravelly, "maybe I'll go back to Cleveland."

As though waking from a dream, Berenice turned to him. She stared at him a long quiet moment. "Do as you like," she said. He sat staring straight ahead, turning his cigarette round and round in his mouth. "Do as you like. You're not a farmer, Lord knows," she said, "though if you tried harder..."

Now he turned to her. "Why? Why try harder? You don't pay me."

"If you marry my daughter, you are part of the family. No one in the family gets paid."

He exhaled a cloud of smoke. "I haven't married her yet."

Berenice stood wearily, set her needlework aside. "If you want to be a hired hand, I tell you we can find better." He was still staring at the wall. "It's up to you. You're free to go." She went past him into her bedroom, then closed the door.

He sat, considering. If I marry the girl, he thought, I work all day and don't get paid. But if I don't marry her, I end up leaving. Well, he thought, at least I know. At least I know where I stand.

***

The next morning at breakfast Berenice answered the phone. It was Joe. He wanted to talk to Mary. No, her mother told him, she's not here. Yet he knew she was; and the thought of her sharing the house with that little Russki enraged him.

He'd tried before, and each time her mother had answered, and each time Mary wasn't in. He hung up. But it built up inside him — no longer could he get away from it. He went out to cut hay, and it followed him out. In the barn that evening; while he was eating his supper; and on into the night he thought of Mary, of the little Russki, of some way out. One moment he would grab hold of one scheme, sure that it was the only way. And then he'd find in it some fatal flaw and have to invent another, and another, until he had to admit there was no practical way out. At last he promised himself he'd go back to his work at the mill, as soon as haying was over. Maybe if he got away from it he could have some peace.

But then he realized that that was only throwing Mary into the Russki's arms.

***

After Frank's death Joe had taken over presidency of the fledgling Union. It seemed now that everyone was too busy with fieldwork to come to meetings. So they'd not sent anyone to the state convention. Ben Lang called, wondering what was going on. Joe was ashamed. It seemed to be falling apart in his very hands. Yet he had to admit he didn't have the experience or command the same respect that Frank did. He tried, as a last — unsuccessful — resort, to talk his father into taking over the presidency.

Joe and Roman Gruba sat on the porch one evening at Roman's, sipping beer. Joe had to get away from the house, had to vent some of his frustration. Roman sat quietly listening to the boy complain about the Union, knowing there was a lot more behind it than that. At last he suggested, in order to test the boy's conviction, that maybe it was time to let it go. "Without Frank it seems the heart's out of it," Roman said.

Joe spat into the grass, drained the last from his beer. "Everyone's back to looking out for number one. Can't they see they've got to work together if they're going to make it?"

"That takes a special kind of vision," Roman said. "A vision not granted to all of us." Roman knew the pressure Joe was under, about the girl. He wasn't the same man he'd been just six months before. But on the other hand, neither of them was. "Look why don't we give them one more chance," he suggested. "Call a meeting for... for Saturday after next. If no one shows, well then, we'll know, won't we?"

"I'll be there," Joe said cynically. "And you will. And maybe Pa, too, if he's not too busy." He spun the empty bottle on the porch deck.

***

The next day was the Fourth of July. It was a clear but hot afternoon. In town there were some small festivities: a parade, some long speeches — longer than the parade, actually — which tended toward the patriotic, and later on some noisy fireworks. But on the farm while the sun shone there was hay to be made. The Stelmachs would finish that day, God willing. George, Joe's younger brother, was on one side tossing up the hay, their father on the other driving the team. Joe was up on the load, tramping it down. They had the wagon stacked high. The horses strained at the harness as they pulled it through the rough and rut-pocked field.

"Enough!" Alex shouted. Any more and an axle might break. George handed his fork up to Joe and clambered up the back rack to ride home. The wagon lurched forward as their father guided the team. The boys were hot and thirsty, each looking ahead to the evening when, after chores, they could sit and cool themselves over beer.

"Almost done," George said eagerly. Behind them they could see the last few windrows which Joe raked that morning. It had been a good year. The mow was almost full. The two brothers relaxed into the pleasure of knowing most of their work was behind them. They were good friends, Joe and George; both amiable and hard-working boys. So when George lifted a big handful of hay and dropped it onto Joe's head, a moment later they were rolling back and forth on the wagon, in the middle of a hard-fought wrestling match. Gripping each other, they rolled clear to the back of the wagon, just missing George's fork.

They broke free and stood up and faced each other, each waiting for the other to make the first move. Their father, from below, looked up and smiled, wondering where they got their energy from. He shook his head, was about to shout something up to them about needing to find more work to keep them out of trouble when the left front wheel of the wagon suddenly dropped into a deep, unseen rut. The horses, feeling the extra tug, leaned ahead. The wagon lurched suddenly, and both boys on the wagon lost their balance.

George fell forward into the hay. But Joe was not so lucky. He tipped backwards; in his fall he tried to grab the rear rack of the wagon, but missed it and tumbled instead right over the end of the load.

George pushed himself up. Joe was nowhere to be seen. He hollered to his dad. But Alex had already seen Joe fall; he stopped the horses and hurried around the wagon. Joe was lying on the ground, his face in the hay stubble, softly moaning. His father bent down beside him. The wagon moved ahead.

"Hold the team!" Alex shouted to George. "Joe! Are you hurt?" Now on Joe's face, pressed against the ground, he could see the pain. And Alex thought, for one terrible moment: my God, he's broken his back. But then he noticed the boy's leg moving back and forth against the ground, and knew that if the back was broken, Joe's legs would be still. He tried to turn the boy; but Joe only moaned louder.

"Run to the house and get Ma," Alex shouted. "I'll hold the horses." He took the reins from the younger brother. It seemed forever — though it was only a minute or two — before Joe's mother, still wearing her apron, joined them out in the field, worry written all over her face.

"Here ma, you hold the team. We'll see if we can move him."

Carefully they turned Joe over. "Where's it hurt?" the father asked. Joe muttered that it was his shoulder. "Can you stand?"

Joe nodded. "I think so."

They helped him to his feet. He stood with his left shoulder hanging far down, wincing from the pain with the slightest move. "Ma, you come here!" Alex shouted. "George, get the car." While his mother and father supported him, George took the wagon and team to the yard and hurried back out with the car. They managed to get Joe into the back seat and started off for the hospital.

It was a fractured collarbone. They could even see the end

of the bone, halfway between the neck and the outside of the left shoulder, where it stuck up against the flesh. The doctor assured them it was a simple fracture — painful but not dangerous. Joe smiled when he was offered a shot of whiskey. "Helluva way to get a drink," he joked.

They had to set it. They could hear the bone grinding against itself; the sound sent shivers down their spines. But Joe only closed his eyes hard and gritted his teeth. Then they wrapped long thin bandages again and again around Joe's chest and under the armpit. They put his left arm into a sling so he wouldn't be moving it. Then came the worst: it would be six weeks or more before the arm could come out of the sling. Meanwhile Joe was not to do any work around the farm.

That evening Sophie Tomczak walked over to the Topolskis to visit Berenice. "Did you hear?" she asked, proudly airing the latest gossip, "about Joe Stelmach?" Mary, ironing in the kitchen, looked quickly up, her heart skipping a beat. "He fell off a hay wagon and broke his shoulder," Sophie pronounced meaningfully.

Mary's hand went to her mouth. Anton, sitting in the dining room, set his whiskey glass down. There was a moment of silence. Mary leaned on the ironing board.

"Too bad," her mother said.

"Yes it is. And in the middle of the fieldwork too," Sophie added.

Mary waited only for Sophie to leave, then marched straight to the phone and asked for the Stelmachs'. She didn't care what her mother, who was sitting there in her rocking chair, might say. Or the other man, propped quietly in the corner.

Joe's mother answered. Mary asked if she could talk to Joe. She stood anxiously waiting for him to come to the phone. Anton pretended not to be listening.

"Joe!" she said, her voice much louder than she wanted it.

"Mary." He sounded glad to hear her.

"I just heard. How are you?"

"Oh, I'll be all right," he said. "It hurts like hell, but I guess I'll live."

"How did it happen?" Mary could breathe easy now. He sounded himself.

"Aw, we were goofing off, George and me. We shouldn'ta done it." There was a long silence. "Worst thing is," he went on, "I won't be good for nobody for a month or two."

"Now Joe..."

"Well, it's true. You know me. I ain't the kind to sit around all summer." He paused, his voice changed from complaint to concern. "So how are you, Mary?"

"All right." It seemed to her that they were almost like strangers now, or friends who hadn't seen one another for so long that there was so much to say there wasn't any sense in saying anything.

"Can I come see you sometime?" Joe asked. "I'd like to."

"Yes." But her voice was complicated with more than welcome.

When she hung up, Mary thanked the Lord he was all right. And yet there was a great uneasiness in her; turning and seeing Anton sitting there, absorbed in thought, only deepened that unease.

The next morning, to everyone's astonishment, found Anton out in the potato field, hoe in hand, drawing dirt up around the big coarse-leaved plants which were already in blossom. He came in for breakfast but didn't speak a word. Mary, Lotti, and Angie went out with him then, and though it didn't take long for them to pass him up and leave him far behind — they'd hilled too many potatoes over the years even to think about — that didn't seem to bother him. Clumsily but doggedly he worked away, driven by a mysterious force even he could only faintly apprehend.

✳✳✳

And so it went. The work was getting done. The Topolskis and their guest moved past one another as though in separate worlds. Nothing, anymore, seemed to be holding the family together — nothing, anyway, beyond the work. And no one seemed in control. Not even Berenice, whose intimations about the wedding made at breakfast and dinner seemed strangely cold and unenthusiastic.

Anton's hands were covered with blisters, and on top of them calluses. It didn't escape Berenice's notice that he was out working with the rest of them. So he's decided, she thought. At last he's decided.

One morning she asked Stash to drive her into Stevens Point. She had shopping to do. She would stop, she said, at Rothman's to look for material for the dress. Mary said not a word. So the mother went alone, and brought home a half-dozen yards of an elegant ivory satin. It was the most beautiful fabric Mary had ever seen. She was drawn to it, to the rich sheen of its texture: but the moment her fingers touched its silky surface, she drew back, as though she'd touched the burning surface of the stove. She turned away.

"Have your own way," Berenice pronounced, setting the fabric beside the sewing machine. "But you're the one who'll wear it. Before threshing begins, as God is my witness, you'll be the one to wear it."

***

Anton was working. Evenings, he was drinking. And there didn't seem to be a civil word in his head. As though working was as much as he could manage; to expect him to be friendly, too, was apparently expecting too much.

Stash spent more and more time at Rybarczyk's. One evening after he came home, his mother was sitting up alone. She asked him to come into the living room for a minute.

"We could have a double wedding," she suggested.

He stood in the doorway, hands in pockets. "No," he said, in his quiet, yet conclusive way.

"Why not?"

He shrugged. "We're not ready yet."

So that was that.

***

It was, for the family, the worst summer they could remember. Even Eddie, so eager for the warm days of June and July, spent his time in the same grim doggedness the rest of the family shared. It wasn't just his father being gone — though that was bad enough. But on top of it all there was that dreary cloud which inhabited the house — which they rightly or wrongly attributed to Walerych's presence — a cloud which seemed to cause everyone to mistreat everyone else, to go through their days in an awful unbroken tension. No one ever laughed anymore. Or teased. Not even Bruno.

Anna and Sophie had decided that Anton was not going to tell on them. They didn't know why, but they felt sure that their secret would remain a secret. Yet it was there, would always be there, that uneasiness which they'd brought on themselves. If their mother ever found out... And the worst was, it had accomplished absolutely nothing. They knew that now, how futile the gesture had been, knew down which path the future would lead.

And Angie and Lotti, knowing that too, could only feel deeply sorry for Mary; and at night in bed whisper to her as reassuringly as they could. And that was all. Beyond that there was nothing they could do.

So Mary was left to herself, to face her destiny alone. She was tired of it all, tired enough to have given up. It was all she could do anymore, drift in the current until she bumped up against the only mooring she could find — her last promise to her father. Her promise to obey her mother. That, now, was what she clung to. It kept her up, gave her life some sense and meaning: that she would be true to him. True to her father. And after the long battle she was thankful for the respite this mooring offered. She would try. God would give her the strength to try. And that, in the end, was all she could do.

✳✳✳

With suntanned faces and skins dried and toughened with long hours in the sun, they sat uncomfortably in their pews. Their muscles, strengthened by swinging scythes, loading hay, pulling hoes, could only relax in the rhythm of work, not in inactivity. So they squirmed minutely in their seats, twisted and twitched like tigers in a zoo trying to contain their excess energies.

Joe sat beside his brother. Under his dress shirt the bandages were thick, his arm slung in front of him. His suffering, of course, was not just this one hour a week — for five days now already he'd had to mope around the house while his brother and father worked, or go outside to shuffle glumly up and down the drive, capable of nothing more than kicking rocks with his boot. And today added to that was the knowledge that he had, that evening on the porch at Roman's, exactly predicted who would show up for the Union meeting: himself, Roman, and his father. He knew that the others, there in church with him, felt guilty about not coming. He wasn't sure, yet, if he should be mad or feel sorry for them.

Father finished with the gospel, closed the book. He wiped his forehead. It was the height of summer. Though the windows were open to let in the breeze off the river, still it was hot and close in the little church. Father had long ago learned that summer sermons were best kept short and simple. Winter was the time to ruminate over the faith, summer the season to live it. And that, in a way, was the theme behind today's sermon: living our faith while we have the strength to do so. Before the frosts came, as surely they would, to finish off the season of their lives. Now, at the height of summer, he would tell them, at the height of our powers, now is the time to do God's work.

But first he had an announcement. His hands held the sides of the lectern. He was gazing over them, to the blank wall at the rear of the church. He had never noticed before how empty that wall really was. "I announce today," he said, his voice cold and official, "the first banns for the marriage of Mary Topolski, of this parish, and Anton Walerych, also of this parish."

There was a slight ripple through the crowd; furtive glances reached the couple. The priest's eyes dropped to stare at his missal. He spoke more quietly now, almost as though afraid he would be heard. "If there be anyone here who knows good reason why this marriage should not take place, let them come forward now or forever hold their peace."

Mary had closed her eyes, wishing herself somewhere else. Oh, she thought, to be somewhere else.

Her mother sat beside her, silent, implacable as the days ahead. On her other side, Anton, erect, self-conscious, proud. And though at shoulder and hips their clothes might touch, there was between the man and the girl some thing — or some nothing — which no ceremony, church-sanctioned or not, could ever bridge.

35

While stars are fading in the dawn
Over the desert they'll be gone
His captured bride
Close by his side
Swift as the wind they will ride...
— from a popular hit of 1922, *The Sheik of Araby*

She could hear them downstairs. She could hear her mother's voice, so familiar it blended sometimes with the voice inside her head; Lotti's shrill reminder to Eddie to hurry up, it's getting late; and Angie, chattering nervously away about probably nothing. This was her home. They were her family. They loved her. And now, they were all busy, so happily busy, with final touches; and it was all for her. While here she sat, like a bump on a log.

She twisted the hankie in her hand, glancing again at the

dress. It was beautiful. She'd never seen such a beautiful dress, let alone worn one. Last week when they were making the final fitting, she'd looked at herself in the dining room mirror. It was beautiful. It made her look like another person.

If only she could be another person.

What did they want? Did they want her to go willingly like a lamb to the slaughter? Is that what they wanted?

She had. She saw that, as much as it hurt her to see it, how little she had fought along the way. It was not her. It was not like her to fight. She trusted them to know what was best for her: her mother, her father, Father Nowak. God.

Once Rose's, the petticoats, all fluffy full, lay waiting for her. The hat and veil which her mother had bought, which with the material for the dress must have cost a whole week's cream. The long white stockings, their heels worn thin. She wanted a new pair. She felt, at least I could have a new pair of stockings. But there was no money left. The old pair would have to do.

She wiped her eyes. The tears were almost stopped. The pain was almost gone. She was glad anyway for that. But instead of the pain she found something far worse: an emptiness, a heavy numbness, like the first week after her father died. Or Rose.

But no one was dying. It was only a wedding.

Only.

A wedding.

She heard footsteps coming up the stairs, sat straight in the little chair, leaned her head against the chest of drawers, wound the hankie round her hand. If it was her mother, she would get it for sure. Let her come, she thought, she won't find me here.

It was Lotti.

Her sister stopped dead in the doorway. "Jesus Marya!" she exclaimed, "you aren't even dressed."

Lotti bent down beside her, lay her hand on her shoulder, bare except for the fine, thin camisole. "Mary, please. Before mother comes up."

And just then their mother did come up the stairs, or anyway, her voice. "Aren't you ready yet?"

"In a minute," Lotti answered, knowing full well one minute wasn't a tenth of what they needed.

"Is he still here?" Mary asked, her voice thin and weak.

"Anton? No. He left with Sophie and Anna a long time ago."

Mary stared into her sister's eyes. Yes. Lotti she could trust. Yes. Lotti understood.

Lotti pulled her up by the hands. "Henry and Gertrude stopped by," she explained, "and they all went together in their car. Come on, Mary, we'll get you dressed."

Anna appeared in the doorway. She and Lotti looked wonderful, were ready to go. It was easier for them. It had to be easier for them.

"Come on, give me a hand," Lotti said to her younger sister. Together they lifted the petticoat and slipped it over Mary; like a tent, at first, it hung on her shoulders. They sat her on the bed. Picking up the stockings, Lotti shook her head, sighed. But then she had an idea. She sat down next to Mary, slipped off her shoes and unfastened her own garters. In a moment she slipped out of her stockings. "Here," she said. "You wear these. They're newer."

Mary meant to protest, but her voice seemed lost somewhere in that deep emptiness inside her. It wouldn't have mattered anyway. They were slipping Lotti's stockings onto her; and when that was done, Lotti took the other pair then slipped into her shoes.

Lotti's tongue clicked against her teeth. "What are we going to do with you, Mary?" She stood back, looked at her. Mary bit her lip, twisted her hankie. "Come on, stand up."

They pulled her up again and managed to get the dress on. She shuddered to feel it drawn around her. When Anna brought the little mirror from off the chest she stared at the image she saw as though it were a picture she were looking at. A picture of someone she'd never had the pleasure of meeting.

"You comb her hair," Lotti said to Angie. They were turning her around as though she were a goose that needed basting. At last Lotti had the dress straightened to her satisfaction.

"Where's your shoes?" she asked. But Mary took so long in first trying to understand the question and then searching for an answer that Anna answered for her.

"They're downstairs."

Lotti, holding the veil and brushing it out carefully, set it for a moment on Mary's head. It was like a net in which they meant to capture her. "Are they clean?"

Again Anna answered. "Eddie did this morning."

"Thank God."

Their mother's voice crashed up the stairs. "Time to go!" Lotti took the veil off so Anna could make final touches on the hair. And now their own dresses and hair had begun to look worse for the wear. Lotti stepped back for a look. It wasn't right. Something wasn't right. But there wasn't time. It would have to do. She took Mary by the hand and led her down the stairs.

"Jesus Marya!" their mother exclaimed. "Look at her!"

It was true. She looked like she'd been stuffed into the dress. And her hair, well, it was good enough for the barn.

Her mother grabbed the brush from Anna's hand and began tugging at Mary's hair as though trying to pull it out by the handful. "We're already late and you're not even dressed," she said. "Ten minutes to ten! We'll never get there on time!"

Bruno came in the back door, swiped a *ponchek* from the kitchen table. His mother, who missed very little, scolded him. "Bruno!" she said. But the boy already had half of it in his mouth. "Where's Stash?" his mother asked.

"Outside," the boy said through a mouthful of dough. Bruno had been busy polishing the Overland. He bent to brush off his very best pants. As far as he was concerned, he'd rather be out cleaning calf pens than stuffed into these clothes facing what he faced.

"Tell Eddie to come in and have Stash start the car."

Bruno hurried back outside. Eddie, who was supposed to help him clean the car, had instead climbed onto his bicycle and was riding in endless circles round and round the yard. "Ma wants you," Bruno shouted. The boy paid no attention. Bruno turned to look for Stash, found him out in the orchard, all suited up as best man, jaunty carnation in his lapel, standing patiently smoking and watching his bees busily bringing in the first of the goldenrod. Bruno waved to him. He stood a few minutes, as though deep in thought, then turned.

"Bring me her shoes!" Anna handed her mother the white dress shoes Mary had worn for her confirmation so long ago. Her feet, from going barefoot all summer, had splayed out. The shoes would be tight.

They sat her into a chair while Berenice and Lotti forced the shoes on. Buckled, they pinched her toes. In an hour, they would hurt almost beyond bearing. Suddenly she remembered the time, years before, when she and Rose and Lotti had dressed

up the kitten with a silly little coat and pants and tied boots on
its soft little feet and let it go. It looked so silly. And all the
poor kitten could think of was how to get out of it. That was
how she felt now. She felt like she was so covered with clothes
she couldn't find herself even if she tried.

"Now the flowers," her mother said. On the dining room
table were three beautiful silk roses, identical almost to those
tied below her parents' wedding picture, only their color was as
yet unfaded. With fumbling fingers Berenice fastened them to
the bodice of Mary's dress. Mary quivered now in fear, expecting at any moment the long pin to reach her tender skin.

The clock struck ten.

"Jesus Marya!" her mother exclaimed, adjusting the three
scarlet roses and turning Mary quickly round. "Get in the car!"
she told her other daughters, then pushed Mary out the door
and towards the car.

Stash had it running and sat waiting for them at the wheel.
He looked handsome — no, more than that, elegant. The car
shone brightly in the morning sun. Everyone looked so nice. It
was wonderful, after all. They all looked so nice.

Mary sat in front between Stash and her mother. Everyone else climbed in back. Eddie was last in. The bottoms of his
pants were dusty from the bicycle ride. Berenice wanted to
brush them off but told him to hurry up and get in.

At last. They were on their way.

Berenice told Stash to hurry. She was almost having a fit.
The girls had never seen her so nervous. Stash shifted the car
into high. As they sped down the hill toward town the car
reached thirty-five, then forty miles an hour. Berenice clung to
the door handle and stared bleakly ahead. "Slow down!" she
shouted. "You want to kill us all?"

In back, Bruno could not suppress a smile. Lotti, holding
the hat and veil on her lap, nudged Anna who, wedged up against
Bruno, slapped him sharply on the head.

✳✳✳

There were not many cars at church — no more than might
show up for a Novena or a First Friday. It would be one of the
smallest weddings the parish had seen in years. The car bearing
the bride was the last to pull in. Everyone else was already
inside. Everyone else was waiting. Stash turned off the motor
and quickly went round to help his mother from the car, then his
sister.

Clouds were building across the river. Before the day was over, the sky too would be weeping. *"Jakie wesele, takie zycie,"* the old saying went. As goes the wedding, so goes the marriage.

Berenice fussed over Mary one last time, setting the hat and veil in place, smoothing out the ivory-sheened dress, straightening the roses on the girl's bodice. Then she bent to slap the dust from Eddie's pants.

Mary glanced quickly over the cars. No. The Stelmachs' Chevy was not to be found. So even his parents, she thought, even they did not come.

The doors into the church were open. Inside it was dark, as though gathering and reflecting the darkness growing in the west. Father Nowak stood at the doorway, smiling and shaking his head.

For a while they'd thought she really wasn't coming. Thought she'd run away somewhere. Unlikely as it seemed. But now she was here.

The priest turned and disappeared into the church.

Stash and Berenice supported her as she walked across the drive, her feet clumsy in the tiny shoes. Already they were hurting. The gravel was rough and it seemed each rock was trying to trip her up. Kind rocks, she thought. Kind rocks, but too late. Too late for that.

Anna stood at the top of the stairs, a big bouquet of flowers nestled in her arm. And Helen, who was waiting for Stash. Thin and frail, Helen would soon be a bride herself. It seemed impossible, she was so small and young and grey.

And Walter was there too, with Stasia, his girl from the city. They'd arrived just the night before. Walter and his mother had gotten into an argument about the wedding. Walter had threatened not to be in the wedding party. But in the end it had worked out. He looked down at her warmly.

Now she was at the foot of the steps. It seemed such an impossible climb, those six easy steps. And the organ music was rolling out of the church like a wind she would have to lean against to make any headway. Her mother took her arm, to help her; step by step they climbed the stairs. Helen and Stash, Walter and Stasia, little Anna with the flowers, they all loved her, they were the ones she loved — and yet she hardly recognized them.

From behind, the deep-throated roll of thunder.

At the top of the stairs she paused. Inside she could see

the meager crowd. For Joe's wedding, she thought, there'd be standing room only.

She saw Chester Tomczak, and Henry and Gertrude — she could always tell Henry by the big bald spot on the back of his head, surrounded by a thin halo of grey hair. She felt a warmth go out of her to them. She knew they'd rather not have come. It was respect for her that brought them. She wanted to cry out: No! If you really love me, go home. Turn and go home.

I want to be alone in my sacrifice.

The music grew louder. Now her eyes adjusted to the darker interior. She could see Sophie, sitting up front but on the aisle, turn to look back, and, beyond her, the altar, covered with flowers, its candles flickering as a breeze followed her in the open doors. Father Nowak, all in white, prayer book in hand, waiting for her. And there, at the rail, Walerych himself.

No. I will not. I will not go.

Her mother held her arm and with a deep breath to steady her own nerves, urged her forward. All she had to do, she knew, was relax, and let the music and the press of those around her carry her in to the farther shore. Twenty steps, no more, and it will be over, and she can rest at last.

She lifted one foot off the stairs and into the church, the threshold almost catching her toe. Her heart was pounding. Stash and Helen, ahead of her, began the slow solemn walk up the aisle. Her mother was firm. The bells rang out.

She felt faint, tried to just let it happen. As though it were someone else. She stopped, just inside the church. The bells, ringing just above them, were so loud.

Then suddenly, through all the noise she heard something. Her ears were trying to tell her something. Stop, they said. Stop. Don't go. She stood still, listening. Stash and Helen were already halfway to the altar.

Yes! she thought. Yes!

She turned. A car horn. Yes!

There at the foot of the steps sits the familiar Chevy, idling roughly as though about to kill. Seeing it, now she can hear it. And there, at the window, waving, is Joe.

"Well Mary," he shouts above the peal of the bells, "are you going in or coming with me?"

She finds herself wheeling around to face him.

Father Nowak, craning his neck to see what was holding them up, has excited the rest of the crowd. They all turn to look.

Sophie Tomczak, near enough to the door to catch sight of the car, stares unbelieving. Her hand goes to her mouth as involuntarily the name escapes her lips.

"Joe!"

A ripple runs through the crowd. They are all turned, staring toward the back. The priest closes the book. Anton moves between Helen and Stash, to walk to the back. But the priest catches hold of his arm.

Mary is frozen to the spot. She is, in the vestibule, neither officially in nor out of the church. She turns her head, like an animal with dogs surrounding her from every side. Anna gapes up at her. She appeals to Walter for help, and Lotti behind him. But they are all too astonished to think, or react.

Her mother grasps her arm, trying to turn her. But she will not turn.

Joe looks up at her, smiling. Though his one arm is bandaged, the hand resting loosely on the wheel, she knows how strong he really is. Knows how kind, how good, how honest he really is.

"Come," her mother says, glaring down at Joe and the puttering car.

"Mary!" he calls out to her, not demanding, not pleading, only with the length and depth of their affection reminding her of who she is. "Mary!"

Yes, she thinks, I am Mary. Mary Topolski. And that is Joe.

There is an instant, then, in spite of the music from the organ, the ringing bells, the rattling car, the muttering crowd, or the distant roll of thunder, an instant of absolute silence. As though they were all, church and crowd and all, transported to another world, another universe, where sound is too trifling to enter. It is one of those moments which jolt God himself into paying attention.

✳✳✳

And what He saw, when He peered down at this pathetic little scene, on the banks of this too-ordinary river, with the mean little church and the shabby cars and trucks parked in its lot, the few, colorful members of the party just inside the church, what He saw first was a sudden blur of white. And out of that utter silence the first sound He was to hear was the thunk of steel against steel, trailing behind it the roar of an engine and the whir of gears.

And He stared then with the eyes of the mother, disbelieving, to see the vehicle recede away up the narrow, winding country road.

While on the church steps, dropped like feathers from a bird just escaped its cage, a scattered spray of roses: tiny, delicate little roses, blood-red little orphans, suddenly discarded, left to be lifted by other, less hurried hands.

36

However different their other features
may be, the eyes of all Polish women have
but one expression, and seem for ever striving
to pierce the black veil of the future...
— from *Polish Experiences During the*
Insurrection of 1863, by W.H. Bullock

The rain began, drop by drop, to patter against the windshield. Mary counted... five... six... seven... then, as they came too numerous to count, watched the droplets which fell on the hood steam quickly away into nothingness. Now big beads were thunking on the roof; as they came down faster and faster the little sedan seemed, for the moment, a sanctuary, safe from the turmoil of the world. But outside the birds had stopped singing, the air was ominously dark and still. The thunder grew louder, and every few seconds brilliant flashes blazed across the steel-grey, pockmarked surface of the river.

Joe drummed his fingers on the steering wheel, stared across the water to the west. Mary, who had long before slipped out of her shoes, sat quietly rubbing her feet. They heard it coming long before they saw it and could only watch it roll upon them, a wall of water rushing madly across the river, then striking the car with a deafening roar. The windshield and the side-windows were useless now, covered thick with water: pervious only to the lightning and the thunder which roared its unfathomable anger.

Joe reached out to touch her cheek. But she pressed against the door, afraid now of even him. He could sense her fear; but if she would not let him, how could he help?

How strange it felt to her, here on the edge of the water,

the storm pouring its vengeance onto them. It was the dress, as much as anything. She hated the dress. Hated it. But there was no way on earth she could get away from it.

She should be married now, she thought. Married and home with the family. Sitting down to eat.

An hour before — it seemed forever ago — she had jumped into the car, scarcely able to breathe, and Joe had sped away from the church, staying on the highway along the river. They rode in silence, each too full of turmoil to trust their hearts to words. They sped south, at first, almost to Point. Mary wondered where Joe meant to go. But when he crossed the river and turned back north she realized he knew no more of their destination than she did. He was just driving, madly driving, for every direction seemed to take them farther from the church.

She glanced at him, then, as he guided the Chevy up the familiar road, and the unspoken triumph and glory she saw shining in his face astonished her. All the while, outside, the sky grew darker.

As they turned off the highway onto one of the many side roads which they had so often traveled, he turned to her. "Mary," he said, his voice gentle, barely loud enough to hear over the shush of the wheels on the dirt and the purr of the motor, "even if you hadn't come, even if you'd turned and walked into the church, I'd still love you."

Tears found their way from her eyes onto her cheek. Joe handed her his handkerchief.

Without even thinking, he was driving straight to this place where they were now parked along the river. A favorite spot of theirs, behind the Wolniak farm, they'd shared many picnics here with Stash and Helen, George and the Wolniak boys; had fished and laughed and grown into love. It was a holy spot, in a way, sacred with the birth of their affection.

But now the rain beat down, and the thunder roared. The storm was on top of them. Joe wondered quietly if the road might wash out, stranding them there along the river. They sat in silence and stared at the blanket of water running down the windshield.

He pushed his door open. It was a pouring wall of water he stepped out into.

"Joe!" she cried.

But he hurried around front, cranked the motor over, ran breathlessly back inside, all wet and dripping. He turned on the wipers. Now they could see. As the rain poured down, big puddles had formed all around them, were growing deeper and deeper.

Joe turned to her. "We'd bettter go," he said. She seemed so frail: a delicate vase teetering on the brink of a long fall. He wanted to hold her. But just to touch her seemed dangerous; she might slip right out of his grasp. He was clumsy at these things, self-consciously clumsy. His heart he trusted, but not his lips or hands, his big hands fit only for cows.

She stared into his eyes, wondering.

Here, she was saying, here I am. Now what will you do with me?

He fought an inner battle; unsure if he'd won or lost, his hand reached for the gearshift. "We'll go home," he said. "We'd better go home."

***

Through the rain they ran into the house. Joe's mother and father stood at the door. When Joe had driven out of the yard that morning they'd had to guess his destination. They were afraid there might be trouble. He'd been like an animal these past days, pacing, pacing, unreachable with word or touch. Now, seeing the couple run toward them through the rain, their hearts leaped with his.

"Mary, come in!" Sophie exclaimed. "You're all wet!" She hugged the girl. Mary lay her head on Sophie's shoulder, shivered uncontrollably. "Joe, get her some coffee."

Joe stood at the doorway, dripping water, holding Mary's hat and veil; suddenly he realized how foolish he'd been to bring them in from the car. He lay them on the table, where they dripped, loudly, onto the floor.

He poured two cups of coffee. His mother had Mary in a chair, with a scarf over her shoulders. She accepted the cup from Joe, smiled weakly, sipped. It was hot and delicious, gave her heart a new life.

Joe backed up and stood by the cook stove. Though it was warm outside, wet as he was, he felt chilled. His father, sitting at the table across from Mary, was rubbing his hands together. Joe could tell he was happy, for his sake. And for Mary's sake, too. But the price of what they'd done would be steep. Alex was certainly considering that now, the social price; yet he felt that whatever the cost, his son's — and the girl's — happiness was worth it.

Joe sipped the coffee, glanced up at the clock. Eleven-forty.

"Did they call?" he asked his father.

"An hour ago."

"What did you tell them?"

"The truth. That we didn't know where you were."

That seemed to satisfy Joe. He was trying now to relax, to gather his thoughts. When he'd left that morning he didn't even know where he was going. All he knew was he had to get away from home. Then, at the last minute, that he wanted to be there. Just in case. He didn't go to make trouble. So he'd spun the car around in the road and sped toward the church, praying he wasn't too late. And he would have been if Mary herself hadn't dragged out the preparations to the last minute. As though, unconsciously, she was giving him that one last chance.

When he called to her, and she stopped, it was almost unbearable. He had to force himself not to throw the car door open and rush into the church to carry her away. But it had to be up to her. When she came, it was the happiest moment of his life — never before had he felt such great joy welling up inside him. Such must have been the glory Christ himself felt as he stepped out of the tomb.

But Joe had not planned beyond that. Once in the car and on the road, he had to decide what to do next. And now, at home, that decision still hung over him. But first he had to relax, to sort things out.

Outside the storm was dying away; the dark grey light gave way to a yellow cast which grew brighter by the minute. Out across the pasture, where the cows had left the protection of the big elms and were already cropping the rain-drenched grass, big breaks could be seen in the clouds. A robin in the yard took up a song.

✳✳✳

His mother sat beside the girl, took her hand in her own. They all seemed affected by a strange kind of paralysis, as though the air around them had thickened into some kind of viscous fluid, making their movements difficult, futile. Joe held his cup, stared out the window. His father sat at the table, only his hands moving slowly over one another. Sophie's heart was turned to the girl, who sat with occasional shivers gripping the half-empty cup.

"You must be hungry," Sophie said, trying to break out of

the spell which seemed to be settling over them. "I'll get some lunch." She stood, her hand lightly touching Mary's shoulder. She turned, stepped toward the stove.

In the yard was the sound of a car.

Alex turned, pushed himself up from the table, pulled aside the window curtain. His voice spoke of its own. "Thought I recognized it," he said. "It's the Overland. Needs a tune-up, it's missing on one cylinder."

No one moved, only stared at the door.

There were footsteps on the porch.

The door was knocking.

"Don't open it," Joe said quietly. "Don't open it. We don't have to open it."

But his father shook his head. "No, Joe. We're not afraid of anyone." As Joe set his coffee down and stepped quietly behind Mary, his father pulled the door open.

She stepped inside; behind her, on the porch, they could see the priest.

Joe thought: If he's here, if that damned little Russki's here, I'll...

"Come on, Mary," she hissed, ignoring everyone else in the room.

Joe put his hand on Mary's shoulder. "Wait, Mary," he said. "Wait."

They could hear the Overland through the open door. Joe, to his own astonishment, was thinking: pa's right. It is missing. He looked past Mary's mother. Stash was alone in the car, sitting timidly at the wheel smoking a cigarette.

"Well?" she demanded. "Look at you!" She stepped forward, lifted the sodden veil from the table. "Are you going to put us all to shame and your father's memory along with us?"

A groan escaped Mary's lips. She stared at the coffee cup, which her hand was squeezing now — any thinner and the timid girl would have shattered it in the press of her grip.

Her chair slid back.

"Mary!" Joe said, his hand tightening on her shoulder. Now his voice, no longer confident and gentle, was as demanding as the old woman's.

37

We stand in front of our future
which closes and opens at the same time.
Do not close the oneness of comings and goings
with willful abstractions:
life throbbed and blood dripped in them.
Return to each place where a man died; return
to the place where he was born.
The past is the time of birth, not of death.
— from *Easter Vigil 1966*, by Karol Wojtyla

A waning moon shed its light onto the warm August evening. From the front porch, the apple trees, their branches slung low with fruit, looked like stoop-shouldered elders gathered to parley over the coming harvest. There, among the trees, two or three or four fireflies — impossible to tell exactly how many — flashed sporadically, as though their hearts were no longer in it. But from under the porch, out in the tall grass and from sanctuaries under the scaly bark of the trees, a chorus of crickets rasped away their lazy romances. The air was still. A dew had begun to settle onto the grass, which would stay long into the morning, to be cold and wet on the bare feet of whatever girls might have to follow the cows out to pasture.

But that was not to come till morning — morning, a far world away. Now, tonight, the little girls and boys were running in and out of the house in a savage game of tag, slamming doors, adding their shrieks to the screech of the Victrola. Bruno, who had clambered up into the big willow above the front porch, waited breathlessly until a figure — it was Julia Tomczak — rounded the house, when he jumped down and screamed like a maddened banshee. Her heart in her mouth, Julia hurtled into the dining room and right into the arms of Bruno's mother, who also had been lying in wait for the poor girl.

"Stop this running in and out!" Berenice scolded her. "You're letting in mosquitoes. And look!" She pointed to the mantle where an enormous moth fluttered around the lamp. Bumping against the wall, the creature fell to the floor, lay with its wings breathing in and out. "Now see if you can catch it," Berenice said. She released Julia, who, having forgotten her game of tag, intently stalked the lovely moth.

It was warm in the house — too warm, really. The air was full of sounds and smells, laughter and a happy jumble of voices. Yet it was an odd congregation, for a wedding party. A *poprawiny* usually brought out every teenager and unmarried lad and lass for a dozen miles. They lasted days. Whole families would celebrate together, going home when at dawn it was time to do the chores, only to rest up and start again.

The Wolniak boys were in attendance, a quartet ranging in age from sixteen to twenty-five, who stood rather solemnly in the corner like so many bailiffs at a trial. The others were mostly Berenice's friends, generally too old and too tired to dance. So only Mary and George Zimmer, the bachelor mailman, whose greatest joy these days was attending others' weddings, circled the floor in slow and cautious circles. Even Henry and Gertrude, who'd been dancing most of the evening, decided to rest this one out. They stood exchanging small talk with the Rybarczyks, along the wall at the back end of the living room. Next to her parents sat Helen, looking out at the festivities as though through a glass wall. Beside her Stash, carnation still in his lapel, was drawing quietly on a cigarette. Though they sat so close together, he and Helen seemed, as usual, hardly aware of each other's presence.

The music died away. Mary broke free from the mailman, whose supply of quarters seemed literally unlimited. She slipped behind Lotti and looked out at the party rather like a child seeing its first lion.

Behind her Julia finally gave up on the moth. Her interest turned to the wedding cake. Quickly looking round to be sure Berenice was not in sight, she lifted a piece and ran with it outside again, having decided that in the balance Bruno was less of a danger than his mother. Julia's piece was not to be missed — three-fourths of the big pound cake, smeared with its sticky sour-cream frosting, remained uneaten. And the same for the cold cuts of chicken, ham, kielbasa, pork chops, fresh-baked bread, the potato salad, beans and applesauce. All had been prepared in quantities to satisfy a much larger gathering.

Though the bottles of beer and whiskey were disappearing rather quickly. But that did not trouble Berenice. After two more nights of *poprawiny*, it would be best not to have any leftover liquor lying around the house.

Father Nowak himself stood beside the food, nibbling a slice of the ham. He came from a sense of duty, having talked his housekeeper Verna into driving him over. For him not to come would have been discourteous. He had, after all, married them. So, in spite of himself, in spite of the liquor in plentiful supply, he made his showing.

He turned to reach a slice of bread, but his leg inadvertently bumped the pile of presents on the nearby table, knocking several to the floor. He bent to slide them back in among the others, searching to find the little gift he'd purchased for the couple, afraid for a moment he might have forgotten it and left it in the car or back on his desk.

But no. There it was. Among the pillowcases and towels, the silverware and pots. From Aunt Mary in Chicago, two large holy pictures, one of the Sacred Heart, the other of Mary's glorious Assumption into heaven. The largest present of all was the big shiny bronze Aladdin lamp, from Edward Ciepalek, with a short note apologizing for his not being able to come.

What a strange day it had been. Father smiled to himself, chewing the ham, as he remembered how astonished they all were to see her run down the stairs and into the waiting car. It was her moment of glory. Like a bird, she had for that glorious moment escaped her cage, flown free in the air.

But he'd ridden back to the church with the bride beside him, all the way not exchanging a single word. Once recaptured, she only sat, staring ahead, with a profound resignation.

By the time they were back at the church, most of the crowd had gone. Only one or two, besides the wedding party, had remained. The church seemed terribly empty. He knew how much it must have hurt her. She didn't deserve that.

But at least she had had that moment of freedom. It was more than many were ever granted.

He never liked doing weddings. Everyone in such a state, impossible to control. Funerals always went much more smoothly. This wedding, it was like nothing he'd ever seen before. Chaos, really. Yet once they'd brought her back and all that nonsense was behind them, it went very well.

It would be a wedding not easily forgotten.

Through the archway into the living room he caught sight of Mary, once again in the zealous arms of the mailman. The poor girl wasn't much of a dancer — how could she be when her mother never let her dance? Ironic, the priest mused: now that she's got permission, it's too late. Too late to learn, too late for fun.

It was insulting, really, under the present circumstances. The Bridal Dance often added life to the party. It gave the local lads one last chance to enjoy the bride's company — and at the same time earned a little extra to help the couple get started. Just twenty-five cents for a dance with the bride. But here it only turned the timid Mary into a commodity, available for the price of a pair of work gloves. Another generation, Father guessed, and it would be a thing of the past. Sometimes, he mused, something's gained when something's lost.

Walter slipped out of the kitchen where he'd been sitting with Stasia and a beer. He picked up a pork chop, nodded to the priest.

"Am I invited to yours?" Father asked.

Walter chewed thoughtfully. "Ah. My wedding. Of course." Nothing was a secret out here in the country.

"In Chicago?"

"St. Hedwig's," Walter nodded. "It's Stasia's church."

"And your brother?"

"Stash?" Walter sipped his beer. "Maybe. Maybe in a month or two. That'll be one for you."

The priest looked the bride's brother in the eyes. Walter, who thought the priest should have held out and refused to marry them, was not being very friendly. Father was all too aware of that coldness.

"Yes," he said. "That'll be one for me."

The music ended and Mary was left to catch her breath. How obviously she'd withdrawn, the priest thought. With no one to turn to. Not even her sisters, anymore. No longer a girl. A married woman, now.

And today, her wedding day, she'd never been more alone.

The front door swung open. Father turned to see. It was Julia again; quietly she slipped beside Lotti and stood watching the older people. She smiled up at Mary, who smiled back. They were playmates no more, the priest thought.

Chester, seeing Julia, waved to her. At just that moment Bruno ran in, dangling a spider from the end of a straw, tormenting her into a corner. In his eyes there was something more than mischief. But she slipped away from him and ran beside her father who, reaching out, tweaked Bruno by the ear and told him to go find work in the barn.

Lotti dropped another record onto the Victrola. Henry Bollom excused himself from the Rybarczyks in order to rescue Mary. He slipped some coins into the hat and took Mary's hand. They walked to the center of the room. He put his arm around her. He could feel how tense she was, how she cringed at the slightest touch. He held her gently. They danced alone, and after several circuits of the room, he could feel her softening. He nodded to George Zimmer, who was trying now to talk Lotti into a dance.

"You're not happy, are you Mary?" he asked softly. She glanced up at him. She was concentrating on keeping her feet out from under his. "It takes time to love," he said. "Did you know that Gertrude and I, well, ours was a wedding of convenience. Arranged by our parents." Mary listened intently. She had no idea. "But if I had to do it over again I would chase the world over to find her." They turned, twirled slowly around. Mary was beginning to feel the rhythm of the dance. "It seems only yesterday we were here, Gertie and I, dancing with your mother and father." He looked down into her eyes. "He was a good man, your father. Don't ever forget him, Mary."

She put her head on his shoulder, closed her eyes.

Lotti, by declining the mailman's offer to dance, had secretly pleased the Wolniak brothers. The youngest, James, was busy teasing Angie, trying to get her to drink some beer. Anton, a little unsteady on his feet, passed by on his way to another drink.

"He's drowning the worm," the older Wolniak said.

"But he got the bride," James said quietly. "Joe's the one should be drowning the worm."

"He is," his brother replied. "He is. But look at Mary. What did the Russian get? He didn't get her love, that's for sure. He knows that. So he's getting drunk." The bridegroom stood with a bottle of whiskey in his hand, filling then refilling the glass. He scowled back at the brothers. "You'd get drunk too if you knew you took second place in your wife's heart."

The music ended. Berenice, at the back door, was already seeing the Klebas out. They had a long drive ahead of them. Father Nowak, too, was preparing to leave. He slipped into the living room, congratulating Henry Bollom on his dancing, and took the bride aside for a few words. He held her hand; it was warm and limp. He assured her that things would turn out.

God is with you, he said. God won't forget you.

He felt better after that. He said good-bye to her sisters, and with Verna at his side headed for the back door. But as he passed the bridegroom, Anton whirled around, bottle in hand, and put his arm around the priest's shoulder.

"What's the matter Father don't you drink?" the Russian said. His words were blurred together. The priest smiled, backed away, trying to slip free. "Too good for drink?" Anton asked. "But not too good to destroy someone else's property?"

Father, with his back to the wall, directly behind him Berenice and Frank's wedding picture, wondered what the man was talking about. Was he crazy? It made no sense. From where came that fire he saw burning in the other man's eyes?

Berenice, in the kitchen, sensed that trouble was brewing. She stepped into the dining room and without a word the bridegroom backed away and slipped off into the living room. Father nodded good-night to his hostess, and he and Verna were out the door.

Stash and Pete Rybarczyk, Helen's older brother, were standing together talking about fishing. Anton joined them. Bruno, with no one in particular left to tease, sidled up beside the little group. Anton put his arm around Bruno who, after all, was actually a little shorter than he was. He started into a story. His meal-for-nothing story. They'd heard it before. Yet Bruno liked these stories of faraway places. We were on leave, Anton began, two of us hiking in the backwoods of Russia, and we were out of food and money. We came into a little village. No bigger than Dancy, he said for emphasis, then sipped his beer. We thought: how can we get something to eat? Then we concocted a plan. In the town's only cafe we ordered two plates of mushrooms, smothered in cream. They were delicious. We stuffed ourselves. Then we fell back off our chairs and began rolling around on the floor, complaining of our stomachs. All the other customers stared. We kept up the moaning and groaning until the owner threw us out.

Once on the street we stood up, brushed ourselves off, and walked happily away, bellies full in spite of our empty pockets.

Anton was beaming with pride. And Bruno, all he could think was that he'd never have the nerve to do something like that. He watched the groom tip his head back, run half a bottle of beer down his throat. Now Anton grew even bolder, his eyes sparkling. Though he spoke more quietly, the spit came in little

sprays from his lips. Bruno kept one eye out for his mother.
"We were pretty loaded this time," Anton was saying. "At
another inn, on furlough. Karamzin pulled out his squeezebox.
The inn-keeper's daughter, the oldest, the one we were plying
with drinks all night, she took a liking to me." He looked at his
friends meaningfully. "We sat at a table. She was on my lap.
We sang while the squeezebox played. She started singing, too.
I had my arm around her." Anton put his arm around Bruno
again. Now the boy was embarrassed. "She knew a few verses
I'd never heard."

He lowered his voice even more.

I've a hole in my shoe, so I can't dance, he sang quietly, clumsily trying to imitate a woman's voice:

But play anyway, Mr. Musician,
Though I can't dance, I'll lift a leg.
I'll start with one, then I'll raise both.
We'll see what we can do...

Anton laughed coarsely, dropped his empty beer bottle.
Stash could only smile, and the Rybarczyk boy, nervously. Bruno
knew full well this was forbidden territory, yet he was enjoying
it to the full.

"She slept with her sisters," Anton went on. "But she
promised me I could come to her in the middle of the night."

Berenice stepped into the room.

Anton, though his back was turned, could sense her presence. Bruno slipped away. The groom bent to pick up his beer
bottle, holding onto the table for support. Standing upright
again he winked knowingly at the Rybarczyk boy, belched, and
turned to find the dining room.

Stash watched him walk away. The Wolniak boys, still
flirting with Lotti, had to part so Anton could pass between
them. Stash wondered if there would be any trouble.

But a few minutes later the Wolniaks were gone. And now,
as though he'd only been waiting for them to leave, Anton returned to the living room and demanded Lotti put a record on.
"I want to dance with my wife!" he crowed.

Though he held Mary away from him, it was obvious to all
how much shorter he was. Though a better dancer, the liquor
had made him clumsy. He was trying to make her follow his
steps, and the more she sensed his frustration, the less able she
was to follow.

The music grew louder, faster. They whirled around, Mary

trying to steer her partner away from the furniture and walls. He interpreted this as rebellion. At last in a fit of anger he let her go and broke into a wild Cossack dance, flinging his feet out, shouting wildly, his boots stomping noisily on the hardwood floor. When the music stopped, abruptly, he stopped too, and collapsed onto the floor panting. "Come here, Mary," he said, gesturing her closer. But she cowered beside Lotti. His eyes closed, his head leaned back on the chair which had been Frank's. Still dressed from church, flower in his lapel, he slumped down, his mouth half-open. Suddenly he looked pale, as though he had died.

Seeing him there, Mary had to look away.

Berenice had shown the last of the guests out of the door. Now only Walter and Stash stood in the kitchen, talking. The younger children were in bed. Coming into the living room and finding Anton asleep on the floor, Berenice shook her head. Without a word the girls began cleaning up, picking up the empty bottles, carrying the food into the kitchen and sliding furniture back where it belonged. Lotti, carrying food to the cupboards, was astonished that it was past eleven.

In the morning it would be chores again. There were two more nights of *poprawiny* left, but Walter and Stasia would leave in the morning. Then Stash and Bruno, with as much help as they could get from the groom, would have the responsibility of the farm. It was time to harvest the oats, which would be piled in tall conical mounds by the barn, waiting until the threshing crew arrived.

Berenice bent to shake the sleeping groom's shoulder. He grunted, his eyes fluttering open. Looking round, as though expecting to wake in an old Russian inn rather than this strange house in Wisconsin, they closed again.

"Get up!" Berenice said. "Everyone else is in bed."

Anton made low noises from his throat, pushed himself onto his hands and knees, then stood and none too steadily headed for the front door. Berenice and Walter's Stasia disappeared into the bedroom, leaving a lamp burning for the groom.

After a long while, the screen door slammed. Anton stumbled back into the house. Berenice could hear him muttering. His boots clomped into his room. First one, then the other fell to the floor. "Mary!" he called out, his voice slurred. Louder now. "Mary!"

Berenice slipped out of bed. She was startled to find him

standing in the living room, in his stocking feet, as though he were lost.

"Where's my wife?" he demanded.

Berenice stared at him. If Frank were here, she thought. If only Frank were here. She walked past the little man, peered into his room. It was empty. She went into the kitchen, then returned to the living room.

"Get to bed," she told him. He turned and disappeared into his room. She picked up the lamp and carried it up the stairs. In the boys' room she could hear Stash's peaceful snoring. In the girls' it was quiet.

Mary lay beside her sister, her eyes wide open, staring up at the light with fear deep in her eyes. Only her lip moved as nervously she bit at it. She blinked, then, and looked away.

Her mother stood beside her. "Come on, Mary," she urged, lifting the summer blanket. Mary was holding Lotti's hand. "You have to, child. You're not a girl anymore. You're a wife."

Berenice took her by the arm, pulled her gently to her feet. Mary's hand disentangled from her sister's. She stood a moment, then her feet began to carry her toward the stairs. Berenice followed her as they went down, step by step, slowly, solemnly.

Partway down, Mary stopped. The house was still and dark. Through the window she could see the moon slipping down toward the west. Her mother gently urged her on.

They stood in the dining room, the silence of the years descending upon them both. "Go on," her mother urged her. They faced the door into Anton's room. Her mother's voice was quiet and uncommonly gentle. "Go on," she repeated.

The lamp her mother carried threw long shadows across the room. Mary breathed deeply and stepped out of the circle of its light and into the darkness of the bedroom. The door closed behind her.

38

And so, leaning over the waters,
we will float away to oblivion
and on earth there will cry for us only
our own shadows which we left behind...
— from *A Little Song,* by Andrzej Trzebinski

T he Stelmach farm entered the fourth decade of the century on solid enough footings to suggest, if not guarantee, its survival through the Depression, just beginning. Joe had taken over from his father, who was semi-retired; meaning he slept through morning milking when he felt like it, but otherwise kept his hand on the pulse of the farm. Alex and Sophie continued to live in the house, with Joe and his family. The Christmas after Mary's marriage to Anton, when he was certain that Berenice had the couple bound irrevocably together, Joe had let it be known that he was looking for a bride. And as Father Nowak had so long before predicted, nearly every eligible girl in the parish applied. He took his time, settled at last on Martha Kuberek, and could not have been happier with his decision. Joe and Martha were already blessed with a boy, Frank, and a girl, Vickie.

A year before Joe was married, his brother George had gone to Chicago to find work and found a job there as a butcher at Arnold Brothers. Now, with work almost impossible to find, George clung to that job like a life raft in rough seas. In Chicago George had also found a wife, Catherine, a lively, energetic, and strong-willed woman. Though a child of the city, when she visited the farm she loved working alongside the men in the barn or out in the field. Her down-to-earth ways endeared her to Joe and his parents.

Just three weeks ago, Catherine had given birth to an eight-pound three-ounce boy, their first child. They named the boy Alex, after George's dad. Over the phone, George sounded ecstatic. Sophie had already taken the train down to Chicago and was helping Catherine with the new baby in their flat on Damen. George asked Joe to be the boy's godfather. So Alex agreed to take care of the farm while Joe went down to the christening. After Joe returned, in four days, his father would take the train down to visit and bring Sophie back. This would be Joe's first trip to the city. Though he worried over being gone that long, he knew he was leaving family and farm in good hands.

✱✱✱

It turned out to be quite a remarkable christening. Unlike so many infants who seem not to realize the importance of the moment, and slide off instead into colicky crying fits, little Alex was fascinated by the ceremony. The priest's colorful garments, the candles and the smell of incense, even the drops of water on his forehead as he received his Christian name, Alex Steven Stelmach, all attracted his close attention. He noted everything with wide-open, studious eyes. After it was all over, and the parents and godparents were in the foyer of the church getting ready to leave, Father O'Malley told them that he'd never seen a baby quite as attentive as Alex. A little cherub, he called him, pinching his cheek, a little cherub who would certainly grow up into a holy and God-fearing young man. And you never knew, Father added, he might even find his vocation in the priesthood.

Afterwards, there was a nice meal at George and Catherine's. Joe basked in the affection the family showed for one another, and could not have been happier for his younger brother. He would be spending the night at George's, then in the morning take the long trip back home. When he'd first agreed to come to the christening, in the back of his mind Joe remembered that Mary Topolski — now Walerych — lived in Chicago, with her mother and sisters.

✱✱✱

For though they had made it into the autumn after Frank's death, things had not gone well at the Topolski place. Joe had been called over time and again to doctor the herd. Eventually his father came to resent all the time he spent there; and just driving in the yard, where Frank had been replaced by Walerych, was hard on Joe. So he told Berenice there was nothing more he could do, and the Topolski cream checks maintained their relentless slide downward. Meanwhile, Berenice had been forced to borrow to pay off the hospital and funeral bills. Verna Las, Father Nowak's housekeeper, loaned her five hundred dollars, with a mortgage on the farm as collateral.

Harvesting and threshing the oats went smoothly enough, aside from getting Walerych to do his part. It seemed the fun-loving threshing crew, mostly young Bohemians from Rozellville, kidded him mercilessly about his clumsiness, and after just one day helping toss the shocked oats into the noisy, smoke-belching thresher, Walerych simply refused to leave the house. Berenice was livid, but he didn't seem to care.

After threshing, the family turned to digging potatoes. More than twenty tons were hauled, wagon by wagon, to the big warehouse in Point, proving Frank right — the certified seed had yielded over a hundred bushels an acre. But yields were up all over the state, and the price fell, to just over thirty cents a bushel. It was a banner year; and as farmers well know, a banner year can be the ruin of the farm.

Walter and his Stasia were married in September, then moved from Milwaukee to Chicago, where Walter found work as a mechanic at the huge Cuneo Press. Stash and Helen, who were married in November at St. Francis Xavier, followed Walter to Chicago. Wages as high as thirty dollars a week were irresistible; Walter found Stash a job working alongside him. So Bruno was left to be the man around the Topolski farm. But by then it was obvious that the inevitable had arrived. Early in 1923 while in Chicago visiting Walter, Stash and her sister Mary, Berenice took an ad out in the *Dziennek Chicagowski:*

> *For sale or trade: One hundred twenty acres of farm with barn, house and outbuildings in good land of central Wisconsin. Write: Berenice Topolski, Box 1, Rt 2, Dancy, Wisconsin.*

Before spring had brought its full palette of greens and its medley of bird song back to Wisconsin, the farm had been traded for a four-story tenement on Chicago's Cleaver Street. The young couple who took on the Topolski place held it for only two years before they too had to sell. County records indicated that in the decades after the death of Frank Topolski, the farm changed hands more often than there were presidential elections. Like the family itself, the little farm on the hill just out of town may have reached its finest hours in the last days of Frank's life.

Berenice, before they moved to Chicago, sat Mary and Anton down at the dining room table and compelled them to set their signatures to a rough sort of contract, which was little more than a deed of indentured servitude. For it welcomed the newlyweds to continue living with her as long as they performed whatever work she asked of them, without wages. And, further-more, that the covenant so attested could only be annulled by mutual consent. Little did Berenice — or Mary or Anton, for that matter — know that more than a century before, in the case of Mary Clarke vs. the State of Indiana, indentured servitude had been declared illegal and all such contracts null and void.

Such subtleties were of little use to Berenice Topolski, left with six children to raise. So, after moving to Chicago, all the girls — except Anna, who wasn't yet sixteen — went to work. Every week they turned their paychecks over to their mother and were given back twenty-five cents apiece. After subtracting trolley fare to and from their jobs, very little was left.

Not long after they moved off the farm, Mary made Berenice a grandmother. Frank would have loved the little girl, Rose, a dark-haired and dark-eyed beauty, whose infectious smile could refresh the most tired heart. Anton meanwhile moved from job to job. For a while he tried selling insurance, spending his evenings in bars where, according to him, he could meet new clients. Another daughter came, then a son. To help support the family, Mary took a job while her mother stayed home with the children.

Berenice had known a Kashub from Junction City, a dis-tant friend of the family, who wrote her after hearing of Frank's death. He had been widowed two years earlier, and needed a wife. For the children's sake — he had four of his own — they decided to marry. So the house on Cleaver Street was sold, and the family moved onto his farm near Junction City. But her new husband did not stand a chance meeting Berenice's impossible standards. The marriage was annulled, the common property divided, and the Topolskis bought a three-story house on Dickens Street in Chicago, where they now lived, and in which at this very moment the telephone in the second floor flat was ringing. Heart in throat, Joe Stelmach had decided to get in touch with Mary.

But it wasn't Mary who answered the phone. It was one of her sisters; Joe was sure it was Anna. He wanted to tell her who he was, and talk openly with her, like in the old days. But he simply asked if Mary was home.

"Oh, she's not here," Anna replied, her voice polite but tinged with a touch of curiosity. In the background, Joe could hear Berenice asking who it was.

"I see. When will she be back?"

"She's at church. It's her daughter Rose's First Communion."

"Oh. Wonderful. Which church would that be?"

"Saint Hedwig's."

"Ah. What time is the First Communion?"

"Two o'clock."

Joe checked his watch. He had almost half an hour. He thanked Anna, hung up the receiver, and asked his brother if he could get to St. Hedwig's before two o'clock. It wasn't far, George said, and gave Joe directions.

✳✳✳

Joe caught a streetcar headed north up Damen. He was amazed, as he had been since arriving in Chicago, at the hustle and bustle of the city. It seemed impossible that any one place could have so many cars and trucks, and such crowds of people, waiting for a change of light to cross the street, getting on and off the streetcars which clanked busily off into the distance or disappeared suddenly around a corner, people hurrying in and out of cars, or into the many shops up and down the street, some carrying bundles, others intent on some important mission only they and God could know. He had never seen so many different styles of dress, of haircuts, of shaving or not shaving. He knew there were bigger cities than Chicago, but he could not imagine it.

It had its own smell, too, this recumbent giant called Chicago, the heavy smell of doughnuts frying, of car exhaust and coal smoke and the sometimes disgusting pollution from factories which burned your nose as you went past, and if the wind was right, the sharp smell of the stockyards and rendering plants to the south. A hundred smells, a hundred sounds, the incessant motion of man and machine, there was an energy to it all that Joe hadn't experienced on the farm, a heady energy which put its arm around your shoulder, said something brash in your ear, then swept you up and dragged you along with it on its way to — who knew where?

He saw, too, a line of unemployed men, shuffling up and down the sidewalk, some with placards begging for work. How difficult it must be, he thought, to be out of work here, where there was no food to raise, no firewood to warm you when you needed it. At least on the farm, the Depression was bearable. Even poor Adam Laska, who continued to scratch a living for himself and his family from the rocky hardpan of Marathon County, was better off than these sullen, angry men.

The city repelled Joe, and it fascinated him. As the streetcar noisily accelerated through the bustling Armitage Street intersection, he scanned his fellow riders for some sense of who they might be. But their lives were a complete unknown to him. A young woman, from under a pretty blue hat, smiled at him, her lips reddened and shiny with lipstick. He blushed, and for an instant saw an advantage to all this anonymity. No one knew you; no one could know what you saw, or did. As he stepped off the streetcar, he understood for a moment why his brother spoke so highly of life in the city. Ahead of him he saw the towers of St. Hedwig's church.

St. Hedwig's was relatively large, as churches went, though from Joe's vantage there seemed to be nothing particularly striking about it. The city held hundreds of churches, of every kind, some much bigger, and some smaller. Neat yellow brick and painted wood-frame houses huddled around the churchyard and its attached school, not unlike the huts and hovels which nestled near churches and cathedrals in medieval Poland. St. Hedwig's, in fact, lay in the center of a sprawling enclave of ethnic Poles. Walk from its steps a half an hour in any direction and you were as likely to hear dialects from Wielkopolska and Mazuria as you were to hear the American tongue. And once inside, this was a church full of color and glory, high Polish Baroque, as though a piece of Heaven had been stolen and was being held hostage under its steeply sloped roof.

***

Saint Hedwig — Jadwiga, in Polish — for whom the church was named, was one of the great personalities in Polish history. Jadwiga was a shy and lovely princess, whose affection for her childhood playmate, Crown Prince William of Austria, received her father's blessing. In January 1378, when Jadwiga was only seven, she and William celebrated their betrothal in a glorious mock wedding which, as was common among the nobility of that time, declared their intention to be married when Jadwiga turned twelve. In the intervening years they played, studied, and prayed together, looking forward to the day they would be finally and eternally united.

But in 1382 Jadwiga's father, King Louis, died. Political intrigue bent Poland's future northward, rather than southward. The now Queen Jadwiga was courted by the Duke of Lithuania, a short, coarse-looking pagan named Jagiello. Lithuania, to Poland's northeast, was a great land, but it was not Christian. And Jagiello had promised, if their countries were united by marriage, to embrace Christianity. The Council of the Crown, Poland's greatest nobles, pressured her to give up William and instead marry the pagan Duke. Jadwiga was torn. She and William considered a secret marriage. Praying one Sunday afternoon in the cathedral of Kraców, she asked for guidance. And God spoke to her, in a voice of terrible clarity. He asked her to sacrifice herself for her country, and her religion. For an instant her heart rebelled, but then, heartbroken but obedient, she relented.

The marriage of Jadwiga and Jagiello, uniting two powerful countries which had for centuries been bitter enemies, began a four-hundred year federation which was unique in medieval Europe. As Jagiello had promised, Lithuania was converted. Jagiellonian Poland became a guiding star of Europe, with its great University, its music, literature and art. Jadwiga herself died an untimely death at the birth of their first child, Elizabeth, who perished with her. But Jagiello continued to hold the country together, and in one of Poland's finest hours, led his forces to defeat the Order of Teutonic Knights, at the battle of Grunwald.

Not many of the years since then had Poland even existed as an independent state. From the modest church in near north Chicago, in the early days of the Great Depression, St. Hedwig's statue reached back through those ages of suffering and futility to the glory of the Polish nation at its height. No wonder Poles had raised the church in her honor, lived in its protective shadow, been baptized and confirmed under its roof, and buried their dead through its doors.

***

Joe walked up the steps a few minutes past two. The door to the church was already closed. He slipped in, crossed himself with Holy Water, and found a place to sit halfway up the aisle. He scanned the congregation, its hundreds of strangers only half filling the pews, for a glimpse of Mary. Finally he saw her, across the aisle and near the front. She stood between her younger daughter and her son. And next to the handsome little boy, who raised himself at that moment onto the kneeler in order to peer around the church, his aunt Lotti.

So she wouldn't see him, he slid to his right, hiding himself as best as he could. She wore a dark dress, bought new, he guessed, for the First Communion. On her head, a bright babushka. In one hand she held her missal while with the other she reached to straighten her son's jacket, then smoothed down his hair, a small gesture of deep affection. Joe knew how flustered she must be by the First Communion ceremony, and by having to be in a crowd of strangers. He wished, though only for an instant, that he could be beside her, to calm her. Then silently he cursed her husband for not being with her.

Her eyes fell back onto her missal, and her lips moved quietly in prayer. It was the Mary he'd known and loved, the same selfless, innocent Mary. Only she looked older than he'd expected. They had both grown up, it was true. They were parents now. His life had gone ahead, after their time together, gone its own separate way. The bitterness he'd felt toward her mother had, in time, slipped off to a quiet corner of his heart. Frank's death had put all that in perspective. In time the love he had felt for her he came instead to feel for Martha.

He wondered, his heart going out to her, what journey her heart had taken. Had she somehow come to feel for Anton what she had felt for him? Joe hoped, for her sake, that she had. Yes, she too had more than enough reason to be bitter. But that was not Mary's way. He could see, from halfway across the church, that in the full gentleness of her heart there was no room left for bitterness. And that the miracle of Mary's heart, which he had glimpsed those years ago, was the quiet strength to change life's burdens into gifts. Only he felt sad, that somehow, except for her children and the constant kindness of her sisters, she had been left alone in the world. She deserved better than that.

But she wasn't alone. For as he watched her, he could see in her, still alive, the simple, soft gestures, the selflessness and the essential goodness which was her father. And he knew Frank would always be with her, and she would be all right.

The choir began a sudden glorious melody. From the back the priest and his altar boys entered, singing with the choir, carrying candles and incense. Behind them the children came, in two long lines side by side up the aisle toward the altar. He turned to see them. There were so many — half a hundred, or more — and Joe knew none of them. First Communions at St. Francis, where his Vickie and Frank had been baptized, were a matter of a dozen or so communicants. There, Joe not only knew each child, but the intricate network of social connections which had brought their parents together. He did not envy Mary for what she had given up.

As they came gracefully forward, he searched the faces of the girls for some sign which might identify the young Rose Walerych. They were immaculately dressed, in fine Communion uniforms — the boys in suits, the girls with white dresses and large bows on their backs which were like cloth angel wings. And in their faces they seemed that, young and impossibly innocent angels. They would in time — as he had already begun — look back to this moment when their souls were as yet unsullied by the great struggle of life.

As they moved past, each carried a single lit candle. On their faces he could read the excitement the ceremony meant for them, an excitement tempered only by concern that the fragile flames they carried not go out. Joe watched as they passed, a long procession of flickering candles moving slowly toward the great altar, ablaze in its own manifold glory. Each face, each child as they passed, was unique, held a unique history — of which he knew nothing — and moved toward a unique future — of which none of them could say. Suddenly, in a petite young girl coming toward him, he saw her. Her hair, dark and shiny, and her eyes, black as gypsy's, were her father's. But something in her face, a soft and subtle strength in the cheekbones and mouth, told him this was Mary's girl. He gasped involuntarily as she reflected back to him his youthful love, not yet dead. He smiled to her as she passed, and she returned his smile, for an instant, without an inkling of who he was or the depth of his attachment to her, through her mother. The connection their eyes had made, and their smiles, closed a chapter in Joe's life. His heart was overtaken with a great flush of love for his Martha and his own children, and he was suddenly, deeply homesick.

As Rose came past, the line of communicants stopped for a few moments, as up front the priest directed them into their pews. He was tempted to reach out and touch her. "Hello, Rose," he would say. But he did not want to interrupt the enchantment of the moment. He sat, instead, and watched as the candle flame she carried flickered and flashed with a sudden unseen wind and, like the flames of their lives — whether Queen of Poland or common farmer — flared and danced its way toward Heaven.